A HOUSE FULL OF SECRETS

Zoë Miller was born in Dublin, where she now lives with her husband. She began writing stories at an early age. Her writing career has also included freelance journalism and prize-winning short fiction. She has three grown-up children.

www.zoemillerauthor.com
@zoemillerauthor
Facebook.com/zoemillerauthor

Previously by Zoë Miller

Someone New
A Question of Betrayal
A Husband's Confession
The Compromise
A Family Scandal
Rival Passions
Sinful Deceptions
Guilty Secrets

A HOUSE full of SECRETS

ZOË MILLER

HACHETTE
BOOKS
IRELAND

First published in Ireland in 2017 by HACHETTE BOOKS IRELAND
First published in paperback in 2018

Cataloguing in Publication Data is available from the British Library

ISBN 978 1 4736 6460 9

Typeset in ArnoPro by Bookends Publishing Services, Dublin.

Printed and bound in Great Britain by Clays Ltd, St Ives plc

Hachette Books Ireland policy is to use papers that are natural, renewable and recyclable products and made from wood grown in sustainable forests. The logging and manufacturing processes are expected to conform to the environmental regulations of the country of origin.

Hachette Books Ireland
8 Castlecourt Centre
Castleknock
Dublin 15

A division of Hachette UK Ltd
Carmelite House
50 Victoria Embankment
EC4Y 0DZ
London

www.hachettebooksireland.ie

Dedicated to my inspirational and hugely supportive agent and friend,
Sheila Crowley

CHAPTER ONE

The lough is still out of bounds.

The forest track leading to the beauty spot where Gabrielle met her untimely end has become impassable. Fallen tree trunks, shrouded with clusters of vegetation and thick tentacles of ivy, block the entrance. Where prisms of sunlight pierce the leafy canopy, clumps of untrammelled nettles, tumbleweed and briars thrust through cracks in the forest floor. It's as if nature has conspired to prevent me or anyone else from trespassing, in collusion with the crude-looking, crumbling 'Danger: Keep Out' sign swaying against a tree trunk. The laneway down from the road is similarly obstructed; here, a wide gate smothered with thorny brambles and wild bushes strengthens the barricade, and the gap in the ditch where her car went off the road is shored up by a sheet of rusty corrugated iron reinforced with barbed wire.

As if this will stop me.

I've waited so long for the truth to be exposed but it's finally going to happen. Lynes Glen has been re-opened for the weekend and the family are gathering. All of us. The broken family, I think, although they don't know who is the most damaged of us all – yet.

Dust sheets have been whisked off furniture, and cleaners have wiped and washed and buffed. I glimpse my shadow moving across the parquet floors and my reflection shimmers as I pass the gleaming woodwork and the sparkling crystal and mirrors. The west-facing windows to the front have been unlocked, the sashes thrown up, and a fresh breeze flows into the rooms, fluttering up to corniced ceilings, surging freely through hallways and swirling up around the curving staircase. It carries a mountainy tang, mixed with the scent of pine trees, and it sweeps away stagnant air, driving any remaining dust motes into a crazy dance.

In the faded splendour of the sitting room, a beam of sunlight slants through the window and glows like a spotlight on the row of polished photograph frames lined up along the top of the piano. The family photos have been taken out of storage and arranged exactly as they were two decades ago, the images caught and frozen by the camera in an innocent fragment of time during the hot summer of 1995 before everything shattered. I step outside myself for a moment, I forget who I am and the scores I have to settle while I stare at the images objectively, as a total stranger might; Alex, Lainey and Niall, followed by proud parents Leo and Gabrielle. There are no hints in any of the faces as to how sharply the bottom was going to fall out of those glittering lives.

First up is Alex, the eldest son, the photograph taken outside on the pebbled driveway that sweeps to a circle in front of the house. He leans back jauntily against the bonnet of his BMW convertible, his red-gold hair flopping over his forehead, his eyes glinting, his whole demeanour infused with the assurance of a young man in his mid-twenties who thinks he owns the world and expects to follow every one of his dreams.

Next to his photograph is one of Lainey, taken inside in the hall. A year younger than Alex, she has a flirty smile on her face as she stands in a sideways pose by the curving staircase, her hair caught into a gleaming barrette. She's wearing a backless red designer dress with lipstick to match, holding a cocktail glass aloft in one hand, silver bangles sparkling on her raised arm, her eyes full of calm confidence as if she had no doubts that life would deliver all the good things she expected.

Then Niall, the youngest, at nineteen years of age, caught in a pulse-quickening image down by the lough. He's posing on the diving board set into a rocky outcrop, his face taut in concentration, his body perfectly aligned in a formation that looks effortless but speaks of hours of practice. He is ready to take flight out into open space, before executing a dive into the still, calm waters of the lough, some thirty feet below.

No matter how arresting they are, these images are eclipsed by those of Gabrielle. The next photograph is a formal one of Gabrielle and Leo, taken at an international literary event just weeks before their world imploded. Tall, spare Leo is dressed in black tie and holding a crystal trophy, awarded for his latest collection of poetry. He looks uncomfortable in the limelight, as though he'd rather be tucked up in his study in Lynes Glen, writing his soul across the page, but standing beside him, Gabrielle more than makes up for his reserve.

Always his muse, forever his beloved darling, she is smiling her brilliant smile. She's dressed in a jade figure-hugging dress, a ruby-stoned pendant gleaming at her white throat, her flame-haired, emerald-eyed beauty frozen in time. Lined up beside Alex, Lainey and Niall, it's obvious that only pale glimmers of her allure are reflected in each of her children, in their green eyes flecked with amber and shades of red-gold hair. Gabrielle's is a luminous beauty that shimmers forever; it will never fade or grow old.

I hate her all over again for this as much as for what she did, ruining the rest of my life in the process. I'm tempted to stamp my foot. I want to raise my arm and send all the frames crashing to the floor. I want to cry out loud. But I've never allowed myself the luxury of tears. I clench my fists and go across to the long sash windows, taking a few deep breaths to compose myself.

From the front of the house, the world stretches away, full of a raw, desolate beauty, an unspoilt panorama of stone-walled fields, gorse-covered hills and glinting streams. It's a patchwork quilt of green, purple and brown granite and flecks of slate, where shadows dissolve into sunlight, and clouds chase their reflections across to the sea. Up above, the skies are limitless. On clear days, high-flying aeroplanes trail needle-thin vapours across the heavens as they head out over the Atlantic, across to America. It's enough to make you dream of running free as far as the sea, like the glinting rivers, or taking flight out into the big, wide world. But those kinds of dreams are long gone.

The back of the house settles into the curve of the forest. Beyond that the mountains form a towering backdrop, their pinnacles serrating the sky. Today the sunlight cloaks the summits in a veil of barley-sugar light. They do not always appear so benign. I've seen the peaks of Slieve Creagh turn into menacing brooding hulks in the blink of an eye when dark clouds scud over, blackening the horizon.

As the family gathers in Lynes Glen this early September

afternoon, everything appears to be calm and peaceful. There are no shadows creeping in corners, no sad whispers wafting through the passageways, no talk of buried secrets, or uneasy ghosts flitting through the rooms or up the curving staircase. That will change within the next twenty-four hours, thanks to what I have planned.

To add to my devilry, a storm is coming. It's seething out in the Atlantic, gathering strength before it hurls itself onto this remote glen in a far western corner of Ireland, expected to hit landfall on Saturday evening.

The timing couldn't be more perfect.

CHAPTER TWO

London: One week earlier

Vikki Gordon had a heightened sense of expectation as she squeezed her way through the Friday evening throng milling around the Thames waterfront bar. Clutching her tote bag, she weaved around stool legs and flailing arms to avoid dangerously tilting glasses of beer and wine, so she felt it was a good sign when she, together with her soft white top, managed to make it to the bathroom in one piece.

She pushed up a basket of paper towels to make room for her bag, glad of the cool quiet after the din outside. She hadn't waited to refresh her make-up in the office because it would have invited comments about why she might be putting on the glam, or, critically, for whom. She slicked some styling wax through her short, dark hair, a touch of fresh mascara that widened her grey eyes, lip gloss, a dab of perfume; nothing too glamorous, strictly effortless. Then she practised her smile in the mirror until she had it right; casual, cheery, relaxed, to suit a casual, cheery friendship.

Dipping into her bag for her sunglasses, she pressed her way through the throng once more, heading towards the terrace at the back and an explosion of late August sunshine, a whiff of Thames-scented air, the blast from a tug boat and shouts floating across the water, conversation humming up around her, laughter and the tinkle of glass – exaggerated gaiety because evenings such as these would soon be gone with the arrival of autumn.

Niall Blake, sitting on an aluminium chair by the railings overlooking a river stippled with sunlight, a bottle of beer on the small table in front of him, was waiting for her.

And her heightened sense of expectation crystallised into all the possibilities coming from this moment.

He stood up. He bent down and kissed her on the cheek. 'Hey, how've you been? I haven't seen you in a while.'

Fourteen days less five hours since she'd last said goodbye to him after they'd been to a movie together, when her tall lean Niall, with golden-red hair and the green eyes flecked with amber had kissed her goodnight, just as chastely on the cheek as he'd kissed her now.

'Haven't you?' she said in a teasing voice. 'I was living it up last weekend,' she continued, as they both sat down.

'Mia's hen weekend in Barcelona – see, I remembered.' He rested his hands on the table and smiled at her. 'How did it go?'

'Great,' she said. 'It's the perfect spot for a party weekend, but unfortunately most of the beautiful architecture went over our champagne-fuelled heads. We were too busy laughing our way up and down Las Ramblas, but I'll be back to nourish my cultural soul another time.'

'Glad it went well,' Niall said. 'Make it a point to return to soak up the Gaudi brilliance. I'm going back as soon as the cathedral is finished, whenever that will be.'

A vision of both of them, going to Barcelona together, swam into her head and she swiftly thrust it away as a wonderful dream. The waiter arrived with a chilled glass of white wine, placing it in front of Vikki.

'I'm impressed with the service,' she said.

'I asked him to bring it out as soon as you arrived. I think you could do with it.' He gave her a long, considering glance. He was not usually given to such contemplative glances and she felt a stab of unease.

'Do you? I'm good,' she said airily, giving him her biggest and brightest smile. The one that covered everything. Taking her cues from him, she wanted to keep it easy and lighthearted. No problems or issues. Nothing for him to fix. And, most of all, no hint of any kind of neediness. She'd learned the hard way; at thirty-six years of age she'd been around that block more than once. She'd already told herself, courtesy of her ever-vigilant inner critic, that if she wanted to keep on seeing him, she had to stick to that script. This was a casual Friday-evening-after-work drink; she was thankful they seemed to be happening with increasing frequency.

Niall said, with a hint of something she couldn't quite define in his eyes, 'I hope you're still good after I ask you a favour.'

She twirled the stem of her wine glass. 'Hmmm. Sounds ominous. My gut instinct is to refuse. What kind of favour?'

'Any plans for next weekend?' he asked.

Her mind went blank. When it powered up again the biggest thing she registered was that he hadn't asked about next Friday or even Saturday night, it was next 'weekend', as in the sum total.

'Why?' she asked, pushing away thoughts of the work conference scheduled for Saturday. The work conference she could only afford to miss at her peril. Niall's next words were so unexpected they put all that out of her head.

'I'm going back to Ireland for an extended weekend,' he said. 'Back to Lynes Glen, the family home in Mayo. There's a kind of get-together; it's been arranged for a while—' he broke off and shook his head. 'Just forget it. I know it's terribly short notice and you'd need time off work – it's Friday to Monday. Anyway you're bound to be busy and you'll think I'm mad for even asking you ...' The way he gazed at her sent her pulse tripping into overdrive.

'What part of what you said are you asking me to forget?' she said, forcing a teasing voice.

He looked as though he was already steeling himself for her refusal. It was something she'd found surprising about this man. Out in company, he was the fun person, never taking life seriously, as he breezed his way through it, but now and again, when they were on their own, she saw glimpses of a different Niall, a man with a hint of vulnerability that found a resonance inside her. A gentle person, he'd always treated her with kindness and respect, unlike some other men who were only interested in how quickly they could get into her bed. If she'd had more than her fair share of relationship disasters, she sensed there was a similar sadness lurking behind Niall, something he'd only hinted at, once.

A pleasure cruiser puttered along the river, the sounds of party laughter coming from the dozen or so occupants out on deck. Niall waited until they had passed. He leaned back in his chair, clasping his hands behind his head.

'Thing is,' he said, looking straight into her eyes, 'I had the mad idea of asking if you'd like to come with me ...'

Come with me ... the weekend ... He'd made sure she'd had

a drink lined up before he'd asked her. In case his mad idea bothered her? Little did he know her thoughts were ricocheting off in a thousand different directions like glorious fireworks.

'But it's probably off the wall,' he went on. 'Lynes Glen won't be remotely like Barcelona, remote being the word because it's quite isolated. Anyway' – he smiled lopsidedly – 'I don't want to mess with your cutting-edge social life.'

He was really asking her. Everything blurred around her, the glint off the river, the drift of laughter and conversation, even her insides felt soft as mush, and then they took shape again, hardening with a daredevil resolve.

'Obviously a glittering social life is high up there on my hierarchy of needs,' she said, sounding as matter of fact as she could. 'But I'm always up for something mad and adventurous to add to my résumé. I've never seen that part of the world, but I believe it's rather beautiful.' She heard the words coming out of her mouth, slightly alarmed at the way she was throwing caution to the wind and performing a kamikaze act on her career, never mind that she'd vowed to put herself and her wellbeing front and centre from now on, after the fallout from her previous relationships.

'You might be up for it?'

'I might.' Go slow, she warned herself, willing her eyes not to appear too eager.

'Before you say yes, let me check out some practical details with my sister ...'

'I should have guessed,' she joked, 'I have to do all the cooking? Your family mightn't want me in their midst?'

'No way! We're getting someone in for the cooking. And my family ...' he paused. 'They'll be grand.'

'Your brother and sister will be there?' Vikki tried to remember what Niall had told her about his family. She knew he was the youngest by four or five years, that he had a sister in her mid-forties who lived in Dublin, and a brother, a year older again, living in New York. Both were married, with children.

Niall stretched out his legs and leaned back, as though to give the impression he was thoroughly relaxed. His face, she thought, was almost too bland. 'Yep, Alex and Lainey will be there with their spouses, Jenna and Ben, and kiddies. And Dad, of course.'

She knew his mother was dead. He never spoke of it.

'My mother died years ago … a car crash – actually, I don't ever talk about it … '

He'd mentioned it early into their friendship, sounding as though he'd felt the need to put down that boundary. She remembered it well, because while she'd sympathised with his loss, she'd also been relieved he didn't want to talk. It gave her permission not to talk about her parentage either.

'I'm sorry to hear that,' she'd said at the time. 'It must have been rough.'

'Yeah.' The closed-up look on his face had been enough to tell her how rough.

'I don't talk about my mother either,' she'd said. 'She's alive and well, so you might find that a bit …' she'd paused. What could she say? Compared to him she was fortunate enough to have Sally Gordon alive, yet she didn't want to speak of her?

He'd looked relieved. 'That's OK, so we're quits.'

Vikki took a sip of her wine and tried to sound as though she was well used to being on the receiving end of weekend invitations to family homes from gorgeous men. 'Your dad – I've never met a real-life poet before,' she said. 'What's he like? To talk to, I mean.'

'Dad?' Niall shrugged. 'You should have something

in common with him.' He gazed at her across the table, disconcerting her.

'Me?'

'You're both involved in the written word.'

'Hah, Niall, you always know how to make me laugh. Being an assistant editor on a beauty magazine who can wax lyrical about ten shades of lip gloss is nowhere near Leo Blake, award-winning poet. It would be wonderful to meet him.'

'He's the same as anyone else's dad I guess,' Niall said.

Oh no, he's not, she wanted to say.

'He's quiet, a bit introverted,' Niall went on. 'After Mum ... he went into himself, but he poured something dark into his poetry that seemed to click with people. His health is not great now, though, which I guess is one of the reasons for the gathering. He's eighty-three this year and his arthritis is seriously bothering him, which is sad to see.'

'It must have been amazing to grow up with him for your father.'

'I suppose ... yeah, when he wasn't out lecturing in universities, he spent a lot of time in his library, Mum playing games with us, trying to keep us quiet. They were mad about each other.'

It was the most he'd ever told her about his family. As though conscious of that, he gave her a careless shrug.

'So yeah,' he said, 'have a think about it anyhow. See if you can get time off work first. If you do decide to come, it's going to be a very relaxing, chill-out get-together, according to Lainey, so just be your usual self.' He pulled a menu towards him. 'Now, down to the most important business of the moment,' he said, as though inviting her to his family home for the weekend was a natural enough occurrence instead of a total game-changer. 'Another drink and maybe a bite to eat?'

'Perfect.'

She watched him summoning a waiter to place their order. There were times when she couldn't take her eyes off him and this was one of them; he'd come straight from the NHS hospital where he worked as an administrator, the sleeves of his blue shirt were rolled up, and red-gold hairs glinted along his forearm. Fine stubble ran along his jawline. He had a very kissable mouth, high cheekbones, a strong nose and a wide forehead. His hair was thick and wavy. His eyes … she tore her gaze away and looked out at the river before he caught her staring at him.

She couldn't pinpoint the moment when her affection for Niall had deepened. Their relationship had begun in a very ordinary way at a party for one of his mates that Vikki had gone to with Mia and Steve, her fiancé. Niall hung around the edges of the same circle of acquaintances as Steve, and she'd found herself chatting easily and naturally to the relaxed Irish guy. They both seemed to have the same attitude towards life – determined not to take anything too seriously and to find the fun element in everything, no matter how ridiculous it was.

They'd picked up where they'd left off when she'd bumped into him at another party, then at the afters of a wedding, then at a concert in Wembley Arena – which they'd both agreed was rubbish, contrary to all their friends' opinions – and feeling like two teenagers on the run from school, they'd sloped off early and gone to the pub instead. He'd said to her at the outset that he wasn't in the market for a serious relationship. She'd said that suited her perfectly as neither was she.

Six months ago, Niall had celebrated his fortieth birthday by taking over the first floor of a Hammersmith restaurant and filling it with mates. 'They're more casual acquaintances,' he'd admitted, when he'd sought her out and they'd had a quiet moment together on the balcony. 'I count you as one of my few real friends. You're like a breath of fresh air to me. You're great. Thing is, Vikki …' he'd paused.

She'd waited.

'Something went badly wrong, years ago,' he'd said, giving her a regretful look as they'd stood together, leaning against the balcony. 'Something I can't bring myself to talk about, but it's the reason why I can't let myself get serious about anyone. I just wanted you to know.'

She'd allowed the silence to rest between them, their arms touching.

'Anyhow,' he'd continued, straightening up, 'birthdays, especially milestone ones, have a habit of making you pause and resurrect old memories. But that's enough about me, we'd better get back to the party.'

He'd had that vulnerable look in his eyes then, and it was significant moments such as these that made her determined never to do or say anything to spoil what they had.

Their friendship had played out against the backdrop of their favourite London haunts, occasional dinners, trips to the movies and the theatre, Friday-after-work drinks, Saturday brunch, then came the odd night when he'd see her home and come up to her Putney flat.

But by degrees, in spite of her best intentions to avoid becoming entangled in any significant relationships, she'd found he was occupying more and more space in her head. A weekend without seeing him was an empty weekend; being in his company filled her with a mixture of excitement and the certainty that this was where she was meant to be. She was hungry to know everything about him, from his opinion on movies and music, books and box sets, his favourite food and chill-out places, to the running of the country.

Then she'd realised that these were all only subtexts to wanting to know how Niall Blake felt deep down inside about big life issues and deeply personal stuff – hopes and dreams, love and death. But these were the places neither of them had gone to yet. Likewise, their past lives were never spoken of; it was as if they'd both come into the friendship as blank slates.

He'd even stayed over the odd time, on the sofa in her flat, looking so ridiculously uncomfortable as well as touchingly vulnerable, with his stockinged feet suspended over the end, that the next time they'd lost track of the hours, chatting until the early morning over a bottle of wine, watching BBC4 on a Friday night, she'd allowed him to crash out, fully clothed, on her bed. He didn't know that she'd spent half the night lying in the dark, listening to him breathe, inhaling his scent, absorbing the precious nearness of him in through her pores and senses until they overflowed.

Then there had been that one night, six weeks ago; she wasn't sure who'd reached for the other first, but they'd slept together as in 'slept together'.

Just be your usual self, Vikki. Oh yeah, easier said than done. She knew how he felt about her: she was his breath of fresh air; he was her London-Irish guy. She sensed there were parts of his life he was keeping under wraps. But, equally, Niall didn't know the real Vikki Gordon, behind the happy-go-lucky face, or the dark thoughts that disturbed her sleep. He didn't know there was a part of her she kept hidden from him, hidden even from herself, squashing it away when it threatened to emerge. Staying light, staying friendly, staying funny, at all costs.

*

He called her on Monday evening. 'Have you a minute to talk?'

'Sure. I'm at home.' *He's changed his mind.*

'I thought you might be out having a ball on the bank holiday.'

'Oh, I was,' she lied. 'I'm at home now, trying to recover.'

She wasn't about to admit she'd spent most of the afternoon in her bedroom feverishly scrutinising the contents of her wardrobe to see what might be suitable when she met Niall's family. Very little. Zilch, actually.

'About the weekend, there are a couple of things …' he said, his voice trailing off.

Things. Here goes. Her heart tumbled down inside her like a brick. 'Go on.'

'I told Lainey I was bringing you; she's organising the arrangements and getting the house in order. It's been more or less unoccupied for the last three years after Dad moved into the town. When she assumed we were an item, I didn't …' a taut silence, then, 'Vikki, I didn't correct her.'

'What does that mean, exactly?'

'Thing is, it means we'll be sharing a room,' he said. 'The spare bedrooms up in the attic haven't been touched in years and are a bit damp so Lainey's just getting the main bedrooms ready. I thought it was only fair to give you advance warning. Scout's honour, I'll behave myself,' he assured her.

'Just as well you did,' she said, her cheerful tone belying the swell in her heart. 'I'll bring my granny PJs in case you hog the duvet and I have industrial ear plugs in case you snore too much. Then again you'd better be warned, it could be me hogging the duvet and snoring my brains out.'

'There's something else …'

*

'What do you mean you won't be at the conference? Are you *mad*?'

On Tuesday evening, in a restaurant tucked into a quaint laneway in Putney, Mia's reaction was just what Vikki had expected. She pushed her pilau rice to one side, took a deep breath and said, as nonchalantly as possible, 'I'm double-booked for next weekend.'

Mia laughed. 'The hell you are.'

'I'm going to Ireland with Niall.' Even saying the words out loud gave her a thrill.

'How nice.'

She knew by Mia's face that she didn't believe her. 'No, seriously … he's actually asked me. Over to Mayo. To meet the family.' She leaned across the table. 'Don't you see what this means?'

Mia sloshed more white wine into their glasses. 'It means you've had far too much of our unseasonal heat and sun. Or wine. Or your Irish guy has turned your head.'

'Maybe he has.'

'Cripes.' Mia put her hand up to her dropped jaw. 'You are serious, aren't you? You're going to miss Saturday's conference because you're going to *Ireland*.'

'Yep.'

Vikki had become good friends with Mia almost ten years ago, when they'd started together in Rosella Incorporated, a large magazine-publishing company, at a time when Vikki had cut all ties to her murky past, changed address, changed job, changed her hairstyle and reinvented herself. Or so she'd thought. Some habits, though, had been hard to break and in recent years, Mia, the older and wiser sister she'd never had, had provided a shoulder to cry on when, one after another, both of Vikki's serious relationships had bitten the dust. Mia had helped her to figure out for herself that she'd been looking for love in all the wrong places; she'd been attracted to the wrong type of guy, giving them permission to walk all over her.

'You need to go out there with a kick-ass attitude,' Mia had said, one of the many nuggets of advice she'd offered to a weeping, snotty-nosed Vikki. Her eyes had been so kind and empathetic that Vikki knew Mia guessed she gravitated towards men who treated her less than she deserved because of a damaging legacy from her past. Mia was the only person in the world she trusted enough to take into her confidence about her feelings for Niall.

Mia shook her head. 'How can you do this, knowing your job could be on the line?'

She wasn't exaggerating. There had been rumours and counter-rumours circulating around Rosella that the magazine *Beautiful Me* where Vikki had a role as assistant editor was going to be subsumed into a sister company magazine, *The Body Perfect*, and Vikki knew there would be no room for two assistant editors. She needed to be there to fight her corner in front of Jo Morgan, the clever, ambitious Rosella CEO.

'This is more important to me than any job. What do you think meeting the family means?'

Mia sat back and studied her face as though she was finally taking Vikki seriously. 'I don't know,' she said, her blue eyes full of warm concern. 'It could mean nothing at all. I'm just being real here. I always had Niall pegged as the kind of guy to run a mile from any kind of serious intention. I've seen you burnt before and I don't want to see that look on your face again. You could lose your job if you don't show this weekend. If Niall was that good of a friend, he'd pick another weekend to introduce you to the family. Of all the crap timings.'

'He doesn't know.'

'The most important weekend of your working life and he doesn't *know*?'

'Before I mentioned the conference, he invited me to the family get-together. I've said "yes".'

There was a long silence while Mia absorbed her words.

'Well then,' she said, 'Plan B. The conference starts at eight o'clock on Saturday morning. We'll be hitting the critical business decisions after coffee break. We can Skype. Jo Morgan doesn't have to know where you are; you could say you were called to a family emergency but you're keeping in touch …' Mia trailed off as Vikki slowly shook her head.

'I can't do that because there's no internet.'

'*What*?'

'Lynes Glen – where Niall is from – is remote. Whatever way the house is situated in the curve of the mountains it's an internet black spot. Even mobile phone signals are non-existent.'

'I do not believe you.' Mia emphasised every word.

'When he called last night he warned me we'll be more or less incommunicado. He's confirmed it with his sister.'

'You think it's OK to lose your iPhone this weekend?'

'I'll hardly need to send out an SOS, will I?'

'So you're just going to commit professional suicide. On account of Niall Blake.'

'Look, Mia, even though I've worked my butt off for the job, I'm still in their firing line. I can't live with the regret of passing up the perfect opportunity to get close to Niall and see where it might lead.'

'Incommunicado for the weekend.' Mia shook her head. 'It'll certainly be a change.'

'I thought it sounded sweet and romantic,' Vikki said

defensively. 'We can have a complete chill, back to nature, walks in the forest, hiking on the mountains. Niall said his sister is arranging a few fun activities. Can't you see, this kind of timeout is just what we need to move the relationship up a gigantic step?'

'OK, I've said my piece.' Mia sighed. She pushed her plate away and rested her elbows on the table. 'If Niall means all that much to you, that not even the prospect of losing your job, never mind the force of my devil's advocate, can rattle you, then I wish you the very best of luck. No doubt you've already gone shopping for a full complement of hiking boots and clothes to suit all weathers. *And* all activities, nocturnal or otherwise.'

Vikki smiled. Trust Mia to come around. 'I'll have them by Friday.'

'It rains a lot in Ireland. Your forest walks could be wet.' Mia picked up her mobile and scrolled through some screens. 'Seems like sunshine all the way for Friday, but Saturday looks seriously rainy.'

Vikki grinned. 'Oh dear, I might just have to tuck myself up in bed. With Niall.'

Mia shook her head and smiled in mild exasperation. 'If I were you, I'd be very careful. This weekend could be a recipe for disaster. Please, for your own sake, do not, in the heat of the moment, mention the L word.'

'I won't make the same mistake twice – or rather three times. It got me into too much trouble before. No way, under any circumstances, will I tell Niall Blake that I love him.'

CHAPTER THREE

On Friday afternoon Vikki watched a small cluster of white airport buildings in the middle of wide open spaces rise up to meet her as the plane screeched down onto the tarmac at Knock airport, Mayo, just ahead of schedule. She pulled on her cream leather jacket, shuffled off the plane, and wheeled her case out into the terminal. Mia was going to make her apologies to Jo Morgan in the morning. Vikki could do zilch. Fate had intervened and all she had to think about was making this weekend work.

Niall had flown into Dublin early that morning because he'd business to do. Right up to the moment she saw him waiting in Arrivals, she'd half wondered if it was all a beautiful fantasy she'd dreamed up during a slow day in Rosella. He was wearing a thick padded jacket she hadn't seen on him before, and she was suddenly shy and overcome by the enormity of it all as their eyes met and held. He came over to her and when he leaned in to kiss her cheek, her breath stopped.

'Thanks for coming. I really appreciate it.'

'No problem,' she said. 'Bring it on.'

'It'll take about an hour and a half to get to Lynes Glen,' he said, leading the way out to his rented car.

Once they cleared the airport, the roads changed; they were narrower and curving, and soon Niall was driving through some of the most spectacular countryside she'd ever seen. She was silenced by the luxury of his close presence as much as the savage beauty in the incredible green and brown and silvery expanses of a huge landscape lit by long darts of sunshine. She caught glimpses of arching stone bridges, ditches brimming with purple heather, hills of yellow gorse, flint-dotted and scree-covered mountainy slopes, where sheep defied the laws of gravity and cast a bored look in the direction of their speeding car. They passed tiny hamlet villages and occasional white-washed roadside cottages, but there were few signs of life. Niall slowed down as they passed through a small, quaint-looking town, where shop fronts and a hotel were still bedecked with the bloom of late-summer flowers.

'This is Creaghbara, the nearest town,' he said. 'It's not much further, ten minutes or so.' They left the town behind, his eyes focussed on the thin ribbon of road that wound around between the purple-grey mountains, mountains that seemed to curve into each other the deeper they drove. It was a road that clung here and there to the edge of a cliff, with Vikki momentarily averting her eyes against the sheer drop to one side. Sitting beside Niall on this spectacular, almost spiritual drive, her senses overflowed.

'Close your eyes,' he said.

She did as he asked, feeling strangely vulnerable.

'Now you can open them,' he said, after a moment.

It took her a few seconds to orientate herself. Overhanging trees on both sides of the road came together in a dark, green tunnel. They came out of the tunnel into brilliant daylight and she blinked.

'It's over there,' he said, sending up chips of loose gravel as he slowed the car to a halt. He turned and stared out her window. 'This is the one spot on the approach road where you can see the house.'

Vikki searched the landscape. The mountains on her side sloped away, a ditch separated them from a sheer drop, and across the valley, about a half a mile away, she saw a stone house with glimmering windows and green lawns unrolling in front. It was set into the embrace of a forest, behind which towering mountains reared up, looking as solid and substantial as though they'd sat there forever.

'Oh, wow,' she breathed out. 'That's it?' She hadn't meant to sound like a small child full of astonishment, but she couldn't help it. Niall's home was in the middle of nowhere, yet in the middle of some of the most raw, spectacular scenery she'd ever seen. It was hard to envisage anyone growing up here, yet he had. She'd always sensed something different about him compared to his London mates; something deep, almost soulful, and it had surely come from growing up in this magical landscape. It was so different to what she'd experienced that she felt a twist of unease.

'Yeah, that's Lynes Glen,' he said.

She turned and looked at his face at the same time as he leaned across to stare out the window. He was so close she could have kissed his mouth, and her head spun. The expression in his eyes was unreadable.

'That mountain peak behind the house is Slieve Creagh. I climbed to the top. Once.'

'I'm impressed.' She added that to her list of things she hadn't known about this man.

'The road is a bit twisty,' he said. 'Are you ready for this?'

'Ready for the scary drive around the mountains or the weekend?'

'Both.'

She looked at the uncharacteristic flickers of hesitation in his amber-green eyes. She sensed something vulnerable about him and had the odd thought that if she said 'no' he'd turn back, no questions asked.

'You know me, I'm game for anything,' she said, looking at him steadily.

'Good. Let's party.'

Niall negotiated a couple of hair-raising, switchback bends. As they turned around another, she saw the signpost; old and mottled with the elements, it swung drunkenly on a rusting pole, wobbling generally to the left. Despite the faded lettering she could make out what it said: 'Lough Lynes'. At first she couldn't see anything, there was a track sloping down off the road but it was blocked with a cattle gate, the once-galvanised bars now corroded and choked with stray bushes and vegetation. Niall swung around another bend and she saw the silvery-white glimmer of water piercing through gaps in the trees. A flock of blackbirds rose up out of the nearby hedgerows, cawing and shrieking as they flapped their wings and tumbled into the sky like dark leaves being scattered off a tree in a windstorm. They cleared the tangle of trees; there was a ditch blocked by a rusting sheet of corrugated iron reinforced with barbed wire, and, over that, she finally had a view.

It was a small lake, lying cupped on three sides in the palm of the mountains, the surface so still it could have been a silvery mirror reflecting the semi-circle of indigo summits and soft, blue sky overhead. It looked so beautiful and pure that Vikki drew in her breath.

Then she saw something silhouetted against the platinum calm of the lake. A long wooden diving board extended from a rocky outcrop, high over the lake. There was someone sitting on it, someone with long, red-gold hair, legs dangling in space. The image seemed so cinematic and surreal that, as they turned the next bend, Vikki craned her neck to make sure she hadn't been seeing things, but her view was blocked once more, this time by the edges of a pine forest.

'What a beautiful lake,' she said.

Niall didn't reply.

'Or is it called a lough? Lough Lynes?'

'It's out of bounds,' Niall said, surprising her with his clipped tone.

'It can't be,' Vikki said.

'What do you mean?'

'There was someone on the diving board,' Vikki said. 'A woman, with long, red hair.'

The car stopped suddenly as Niall jammed on the brakes, throwing her forward.

'What's up?'

'You must have been seeing things,' Niall said, his voice firm. 'It's been blocked off for years.' He stared ahead through the windscreen, lost somewhere in his own thoughts, his face wintry. For the first time since she'd arrived in Ireland she felt a sliver of cold anxiety in her stomach and her confidence dipped.

'Is that the only access?' she asked, hoping to bring Niall back from wherever he'd disappeared to.

He gave a curt shake of his head. 'There's a track through from the forest close to the house but that's also closed up.'

'Any reason why?'

Again, a taut silence. He didn't meet her eyes. 'Vikki – look, just forget what you saw. There couldn't have been anyone there, it was a trick of the sunlight. Or the mist … you're in fairy country now, as my ancestors would say. It was a banshee or something.' He managed to sound like it was a big joke as he put the car into gear and they moved forward, tyres crunching against the edge of the narrow road.

Vikki bit her lip. She was susceptible to atmosphere but didn't believe in fairies or any of that stuff. And there was no mist. The sun glinted across the panorama of slopes and valleys, and in her mind's eye, with crystal clarity, Vikki saw the dream-like image of the woman sitting on the diving board.

'What's a "banshee"?' she asked eventually, annoyed that she had allowed the incident to put a dent in her confidence.

'Nothing much,' Niall said, his eyes focussed on the narrow road. 'I was just talking off the top of my head.'

'Sure, but what is it?'

'It's old Irish folklore … the kind of fireside tale my elders would have been raised on in the days of no television …'

'You still haven't told me what it means, it must be an Irish secret,' she said lightly.

'It's classified information,' he said in a jokey voice. 'Folklore has it that the banshee could be a beautiful young girl or an old hag, and her cries and wails are supposed to herald a death in the family.'

Vikki suppressed a shiver. The glimpse of the woman had been too far away and fleeting to judge if it was either of those, but the long, red-gold hair suggested someone young and beautiful.

'Scary,' she said. 'Is this my London Niall talking? Or have you reverted to type since we arrived in Mayo?'

'After over twenty years in London, I doubt I'd revert that easily ...'

Twenty years? She knew so little about him and she wondered what had prompted his departure. 'You must have been very young and innocent when you left all this behind.'

'Young, yes, innocent, definitely not,' he said tersely. Then after a pause, 'Do me a favour though, will you? Keep what you ... what you thought you saw to yourself.'

'You don't want your family thinking I'm a crazy little cockney gal?'

'They won't mind you being crazy. Crazy is good; you might need to be slightly bonkers to survive the weekend in Lynes Glen with my family, but no banshees, OK?' His eyes, when they shifted off the narrow road long enough to glance at her, were warm.

'If it means that much to you, and so long as I don't see a leprechaun jumping out of the bushes ...'

'You won't see any leprechauns, promise.' He pitched his voice in low, sombre tones, as though the whole thing was to be treated as a joke.

They were approaching the house, driving between wrought-iron gates that hung lopsidedly against paint-peeling pillars, tyres scrunching up a rutted drive that was hedged with beech and pockmarked with weeds sprouting between potholes in the gravel. Behind the hedge a wide lawn ran down to the boundary wall, unkempt grass riffling in the breeze. One upon a time, the entrance would have been impressive; now it looked neglected. The drive ended in a circular flourish by the steps to the hall door.

The exterior of Lynes Glen reminded Vikki of a small Victorian hunting lodge she'd stayed in once outside Inverness. It had a stone front that blended perfectly into the landscape, a heavy black door, two storeys with long sash windows, and above them, two dormer windows set into the attic. She saw a terraced garden running the length of one side. The house had a cosy and sheltered position, tucked into the curve of the forest. Up behind the forest, the barren peaks of Slieve Creagh towered in shades of blue and grey, yellowed now, with pale afternoon sunlight. She sensed someone watching their arrival, but when she ran her eyes along the windows, all she could see was the reflection of the sun and the sky.

Niall ran a hand through his hair and let out his breath. 'Jeez, it hasn't changed a bit. Apart from the gardens needing attention, it looks the exact same.'

'How long is it since you've been home?'

'How long did I say I'd been living in London?'

'You can't mean – you've never been back?'

'Home to Ireland, yes, but not Lynes Glen. That's why I'm glad I have my best mate with me.'

'Is it that bad? Lynes Glen? Or your family? Should I turn and run now?' she asked, forcibly injecting some humour into her voice.

'Actually, Vikki, I haven't been back here since Mum died,' he said quietly.

Vikki bit her lip. 'Gosh, sorry if I said the wrong thing.'

'You didn't, so no worries. Hey,' he said, grinning, 'it'll be different with you here, you and me against the world. Just stick close to me and it'll be fine.'

What did he mean by 'you and me against the world'? Possibly different to what she had imagined and little to do with wanting to show her off to his family. Why hadn't he been back since his mother had died? Another wave of unease slid through her as Niall switched off the engine. The heavy black door swung open and a woman stood in the doorframe. She was tall and slim, wearing figure-hugging indigo jeans and a thin, cream sweater. Her hair was the same burnished russety shade as Niall's, only hers swung down sleekly to her shoulders. Vikki guessed she was in her mid-forties, and as she stood in the framed doorway, she looked like a painting that was fixed and somehow untouchable until Niall stepped out of the car. Then, as though she remembered her manners, she seemed to step out of that tableau, coming down the steps, arms outstretched in welcome. In the moment before she was wrapped in Niall's embrace, Vikki saw that she had the same shade of beautiful eyes.

She couldn't have been anyone other than Lainey, his sister. Otherwise Vikki would have been very jealous of the warm welcome they exchanged. They spoke together for a short while, Niall's head bent attentively towards hers. It was a striking image, both tall and slim and with that unusual shade of hair, framed against the stunning background. Vikki was unable to hear the conversation but there was no doubt Lainey was reassuring Niall about something. She felt a little disorientated as she picked up her handbag and got out of the car. She took a gulp of crystal-clear air and felt the pine-scented breeze riffling gently against her face. The late afternoon was brighter here than it would be in London. The breadth of the landscape stretching on forever under boundless skies was so huge she could have been thousands of miles from the teeming bustle of that city.

Lainey came over to Vikki and gave her a hug and a big bright smile. 'Hi, you must be Vikki. I'm Lainey, Niall's sister. It's lovely to meet you.'

'Hi, Lainey, nice to meet you too.'

Lainey was even more striking up close, with her translucent, porcelain skin and that colouring. Her smile brought out the fine lines around her eyes and made her seem human and more approachable.

'I was beginning to give up on this brother of mine finding a woman,' she said, her voice slightly inflected with the same tones as Niall. 'I haven't a clue how he managed to drag you away from London and over here into the wilds of nowhere. And if we all get too much for you and you want to phone a friend, it isn't going to happen.'

'Yes, Niall explained all that.'

Lainey smiled. 'There should be no need for us to have to phone any friends, isn't that right, Niall?' She looked pointedly at her brother. Something silent passed between them that made Vikki feel oddly excluded.

Get a grip, she admonished herself. They were family.

Still, Niall flicked a look at Lainey that she couldn't decipher. 'That's right, Lainey,' he said evenly. 'We'll all be perfectly well-behaved.'

'Anyway, it'll be good for us to have an "unplugged weekend",' Lainey said. 'We'll be more present to each other instead of communicating through our screens.'

'Great stuff,' Niall said.

'Glad that's all agreed,' Lainey said. She turned back to Vikki. 'You're very welcome, Vikki; welcome to Lynes Glen.'

CHAPTER FOUR

Niall lifted out the cases and shut the boot of the car, the sound echoing in the clear air like gunshot. A flock of birds exploded up out of the trees, their black shapes circling overhead against the clear, blue sky before drifting back down to settle in the treetops.

'Is everyone here?' Niall asked Lainey, nodding to the cars and jeep already parked up to the side around by the outbuildings.

'We're waiting on Alex and Jenna; they arrived into Shannon early this morning and stopped off in Galway,' Lainey said. She spoke, Vikki thought, as though she'd rehearsed the words in advance. 'Dad's delighted everyone is coming.' Lainey continued in that smooth tone of voice.

'We didn't get much choice, did we?' Niall muttered.

'Look, Niall ...' Lainey began.

Again, Vikki saw a meaningful look pass between them. Niall shook his head. There seemed to be a silent conversation going on that she knew nothing of.

'How is Dad?' he asked.

'He's resting at the moment,' Lainey said. 'He'll talk to the three of us before dinner and meet the full gang at dinner. We're having an early meal. I'm hoping to fit in a walk outside after that.'

'Yes, I think we all have the timetable.'

Timetable? For a relaxing get-together? Vikki tried not to let the surprise show on her face.

'Dad's particularly glad the grandkids will be here,' Lainey went on. 'It means a lot to him.'

They went up the granite steps and into the house, and Vikki felt something squeezing her chest as she stepped into the tiled hallway. She was on Niall's territory. His home. She felt she was walking across a threshold into an irresistible, mysterious space, or through the magical wardrobe in Narnia.

The hallway opened onto a square that was full of faded, old-world charm, with a high, ornate mirror over a big marbled fireplace, a small mahogany bookcase crammed with books, and two assorted wingback armchairs with huge shabby cushions. There were panelled doors to the left and right. A glittering chandelier hung in the hallway from high, corniced ceilings. A staircase covered in a dark flowery carpet, with filigree wrought-iron banisters curved up to the right. Straight ahead, and to the side of the staircase, passageways led to other rooms. This was where Niall had grown up; he'd spent his childhood and adolescence moving around in this space. She felt the walls vibrated with the essence of children past, the laughter and the shouts, the host of family memories.

Good memories. Unlike her own.

'I've put you both in the main guest bedroom,' Lainey said. 'The children are all bunking in together in my old room.'

'Grand.' Niall darted a glance at Vikki to check she was OK with that.

'And here come the terrors,' Lainey said as two young children came barrelling up the hallway.

'Hi, Niall!'

'*Nially!*'

A young boy and a slightly older girl came running up and launched themselves on Niall, and Vikki's heart was warmed by the way his face lit up with love and tenderness as they entangled themselves around his torso.

'What did I say about running around?' Lainey said. She turned to Niall, smiling as she spoke. 'Great to see some life about the house,' she said quietly.

Niall scooped up the young boy in one arm and put his other arm around his niece as they cuddled into him.

'Hey, don't mind your mom, you can run around as much as you like. Vikki, meet my two favourite people in the whole world, Charlotte and Harry. Say hello to Vikki.'

Two pairs of eyes looked curiously at Vikki. Charlotte's were bright blue, and Harry's were green like his mother's.

'Hi, Vikki,' Harry said.

'Hi, Vikki. Are you going to marry Niall?' Charlotte asked.

'Charlotte! You don't ask questions like that,' Lainey admonished.

'But I heard you saying it to Dad—'

Vikki felt her face flushing.

'That's enough. Sorry, Niall, and you're only in the door.' Lainey rubbed her brother's arm in a warm gesture, looking up into his face as she did so. There seemed to be a slightly inquisitive glint in her eyes as though she was trying to glean if a wedding might be on the cards, but Vikki dismissed it as her imagination.

Niall levered Harry to the floor and gave him a high five. He bent down so he was on a level with Charlotte. 'If ever I am, you'll be the first to know,' he said. 'Is that a deal?'

'Can I have a high five too?'

''Course.' Niall obliged.

'Will you play hide and seek?' Harry asked.

Niall smiled. 'Later.'

'Come on,' Harry said, pulling at his sister. 'We'll find some good places where Niall will never find us.'

'There are great hiding places in this house,' Charlotte said, doing a twirl before running off after her brother.

A tall, well-built man came out of the same door that the children had rushed out of and ambled up the hallway, extending his hand to Niall. He had a kind, lived-in face, brown eyes that looked ready to share a joke, and Vikki liked him on sight.

'Hi Niall,' he said. 'Good to see you. And' – he turned to Vikki – 'you must be the woman who's keeping this guy in check.'

Lainey broke in. 'Vikki, this is Ben, my husband. Don't mind him. You're here as Niall's guest.'

'Nice to meet you, Ben,' Vikki said.

Ben leaned across and gave her a kiss on the cheek. 'You too, Vikki. Good to have someone on my side against the combined force of the Blakes.' He turned to Lainey. 'Any sign of Jenna and Alex?'

'They're due anytime,' Lainey said. 'I've no way of knowing if they were delayed.'

'The perils of being disconnected,' Ben said. 'We'll all have to talk to each other instead of losing ourselves in our phones. I can't think of a better recipe for perfect family harmony.'

'Ben!' Lainey admonished.

Ben lowered his voice theatrically and his eyes were full of laughter as he said to Vikki, 'Welcome to Lynes Glen, better known as the lion's den.'

'Ben, that's enough.' Lainey tossed her head in exasperation as though she was used to hearing this expression and it was wearing thin. 'Go on up and settle in,' she said to Niall. 'Then come down for drinks. We're slumming it in the living room for now, but we'll eat in the dining room later.'

Slumming it? In this house? Vikki got the sense that Lainey was going a little overboard in her efforts to sound relaxed about the weekend.

'I know you said Dad was covering the food and wine expenses, but I'd like to make some contribution,' Niall said quietly.

Lainey shook her head. 'Alex said the same to me when we spoke last week, but absolutely not, Dad's insistent it's his treat. He's received some unexpected royalties from America. The best contribution you can make is by being here, and helping to make it a good weekend for everyone. OK?'

'Right. OK.' Another look passed between the siblings. Then Niall grabbed the cases. 'Come on, Vikki,' he said. 'I'll show you around when we've sorted these out.'

Vikki had taken two steps up the stairs when Lainey said, 'You're both sharing a bathroom with the kids, is that OK, Vikki?'

'Sure,' Vikki said, feeling on the edge of hysterical laughter. Sharing a bathroom with three small children was insignificant compared to sharing a bed with Niall. As she went up the stairs, she heard Lainey say to Niall in a quieter tone of voice, which was loaded with something Vikki couldn't define, 'Ben and I are in your old room, and we're sharing a bathroom with Alex and Jenna. I thought that was the best way to manage it.'

Manage what, Vikki wondered, as she followed Niall up the stairs.

'We're first on the left,' he said. Behind them, the staircase continued on up, leading to the attic rooms.

Vikki opened the heavy mahogany door and stepped inside. She sensed a ripple of expectation in the still air and had the odd feeling that the room had been quietly waiting for this moment. She shrugged off the sense that she was being watched. The room was beautiful and more than half the size of her London flat. Two long sash windows looked out over the front gardens, cream-shaded curtains held back by swags. A rug covered most of the floorboards, there was a wardrobe, matching dressing table, chest of drawers, and a big high bed, covered in a thick duvet with extra blankets folded on top. A side table held a bottle of water and glasses, and a jug of wild flowers, a small box of chocolates and magazines. Fluffy towels were piled on top of the chest of drawers.

'Lainey did an amazing job,' Niall said, opening a door opposite the bed. 'This is the bathroom.'

The bathroom was generously sized as well, almost the size of Vikki's entire living area, with a black and white tiled floor, a huge claw-footed bath and a shower over the bath. It was interconnected between their bedroom and the children's bedroom. Niall threw open a door to that bedroom and Vikki peeked inside. The double bed and single bed were covered with cartoon duvets.

'Lainey must have brought the duvets from home, fair dues to her,' Niall said.

The amazing Lainey must have thought of everything, Vikki thought, surprising herself with her prickle of annoyance. Niall showed her how the bathroom could be locked from either side for privacy.

'It's the same setup across the corridor,' Niall explained. 'So don't worry about coming face to face with anyone else on your bathroom trips. Come on, we'll have a quick look.' He brought her through the children's bedroom and back out onto the corridor, throwing open the door to the room opposite.

'This is Alex's room,' he said. It was a room much like theirs except it faced the back of the house and the mountains. Vikki followed Niall through the room and into another bathroom, then he stopped at the threshold of the bedroom beyond that, which Lainey and Ben were using.

'This used to be my room,' he said.

'They're all beautiful,' Vikki said. 'But no old aeroplanes hanging from the ceiling? Or school books, or marks on the wall from posters of Prince or whoever you might have followed then. Oasis, maybe?' she prompted, hoping to get more insight into this man. There was nothing to show in any of the bedrooms that a family had grown up here. Any trace that Niall or his siblings had inhabited them during all the childhood and adolescent years was long gone.

'Ah, here.' Niall laughed. 'God forbid. The rooms were all cleared out a few years after we left. There are probably boxes of my stuff up in the attic but they can stay there. At one stage Dad used to have the occasional writer and poet stay over as a sort of retreat. Lynes Glen was perfect for that kind of thing and it gave him something to talk about. Lainey was the driver behind it to give him another interest and she got the house organised at the time. But it didn't really take off. Then about three years ago the house got too much, his age caught up with him so he moved to an apartment in the town and Lainey arranged day-to-day help for him, to maintain some independence.'

'It must have been far too big for him on his own,' Vikki said.

'He loved this house,' Niall replied, throwing his case down on a chair and zipping open the lid. 'It was his parents' home as well, and his paternal grandfather's, who made a fortune in America before coming back home and buying it. Dad was an only child, so it was always part of him, and in his blood.'

'How about you?' Vikki asked, disconcerted by the unusual familiarity of Niall picking out some jeans and tops and putting them on the bed. 'Did you miss not coming back here in the last twenty years?'

'Not a bit,' Niall said easily. 'I caught up with Dad along with Lainey in Dublin, and they popped over to London now and again.' He opened the wardrobe, sending clothes hangers jingling together in the space, pulling a couple of pairs of trousers and tops through some hangers. 'Plenty of room for whatever you want to hang up.'

She was unable to speak for a moment. It would be the first time they'd shared a bed since the night they'd made love. Niall came over to her, putting his arms loosely around her.

'Hey, having second thoughts?' he asked.

'Absolutely, just what have I signed up for here?'

'I'll keep to my promise, no messing,' Niall said, his eyes warm. 'I'll stick to my side of the bed and I won't even sneak a peek at you in your nightie. OK?'

'And I won't look at you in your ... whatever.' She grinned, her mouth wobbly with nerves.

He tightened his arms around her. He bent his head so that their foreheads touched. She inhaled the nearness of him and longed to melt into him. The edge-of-senses pleasure and the heat and warmth of the night they'd spent wrapped up in each other flashed between them. She wasn't sure who'd reached for the other first; it had been slow and sensual and achingly perfect, almost like a dream sequence, until the next morning when he'd sat at the edge of the bed, his head in his hands, and said it shouldn't have happened, it had been a mistake. The last thing he'd wanted to do was take advantage of her, or ruin their friendship – she was a brilliant person, wonderful and warm, and far too good for him.

Too *good*? Nausea had risen in her throat. His gut-wrenching words and the look on his face had silenced her.

'Look, Vikki, I think you're—' He bit back whatever he'd been about to say. He pulled away slightly and went on, 'You're my best mate. I appreciate you coming to my rescue.'

She tilted her head back. 'Your rescue? From what?'

He gave her a quirky smile. 'My family.'

He didn't sound like he had brought her here to show her off, let alone move things on between them in the big wide bed. 'I don't blame you,' she said, swallowing her disappointment. 'They seem like a load of monsters and I'm actually quite terrified.'

'You haven't met Alex,' he said quietly. He smoothed her hair, taking a deep interest in fixing strands of it behind her ears, sending delicious shivers through her scalp.

'Would he terrify me even more?'

'Thing is, I suppose it's best you know – I haven't seen Alex since I left here.'

'But that was …'

'Twenty-one years, actually,' he said.

Her heart stilled. 'I don't understand. Your own brother? You haven't seen him? In all that time?'

'No. There have been occasional emails, but very occasional.'

'Emails?! No phone calls? Texts? Skype?'

He shrugged. 'I know it sounds mad, but it was just a situation that … evolved.'

'Are you going to tell me why?'

'It's something I can't talk about,' he said, his face a mask of regret. 'What happened between us – I'm not very proud of it to say the least, can we just leave it?'

'*Leave* it?' Her total bafflement must have shown on her face.

'Look, we all have baggage ... something ...' he said, giving her a sober look that cut straight to her heart. 'We're all, to some degree, operating as best we can with a safety net drawn over certain things. Alex and I – what happened was total crap and I hope we can just park things for the weekend. Can you try to understand?'

She understood that they both had things they were keeping from each other. She'd never spoken to him of her mother, Sally Gordon. He'd never told her about the rift with his brother. And so what if Niall had family stuff he was keeping from her? After all, he knew next to nothing about her family. Whatever about him not being home for over twenty years, she hadn't been home for ten years.

But where did that fit with wanting to deepen their friendship? How could you form a committed, loving relationship if there were big parts of each other about which you knew nothing? They might be good friends, but their friendship was built on shaky ground. Tear away the safety net and everything would all fall down. Vikki shut her ears to the voice in her head.

Niall put his hands on her shoulders. 'I just need to have my best buddy at my back. OK?'

'Short of taking the car and attempting to find my way back to civilisation, which would be impossible, it seems I am going to be here.' She tried to sound bright and breezy but she failed miserably to get beyond the lump in her throat at the thoughts of how fragile their relationship actually was. She'd also harboured the faint idea that maybe she could have driven to a nearby village in the morning to connect even briefly with Mia and the conference in London, but that wasn't going to happen.

'Thanks, you're a star,' he said, giving her a squeeze. 'I'll leave you to unpack. Come downstairs when you're ready and I'll show you around.'

*

Vikki felt hollow inside as she unpacked her clothes: pencil-slim jeans and soft sweaters, a cherry-red and deep-blue for day time, and just in case, a couple of lacy and chiffony tops for the evening. She'd maxed out her credit card with new hiking boots, as well as frothy underwear and white lacy PJs, bought in a haze of feverish anticipation during a rushed lunch hour on Thursday. She left the underwear in her case for now.

She went out to the landing, pausing to admire the stained-glass window set into the alcove in the wall at the end of the corridor. Full of colourful leaded glass, it sent beautiful prisms of light playing along the wall. There were candles on the windowsill, a bookcase underneath filled with assorted books, and beside that, a comfortable armchair making it a perfect reading spot. The cosy look of it sent something soothing into Vikki's jangled nerves as though she was in a good place and she wondered if Niall's mother had arranged this years ago.

She *was* in a good place, even if she sensed the atmosphere was thick with memories and secrets. All families had them, concealed in their hearts. She took a slow, deep breath. Maybe the weekend hadn't started out as she'd hoped, but it was just the beginning. She had three nights when she'd be lying next to Niall in the king-sized bed, mornings when she'd wake up beside him, warm and cosy. Something good had to come out of those sleepy, unguarded moments.

She heard voices coming from below her. Quiet tones, as if anxious not to be overheard, but they carried straight up the stairwell to where she was standing.

'So she doesn't know …' It was Lainey speaking.

'No, I promise, not a clue.' Niall's voice.

Vikki froze.

'Good. Let's keep it like that.'

'How about Alex?'

'He feels the same as we do – honestly, Niall.'

'I hope so. It'll be bad enough facing him as it is.'

'It'll be fine. We're all agreed. Total silence. It never happened.'

'I got a bit of a start on the way here …'

'You did?'

'Vikki thought she saw something … someone on the diving board by the lough …'

'Go on.' A trace of ice in Lainey's tone.

'Someone with long, red hair.'

'For Christ's sake, tell me you're joking …' Her response was instant and sharp, the language a surprise coming from perfectly polished Lainey.

'I'm not. I told her it was a trick of the light, that we're in fairy country now.'

'You big eejit.'

'I panicked. I couldn't think straight. I nearly crashed the car as it was. Supposing she hadn't been seeing things? That someone – or something – had been there?'

'Jesus, don't start. There couldn't have been anything there. It's all blocked up.'

'That's how it looks but I'm sure you can still get through somehow.'

'It would be difficult but not impossible. Still, as far as we're concerned, it's all blocked up, right?'

There was a short silence.

'Right.'

'Vikki seems like a nice girl but I can't understand why you wanted to drag her over here into all this.'

'She's a good friend. She's very special to me.'

'Did you really have to bring her this weekend?'

'Coming back here – I felt I needed all the support I could get.'

'*I'm* here—'

A door opened downstairs and one of the children called out. There was the sound of footsteps fading away. Vikki put her fist to her trembling mouth, tiptoed back along the corridor and went into the bedroom, her face stinging. She needed a few moments to compose herself before going downstairs. And she needed to shove what she'd heard into a far corner of her mind, otherwise she'd drive herself mad wondering what had gone wrong in this family and why Niall needed her support.

She went across to the dressing table and checked her face in the mirror. She looked OK, didn't she? Just a tiny telltale tinge in her cheeks. She went over to the window and rested her hot cheek against its coolness. Outside, the surrounding countryside was veiled in afternoon sunshine and, despite her misgivings, she felt a lift of pleasure at the beauty of the scene. In the distance, she saw the glint of something sparking against the grey-blue shale of the mountains. It came again, a quick flash, then she realised it was a car travelling along the approach road to Lynes Glen that Niall had taken earlier that afternoon. Alex and his family? Alex, the brother Niall hadn't spoken to in over twenty years, for whatever reason he was unable to say …

CHAPTER FIVE

New York: Two months earlier

Her arms laden, Jenna Blake shouldered her way into the kitchen of her Manhattan apartment and dropped a box of groceries along with a bouquet of flowers onto the brushed granite counter top. Sunshine flooded the kitchen so that the shiny surfaces gleamed and sparkled. She was thankful the air conditioning was cool and comfortable after the humidity of the July afternoon outside. Six-year-old Jack had run into the living room and she heard the rattle as he pulled his storage box of Lego over to the low table, and knew he'd be engrossed in it for a while.

She filled a vase with water and opened the wrapper on the flowers, arranging them in the vase, placing it in the middle of the table. An assorted bouquet of blooms to add a splash of colour against the clean, white tones of the kitchen and a splash of cheer to herself. Not that anything was going to erase the thin thread of anxiety that had taken up permanent residence in her stomach.

She unpacked the groceries and put them away. Closing the fridge door, she glared at the invitation attached to the front by a magnet bearing the highly unlikely legend that she was the best cook in the world (a joke magnet that Alex had picked up in a souvenir store one holiday when they had taken refuge out of the rain), an invitation that was far more of an aberration than the fridge magnet.

She'd be forty years old next year, but instead of feeling any kind of maturity, she found everything was becoming more complicated. She knew life could throw you curve balls, that there were times when you were floundering along trying to figure things out and keep your head together, times when you were holding your breath as you tried to slip quietly through the days without drawing any attention to yourself in case the universe remembered you were there and fired something else at you.

She was already at that stage, juggling a load of curve balls, when the invitation to Ireland had arrived out of the blue. Alex had put it on the fridge, marking his intent. As if she'd needed reminding. The white card with the printed invitation, signed in Leo's faltering handwriting, inviting them for a family get-together at the beginning of September, was innocuous in itself, yet the significance of the invitation was the equivalent of a grenade going off in their already rocky lives. She still couldn't believe Alex had accepted it, his casual tone of voice making light of the total enormity of this.

'You can't mean we're going to Ireland, as in *actually going*?' she'd said when he'd told her he'd already phoned his father to accept.

'Why *actually* not? I thought you'd be happy to see where I grew up,' Alex had said, sounding as though it was a trip to the movies. 'And Jack would enjoy being with his cousins.'

Jack had never met his Irish cousins.

'At least you've plenty of notice,' Alex had continued. 'You're not usually booked up two months in advance, are you?'

'No, but ...' Jenna had struggled, her mouth opening and closing ineffectually, unable to find her voice as she stared at Alex, her mind racing.

Because in all the years I've known you, she thought, *you have never accepted any invitation for both of us without checking it with me first. But that's only trivial compared to the rest:*

Because you've never been home since you relocated to New York.

Because your mother, the beautiful Gabrielle, died years ago in a car crash and it was a terrible tragedy. But you don't talk about it. Ever.

Because I know you had some kind of a bust-up with your brother – a difference of opinion, you said, old history, it didn't matter anymore, it would never affect the both of us – but you still won't tell me why you haven't talked to him in all that time, except through your sister. I wouldn't even count the two or three emails you have exchanged because they were also replies to Lainey's emails, when she copied the both of you.

Because sometimes in your nightmares you call out Niall's name. But you never talk about your nightmares either.

Because we've ignored these things for so long and accommodated them into the fabric of our marriage it's become part of our tapestry, like a dark threading in one corner that we've tacitly chosen not to unpick.

The words swirled, unsaid, in the air between them. She knew she'd been partly complicit – so wrapped up in the hot glow of loving Alex Blake, of marrying him, that she'd readily agreed to whatever he wanted.

*

He came into her life seven years ago like a ball of energy and fire, sweeping her off her stilettoed feet the day he'd walked into the Manhattan accountancy office where she'd then worked. He was the director of a consultancy firm that had been engaged to upgrade their cyber security systems, and, as they sat in a meeting, she found herself drawn to the Irishman with the taut, rather intense face, as if to a magnet. His combination of startling green eyes, thick, dark-red hair and an attractive, quick-fire intelligence sent something hot rushing through her veins. At thirty-two years of age she felt like a teenager all over again.

During the upgrade project, Alex's lead consultant became unexpectedly ill, so he stepped in for him and Jenna was assigned the role of liaising with him. They had three weeks of shared morning coffees and snatched takeout lunches at the desk, long evenings spent hunched over computer screens, late nights thrashing out solutions on whiteboards. Then one night when they stayed back together to solve a particularly messy problem, Alex lifted her up spontaneously and hugged her. She felt the sexual tension leap between them and he put her down hurriedly as though he'd been scorched.

'Oops,' he said. 'I don't think that's very compatible with our business relationship.'

'I agree,' she said, staring into his eyes, weak with longing. 'We're going to have to re-negotiate that contract, beginning immediately. I'm just wondering if there are any other areas where we might need to – ah – explore our degree of compatibility.'

She moved closer and kissed him. He kissed her back. A long, sensual, high-voltage kiss that had no place in an office environment. They went for a drink after work, neither of them wanting to pop the bubble of charged expectation that glittered around them. They didn't bother with a second drink as they couldn't wait to be alone, and Jenna brought him back to her apartment, her anticipation at fever pitch.

'I still don't know,' she said, the following morning as they sipped coffee in her tiny galley kitchen, both of them giddy with the knowledge that something wonderful was happening between them.

'Know what?' He'd come from the shower, a blue towel wrapped around his waist. He smelled of almond-scented shower oil. His eyes were warm with satisfaction. His hair was damp and messy.

'If my findings are conclusive ...' she said, biting on a corner of her lip because it was the only way she could prevent herself from leaning over to kiss him.

He smiled at her over the rim of his cup. 'Even after all those test runs?'

Four times. Starting in the hallway, barely inside the door before they'd come together, he holding her up, balancing her against the wall as they shoved clothing aside and he'd kissed her hard before powering into her, then moving onto the kitchen – she, sitting on the edge of her counter wrapping her legs around him, oh, dear God – and then, finally twice in the bedroom. Each time more intense, more explosive, more satisfying than the previous. Now, remembering, her body was liquid fire.

Alex put down his coffee, looped his arms around her and kissed the top of her head. 'We'll just have to test it again, won't we?'

She went to his place that night and they barely made it into the office on time the following morning. In work, they kept their relationship under wraps and managed to keep their hands off each other, but after four weeks, when the project was completed and Alex and his team had left, they finally met each other's friends and let everyone know they were a serious item. They were six months into their relationship and Jenna had just moved in to Alex's apartment when she became pregnant.

Alex insisted on marriage.

'I don't want you to feel you have to,' she said. 'We're not living in the olden days.'

'I don't feel I have to, I love you, I want to marry you, baby or no baby, and I want to be married to the mother of my child.'

'I need to be sure you are not asking me in the emotion of this moment,' she said. 'Ask me again, ask me again in a month when my hormones have settled down.'

He didn't wait that long. He asked her the following week, and the week after that, and she still put him off. She held out until the three-month watershed, by which time he had bought a ring, and he surprised her with it at 30,000 feet as they flew down to San Francisco to visit her mother and sister, kneeling down in the cramped cabin. This time she agreed.

They had a small wedding in New York, with immediate family and friends.

'No brother, not even to our wedding?' she asked.

'No, but it's cool. I'm not disappointed and I don't want you to be either.'

She knew by then that they hadn't spoken in years. He told her she knew all the important stuff; that he loved her and wanted to take care of her forever, that their marriage was a fresh start for both of them and nothing that had happened in his life up to now was of any consequence. She could have dug deeper, asked more questions, but something in Alex's eyes forbade her to, unequivocally.

Then Jack arrived within a month of Alex's fortieth birthday, perfect, adorable, wonderful Jack, and the sight of him nestling in Alex's safe arms brought a tidal wave of happiness and contentment.

'My dad and Lainey can't wait to meet you,' Alex said to his son. 'They'll be over to visit as soon as we're ready for them.'

Wrapped up in the mix of first-time motherhood combined with crippling tiredness and an unexpected lack of confidence in her maternal skills, Jenna didn't question why Alex hadn't chosen the milestone occasion of his son's birth in order to mend the rift with his brother. But once more, rather than sully their new gloss of parenthood, any more than she'd wanted to spoil their wedding day, she chose to ignore it and avoid confrontation.

Four months later she was back at work, and juggling motherhood with a fast-paced career was all she had the energy for. However, she was overdoing it, and found herself having a full-blown panic attack one morning when she was late for work thanks to a disturbed sleep as Jack had been sick the night before.

The reality check she gave herself resulted in walking away from twelve-hour days, deciding to change direction and set up in business for herself as a personal stylist, so that she could be there more for Jack and follow her own dreams. Time slipped past, and she was so caught up in her daily routine that it took her a while to realise all was not well with her and Alex, as well as Alex and his IT security company.

She wasn't sure when late nights at the office, weekend

working, and a constant stream of calls to his mobile began to take over their marriage. Alex became irritable with her and refused to talk about things when he came home late, white-faced and dishevelled. He missed plenty of date nights and social occasions as he was 'far too busy' or 'snowed under'. She couldn't remember the last time he'd complimented her, or looked at her with some affection, any more than she could remember the last time they'd made heart-warming love as opposed to using each other for the release of quick, mindless sex.

She could have suspected he was having an affair, except she overheard some of his phone calls and knew there were problems in his company. Disappointed with the way he pushed her aside and shrugged off her concerns, she began to wonder how much he loved her. They were supposed to be a partnership, weren't they? Yet he didn't seem to trust her enough to confide in her. She was afraid – afraid to push it, to antagonise him further, to put more distance between them. In case what? Because sometimes she found herself questioning if he'd only married her because Jack had been on the way. Alex's pride ran deep, and she knew he'd want to be married to the mother of his child.

*

That evening, Jenna waved the invitation in the air and brought up the subject again when Alex came home from the office later than ever.

'I just want to make sure I have this right,' she said. 'So your plan is, we're all flying to Ireland.'

'Yes, so?' he said, putting down his briefcase and reaching inside it for his iPad. 'It's about time we went over there for a change.'

His father and Lainey had come over to meet baby Jack soon after he was born. Since then, his father had visited twice, and Lainey and Ben had escaped to New York for a couple of long weekends without the children, most recently four months previously. They kept in touch on Skype, by email and the occasional phone call.

'Can we talk about this?' Jenna asked.

'What's there to talk about?' he said. 'We'll stay on an extra few days and do some touring when the family thing is over. No sense in going over just for a weekend.'

'You'll have time for this? You won't be "too busy", or "snowed under", or in the middle of "work overload"?'

'I can plan ahead, just as you are doing, aren't you?'

She ignored his comment. 'So I'm finally going to meet your brother?'

'Yes, I guess you will,' he said easily.

'He'll be there?'

'I think so.' He sat down at the table and flipped open his iPad.

'And this will be the first time you've seen him in … how long?'

He stared up at her for a long moment. 'You know as well as I do,' he said irritably.

'Why won't you talk about it?'

'I told you, it's all fine, it's chill, but it's not up for discussion. Just leave it, Jenna, please. Anyway, I've work to do,' he said, scrolling through his screen.

'Don't let me disturb you,' she said.

She marched out of the kitchen, her mouth dry, and she wondered what had gone wrong with the couple who hadn't been able to get enough of each other in those early days. She felt a slow anger trickling through her that now, all of a sudden, and without explaining why, it was fine to go to Ireland, to meet the brother he hadn't spoken to in years, no sweat. Her anger was mixed with trepidation, because it meant she would be meeting family members she didn't want to meet right now. Ben Connolly, for example, Lainey's husband.

The following week, she overheard Alex on the phone to Lainey and suddenly knew exactly why he was making the journey back home ...

CHAPTER SIX

'We're here,' Jenna said, as the car turned in between two shabby gateposts. She congratulated herself for stating the obvious, especially when a mottled plaque on one of the pillars bore the legend 'Lynes Glen'. But she'd had to say something to break the tension before they faced the family.

It wasn't just Alex's tension she was trying to abate, it was also hers. She'd even snapped at Jack in JFK airport the evening before, and instantly hated herself when his face had dropped. She'd tried to relax and catch some sleep on the night-time flight over, but it had been impossible, and she'd sensed that, like her, Alex was feigning sleep, lying back with his eyes closed to save from having to make any kind of conversation. At least he'd had the foresight to book a hotel room on the outskirts of Galway. It had taken them an hour to reach there from Shannon, but it had given them valuable time in which to grab a few hours' sleep in a proper bed, have some food – not that she'd eaten much – and freshen up before continuing their journey. The journey from Galway up through Connemara had taken longer than Jenna had anticipated, but not long enough, because she didn't want to arrive. She'd found herself silenced by the pure solitude of the road they were on. Any further, and they'd surely be driving over the edge of Ireland. But what a beautiful world it was; she'd never imagined a landscape with this perfection, stillness and colours, coming at her in wave after wave with each bend they rounded.

Oddly enough, she'd used her husband's face as an indication of how close they were to Lynes Glen. He became more and more grim-faced, finally snapping at her as they passed by Lough Lynes. At least she'd guessed that was what it was called, thanks to the rusty signpost. Alex had been tight-lipped when she'd asked him about it. Thankfully, Jack had fallen asleep, still clutching his favourite teddy, Beanie, worn out from all the excitement, so he'd been spared the taut silence between his parents, which was so much at odds with his bubbling enthusiasm. Now, as they turned in off the narrow lane, she was in such an anxious sweat she badly needed another shower.

Alex cursed as the car jiggled and bumped its way up the pot-holed avenue. 'Has no one bothered to fix this? It's ridiculous.'

She knew he didn't mean it literally. It was everything about the situation that was fraught-filled: the problems they were leaving in suspension in New York, facing into a weekend in a home Alex hadn't visited in twenty years, with a family Alex had barely kept in touch with, one of whom Jenna was very wary of facing. She would have given anything to close her eyes, stay in the car and wake up when it was all over. But instead, as Alex switched off the engine, the hall door opened, and Lainey came down the steps, followed by two young children.

Alex got out and hugged his sister. They chatted for a while, Lainey stroking his arm as though she was reassuring him about something, Alex's head bent towards her as though he was listening very closely to what she had to say. He came back to the car where Jenna was unbuckling her seat belt, and to her astonishment, he looked relaxed in a way he hadn't for weeks. He even had a smile on his face as he looked at Jack and murmured, 'Jack, honey, wake up, we're here ... your cousins are dying to meet you ...'

She wondered what magic words Lainey had said to have worked this transformation.

*

The children were giddy. And a blessing. With unconditional enthusiasm, Charlotte and Harry almost bore Jack aloft as they scrambled back up the driveway with him, through the doorway, straight down the hall as though he was a much-treasured guest. She heard Jack telling them in his high, childish voice that Beanie had come on his holidays too.

Jenna followed, finding herself in a roomy living area, with a view through big windows out to the forest and mountains at the rear of the house, and French doors to the side, leading onto the terrace. A few people were grouped around the sofas, sipping drinks. From behind her she heard Lainey talking about having the introductions first before going upstairs. She knew Alex had come into the room behind her. She knew by the way the group in the room seemed to be suddenly frozen in a tableau, but mostly from the look on the face of the guy who was standing by the French doors. He had coppery-red hair not unlike Alex's and the same shade of eyes. He was slightly taller and leaner than her husband and she knew he had to be Niall.

It was disconcerting to see a younger version of her husband. It was only when she compared the two brothers that she realised how fatigued and strained Alex's face was, a permanent feature it seemed to be set in nowadays. But if she'd expected some kind of emotional reunion, she was disappointed. There was no sign of any animosity. Neither was there any back-slapping or hugging. For an infinitesimal moment Niall seemed to be holding himself very still, like an animal on full alert – even the dark-haired woman beside him, whom Jenna didn't know, seemed to be holding her breath – then something flickered in Niall's eyes and then she saw his gaze shift a little as Lainey came forward, chatting brightly as though there were no undercurrents at all, and they had simply gathered for a happy occasion like a wedding or a birthday party.

'Hey, this is great,' Lainey said in a cheery tone, 'all together at last. Jenna and Vikki haven't met everyone yet, so I'll go around and make sure everyone knows who's who.'

Jenna glanced at Alex, to see how he was taking this. His face was bland and unconcerned.

Lainey raised her voice and called over the children. 'We have Vikki and Niall over from London,' Lainey said, indicating Alex's brother and the thirty-something attractive woman who was with him.

Vikki gave a quick smile and a little wave of her hand. 'Hi, all.'

Niall's glance flickered around and Jenna noticed that it slid carefully and neutrally over Alex. 'Hi, everybody.'

Then Lainey's gaze moved to Jenna. 'We have Jenna and Alex and Jack, all the way from New York …'

'Hello, everyone.' Jenna's words were echoed by her husband

so that they both spoke at once. Jack clapped his hands in glee as though it was a party of sorts.

'It's a long way from New York, so it's great to have you here,' Lainey said, beaming.

'We hope to do a bit of travelling around after the weekend,' Jenna said. 'The scenery is totally awe-inspiring. Alex has promised to show me some more of this beautiful country, unless he gets a crisis call from the office.'

There was a tiny silence and Jenna knew she'd said something wrong. Out of the corner of her eye she saw Alex dart a glance at Lainey.

'Well, rest assured Alex won't get a crisis call while you're in Lynes Glen,' Lainey said smoothly. 'Didn't he tell you we have no WiFi or mobile coverage?'

'What? You're not serious?' She looked from Alex to Lainey. Alex wouldn't meet her eyes, Lainey had a bright smile on her face.

'I expect Alex forgot that minor detail,' Lainey said.

Jenna laughed. 'Minor detail? My husband is a slave to his smartphone. I don't know how you coaxed him to go cold turkey for the weekend.' She eyed Lainey closely. 'You must be very persuasive, Lainey, or else he has a pressing reason for agreeing to lose a limb.' She glanced at Alex again but once again he was wearing a perfectly bland expression that gave nothing away.

'I hope you won't suffer any separation anxiety, Jenna; some people pay a fortune to go on digital-detox breaks,' Lainey said, her voice brimming with enthusiasm. 'It means we'll be undisturbed all weekend.'

'Good luck with that,' Jenna said quietly.

Lainey ignored her. 'Getting back to the introductions ... in the rest of our group there's me and Ben, with Charlotte and

Harry from Dublin.' This time Ben took a bow, with Charlotte and Harry following Jack's example and clapping their hands.

'Then out in the kitchen,' Lainey said, 'we have Niamh and Erin, who'll be here from early in the morning until after the evening meal, looking after everything, including Dad. Erin manages Dad's cooking and cleaning and day-to-day needs back in the town, and Niamh is here to help with the cooking for the larger group.' Lainey raised her voice. 'Ladies, come on out and meet the rest of the family.'

Jenna was introduced to both Erin, a forty-something, trim-looking woman with a soft Donegal accent and Niamh, slender and blonde, who seemed to be about half her age.

'Roast beef and all the trimmings for this evening,' Erin said. 'Niamh's training to be a chef in a catering college in Galway and she's playing a blinder in the kitchen. I'm just lending a hand with the gravy.'

'What about your famous apple tarts?' Lainey said, with a gleam in her eye.

'Och, I might throw one or two together,' Erin said, smiling, as the two women went back into the kitchen.

'There's plenty of fruit, chilled water and snacks out in the kitchen, just help yourselves,' Lainey said. 'Beer and white wine in the fridge, red wine and spirits out on the counter and back-up supplies in the utility room. Sorry if I sound like a holiday rep but it's the easiest way to let everyone know what's what. Jenna and Vikki, you haven't been here before, please make yourselves completely at home. I checked with my brothers in advance, but if there's anything you need that we haven't got, either Niamh or Erin can bring it up from the town in the morning.'

'And unlike Big Brother,' Ben said, looking totally comfortable in himself as he stood slightly apart from Lainey, a bottle of beer in one hand, 'you won't have any tasks to perform in order to eat, there'll be no evictions, and Lainey has assured me there are no diary room chairs, hidden cameras or tiny microphones. Anywhere in the house. So if you are doing anything you shouldn't be doing' – he flashed a grin at Jenna – 'you won't be caught.'

'I'm not even going to acknowledge that,' Lainey said, throwing him a haughty glance.

'You just have,' Ben said, with a devilish grin on his face.

Jenna lowered her eyes and dug her nails into the palm of her hand. It was happening. The one thing she feared. Behind his banter, she found something calm and relaxing about Ben. It drew her in, and like a soft balm trickling through her, it eased the little anxieties that nibbled at her heart. She'd felt it in New York the last time he and Lainey had come over for a long weekend. She'd been surprised at how much she'd enjoyed having him part of her life for a few short days, and the apartment had seemed empty, and she bereft, when they'd left for their flight home.

She wanted to weep at her foolishness for feeling like this about another man, she couldn't seem to prevent her feelings any more than she could hold back the tide, but what also shocked her was that nothing about it seemed wrong or out of place; she didn't feel the least bit disloyal to Alex. An Alex who had grown distant and out of reach. Here, this weekend, she was afraid she might reveal something, not only to Ben but to everyone else.

It was a relief to get out of the living room. They left the buzz of conversation behind, including the chortles of Jack engrossed in a game with his cousins.

Jenna followed Alex up the hall and he showed her the rooms downstairs, the formal dining room on one side of the hall and a faded but beautiful sitting room opposite, with sofas and bookcases, occasional tables and photographs arranged across the top of an upright piano. Beyond the dining room, he brought her into a small, cosy library, also looking out over the front gardens, with a mixture of high, wing-backed armchairs, more bookshelves, and close to the window, a mahogany writing desk.

'This is lovely,' Jenna said.

'It is,' Alex replied. 'Dad loves this room, it's where he did a lot of his work.'

When Alex went out to the car to get the cases, Jenna stood by the open door, looking out at the stunning landscape, imagining a young Alex growing up here, coming and going through all his childhood years, attending school, then college in Galway. A part of Alex she knew little or nothing about, a whole chunk of memories he never opened, that were surely ingrained in the fabric of this beautiful and striking house.

Upstairs, Alex threw open the door to the last room on the right, and let out a low whistle. 'It's different and yet it's still the same. God, this brings me back,' he said going across to the window and looking out.

'It's lovely,' Jenna said, admiring the view of the mountains up beyond the rim of the forest. 'Good memories?' she asked.

Alex barely paused before he answered. 'Of course.'

How could they have been good, she wanted to ask, if he hadn't been back, let alone spoken to his brother in so long? He opened another door and showed her into a bathroom. There were signs of occupancy, toilet bags and toothbrushes, a razor in a glass.

'You're OK sharing a bathroom? It's just for a couple of nights.'

'Yes, sure,' Jenna said.

She was fine with it until Alex explained the setup and she

realised with a lurch that it meant sharing with Ben and Lainey as they were in the connecting bedroom on the other side.

'Have you always shared a bathroom with Lainey?' she asked, trying to take her mind off the vision of opening the bathroom door to find Ben in the shower. Or vice versa. She just had to remember to ensure the door was locked.

'No, that used to be Niall's bedroom.'

'How come Lainey and Ben are in it?'

'Does it matter? None of us have lived here in so long, I wouldn't be surprised if Lainey forgot which was which.'

Somehow Jenna doubted that the highly organised Lainey would make such an elementary mistake. It was more likely that Lainey was keeping Niall and Alex apart in this small way, which was going to make it more difficult for Jenna to keep as much distance as possible from Ben.

She followed Alex across the corridor into the room Jack was sharing with Lainey and Ben's children. He was staring out the window, which had the same mountainy aspect as their room. When he spun around at her approach, she was surprised to see something sad flickering in his face before he rearranged his features into the bland look he had adopted down in the living room.

He strolled around the room, idly picking up children's toys before putting them back down again. 'It'll be good for Jack to get to know his cousins.'

'Alex …' she hesitated.

He looked at her, eyebrows raised, a Lego helicopter in his hand.

'What's going on with you and your brother?' she plunged on, unable to hold back. 'He seems nice, no devil's horns at all. Why don't you talk to each other?'

'We were talking fine downstairs.'

'That's what I don't get. What happened to the last twenty years? It's as if' – she laughed hollowly – 'it never happened.'

'That's all water under the bridge.'

'I don't believe this. You're brushing it aside as though it was nothing.'

'It's over and done with. We all agreed to draw a line over it.'

'Who's "we all"?'

'Me, Lainey and Niall. So … end of story.'

'I'm your wife, why are you shutting me out?'

'You're not being shut out. Everything's fine.' The helicopter broke apart in his hands, pieces of it dropping to the floor.

'It sure is fine, Alex. If that's the way you want to play it. I obviously need to get with the programme. Or rather, the timetable. And thanks for letting me know about the mobile phones, by the way. Another minor detail you conveniently forgot to share with me.'

'It slipped my mind.'

'I don't think so. You just avoided telling me. Like you're avoiding lots of things. It's great. We ignore a major rift so we can all play happy families this weekend. Even Lainey—'

'What about Lainey?' His eyes narrowed slightly.

'The way she glossed over it all: "Jenna hasn't met everyone yet". *Met* everyone? Talk about an understatement of the decade. What a most convenient way of ignoring the fact that your brother didn't even come to our wedding. Still, we've been avoiding it all our married lives, so why should this weekend be any different.' Her voice shook and she was annoyed with herself.

His face was perfectly smooth, as was his voice. 'I haven't been ignoring anything. It is what it is. I've been getting on with my life … our lives. I don't know what has you so tetchy. I thought you'd be delighted to be part of a family reunion, and even more delighted to have a holiday with me and Jack.'

'Sometimes I wonder if I know you at all,' Jenna said.

'Why? What have I done now?'

'Come on, Alex,' she snapped. 'What's this weekend all about, really?' She wondered if Alex would bring himself to finally admit to her what she'd heard over the phone.

'Don't be absurd. You know full well we're here at Dad's invitation, nothing more.'

She felt a stab of disappointment at the way he was glossing over everything. 'I think it's a bit weird to start playing happy families all of a sudden. You and your brother …' she shook her head. 'I can't imagine not talking to my sister for twenty years. But if that's what suits you, great, wonderful, let's go with the flow. Let's play the game of make-believe. I hope you get what you want from this weekend,' she added, with meaning.

'I'm sure I will,' he said, in that mild tone she was beginning to find infuriating. He left the room and she heard him going downstairs, whistling as though he hadn't a care in the world.

Her head felt like it was going to explode as she opened her case and unpacked the clothes she had set aside for Mayo. She couldn't believe how uneasy she felt, here for the weekend with her marriage on a tightrope, and a man downstairs who only had to glance in her direction to send feelings running through her that had no business being there.

And a husband who couldn't bring himself to admit why he'd really come home.

CHAPTER SEVEN

'We outlaws have been left to our own devices,' Ben said, looking, Vikki thought, quite satisfied with the situation. 'You don't mind me including you in that, do you, Vikki?'

'I don't have much choice, do I?' She grinned, sensing she could talk to laid-back Ben like this. Being included with Niall's relations made her feel slightly less of an interloper, especially after the way Niall had disappeared with his brother and sister to have a chat with their father. He'd pushed another glass of wine into her hands, ruffled her hair, and said he wouldn't be too long.

Leo Blake's room was on the ground floor and she'd had a funny sense of exclusion, watching him and his siblings heading off, Niall opening the living-room door and ushering them through, Alex with his hand resting lightly in the small of Lainey's back, Lainey reaching around to loop her arm through Niall's, as if to ensure there was no doubt in anyone's mind that they were all united. Individually the Blake siblings were striking to look at; up close together like this, they were a beautiful force of nature.

Vikki thought there was something a little too bright, too energetic about Lainey and the way she flitted around her brothers. When Alex and Jenna had come back downstairs, she'd uncorked the bubbly, Niamh had come out from the kitchen with a selection of nuts, canapes and morsels of fruit, and the conversation in the living room had flowed easily, the brothers chatting casually as though they were taking their cue from Lainey. To all appearances, it could have been a matter of weeks since they'd spoken. In some weird way, Vikki sensed, the Blakes seemed to have closed ranks; it was like they had slipped back to the time the three of them had lived here, thanks to the seamless way they had reconnected with each other.

'Why don't we take our drinks outside while the others are with Leo?' Ben said. 'We can keep an eye on the children from the terrace. It's a beautiful evening, shame to miss the sunshine.'

'Is that allowed?' Jenna asked, half laughing. 'Or do we need permission?'

Vikki didn't realise how tightly she'd been holding herself until Jenna's comment loosened something inside her. Although everything seemed fine outwardly, Vikki sensed a gossamer-fine thread of tension lying beneath the surface. Getting out to breathe fresh air, with or without so-called permission, was appealing.

Ben chuckled. 'We probably do, but I won't tell if you don't.'

Jenna touched her glass to his. 'Right so, if we're caught we'll blame you for leading us astray. Jack, are you OK with your cousins?'

The children were clustered around the low table, engrossed

in a Lego creation. Jack nodded his head without looking up. 'We're making a gigantic battleship.'

'It's going to be way cool,' Harry said.

'We'll be just outside if you need us.'

Ben went into the kitchen for more beer, and, juggling that with a bottle of white wine, he led the way across to the French windows.

Turning to Vikki, Jenna said, 'I'm looking forward to chatting to you about emerging fashion and beauty trends.'

'I should be asking you about that,' Vikki said, having found out that Jenna was a personal fashion stylist when she'd told her about her job with Rosella. 'You must enjoy your career.'

'I'm one of the lucky ones,' Jenna said, her deep, blue eyes sparkling. 'I get paid for doing what I love, which is helping women of all ages with their occasion wear dressing and advising on their wardrobes. Plus, I spend a lot of time flitting in and out of Fifth Avenue stores and boutiques.'

'Nice one,' Vikki said.

Alex's American wife was slim and blonde, and a perfect advertisement for dressing to suit your figure. She was wearing neat black boots, ankle grazer jeans showing her trim figure, and a fine, pale-blue sweater. She was beautiful, Vikki thought, but in a soft, glowy way. Together she and Alex had made a striking entrance as they came into the living room in Lynes Glen, a couple you would turn your head to look at, and want to be sitting at the same table with. At first Vikki had thought that Jenna seemed a little standoffish, but when she'd talked to her on a one-to-one basis, Jenna exuded warmth that was attractive and Vikki knew she'd feel confident that she'd take her under her wing and look after her fashion shopping in a friendly, non-intrusive way.

Vikki stepped through the French doors, out onto a terrace that ran along the side of the house. There was assorted outdoor seating spread across the terrace and steps leading down to a wide, tiered garden in front. It had seen better days when the family all lived here; now the tubs of climbing plants and shrubs that had been trailed up along the terrace were empty, and the trellises were scarred from years of old foliage and twisting vines.

The tiered garden showed signs that someone had given it a hurried tidy-up, which did little to mask all the years of neglect. Down at the perimeter of the garden there was a stone wall marking the boundary between it and the rim of the forest, and a gate, giving private access to the forest, set into this. The whisper of the trees in the evening breeze was soothing; to her right she saw the shimmering, blue-grey folds of the lower mountain slopes and Vikki could imagine how special it must have been to sit out here in the days the house had been bursting with energy and life. For all its faded splendour, it was a sad house, and the realisation came to her as soft as a murmur. No amount of forced gaiety could make up for the long years it had sat here after Gabrielle had died, and the children had scattered, leaving Leo alone.

Ben sat down on a wrought-iron bench that was padded with cushions, and patted the spot beside him. 'Sit here, Vikki, I know Jenna won't mind if I delay your beauty and fashion discussion,' he said with a twinkle in his eye. 'I need to ask you a few things. I've already interrogated Jenna when I was over in New York and now it's your turn.'

'I'm not sure I like the sound of that,' Vikki said.

Jenna curved her mouth in a small smile that didn't quite reach her eyes. 'It's OK, Vikki, Ben didn't manage to get close to any of my secrets, no matter how good his interrogation skills were.' She put down her glass of wine on a table, and drew up a garden chair.

'Didn't I?' he said.

A look passed between Jenna and Ben that Vikki was unable to decipher. It was as though they knew each other well and had bonded together by virtue of having married into the same family.

Ben turned to Vikki. 'I'm going to jump right into it – maybe you know something we don't.'

'About what?'

'The big Blake family secret.'

'So there's just one?' It came out off the top of her head, intuited by her gut feeling that there was more going on in the background of this complex family than she realised, fuelled in part by the conversation she'd overheard between Niall and Lainey at the bottom of the stairs, the semblance of unity that seemed a little forced to her, and Niall's own admission that he needed her at his back this weekend.

'Hah. Right there, Vikki.' He looked amused. 'You get the picture. How long are you hooked up with Niall?' Without waiting for an answer he went on. 'You caught Lainey by surprise, she didn't know of your existence until last weekend. She was quite put out, and' – he laughed – 'you don't want to meet my wife when she's in that mood. She thought Niall was holding out on her. They mightn't see each other that often, but they're very close; blood is thick as they say, but Blake blood seems to be thicker than most.'

'In the ranking of understatements,' Jenna said, refilling her wine glass, 'that's off the scale. I couldn't have put it better myself.'

Ben grinned at her.

'I met Niall about a year ago,' Vikki said, her tone implying she knew him better than she actually did, hoping her desire to mean more to him wouldn't reflect in her eyes and her voice.

'A year?' Ben whistled. 'Niall sure kept you to himself. How did he get that by Lainey? I thought there were no secrets between the Blakes, even if they have family secrets they guard tightly, ones we hoped you might be able to enlighten us about.'

'"Us"?' Jenna said. 'Speak for yourself, Ben. Personally, I couldn't give a damn.'

He looked at her steadily and their gazes held for a moment until Jenna looked away. They seemed to have forgotten about Vikki.

'Don't tell me you don't want to know.' Ben looked at her shrewdly. 'Like, for instance, why Niall and Alex have avoided each other for years.'

Jenna shrugged her shoulders. 'At this moment I couldn't care less.'

'Yeah, right. Or maybe you know and you're not telling,' Ben went on.

'I don't. And we've already had this conversation.'

Vikki broke the ensuing taut silence by laughing lightly. 'Sorry, I can't help you there, Niall never talks about his family.'

Ben took a glug of his beer. 'Lainey has spent the last twenty years playing go-between for her brothers and still won't tell me why. Old family history, she says. Nothing to do with the two of us.'

'It's got nothing to do with me and Alex either,' Jenna said.

'According to you or according to Alex?' Ben asked.

'Does that matter?' Jenna said.

There was something unhappy in her blue eyes that flickered momentarily to Ben before she turned to Vikki.

'Sorry if we're putting you on the spot, Vikki,' she said. 'You hardly know us, and we must seem terribly rude, but Niall didn't come to our wedding, and Alex wouldn't enlighten me as to the reason why.'

'Hang on,' Ben said. 'Lainey and I got married in Rome and invited no one. It was all kept very small and contained. How's that for avoiding favouritism or confrontation? Sorry if we're overwhelming you, Vikki, but Jenna and I have worked out so far that the brothers had a falling out sometime soon after their mother died. We can't help being curious. Even Jenna is, if she's pretending otherwise.' A smile played on his lips as he flashed Jenna a glance. She stared back coolly at him.

'And watch out for Lainey,' Ben said to Vikki. 'She might try to give you the third degree over the weekend as to your intentions with Niall.'

'You mean this isn't it? In a roundabout way?' Vikki asked.

'Nah.' Ben grinned. 'This isn't even a warm-up. Are you sorry you came now?'

'I dunno, it all depends on whether I get out in one piece.'

Ben laughed a rich laugh. 'What about you, Jenna?' he asked. 'Were you looking forward to the weekend?'

'What do you think?' she said.

There was a perceptive look in his eyes. 'Thought you'd be intrigued to see the place where Alex spent his childhood. And meet his brother at last.'

'It's a beautiful spot,' Jenna said. 'Quite awesome. But I'd rather have stayed put in New York. There's too much intrigue going around here.'

'So you do have a bee in your bonnet,' Ben said affably. 'It's only a weekend. And it's nice for the cousins to have time together, as well as the outlaws.'

'I think that remains to be seen,' Jenna said.

Once again, there was a tension Vikki couldn't decipher. She sensed an undercurrent of sorts between the two of them, edginess in Jenna, perhaps something that was bound up with them being married into this enigmatic family. They had a shared history she wasn't aware of, yet it was a bit disconcerting to know that, once again, they'd forgotten she was there.

Ben looked at Jenna, concern evident on his face. 'It can't be that bad. Go with the flow. Relax.'

'I *am* relaxed,' Jenna said tersely. 'It's all brilliant. Happy clappy. Not even a digital distraction. I'm sure Alex will be practically horizontal without that stress. And if the Blakes don't want us to know old history, well, who cares? I don't give a sugar.'

'Maybe they have good reasons.'

'Like what?'

'They could be afraid of what we'd think of them if we found out.'

Jenna tilted her head and scrutinised Ben. 'Do you seriously think Alex is bothered about your opinion of him?'

Vikki thought she heard him mutter in a low voice, 'Maybe he should be.'

Jenna was still staring at him when the French doors opened and Lainey breezed through. She had changed her cream jumper for a black scalloped-neck jersey top. Gold jewellery glittered at her creamy throat and at her ears.

'So this is what you're up to,' she said, 'enjoying your own private party …' Her eyes darted around the three of them and Vikki had the feeling she was sizing them up.

'Yes, sorry you missed it,' Jenna said.

'Glad you're all enjoying yourselves,' Lainey replied. 'Dinner is being served in five minutes,' she went on, announcing it as if it was a summons.

'All good with the council of war?' Ben asked, lifting an eyebrow.

'Of course.' Lainey looked at him sharply as though he shouldn't have asked that question. 'And it wasn't a council of whatever. Dad just wanted to see us for a chat. He's delighted we're all here under the family roof at last, and he was more than a little emotional. Apart from that, there was nothing said that couldn't have been said in the bigger group. He wants to talk to us on Sunday morning. So we'll have to wait until then to see if there's any particular reason he brought us all together this weekend.' She put a bright smile back on her face and Vikki sensed she was forcing it. 'For our first sit-down meal, I've put out place settings on the table; it will give everyone a chance to get to know each other.'

Vikki went upstairs to use the bathroom. Place settings? What was the betting she'd be seated away from Niall. They were supposed to be family. They shouldn't even be at the 'getting to know each other' stage. Just as she reached the landing, Niall came out of the bedroom, the sight of him sending a hot jolt of pleasure through her. He'd taken off his jumper and put on a navy shirt. Here in his home, the veneer of London had dissolved and he seemed softer and more unguarded. He gave her a big smile, looking so fresh, clean and gorgeous that she wanted to lean over and kiss him and her heart quivered at the thoughts of sleeping beside him tonight.

'Fancy bumping into you here,' she said, deliberately cheery.

'You too, lovely to see you like this,' he said, his eyes scanning her face. To her delight, he reached out and brushed his hand along the curve of her cheek. 'Can't believe you're actually here.'

She smiled at him. 'Well, I'm not a mirage …'

His gaze held hers. Her cheek burned under his touch. 'Sometimes I wish things in my life had been different.' He said it so softly she barely made out the words. 'Sometimes I wish … oh, Vikki—' He broke off and, leaning forward, he kissed her forehead so tenderly she felt it ripple into every cell of her body. He was so close, her insides pulsed with longing. When he stepped away, she felt cold.

'Sorry,' he said. 'I got carried away for a minute. I'm not being fair to you. I haven't forgotten you said you're not up for a serious relationship either. Don't mind me.'

'I'll do my best to ignore any lapses,' she said jokily, her own words coming back to haunt her.

'Food's almost ready,' he said. 'I'll introduce you to Dad as soon as you're back downstairs.'

'Great, I'm looking forward to meeting him.'

'He's in good humour,' Niall said, heading down the stairs.

Her legs were wobbly as she continued on up. She put on a pair of black velvet jeans and a scarlet chiffon top, as well as fresh lip gloss and a squirt of scent. Her mouth felt dry as she looked at the bed before she went downstairs.

The dining room was another beautiful room, the walls covered in pale-blue wallpaper etched with a silvered floral pattern that would now be considered vintage and highly chic. An oil painting of Slieve Creagh dominated one wall, and there was a mahogany cabinet and matching bureau bookcase with leaded glass doors set against the other walls. It was a room perfect for formal dinner parties of bygone eras, and Vikki could just imagine what it might have been like back in Leo's parents' day. Two long sash windows, framed by silvery blue brocade, looked out onto the side of the house. The long mahogany table with matching upholstered chairs could comfortably sit twelve to fourteen. It was arranged with a crisp Irish-linen runner placed down along the centre, and set with small wildflower posies, high silver candelabra, and crystal glasses and cutlery that caught the light twinkling from the overhead chandelier drapes.

When Vikki saw the seating arrangement she guessed Lainey's place settings were a deliberate ploy to keep Alex and Niall apart and maintain the semblance of family unity. She was seated between Alex and Ben, with Lainey, Jenna and Niall on the other side of the table. The children were sitting up near the head of the table, chatting animatedly to an elderly gentleman, who was seated at the top. He had a mane of thick, grey hair, a hooked nose and, though still in his eighties, piercing blue eyes: Leo Blake.

CHAPTER EIGHT

When I read her diary, I knew.

Everything.

It had the effect of pulling the plug from under the life I had known up to then, changing it completely, so that everything was sucked down into a dark and narrow vortex. Yet when I eventually came up for air, choking and struggling, I realised it had opened up a whole new world, one that was thick with intrigue, misplaced love, jealousy, fleeting passion, the ultimate rejection and a painful loss.

I hadn't been expecting the diary to land in my arms. It was contained in a padded envelope along with some mementoes, most of which I was too shaken to examine at first. When I was over my initial shock I laid them out again, trying to make sense: a lock of dark hair twined with one of red-gold; a small, square, grainy photograph taken with a cheap camera, the colours faded now with the passage of time; a video tape; a pendant with a glowing, heart-shaped ruby.

But I was more transfixed with the written account of her life. I liked to think she had recorded it with me in mind, a way of communicating with me through time and space. A chronicle of the truth, exposing it for me to see, so that I could choose to do with this knowledge whatever I wanted.

It wasn't a proper diary insofar as most of it hadn't been written chronologically at the time. She'd bought a 1995 hard-backed A5 diary, in a sale obviously, because it had a vastly reduced price sticker on the front. On the inside of the front cover and spread across two pages was a 1995 date planner. This was blank, except for a few scrawled words in thick black writing that jumped out at me:

'This is the true account of what happened'

A shiver ran down my spine; it seemed she anticipated not surviving the year. The first quarter of the diary had the dates crossed out and contained a summary of her life spanning several years up to 1995. Then followed a large section when the pages were blank, and from the end of July, entries written in real time on the corresponding pages over the next four to five weeks. After that, the pages were again blank.

Had she feared that things might go wrong and she'd need to put it all down? Just in case? I think so. I know she wanted me to have this and I've read it four times so far, staying up late that first night to try and get my head around it all, fingers trembling as I turned the pages, shocked and saddened in turn by the narrative and later entries.

Even if I hate her for what she did, and the way she ruined my life, I know exactly where the blame lies for her early death, who is responsible, and who carries the ultimate guilt – I will never come to terms with that, let alone forgive.

The truth doesn't always set you free. Sometimes it nails you to a cross. It can make the path you were on crumble away in front of you, leaving you frightened and desolate. It opens your eyes to things you mightn't like, forcing you to confront knowledge that alters everything you've ever known, and causing you to act in a way you'd never have imagined.

But knowledge is power. And in a life that had become stale and unfulfilling, it has given me a brand-new purpose. I can't change what has happened, nothing will ever bring her back, but I can change the future and avenge her death.

Right now, Friday evening in Lynes Glen is going according to plan. Nobody suspects a thing. By Sunday, it will all be over and I'll have my revenge.

CHAPTER NINE

'Drink up, Vikki, plenty more where that came from,' Ben said, emptying the last of the white wine into her glass. He'd taken it on himself to keep the wine flowing during the meal. Lainey had helped Erin and Niamh to serve the food, and she was keeping an eye on the table while the others returned to the kitchen, leaving the family to chat in peace, or as Lainey had put it, 'get to know each other'.

'Thanks, Ben,' Vikki said, although she was determined the wine wasn't going to be flowing freely in her direction. She couldn't afford to drink too much. Since she'd bumped into Niall on the stairs, something she normally kept under a tight rein inside her – an inner guard against allowing herself to respond too warmly to him – had started to unravel. She took a few slow breaths, trying to centre herself and avoid being acutely aware of his every move and tilt of his head, every smile, his hands, his eyes, trying desperately to pretend he wasn't sitting across the table from her, looking far too utterly desirable in his crisp navy shirt. Trying to forget she was here in the bosom of his family – his actual *family* – because when she thought about it, it was so alarming and wonderful it made her giddy.

Leo Blake had approved of her. The elderly gentleman had kissed the back of her hand and excused himself from rising to his feet. 'It would take me so long to get upright on my unsteady pins that I'd be afraid the dinner might get cold,' he'd said, with a surprisingly warm smile. 'I'm glad Niall has a good friend like you. He's one of the best, and you look like a lovely young woman, if I may dare to say so.'

She'd felt herself blushing as she'd bent to kiss his cheek.

'Whatever you do, Niall,' he'd said to his son, 'don't let this lovely lady get away.'

Vikki's face had reddened further. Sitting at the top of the table, Leo was now engrossed in his grandchildren's conversation. Ben went out into the kitchen and came back with a fresh bottle of wine, which he dunked into the cooler. Then he picked up the red wine and passed it to Alex.

Alex topped up his glass and studied the label at the back of the bottle. 'Thanks, Ben, good choice.'

'I hoped it would meet your approval,' Lainey jumped in. 'We're not exactly wine connoisseurs so I asked for recommendations.'

Ben looked pointedly at Lainey. 'Hey, less of the connoisseur. You make it sound like we don't touch a drop.' He looked around the table. 'Give me a few pints of Guinness in the Stag's Head in Dublin any Saturday evening.'

'I prefer the bar in the Shelbourne or the upstairs lounge in the Westbury,' Lainey said sweetly, her tone of voice belying the look she gave Ben.

'And would you have a pint there?' Jenna asked Lainey, tongue-in-cheek, putting down her knife and fork.

'Good grief, no,' Lainey said. Her face flushed when she realised Jenna was pulling her leg. 'A gin and tonic; Hendrick's, preferably,' she said. 'We have wine regularly, with meals, but it's usually whatever has been gifted to Ben by his clients. I don't buy it often enough to appreciate the difference between a Malbec and a Merlot. Although you could probably do that blindfolded.'

'Who cares what variety it is,' Jenna said, lifting her glass and taking a very long slug. 'It all goes down the same way and thankfully it has the same boozy effect.'

Vikki saw Jenna raise her eyebrows at Alex, as though she was challenging him to say she was drinking too fast.

'What about you?' Lainey asked Jenna smoothly. 'What's your favourite tipple and where's your favourite spot?'

'Champagne,' Jenna said, without hesitation.

'That figures,' Lainey said.

'Oh, really?'

At the top of the table, the children were chatting to Leo about *Star Wars*. In the middle of the table, all eyes were on Jenna and Lainey.

'You're kind of cool and elegant yourself,' Lainey said, 'so it suits you.'

'I don't see it as a fashion accessory, I just like the taste of the fizz,' Jenna said.

'And your favourite spot?' Lainey went on. 'Somewhere classy and sophisticated?'

'Nah, San Francisco,' Jenna said.

'Oh, what part?'

'My mother's back garden.' Jenna smiled easily. 'She usually opens a bottle of bubbly when I go home for a long weekend and we sit out in the shade and catch the breeze coming up off the bay. My sister Ruth would come around as well. Being there relaxes me instantly. It sometimes makes me wonder what I'm doing in New York.' She flashed another glance at Alex.

'How interesting,' Lainey said. 'Alex, we might as well see this through … we can guess your favourite drink is red wine but where's your favourite bar? Now that has to be the Upper East Side or a cool, funky spot in Tribeca. Am I right?' She gave him a big smile, fully expecting his approval.

Alex held his glass up to the light and twirled it around. 'This isn't too far off my favourite, which is a decent Montepulciano. I'd forgotten we had these beautiful glasses; it makes it seem more of a luxury. But my favourite bar?' He grinned at Lainey. 'Sorry, sis, you're way off the mark.'

'I can't be.' Lainey gave a fake pout.

'My favourite place to relax over a glass of red is none other than Battery Park.'

'That nice hotel we were in for a meal? The Ritz-Carlton?'

'No, our very own apartment. I find nothing more relaxing than being at home in the evening, when Jack's safely tucked up in bed after his bath and story, and I take a glass out to the balcony. It's tiny but if I stick my neck out far enough I can catch a glimpse of the Hudson.'

In the middle of the table, silence fell. Vikki couldn't decipher the glance Jenna darted across at her husband, but Lainey seemed happy enough to pretend that everyone was enjoying the food, wine and conversation, because she turned to Vikki and said, her voice bright, 'Vikki, you're next – what and where?'

'The "what" has to be a mojito,' Vikki said, caught on the hop as she swiftly calculated what would sound sophisticated enough for the Blakes. 'As for the "where", well, there's this dinky little bar in Covent Garden that's just perfectly cute. A fave hangout for lots of celebrities.' The minute the words were out of her mouth, she knew they sounded all wrong.

Niall looked across at her, a frown on his face as though he didn't recognise this side of her. She could almost hear the words running through his head: *since when did you like a cocktail? Don't they usually make you sick? We've never been to that bar, where is it? I didn't think 'cute, dinky bars' were your thing.*

She stared back at him steadily and, as a defensive gesture, she pre-empted Lainey. 'Your turn, Niall,' she said, privately wondering what he'd come up with.

'Yes, come on, Niall,' Lainey encouraged.

Niall sat back, looking perfectly relaxed. 'As you know, I drink anything with a decent alcoholic content, but the "what" and "where" that I recall being my all-time favourite is' – he paused, scanning the table while he considered his words, and Vikki felt herself tense as his eyes settled on her – 'a bottle of chilled beer, sitting on a rickety chair outside a tiny pub on Achill island, as the sun went down. I was about eighteen at the time and I remember thinking that the world right then was a glorious place and full of possibilities.'

His words were like a shock of icy water to Vikki because, as well as the wistful expression in Niall's eyes as he stared at her, coming on the cusp of what she'd said, they made her feel doubly like a fraud.

Just be yourself, Niall had said, the previous Friday night. Which self though? She felt cold inside, because she couldn't remember the last time in her life she'd been 'just herself'. She'd lost touch with the real Emily Victoria Gordon long ago, when that hurt young woman had pulled a door closed behind her at eighteen years of age. Vikki Gordon had ventured back once, just over ten years ago, but it had been a mistake, and since then she'd never returned. Even though she'd built a new life for herself, it had been fabricated on a denial of her past and, deep down inside, she didn't know who she was anymore.

They were talking about holidays now, led by Lainey, as though she was determined to keep the conversation going. Vikki listened to them, realising that the Blakes were grounded in this place no matter how far they'd scattered around the world. They were united by their mutual genes and multi-layered shared history, no matter how sad parts of that history might have been. They all belonged to the same tribe – the tribe who inherited their privilege from childhood and took it for granted, and, confident in their skins, they didn't feel the need to impress, and this included their spouses. Jenna came from a solid background that included her thriving business, and a mother and sister who, she'd discovered, owned a successful spa and wellness sanctuary in San Francisco. Lainey was an English teacher in a privately run, exclusive girls' college. Ben, between his senior role in the management arm of a techie company, and his ease and affability, was someone else with a stable and secure upbringing.

She'd gone to work in a local newspaper at eighteen, taking down copy for small advertisements, working her way up and across into magazines and features until she'd reached the grand heights of Rosella. She thought she'd have been able to carry off this weekend with her usual carefree façade – the Vikki Gordon who was always ready to laugh at life – but surrounded by this colourful family in this atmospheric but beautiful house, her lack of authenticity felt even more pronounced.

Had she been sitting beside Niall, she could have exchanged

soft banter with him, but he was too far away for that kind of repartee. To her acute discomfort, she was aware she hadn't contributed to the conversation for some time; she couldn't think of any suitable or interesting topics of conversation. It brought her back to being an insecure sixteen-year-old once more – days she did so not want to recall, where she'd stuck out like a sore thumb in the company of her peers, thanks to her lack of self -worth, her crippling shyness, and being clueless of the teenage culture of the day.

Sitting at the top of the table, Leo was having great fun chatting to his grandchildren, the rise and fall of their bright young voices cheerful and unaffected. They certainly livened up the atmosphere. Surely children were a safe enough topic? You couldn't go far wrong there.

As soon as there was a pause in the conversation, Vikki summoned her brightest smile and jumped in, beaming across the table at Jenna. 'I love Jack's curls, they're fab. Has he always had them … ?' She broke off, feeling flustered. Of course he must have always had them; a six-year-old child had hardly had a perm. To her surprise, Jenna came to her rescue.

'Actually no, he hasn't,' she said, smiling warmly at Vikki. 'For the first eighteen months he had practically no hair at all. I was in despair. But then it began to grow and by the time he was two, he was a right little curly top.'

'It's gorgeous,' Vikki said, feeling she'd been sent a life raft in the form of Jenna's smile.

'He takes after his mother,' Ben quipped, winking at Vikki.

Vikki looked at Jenna's sleek blonde hair at the same time as Jenna made a face at Ben and she allowed herself a giggle.

'He takes after Gabrielle, Alex's mother,' Jenna said.

There was a lull in the children's excited voices just as Jenna spoke and her clear American tones carried the length of the table. Alex and Lainey stared at each other. Niall paused in the act of helping himself to more gravy, the china gravy boat held aloft in his hand, his green-gold eyes looking at Jenna cautiously. Up at the top of the table, oblivious to the moment, Harry began recounting something of huge significance to his grandfather, to judge by the serious tone of his seven-year-old voice, and from total absorption on Leo's attentive face as he looked at his grandson, he was equally oblivious to the undercurrents spinning around the middle of the table.

'She's inside,' Ben said to Vikki, as though there was nothing of consequence in the moment. 'On the top of the piano. Gabrielle. Her photograph, I mean. You should take a look; she was beautiful.'

'Yes, I saw her,' Vikki said. She'd spotted the photographs arranged along the top of the piano. It had been a quick glimpse, though, because Niall had moved her swiftly along in his tour of the downstairs, not giving her any time to linger over them. She'd been struck, all the same, by the beauty and vitality evident in all the images, the one of a youthful Niall posing on the diving board over Lough Lynes zinging straight into her heart. She'd wanted to ask him about it but had held off, reluctant to get into another discussion about Lough Lynes or about a skill he'd never mentioned.

'Yeah, who put those out?' Niall asked.

'I thought it was a nice touch,' Lainey said. 'They're good memories of the way we were. No harm in recalling those great moments.'

Niall inclined his head towards his sister, but Vikki wasn't sure whether he agreed or disagreed. He seemed distant, a man with something going on in his head that she wasn't part of.

'They're great photos,' Jenna said. 'Capturing you all in different ways. My husband looks so young, young and enthusiastic, don't you, Alex? Ready to take on the world and taste everything life had to offer as though it was your due.'

There was no response from Alex. Vikki glanced sideways at him and saw him stare across at Lainey as though she was responsible for the way the conversation had headed, before he looked back at his wife.

'There's something about that age,' Jenna went on smoothly, as if she was perfectly aware of the slight tension around the table – coming in particular from the way her husband was watching her – but had decided to ignore it. 'Oh, to be in your early twenties, when so much is still ahead, before life manages to dull your passion or knock the idealism out of you. I bet you never realised how beautiful you looked, Lainey.'

Lainey shot her a look of surprise.

'And still do,' Jenna said, moving on swiftly. 'But you radiated carefree youth in that photo.'

'And then she met me,' Ben said, in a deadpan voice.

Jenna was the only one who laughed. 'Oh dear, is that what happened next?'

'Not quite,' Lainey said, snappily, her mask slipping for a nanosecond.

But Jenna wasn't finished. She leaned back in her chair and turned sideways towards Niall. 'Of them all, I think your photograph was the most striking.'

Niall looked at her steadily and Vikki held her breath at the guarded expression in his eyes.

'If you say so, Jenna,' he said, sounding a little bored.

He was putting it on, Vikki realised. There was something in the clench of his jaw that told her he was on edge.

'It looks like sheer, thrilling fun, diving into that lake,' Jenna said chattily. 'It seems to be quite a drop, so you must have guts as well as skill. My cousin dives off Florida, so I have an idea of the dedication involved. Have you ever—'

'I don't dive anymore,' Niall said, cutting across her.

Lainey cast a worried glance down the table that Jenna didn't appear to see.

'Don't you? That's a shame,' Jenna went on, looking at him quizzically as though she was expecting some elaboration. An accident, an injury, something that must have forced Niall to abandon such a fascinating pastime. None was forthcoming.

Vikki chewed on a piece of carrot, not tasting it. What was all that about? '*I don't dive anymore.*' Since when had Niall stopped diving? It was something he'd never spoken about to her and it sounded like it had been a deliberate decision on his part rather than an activity he'd allow slacken off over the years.

'Lainey, I know you have some stuff planned for the weekend,' Jenna went on, undeterred by Niall's silence. 'It would be fun to go down to the lake. Is that on your – ah, timetable?'

There was a deathly silence, broken only by Charlotte at the other end of the table, hotly disputing whatever Harry had just announced. 'Don't mind what Harry says, I do *not*, Grandad,' she said in an indignant voice.

'Yes, you do,' Harry said mischievously.

Almost in unison, Alex, Lainey and Niall spoke.

'It's all closed up.'

'The track is impassable.'

'It's been out of bounds for years.'

Jenna's forehead wrinkled. She said, to no one in particular, 'It couldn't be. I saw someone sitting out there on our way up here this afternoon. Near the diving board.'

Vikki felt something crawl at the back of her skull.

'That's impossible.' Lainey shook her head.

'You never said anything to me,' Alex said.

'I mentioned the lake as we were passing by,' Jenna said, 'but you asked me not to distract you. You were quite … focussed on that narrow twisty road.'

It was clear from the way she spoke, in exaggerated calm tones, that the exchange between them hadn't been so polite. Vikki intercepted the warning glance that Alex threw at his wife, and as they stared at each other, Jenna with a trace of defiance, the tension around the table mounted.

'I thought it must have been a relation of yours with her hair,' Jenna said. 'Is it a Blake family tradition that almost everyone around here has that reddish-gold hair?' She looked around the table as if seeking an answer to her perfectly innocent question.

Vikki did her best to keep her gaze away from Niall. Pinpricks of unease were shooting around the back of her head. She waited for him to say, with an easy laugh, something like, 'Hey, we got this wrong, Lough Lynes is not closed up after all, and guess what, Vikki also saw a woman sitting on the diving board there when we were driving past.'

She felt him staring at her and when she caught his gaze, it was clear by the appealing look on his face that he was willing her to stay silent on the matter. What was the big deal? It was clear that Jenna wasn't afraid to pull her punches. Comfortable, confident, she didn't seem to give a toss if she was upsetting the tranquil façade. It made Vikki feel meek and mousy by comparison for sticking to the script and being nervous of putting a foot wrong. Still, a sense of loyalty to Niall made her do just that. She so wanted to be liked and approved of by Niall and his family. She met his gaze with a tiny nod of understanding, then took a studied interest in helping herself to some more vegetables, watching him out of the corner of her eye as his tense face relaxed a fraction.

Lainey laughed, breaking the uneasy atmosphere. 'Oh, Jenna, it would be lovely to be that unique, but it's not just the Blake family trait. Ten per cent of the Irish population has red hair, and a third carry the gene. And it's not always admired either ... the number of times we were all slagged over our hair in school, carrot top, ginger man, red-head, you name it ...' Her voice trailed away and she shrugged and stared at Jenna as if that was the end of it.

'I can't understand that,' Jenna went on. 'I think it's beautiful, your mother Gabrielle, especially, had fabulous red-gold hair.'

'I don't think any of us managed to inherit her particular shade,' Lainey said. She had a ready smile but there was a tiny edge in her voice. 'I'm glad to see it's coming up in the next generation; Jack is the spit of his father at that age with his curls. Even Charlotte has a trace of strawberry-blonde, so the family trait lives on.'

'Some distant family member was lucky enough to have inherited your mother's beautiful shade,' Jenna said, 'because that's what I noticed the most, down by the lough, the way the colour of it gleamed in the sunshine.'

Lainey gave Jenna a strained smile as she picked up her glass of wine. It slid sideways from her hold and she jumped to her feet, grabbing a napkin and dapping ineffectually at the puddle of wine edging towards the table runner. 'Sorry, folks, an accident. Back in a sec.'

She hurried out into the kitchen.

'Oh dear, why do I feel I said something wrong?' Jenna looked around, glancing in turn from Alex to Niall. She reached over and removed some serving dishes, pushing the linen away from the pooling wine.

Erin came bustling into the dining room, a cloth and spray in her hands, Lainey following. By the time the table was treated, to the accompaniment of Erin's chatter and enquiries about the meal, the tension had diffused.

'Sorry about that,' Lainey said. 'Where were we?' She looked around the table brightly. 'Oh yes, we were talking about activities for the weekend.'

'What kind of activities exactly?' Vikki asked, feeling the need to contribute.

'The fun things we did when we lived here.' Lainey's bright smile slid from Niall to Alex. 'All those years we were growing up, we had to make our own entertainment. Because we lived so far away from other kids, we were left to our own devices a lot. We had midnight feasts in the forest, treasure hunts, and endless board games.'

At the other end of the table, the children exchanged whoops of pleasure.

'What kind of game is a board game?' Vikki heard Jack say.

'It's where you pretend things,' Charlotte said.

'You're hardly suggesting we all go on a midnight feast?' Jenna looked at Alex.

'Not quite.' Lainey answered for him in a tone that brooked no argument. 'I've arranged for us to have our cheese and wine up in the fairy fort.'

'So it's still there?' Niall said.

'Of course,' Lainey replied. 'Then tomorrow we're going on a picnic up to Infinity Hill and the waterfall,' she went on, still with that air of authority. 'I think there's some rain on the way, so we'll get out while we can and Dad's OK with this, aren't you, Dad? Erin and Niamh will be here until we come back.'

'Sure.' Leo beamed down the table. 'Go out with the little ones and let them run around. Being here with everyone ...

it's wonderful. I'll be happy to sit in the library for an hour and remember all the good times, if someone is kind enough to help me in. I'll join you for a night cap later.'

While they were getting up from the table, Vikki overheard Jenna talking to Alex and knew she wasn't the only one who felt a little ruffled by Lainey's air of command.

'Are we seriously doing this?' Jenna asked. 'Bringing Jack out at this hour? Taking our cheese and wine into some kind of fairy fort?'

'Why not?' Alex's tone was hostile. 'It's a beautiful evening and we've a good hour before it will start to get dark. Lainey's put a lot of thought into the weekend, so it'll all go smoothly.'

'She certainly has,' Jenna said smartly. 'The timetable sounds like it has been planned with military precision. I hope, for her sake, it stays smooth.'

'So do I, for my sake,' Ben said as he strolled past.

Vikki watched Niall gently escort his father from the room, observing the way he tipped his head towards him, his eyes kind and attentive. She knew how good it felt to be on the receiving end of that thoughtfulness. Whatever about the outlaws and the in-laws, she hoped the weekend would go smoothly for her and Niall, although now she was in the bosom of the enigmatic Blakes, she was beginning to wonder what exactly it would bring.

CHAPTER TEN

Vikki and Niall went ahead of everyone else as they walked around by the side of the house, across the terrace, down the garden, and out through a gate in the wall, taking a track that led around by the perimeter of the forest. The sun was sliding down out of the sky, bathing the landscape in a marmalade sheen. Vikki took deep breaths, inhaling scents of pine and bracken, and she soaked it all up; the deep and silent forest to one side, occasional glimpses of Slieve Creagh through the lattice-work of treetops, and the undulating flow of the green and gold terrain and rough tumbling walls of the countryside falling away to her right. Most importantly, this man, walking beside her, making her senses swim. Only for the voices of the children, streaming in the clear air from somewhere behind, they could have been all alone.

After a short walk they came to a junction in the trail. Straight ahead, a path led into the centre of the forest itself; to the right, the path continued to skim the perimeter of the trees, and a track to the left, which also dipped into the forest, looked as though it hadn't been used in a long time, because it disappeared into a tangle of wild undergrowth, thick furze bushes and desiccated tree trunks. Peeling lettering on an old wooden sign caught up in a decayed tree warned about the danger of trespassing. She wondered why it was needed in the middle of nowhere.

Niall took the path to the right.

The only problem was that her brand-new, ultraglamorous hiking boots, specially bought on Carnaby Street for tramping the Mayo woods, could have done with being broken in. Even after a few minutes her feet were chafing in places she hadn't known existed. She'd have to go searching for plasters – discreetly, of course – as soon as they got back to Lynes Glen. She'd noticed that Lainey was wearing a comfortable-looking pair of knee-length black leather boots with thick soles, similar to what she had back home in her London flat. Even Jenna, stylish as she was, was wearing a pair of chunky padded boots. When she stumbled on the stony surface, Niall held out his hand to her.

'Hey, can't have you getting an injury.'

Her hand felt warm and secure in his as he tucked both of them together in the pocket of his padded jacket. She took measured footsteps, ignoring the pain, telling herself this was worth it.

'Just another five minutes,' he said.

Five precious minutes to have this man to herself.

'Was this one of your childhood haunts?' she asked.

'Yeah, we spent as much time as we could outdoors.'

'Imagine having this for a playground,' she said. 'What is a fairy fort anyhow? Do they really exist?'

'It's so-called because it's something like a circular kind of mound or imprint left on the landscape where there once was a fort of some kind. It could have been put together with ditches and bushes, back in the year dot. There are lots of them scattered round the country.'

'But they have nothing to do with the fairies.'

'Nah. But it all depends on what you want to believe. Legend has it that there's some kind of magic attached to a fairy fort so they're best left alone. In some parts of the country there's a mad outcry if someone wants to demolish one to build on the land, even to this day. It's supposed to bring bad luck.' His eyes were gleaming with mischief, giving her a glimpse of her London Niall.

'Oh dear, I hope I don't get on the wrong side of the fairies.'

'You're doing great so far. You're OK with everything else?' he asked. 'This weekend, I mean. Not missing the bright lights too much?'

'How could I miss the bright lights with all this?' she said, sweeping her arm out in an expansive gesture. 'It must have been wonderful as a child, growing up here and running free in the mountains and the forests. Then you had the lough. Did you go diving much?'

She hadn't meant to ask so bluntly; she'd planned on leading up to the subject as it was clearly sensitive, and she just wanted to enjoy these moments with Niall, but the words had slipped out. Well done, Vikki.

A shadow crossed his face, and although he was staring ahead she knew he wasn't seeing anything, and she could have kicked herself. Then they rounded another bend, came into a clearing and he said, 'I think we're here, this is it. Wait, though—'

Vikki looked round at the clearing, a sense of foreboding gripping her. 'What's going on here?'

*

Jenna found herself taking up the rear of the group with Ben. Up ahead were Lainey and Alex, the children skipping around them, heeding Lainey's urgings not to venture too far in front.

'What's up with you?' Ben asked.

Jenna was surprised by his frankness. 'What do you mean?'

'You seem … unhappy. Both out on the terrace this evening, and then at the dinner table.'

'You mean I was a little bit snippy.' She met his candour with a directness of her own.

He didn't disagree. 'Is being here all that terrible or is anything wrong?'

They had fallen behind the others now, and because the track curved ahead they couldn't see the rest of the group although they could hear the children's excited voices and laughter coming from Lainey. Jenna was surprised at the rush of emotions she felt in Ben's company; her pleasure at being with him mixed with unexpected nerves now that they were alone. Lainey was his wife, she reminded herself.

'I'm a bit out of sorts,' she admitted. 'Ignore me.'

'Hmm.' He smiled at her. 'Pretty difficult, seeing as we're likely to be thrown together over the weekend.'

Exactly what I'm afraid of. She'd never had much opportunity to talk to Ben alone. The couple of times he'd been over in New York, either Alex or Lainey had been around, leading the conversation; mostly Lainey, she realised, when she looked back now. The couple had seemed inseparable. She'd thought at the time that Ben was being an ultra-attentive, devoted husband. Now she had a gut feeling that it had been the other way around – Lainey keeping close tabs on Ben. In case he spoke out of turn? Or said something that went against the Blake code of secrecy? Once, they'd been left alone in the booth of a New York restaurant when Alex had gone across to another table to chat to an acquaintance of his soon after Lainey had gone to the bathroom. In that ten-minute space of private conversation, Ben had asked her about the brothers' falling out, a question she'd been unable to answer.

When they came to the break in the path, they saw Lainey waiting up ahead, looking behind to make sure everyone was following. 'This way,' she called out, veering right.

Yes, sir, atten-shun, Jenna thought.

Lainey's eyes rested on Jenna for a moment. She looked like she was about to double back to them, but Alex said something to her and she fell into step beside him again. By rights, Lainey should have been nervous of Jenna alone with her husband.

'You've been along this trail before?' she asked Ben.

'A few times, but not after Leo moved down into the town. I come back to Lynes Glen with Lainey a couple of times a year, just to check on the house. Leo arranges for it to be checked for maintenance, but Lainey likes to satisfy herself that everything is OK. You'd get occasional hill walkers and hikers along here, both up to Slieve Creagh and into the forest. It keeps the trail open. Getting back to you, is there a problem?'

'Does it bother you if there is?'

He stopped and looked at her, a hint of annoyance on his face. 'Jenna. Don't insult me, please.'

'Where will I start?' she said. 'Number one, why do I feel the family are all acting a part, pretending everything is perfect and has always been perfect? From the way Alex and Niall are carrying on you'd never think they'd had a bust-up. In the few hours since we've arrived here, it's as if Alex has morphed into someone else. He won't level with me about why we're here, or why he has conveniently forgotten he fell out with Niall.'

'I didn't want to be here either,' Ben admitted.

'Didn't you?'

'It's been bad enough watching Lainey run between her brothers for most of our marriage,' he said. 'I've had to accept that Lainey is ultrasensitive when it comes to her brothers. She loves them, fine, but there were plenty of times over the years when I got pissed off playing second fiddle to the all-important Blakes. Even this weekend – she's been thinking of nothing else since Leo fixed the date, almost to the point of obsession. I resent being dragged over here to be part of some kind of peace-making effort when I don't know what the hell went on years ago. It makes me feel like a proper gobshite. Lainey has probably warned Alex and Niall to behave. I know how much this reunion means to her.'

'I'm beginning to gather that myself,' Jenna said.

'Maybe we're the ones who are being too sensitive. Do husbands and wives share everything? I dunno. Have you any secrets you're keeping from Alex?'

The bluntness of his question surprised her. She was keeping a secret – very close to her chest – the fact that she found this man far too attractive. So attractive that she was in danger of committing virtual adultery. If there was such a thing. How much difference was there, in essence, between the lustful thought and the deed?

'Maybe I shouldn't have asked that,' he said.

She laughed. 'You don't look a bit sorry. It's no secret to Alex that I didn't want to be here this weekend. He's had no time for me for months, he's totally obsessed with his business problems, which is something else he won't talk about either, and thanks to all that, our marriage isn't what it should be. There, I've said it.'

To her surprise, Ben gave her shoulder a reassuring squeeze. 'It makes you ask yourself why Alex came home at all.'

'Oh, I know all about that, not that Alex will admit it. I heard him on the phone, discussing it with Lainey.'

'Oh? Eavesdropping?' His eyes gleamed.

'Not intentionally.'

'You might as well tell me, so.'

'This weekend has nothing to do with mending a rift, believe me. That's why I'm cynical about the sudden outpouring of family unity. It's everything to do with Leo's will.'

'Leo's *will*?'

'Something to the effect that if they didn't show up for the weekend they'd be cut out of the will.'

Ben whistled. 'That sucks. I'd never have thought Leo was capable of sending out that kind of a summons. Are you sure?'

'Absolutely. I heard Alex speaking to Lainey about it.'

Ben shook his head. 'That explains a lot.'

'Sorry if I've ruined any of your cosy family-unity ideals. The scent of money, or fear of being denied it, brought Alex running home where wild horses wouldn't drag him before now.'

'And you're objecting on principle.'

'What can I say? Leo won't be around forever. There will be a legacy of some description, and I guess Lainey should be entitled to a decent share as she's the one who keeps an eye on Leo. But Alex is entitled to a share as much as Niall. On the other hand, I'm disappointed because I thought my husband was nobler.'

'That's a big ask,' Ben said. 'Especially if he could do with some capital. Lynes Glen would be worth a fair whack on the market, I could see it being snapped up and turned into a boutique hotel or an intimate wedding venue, especially with that setting around it.'

'Money always talks, doesn't it?' Jenna said bitterly. 'No matter how highly principled we think we are. In a way I see Alex's point of view, but why couldn't he be honest with me? That's what hurts me most. Sorry if I'm spouting off too much but you asked why I was out of sorts and I'm finding it all a little overwhelming. I didn't want to be here – for several reasons – and the happy family charade is doing my head in.'

He stopped and put a hand on her arm. He smiled at her. 'You can spout off to me anytime, Jenna. The Blakes, all together, can be more than a little overpowering.'

They stood there for a moment. Did he feel it too? The pull between them? Every cell in her body went into a meltdown of sorts. She could have stood there forever. She was overcome with a mixture of heady excitement and dizzy fear, and she struggled to prevent her face, her eyes especially, from mirroring her thoughts.

Then, from up ahead, they heard a shrill scream.

CHAPTER ELEVEN

Vikki put her hands up to her mouth, but it was too late to stop the scream that rushed up her throat and hurled itself out into the cool, clear air. She tried to look away but her eyes were drawn down as if by a magnet.

They were lifeless sparrows, with clenched grey claws; their brown feathers flattened and unmoving, enclosing them like stiff veils, while their sightless eyes and fixed gaze glared like shiny pebbles. Dead birds. Three of them, lying together in a row, placed in a slightly battered fast-food carton, waiting to be found.

'What the hell …' Niall said, catching her by the shoulders, his eyes following the direction of hers.

'Tell me I'm not seeing things,' Vikki said, nausea rising inside.

'You're not.'

She closed the lid hurriedly. It wasn't only the ugly contents of the carton ... something sinister had happened to the landscaping that had chilled herself and Niall as soon as they'd arrived in the clearing. What appeared to have been a circle of bushes rimming a slight knoll had been hacked away, and all that remained of the bushes were crooked bare stalks that poked at angles out of the earth like bleached bones. When she saw the carton lying just inside the rim of hacked bushes, she thought she'd be doing the Blakes a favour, getting rid of someone else's litter before the rest of the group arrived. Now she was sorry she'd touched it.

Alex and Lainey arrived, Lainey slightly out of breath. 'Vikki, what's wrong? I thought it was Charlotte.'

'No, it was me,' Vikki admitted, embarrassed to be caught in the spotlight and have caused a fuss like this. She wished she'd had the presence of mind to simply show the carton to Niall so that both of them could have disposed of it safely before anyone else arrived, but she'd got such a fright when she'd opened it that she'd automatically let out a scream.

'What the hell happened here?' Lainey asked, looking around at the damaged bushes.

'It's not just the bushes,' Niall said. He used a twig to flip open the lid of the carton. Both Lainey and Alex leaned forward and shrank back immediately, Lainey stifling a cry. There was a mound of shrubbery heaped up several feet away. As Vikki watched, Alex marched over to it, kicking at the pile savagely, scattering the twigs. Charlotte and Harry picked some up and, holding them aloft like totem poles, they ran around the perimeter of the rise making whooping sounds, Lainey too upset to check them.

'When is the last time you were up here?' Niall asked Lainey.

'Years,' she said. 'I know it's off the beaten track but I'm sure there were occasional hikers up here during the summer.'

'This happened only recently,' Alex said. 'That shrubbery is freshly hacked, and as for the birds ...' By now the children had stopped their running around and had joined the adults, Alex doing his best to hold back Jack.

Ben and Jenna arrived, Charlotte skipping up to her father. 'Three dead birds,' she said, 'wait til you see them. Vikki screamed and gave us all a big fright. Even I got a fright when I saw them, but I'm OK now.'

Harry used his piece of twig to turn over one of the dead birds.

'Harry! Stop that,' Lainey admonished, grabbing the stick, trying to flip the lid back on, but it fell to the side.

'I'm only looking, Mum. I wanted to see if he was hurted.'

'Of course he was hurt,' Lainey snapped. 'He's dead.'

'It could be a girl bird,' said Charlotte, peering in. 'How do we find out?'

Lainey put a hand to her head. 'Oh, for goodness' sake. Ben, sort out your children.'

Ben duly obliged, drawing the children away from the rise.

'What are we going to do with these ... with this?' Lainey asked, looking distraught as she gazed from Alex to Niall. 'Could it have been a stray hiker? God ...' her voice cracked.

'Or was this set up to rattle us?' Niall said.

'Christ, Niall.' Alex put an arm around Lainey's shoulder. 'It's OK. Of course it was a stray somebody who wasn't bothered disposing of them properly. You can't think they were put here on purpose.'

Beside her, Vikki heard Jenna swear very quietly.

'What the hell is this all about?' Jenna said to her, as they moved slightly away from the group. 'It's only a few bushes.

Whatever about the birds, which is a shame, Alex hasn't given a damn about the state of the flora and fauna around here in two decades.'

'This isn't an ordinary clearing,' Vikki said. 'It's a fairy fort. Or at least it was.'

'So this is it?' Jenna said, her brow wrinkled. 'Where we're supposed to be having our cheese and wine? Just a circle of bushes? Mind you' – she wheeled around – 'the view from here is amazing. Those fairies sure knew what they were doing, building their fort here.'

'Apparently it's an Irish superstition that it's bad luck to damage these in any way,' Vikki told her.

'Ah-hah. Get you. Although I wish I could "get" a few other things about the weekend. Do you think Lainey would notice if I sneaked off and nipped down to the town? There's bound to be an internet facility somewhere. I'd like to google some stuff in more detail – although google hadn't been invented around the timescale I'm interested in.'

'Same here, actually.' It was exactly what Vikki itched to do – find out more about Leo and Gabrielle, although Niall had said his father had always guarded his privacy fiercely and had little or no internet presence. She also wanted to see were there any references to Niall as a diver. Had he won any medals or competitions? Then again, twenty-year-old-plus editions of the local newspapers scarcely had a digital imprint.

Alex and Niall spoke to Lainey, the three of them in a huddle, and there was a decision of sorts made because the two men went over to a ditch and, using pieces of broken branches, dug a shallow hole. They placed the carton of dead birds into it, which they covered up again, Niall stamping on the earth to compact it down.

'Right. Back to the house, everyone,' Lainey called out. 'The children can have their treats in bed,' she added, to the accompaniment of their cheers. 'Once they clean their teeth afterwards,' Lainey cautioned. 'Is that OK with you, Jenna?'

'Of course.' Jenna said. 'I didn't expect to have any say in that.' Lainey gathered the children and Jenna turned to Vikki. 'Are you OK?' Jenna asked. 'I don't mean the fright you got … are your boots hurting?'

'Murder,' said Vikki, trying to smile but gritting her teeth instead.

'Oh dear,' Jenna sympathised. 'I can lend you a pair of socks? It might help to get you back to the house. I've double socks on, but one pair will do me fine. I was expecting the Irish weather to be colder.'

'Actually, thanks, I'll take you up on that,' Vikki said gratefully.

'Nothing worse,' Jenna said. 'Sit on this fallen log and we'll fix you up.'

Vikki sat down beside Jenna and inched off her boots, grateful for the extra pair of knee socks that Jenna peeled off and handed to her.

'Hey, Vikki,' Niall said, walking over to her. 'Anything wrong?'

'I'm grand,' she said, once more feeling a touch of embarrassment. 'Just getting more comfortable.'

'I'm walking back with Lainey, if that's OK with you,' he said. 'She's a bit upset.'

'Of course, Niall, no probs,' she said, ignoring the lurch in her chest.

'A bit weird, all the same,' Jenna said, when Niall had gone across to his sister. 'Three dead birds, lined up like that.'

Vikki shivered. 'Don't.' As well as being spooked, she felt hugely uncomfortable that she'd been the one to draw attention to them. She could imagine how annoyed Lainey was that this special childhood place with all its superstitions had been spoiled.

'Sorry.' Jenna pulled a face. 'Don't mind me, I'm not in the least bit superstitious.'

Vikki eased her boots back on, the additional layer helping a little to cushion her feet. The Blakes led the way back to the house, the children skipping alongside them, laughing and chattering. Ben followed them, slightly ahead of Vikki and Jenna.

'So now we've something else to figure out,' Jenna said. 'Who wrecked the fairy fort? And what bad luck is going to follow us forever more?'

'None, I hope,' Vikki said. 'I need all the luck I can get in my life right now,' she went on, unburdening herself a little, much to her surprise.

'Niall?' Jenna flashed her a grin.

'Yeah, Niall ... and other things,' Vikki said, thoughts of the missed conference flickering in her head. Because of Niall, she'd put her career on the line. She didn't know if she'd have a job to go back to next week. By now Jo Morgan would know she'd been 'unavoidably called away' because of 'urgent family business'. Urgent business of the family she hoped to belong to, even though it seemed like a ridiculous dream. Watching him up ahead, loping along with his sister and brother, he seemed a stranger to her, with no common ground between them other than the times they laughed and joked their way around London. Apart from that one special night, it was always fun – superficial, careless and carefree fun; their biggest disagreement to date had been about the ingredients that went into making a lasagne. This was Niall's home territory, he had breathed it into his bones so that it was part of him, but it couldn't have been further from the London streets of her childhood. He had history she knew nothing about, he had hopes and fears and dreams he'd never spoken of.

'The best of luck,' Jenna said, 'whatever it is you want.'

Vikki took a breath and said, 'There was something you said, earlier this evening. About seeing a woman by the lough.'

'That's right. Why?'

'I saw her too. When we were driving past, a woman, sitting on the diving board.'

'Did you? So I was right. Although it went down like a lead balloon,' Jenna said, a hint of laughter in her voice. 'Lainey spilt her wine most conveniently. I wonder why the lough has been closed up. From the glimpse I caught, it looks incredibly beautiful. Probably another Blake secret that will never see the light of day.'

Ahead of them Ben stopped and half turned, waiting for them to catch up.

'Sorry, Jenna, I couldn't help overhearing. Don't you know? Or Vikki?'

'Know what?' Jenna said.

He stared at both of them for a moment before saying, 'The lough has been closed up for years, because that's where Gabrielle died.'

'*What*?' Jenna said. 'Alex told me it was an accident. That her car went off the road.'

A shiver ran down Vikki's spine. 'That's what I heard too.'

'Technically, it did,' Ben said. 'Gabrielle's car went off the road on her way back to Lynes Glen, but it then went through the ditch and down the slope into the lough. You can see the actual spot on one of the bends in the road. It's blocked up with corrugated iron and barbed wire. The laneway down to the lough is also closed up, as is the pathway through the forest. Leo had that done soon after the accident and it's been like that ever since.'

'Christ. I didn't know,' Jenna breathed. 'Why the hell did Alex keep that crucial detail from me?'

'They never talk of it,' Ben said. 'Lainey happened to tell me on one of the anniversaries of Gabrielle's death. Her tenth, I think. We were a steady item by then and down here for the weekend; she'd had far too much to drink and was all emotional because it was a milestone anniversary for her. The next day she even brought me to the lough, there's a way around through the forest, but then she said she wanted to forget it had ever happened. I went along with her, although I know it's not good to blank things out.'

Sometimes you need to blank things out, Vikki almost contradicted him.

'That's dreadful,' Jenna said. 'It makes it seem more tragic. And tough for the Blakes, passing that spot on the way to Lynes Glen. I sure put my foot in it this evening, sounding like I saw a real, live ghost. Je-*sus*.'

Ben smiled. 'A real, live ghost is a contradiction of sorts. But yeah, I wouldn't say it went down too well.'

'That's one very diplomatic way of putting it,' Jenna said. 'At least you stayed quiet, Vikki, you didn't land yourself in it, like me.'

Vikki shrugged. 'Niall gave me a look that asked me to say nothing. Now I see why.'

'It seems strange that just you and I saw her,' Jenna said. 'Although Alex's attention was focussed grimly on the road as we passed by the lough.'

'Same with Niall.'

'Gabrielle was quite young when it happened,' Ben said. 'Just forty-eight. She'd be seventy next year, if she was still alive. I know it was over twenty years ago, but there's a sense that the tragedy has left a lot of raw edges and, for reasons of their own, the Blakes are still hiding their wounds.'

Vikki gazed ahead to where the trio were just disappearing around a corner, marching together with Lainey in the middle, linking her brothers. No wonder Niall had jammed on the brakes when she'd mentioned the woman to him. She and Jenna had hardly both seen a ghost. But looking about her now, at the still, watchful mountains and the deep, silent forest, a mystical landscape that seemed to be thick with secrets and shadows, never mind the air of enigma surrounding the Blakes, the ghost of vibrant Gabrielle didn't seem inconceivable at all.

CHAPTER TWELVE

1968

She was all light and fiery gold; it shone out from her face and formed an aura around her. She glistened, she glowed, and even her hair rippled around her shoulders like a sheet of sun-kissed flame. He wanted to bury his face in the wonder of it, exult in it, and soak up all that life and colour so that it might infuse the greyness of him and his life, and lift him away from his dusty books and the sadness that had engulfed him since his parents had died the year before.

Her laughter sounded like the joyous bubbling of a mountain spring tumbling down from the peak of Slieve Creagh, gurgling under stone arches on its journey out to the Atlantic. He wished he was the sole recipient of that laughter; he found himself insanely jealous of anyone else it was shared with. She was younger than he was. A lot. He found out she was fourteen years younger, when someone spoke to her of her recent twenty-first birthday. *Fourteen years*? What would she be doing with someone as ancient as he was? In five years' time he'd be forty. He was mad, foolish to be having such ridiculous thoughts.

Yet, for the third day in a row, he found himself making the journey from Lynes Glen into Creaghbara and lingering over his dinner of chicken and ham with mashed potatoes and all the vegetables in the town centre hotel, feeling he was soaking up the sun each time her bright smile drifted in his direction. He told himself he was crazy and delusional. It was her job to smile at the customers. She was being paid to do this, in addition to serving the tables. It wouldn't be good for hotel business to have a new waitress who was scowling and unfriendly. So why should he think he was getting any preferential treatment or imagine her eyes were gazing purposefully in the direction of his table? And why were wonderful dreams of her filling his thoughts and causing his blood to rush to his head, dreams of twirling her around, arm in arm on the dancefloor on a Saturday night?

As if she'd even bother with that. She probably wanted to kick up her heels to some pop music. The Beatles or Elvis Presley.

It was the summertime, and he was taking it off. No university lectures or class preparation for three whole months. No exam papers to correct, not even a summer conference or poetry festival to attend. He could write to his heart's content in his library at Lynes Glen. Make shape of the words streaming through his head.

At least that had been the plan.

Except, sitting in his study in Lynes Glen, her smile kept getting in the way, superimposing itself on the terrorising blank sheets in front of him. He broke the lead on his pencil several times, taking his time to sharpen it, and wished he was able to write music because he might have been able to echo her laughter in the true, clear notes of a flute composition. He wished he could paint, so he could copy her likeness on canvas, and imitate even a small fragment of her spirit in outlining the soft curve of her face, the hint of rebellion in the tilt of that chin. Despite her slight figure, she looked like the kind of woman who could have enticed an army of men into battle, leading the charge with her standard bearer flowing out behind her along with her glorious hair. For once he resented all the shortcomings of his craft, because no words of his, no matter how lyrically arranged, could do her justice in any shape or form.

'Gabrielle.' He heard her name being called by the manager. It was market day and the dining room was extra busy. A table was looking for a jug of water.

Gabrielle. It sounded beautiful; the name enchanted him like the charm of a glockenspiel being struck gently, and it resonated in his head. He watched the way she turned in response to the call, and stood poised, slim and neat, yet energy vibrated from every cell of her body, like a dancer in the wings awaiting her cue before pirouetting across the stage. How he wished he could take the liberty of calling her name and having her turn to him in response. He would lift her off those perfect feet and spin her around and around for the sheer joy of it. Because everything about her filled his senses with a bubbling, vital joy.

And shy, scholarly Leo Blake, lonesome bachelor, nerdy university lecturer in English literature and Classical studies, struggling poet, realised that, for the first time in all of his life, he'd finally and irrevocably fallen in love.

*

'Here again? We'll have to start charging you rent.'

His dessert spoon clattered to the floor. He felt the heat of colour rising on his face. Had she really spoken to him? He'd sat at his table so long that the lunchtime crowd had dissipated and the waitress who served this side of the room had gone on her break.

He'd deliberately stayed away from Creaghbara for almost a week, wrestling with his heart and his imaginings, but he found himself drawn back again, and once more, it was the third day in a row that he'd occupied the small table close to the window. Gabrielle had brought a tray over to a table next to his to clear it off when she'd spoken to him. They both bent down at the same time to pick up the spoon. He caught the drift of her light fragrance, and his head came so close to hers it was like an electrical charge to his skull.

'Sorry,' she said, smiling at him. She had tiny freckles chasing each other across her pale skin. He astounded himself with the urge he felt to put his fingers to them. Not only his fingers but also his lips.

'Get you a fresh one,' she said.

He couldn't bring himself to admit that he was long finished his meal and didn't need the spoon replaced as he wasn't having dessert. He watched her walking across the room, the knowledge that she would be returning to his table filling him with trepidation and excitement. Hoping it wouldn't show on his face, he tried to compose it into a suitable relaxed state. *Smile*, he urged himself.

'There you are,' she said, placing the spoon down on his table along with a fresh napkin.

'Thank you,' he said, smiling up at her, although she was so petite compared to his lean, awkward height that he hadn't too far to crane his neck. He wondered why there were no other words in the English language that he – a man of letters, supposedly – could think of saying right then.

'Can I get you anything else, sir?'

Sir? She was being polite and friendly, but the formal title unbalanced him and forced him to speak.

'It's L-Leo, my name is Leo.'

'Well then, can I get you anything else, Leo?' Her voice washed over him like soft music.

'I'm fine, thanks.'

He was anything but fine. He was a long, lean, gibbering mess, thanks to the way he'd allowed this young woman to inhabit his every waking moment. He waited until she was busy clearing the table beside him before he got up to go, bumping against his table as he stood up – naturally enough – rattling the water jug and the condiments. He hoped he might be able to skulk away unobserved, especially after being so clumsy, but she turned and smiled.

'Bye now,' she said, her voice a soft lilt.

He carried the sound and that smile all the way home. As he neared the house, he turned down the narrow track to Lough Lynes, parking on the grassy strip overlooking the edge. It was the sanctuary he had always come to when he sought peace and inspiration in a world that didn't always appreciate nerdy poets, and it had never let him down. The glacial lough had been hewn out of nature thousands of years ago. The shallow shelf close to the shore quickly dropped away and the lough was deceptively deep. He could have climbed up the nearby rocky outcrop for a better view, or to access the diving board, but he was happy to stay where he was, watching the play of sunlight on water, and the rippling reflection of the mountains and the sky on the luminous surface. He sat for quite some time, realising there was no point in trying to analyse, in any rational way, what was happening to him. It was beyond coherent explanation.

When he eventually went home and walked into the hallway at Lynes Glen, he knew that, for the first time since he'd buried his parents within six months of each other, he didn't feel quite so alone.

Still, the following week he rationed himself to two visits to the hotel dining room, soaking up the sight of her, stalling until the lunch hour was almost over and the dining room was quiet enough for her to notice when he got up to leave, and he was uplifted with another smile and another 'Bye now.'

And the following week, the poster appeared, advertising the dance.

CHAPTER THIRTEEN

Vikki was relieved to see the chimney tops of Lynes Glen appearing between the trees as the group returned from their curtailed Friday evening walk. She envied the children racing each other down the final stretch, up through the garden and around by the terrace, colourful bundles of energy and life streaking joyfully against the gathering evening. The sun was dipping low in the sky, and, in the draining light, the forest appeared darker and denser. She fancied it encroached more on the house, as though the trees were reaching out their tentacles further towards it with the coming of night. Even the house set against the darkened backdrop appeared more sombre and melancholy. She reined in her imagination; as a form of escape, she'd read far too many fairy stories as a child. Reaching the entrance hall, she subsided gratefully onto one of the faded armchairs and gingerly eased off her boots.

Immediately, much to her renewed embarrassment, she was once more the sole focus of attention from the Blakes, who were moving round the hall, divesting the children and themselves of coats and jackets with a little more enthusiasm than was warranted. Whatever the three siblings had said to each other on the homeward journey, they had obviously agreed to forget the unpleasantness that had awaited them at the fort.

'Vikki, you poor thing, you should have said something,' Lainey gushed, untwisting her scarf, her pale forehead creased with concern. 'I hope it didn't spoil your walk.'

'I'm fine, really,' Vikki protested, acutely uncomfortable at being viewed as Lainey's 'poor thing', or being responsible in any way for further marring the trip to the fort, never mind bringing unwanted attention down on herself. 'It's just a couple of blisters,' she went on. 'Nothing as bad as …' she paused and bit her tongue.

There was a tiny silence and Vikki wished she could take back her last words. Compared to the disappointment the family had faced at the fort, Vikki's sore feet were a minor nuisance, but she hadn't needed to emphasise that. Lainey took off her jacket and scarf, sighing quietly as she handed them to Ben, and, in that unguarded moment, Vikki sensed something vulnerable, a tiny hint of helplessness, about her. Then Lainey turned to Niall, her moment of fragility covered up so comprehensively that Vikki wondered if she'd seen it at all.

'There's a first-aid box in the kitchen,' she said, back in control once more.

'Stay where you are,' Niall said, when Vikki went to get to her feet.

'I'm well able to get down to the kitchen,' Vikki said, not wanting to be left sitting in the hall in the role of Lainey's poor wounded thing.

'I'll have a big glass of wine ready and waiting for you,' Alex said, giving her a wink, as though he sensed Vikki's discomfort. His kindness was unexpected. Of them all, Alex was the one she was the least able to figure out. There was a mercurial tension about him that totally unnerved her. Jenna, she sensed, would be well able to handle the fidgety energy of this man and be a grounding force. She wasn't afraid of speaking her mind, unlike Vikki, hell bent on approval.

In the kitchen, Niall opened drawers and poked around to no avail. 'I'm sure there are plasters here somewhere,' he said.

Vikki was quite happy to sit for a while. The kitchen in Lynes Glen filled her with ease and she had Niall to herself once more. A relaxed place adjacent to the living room, the room was an eclectic mix of retro and more modern design. It had a red-tiled floor, scrubbed spotlessly clean, which must have been laid in the time of Leo's parents, to judge by the faded patina, and a deep Belfast sink from the same era. The farmhouse-style kitchen cupboards were an updated addition – during Gabrielle's time, Vikki guessed – along with a matching table and six chairs with assorted seat pads that looked perfect for casual breakfasts and lunches.

This evening, the room was pleasantly warm, and redolent of cooking aromas as well as a citrus-lemon scent. A dishwasher hummed as it went through its cycle. Fresh tea towels were folded over the door handles of the big cooking range, and a rack overhead held gleaming pots and pans. The windows, with their cheerful, red-checked curtains, looked out onto the forest and the mountains. Cookery books were stacked in a shelved niche, and pottery jugs and vases stored away on top of a press. Her heart tugged as she imagined Gabrielle moving around this space, flicking through the cookery books, filling the kitchen with wonderful aromas, arranging jugs with flowers and greenery, filling the house with colour and love and warmth.

It made her realise how little physical evidence there was that Gabrielle had lived here, yet Vikki sensed her presence everywhere. She imagined Niall too, bursting in here, raiding the fridge, and while it made her feel close to him, it brought home to her the huge difference in their childhoods. The kitchen in Hackney had been nothing like this. Her guard was down for a moment and the dark image of it rose up from its hiding place and played at the edges of her mind. She blinked hard, trying to blank it away.

'What are you looking for, Niall?' Erin said, bustling in from the dining room through the connecting door. Niamh was still in there, cutlery chinking as she set the table for the following morning's breakfast.

'Vikki needs something for her blisters,' Niall said.

'I'll look after her,' Erin said. 'See if your dad needs anything before Niamh and I go home. Now, pet' – she turned to Vikki, her arms akimbo – 'did they really drag you out for a walk without proper footwear? Tsk, tsk!'

'It was my fault,' she admitted. 'I bought new boots for the weekend, but they're not broken in yet.'

'Oh dear, nothing worse,' Erin said, opening a press and putting her hands on the first-aid kit immediately. Lainey's clear tones floated in from the living room, her voice full of relentless cheerfulness as she chatted to Jenna and Ben. To Vikki's ears it sounded brittle and forced, and it gave her a twist in her stomach. She'd listened to that kind of voice before, using contrived cheer to pretend all was well, when it had been anything but:

'Emily Victoria, say hello to your new daddy. He's going to look

after us, aren't you, John? Your last daddy was mean so I sent him away. Give him a hug and a kiss ...'

'Emily! Be nice to your new daddy, Simon has got you a lovely present. You're a very lucky girl to have such a wonderful new daddy ...'

'Your mummy said you'd be a good girl for me ...'

Vikki felt the blood draining from her face and she leaned forward, resting her dizzy head between her legs. Where had that come from? After all this time?

'Lainey is some woman,' Erin was saying. Vikki heard the sound of her setting the box down on the table. 'Always positive and upbeat. Had you met her before? I don't remember her mentioning your name until this week. Hey, Vikki? What's happened to you?'

Vikki raised her head and took a deep breath. 'I'll be OK in a minute.' She was relieved that none of the Blakes were around to witness her moment of weakness. 'This is my first time to meet the family,' she went on, trying to sound calm and neutral but something in her face caused Erin to give her a studied look and Vikki flushed.

'It means a lot to you, I see,' she said. 'I'm used to Leo and his ways, I'm with him almost a year now, and I've met Lainey a few times. All together in the same place the Blakes might seem a little overpowering, but behind it all they're no different from anyone else.'

Yes, they were, Vikki wanted to say. Even this kitchen spoke to her of an idyllic childhood, and while it filled her with comfort to think of Niall experiencing this as he grew up, the cold realisation that she'd never had anything like it caused a funny catch in her chest. Still, all the security in the world hadn't saved Niall or his siblings from heartbreak, or from being so cut up about the tragic way they'd lost their mother that they still couldn't bear to speak of it. She wasn't alone in wanting to keep certain things hidden behind a securely locked door.

There were times when it was better not to talk. She hated the current-day expression of opening oneself up, as though it was mandatory for the social conversation that people bared their vulnerabilities and deepest sore spots for general, often lascivious, consumption. It made her think of hacking open a tin with a blunt opener and peeling back the serrated lid to expose the defenceless contents. Who wanted their sad history laid bare like that? There was a lot to be said for just getting on with it, accepting things the way they were, accepting people the way they were and letting them be, without ripping away protective scabs.

Unless, of course, those scabs were hiding things that might hold you back.

'You're from London, aren't you? What part?' Erin said chattily as she riffled through the contents of the first-aid box.

'Putney,' Vikki said.

'Here you go, these should sort you out,' Erin said, handing Vikki some plasters. 'Have you always lived there, in Putney?'

'Oh yes,' Vikki said, hoping the lie wouldn't show on her face. 'Thanks, these are perfect.'

'If you need more, just help yourself,' Erin said, showing Vikki where the box was stored. 'I've been to London, just the once,' she went on, untying her apron. 'It was enough for me. It's a mad busy city, and as for the Tube – I don't know how you find your way around.'

'I suppose it's easy enough to get lost,' Vikki said. And even easier to lose yourself too, if you wished, she could have added.

'Niall is happy there according to his dad, but give me my hills of Donegal any day of the week,' Erin said.

'You Donegal natives are all the same,' Niall said jokily, as he came into the kitchen. 'You think there's nowhere like it on earth.'

'That's because there *is* nowhere like it,' Erin said firmly, 'although Mayo comes close enough. Have you ever been to Donegal, Vikki?'

'No, not yet.'

'I must bring you up for a visit sometime,' Niall said, surprising her. 'Erin is right, it's all beautiful ... Inishowen, Glenveagh, Dunfanaghy beach. We holidayed a lot there as children.'

'Sounds magical.'

'It is. Almost as magical as Mayo,' Niall said.

She felt warmed by the light in his eye and she wanted to hibernate in the kitchen with him for the rest of the evening.

'Dad's fine,' Niall said to Erin. 'He doesn't need anything for now and one of us can organise him later.'

'Right so,' Erin said. 'We'll be here bright and early in the morning. Niamh?' She called out to the younger woman, winking at Vikki as she said, 'That job should be well done by now. Get a move on.'

In the quiet of the bedroom, Vikki treated her blisters, the noise of the children trooping upstairs and being organised by Alex and Lainey for their bedtime treat floating through the rooms. It sounded like they were having a lot of fun and she could imagine Lynes Glen echoing to a similar noise when the Blakes were young. She put on a pair of slippers and went downstairs. The door to the living room was ajar, and she heard the rumble of Leo's voice, followed by Niall's comment and Jenna's answering laugh. She felt suddenly shy at the thoughts of joining them. On impulse, she slipped into the sitting room, admiring the collection of photographs on the piano, trying to associate the images of the twenty-somethings with the present-day Blakes.

With the exception of Leo, who wore an expression bordering on total awkwardness at his moment caught in the glare of the spotlights, they all had something in common, something Vikki had never had at that age. They looked so sleek and polished, privileged and sure of themselves, as if the sun would always shine on them and the dark underbelly of life would never touch them. And she'd been wrong about the lack of physical evidence of Gabrielle's presence in Lynes Glen. The image of her in this one photograph was so vibrant and alive it seemed to swirl out of the frame and resonate throughout every corner of the house.

She had a sudden feeling she wasn't alone in the room, that she was being observed, and the hairs rose on the back of her neck. She remained motionless for a moment but when she turned around, a forced, half-smile on her face, there was no one there. Yet the eerie feeling persisted. She'd heard Erin and Niamh's car crunching down the driveway earlier, and knew that everyone was either upstairs or in the living room but, for some reason, she didn't feel inclined to leave the room and go out into the hall.

Instead she went to the window. Outside, the setting sun was slipping down the horizon behind a bank of fluffy white, full-bellied clouds; it threw out shards of light into the western sky and it looked incredibly peaceful. Growing up in a house like this, with a beautiful and vivacious mother like Gabrielle, and a gentle, self-effacing father like Leo, Niall had probably taken it all for granted as part of his birth right. Just as she'd taken certain things for granted as being a normal part of life when she was growing up. Until she found out otherwise. Niall's happy childhood in this idyllic place had been so much at odds with her childhood – brought up on a deprived London council estate, her mother had cared far more about pleasing her succession of boyfriends than her skinny, timid daughter.

Vikki felt a shiver run through her. Never had she felt more disconnected from Niall than she did at that moment. The cold reality washed over her that she'd been deluding herself where their relationship was concerned. It had all been very well indulging in wonderful dreams of taking things further with him, but how could she ever bring Niall home to witness where she'd grown up when it was something she was determined to leave behind locked doors? Yet what kind of a future could they have if she didn't let him in to see the truth of who she was and where she'd come from?

She heard Alex and Lainey talking in low tones as they came down the stairs, passing by the sitting room on their way to the living room, and one of them must have spotted her because, a couple of minutes later, Niall appeared in the doorway.

He waggled a bottle of beer. 'Here you are.'

'I was admiring the photographs. Your mother was beautiful,' she said, feeling her way, conscious that he'd whisked by these as he'd showed her around.

'She was.' He put the bottle of beer to his mouth and demolished half of it.

'And look at you,' Vikki went on, 'I never knew you were into diving.'

'That was years ago. I thought those photographs had all been packed away.'

Lainey glided into the room. 'So this is where you're hiding. Aren't you happy to be reminded of all that is great about us and our family?' Vikki hadn't heard her approach. Niall's sister had taken off her boots and was wearing a pair of chunky socks with a thickly padded sole.

'Once upon a time, you mean,' Niall said.

'There's no reason why we can't remember the good times. That's what this weekend is all about, remember?'

'Is it?'

There was a charged moment between them. Vikki sensed something thick hanging in the air.

'Of course,' Lainey said silkily, hooking a strand of her coppery hair behind her ear.

Niall gave a short laugh. 'You're hardly suggesting we can go back in time?'

Lainey's unblinking gaze slid to Vikki. There was something calculating in the way those green-gold eyes settled on her as if trying to figure out how well she knew Niall, how much she knew of his past, how much he'd told her of his family.

Vikki returned her gaze as blandly as possible.

Then, like the moment earlier in the hall, Lainey's automatic smile switched back on so swiftly that Vikki wondered if she'd imagined that searching look.

'Of course not,' Lainey said smoothly, her gaze moving to Niall. 'But we need to celebrate where we came from, and acknowledge our wonderful childhood. We had some fantastic times and there's no reason why as a family we can't have more fantastic times.' She reached out and rubbed his arm.

'So what's up for the rest of this evening?'

'Monopoly? Or Scrabble?' She looked from Niall to Vikki. 'I hope we're not boring you, Vikki. I'm afraid there isn't a lot of excitement to be had in Lynes Glen, compared to the glittering lights of London.'

'I'm not bored in the least,' Vikki said, wishing she sounded more positive. She felt out of place and on edge, unsure of what she was doing here, never mind being forced to face the yawning gulf between her and Niall's background.

'I hope we have a chance to talk,' Lainey said. 'I'd love to know how you pair met. Niall never mentioned you until we were making the arrangements for this weekend. He kept you all to himself.' She shook her head disapprovingly. 'I'm looking forward to getting to know all about you.'

Vikki lifted her chin. 'Same here, Lainey, I'm looking forward to getting to know you too.'

There was a short silence. 'Right then, that's sorted,' Lainey said. 'Will we move inside?' She marched out of the room, fully expecting them to follow in her wake.

'You don't feel like running away yet?' Niall asked Vikki.

'What if I did?' she said, forcing a playful voice, unable to resist looking at him from under her lashes. 'I haven't a clue how to get back to civilisation, neither can I make contact with the outside world, so I'm well and truly trapped. I'm totally at your mercy, Niall Blake.'

He wrapped his arms loosely around her and his eyes searched her face. 'So you are. Don't be looking at me like that.'

'Like what?'

'Tempting me to do something I promised I wouldn't.'

They stared at each other and Vikki's breath quickened. He ran his fingers lightly through her hair. Her scalp prickled. Then Lainey called out and asked what was keeping them.

He squeezed her shoulder. 'Come on, let's go play Monopoly.'

CHAPTER FOURTEEN

1968

The poster in the window of the Creaghbara Hotel foyer jumped out at him when he arrived for lunch. Big Jack and the Western Cowboys were coming on Saturday week. The Country and Irish showband were appearing in the local dancehall as part of their summer tour. Leo knew it was a regular enough occurrence; he'd seen such posters before, but he'd never taken much notice of them. Now it was different. He itched to know if Gabrielle might be there, already taking mental stock of his limited wardrobe. It was a long time since he'd bothered with a dancehall night and he wasn't sure what the dress code entailed. He wasn't even sure if he had the guts to go.

Gabrielle was serving his table and he felt a spasm of anxiety as he let the paper menu slip out of his grasp when she came over to take his order.

'It is your usual, sir?' she asked. 'Sorry … Leo.' She smiled as though she thought she'd made a joke, but in a kind way.

'Yes, please,' he said, wondering if this was a good thing or not. Good that she had noticed he had a usual order, or did it make him appear dull and boring?

He imagined her thoughts; *the oul fella by the window is not a bit adventurous.*

The oul fella by the window will turn into a chicken, he eats it so often.

'We have cabbage on today,' she said. 'Would you like some?' She was so lovely she could have offered him muck and he would have said yes.

'I'll give it a go,' he said. What a stupid answer. As though a portion of cabbage was propelling him out of his usual comfort zone. She must really think he was a no-hoper. So he got the shock of his life when she returned bearing his plate, and as she set his dinner carefully before him as though it was a feast for a king, aligning his cutlery on the table beside it, then filling a glass of water for him from a small jug, she said, 'I don't suppose you're going to the dance next week?'

He didn't know what to say; then, even though he felt his face scalding to the tips of his ears, he forced the words out. 'Do you know, I might be.'

'So might I.' She laughed as she picked up her tray and went across to another table.

If his head had been full of her before, now it was overflowing.

But the dancehall night was a disaster. Packed to capacity, he could only watch from the sidelines as she whirled around the floor in one fella's arms after another. She knew how to jive, twisting easily under the fella's arm like she'd been born to it, looping around and back, her feet barely touching the floor as she spun, hair flying like a golden flag under the glittery disco ball, her face alight with laughter. He watched for a while, his heart heavy, his stiff shirt constricting his neck – the kind he never wore, it was new, and straight from the wrapping, and he saw in the men's bathroom mirror that he should have ironed it first, because it bore all the creases of the packaging, flagging his desperation. When the music slowed and he saw another fella approach her and lead her out onto the dancefloor, he was unable to bear it any longer and he slunk home.

*

Then the unexpected happened. He stayed away from the hotel for a week, cooking the minimum for himself in the splendid isolation of Lynes Glen. He went into Creaghbara on a Saturday morning to buy a fresh typewriter ribbon and some carbon paper, and just as he came out of the stationer's store, a drizzle of rain began to fall and he bumped into her passing by.

'Leo.' She had to tilt her face to look up at him. Beside him, she barely came up to his shoulder.

'Gabrielle.' It came out fine, considering it was the first time he'd uttered it in all the times it had flitted silently through his head.

'So you do know my name.'

'I've known it from the very beginning.'

'The beginning?' She gazed at him.

The beginning of what? He sensed her question. Had he said too much? Maybe he had revealed something but right then, as he stood with the rain sprinkling his dark hair and shoulders, and as she too allowed it to fall on her upturned face and veil her hair with tiny beads of moisture – she didn't attempt to wipe it off or move away seeking shelter – he was possessed by a sudden calm.

Afterwards he decided that fate had stepped in. Or some kind of guardian angel decided he had been alone for too long and gave him the power to continue.

'From almost the first time I saw you, I've known your name,' he said.

Her beautiful eyes widened. Out here, in the daylight, he saw that they were shades of deep green and gold, like the sea off Achill in sunset.

She looked away for a moment and then she looked back at him. 'You never came.'

'Sorry?'

'The dance. Last Saturday night. I didn't see you.'

His heart swelled. Even though she'd been with others, she'd looked for him.

'I went but you were ... you seemed to be—' What to say without the risk of revealing the burning envy that had consumed him. 'In great demand, on the dancefloor ...' he finished lamely.

She shook her head. Disappointment tinged her face. 'Didn't you want to ask me up? You hardly let that stop you.'

He cursed himself for putting that look there. 'I can't jive. I can do many things,' he reassured her. 'I'm not as useless as I appear, but I can't jive.'

'Is that all?' Where there had been disappointment, now there was hope. 'And anyway, you don't look useless to me.' She gave him a shy smile.

Say something, he urged himself. Don't just stand there feeling inadequate.

'Sometime, maybe, you might show me ... how to jive ... so I'll be ready for the next time.'

'I'm off on Mondays,' she said, her face so full of a happy expectation that he couldn't but respond to that.

'So am I, for now. That sounds like it could be a plan.' He fell silent, then he forced himself to say, as lightly as possible, even though his heart was hammering heavily, and he prayed his voice wouldn't crack, 'We're getting wet. Have you time to go in somewhere for a cup of tea and maybe we could talk about it more?'

She had an hour to spare before the lunchtime shift. He brought her to a café where they sat by the window and he was conscious of how they appeared to passers-by – a thin man wearing jeans and a grey jumper, and, opposite him, a beautiful young woman with hair the colour of burnished sunsets and eyes of the sea. He marvelled that they looked as though they were doing something very ordinary, just sitting over tea and scones, cream and jam, at a table covered with a red-checked oil-cloth and boasting a tiny jug of wild mountain heather, whereas for him it was the most wonderful few moments of his life so far.

And more wonderful moments were to come. He felt he was touching a priceless piece of delicate Dresden china when she put him through his paces on the tiny living-room floor of the flat she shared with two other female hotel employees the following Monday afternoon. She clasped his hands and any fears he'd had that he was too tall and ungainly in comparison to her petite frame or that he might hold her too tightly vanished in the fluidity with which she twisted and circled about him, slowing her movement every so often to show him exactly how it was done, and his heart soared with the joyful way she tipped back her head and laughed as though she was enjoying it. He came two Mondays in a row, and after the second week she made tea and served apple tart and they sat and talked until his throat went dry.

He told her of his father and mother, dying within six months of each other from cancer and a heart attack respectively, of his university work in Belfast and Galway, his love of literature and his poetry. He held out all of himself for her inspection, as opposed to a watered-down or sweetened-up version, not holding back any of his hopes or fears, risking her rejection and wondering if she'd shy away from him for not being 'with it' or 'groovy' as he sometimes heard his students speak.

She wasn't much older than a lot of them.

To his utter happiness, Gabrielle sat there, elbows on the table, her face cupped in her hands, and she listened quietly and sounded encouraging when he spoke of his poetry dreams. 'I'd like to hear your work,' she said. 'Hear you read it out, I mean.'

'Some day,' he said, wondering if he had the guts to bare the depths of his soul with her as a captive audience. 'Tell me about you,' he said, wanting to know all about her, feeling as heady as if he was unwrapping a very special gift.

Nothing as exciting as him, she said. He shook his head at her words. Everything about her was thrilling. What she had for breakfast, the way she might hold her toast between her pale, delicate fingers, where she went grocery shopping, or clothes shopping, how she might look against the colours of autumn, even watching her neat movements as she poured the tea and sliced up the apple tart, arranging his carefully on the plate, coming around the table to put it in front of him – it all sent warm darts of happiness shooting through him. She was from a small village in Sligo, she told him, her father had left her mother years ago and her mother had recently moved to Australia with her new partner for a brand-new life.

'Seeing as the whole village, as well as some of her family, are condemning her for living in sin,' Gabrielle said, 'she decided to get as far away as possible from Ireland.'

'Did you mind?'

'I minded the narrow-minded village people who looked down on my mother,' she said. 'I hated all that,' she went on with a sudden flash of anger. 'It was my father who deserted her, not the other way around. He left her years ago. By all accounts he's living a great life in England, in Manchester, with a new family. Why shouldn't she find happiness again? She's barely forty years of age. I'll miss her, certainly I will, but I like Patrick, he's good to her, and I was glad she took the chance of a new life with him.'

'So you're more or less on your own?'

'I have some friends, and some cousins, those who also think my mum has done the right thing. I was happy to put the village behind me too. Mum didn't want to go away until she knew I was settled, so I took the job in the hotel serving the tables for lunches and the evening meals. Creaghbara is fine,' she said, 'I have my own tiny bedroom and my independence.'

'You like independence?'

She was young, he reminded himself. Of course she wanted to be free and single and enjoy life.

'Things are changing for women,' she said. 'The sixties have shaken everything up, who knows what the seventies will bring? Even here in Ireland. Equal pay, perhaps. An equal share in the family home. The contraceptive pill.'

He felt himself blush, even though he'd noticed the waves of unrest on the university campus and seen the difference between what was allowed to take place quite freely in Belfast compared to the west of Ireland.

'All of these will bring far-reaching and liberating changes for women,' she said gently, as if she'd noticed his rising colour. 'But some things will never change. Women will become more independent and have more choice, but the majority will still choose to fall in love, marry, and have children.'

She looked at him directly as she spoke.

He swallowed. 'And would you put yourself in that majority?' he asked.

'I might.' She gave him a cheeky grin. 'But he'd have to be a really decent soul and a kind person.'

When she looked at him as though he might possess those attributes, his heart sang.

He kissed her goodbye, loving the way she clung to him and kissed him back. During those early weeks he hugged their friendship to himself like a secret. In the hotel dining room, she treated him like any other customer, but now and then darted private smiles in his direction that made him feel ten feet tall. Then, as though it was the easiest and the most natural thing, they began to go out together. On Gabrielle's day off, Monday, and on evenings when she finished early, they went to the pictures, out for meals, out along the coast for drives, stopping to go for a walk, over as far as Achill for the day, up to Sligo where they passed the house where she'd been born, and for him the final month of the summer was full to the brim with the look in her eyes, the swirl of her hair and the feel of it under his touch, their hugs and kisses, their chats.

The first time he brought her back to Lynes Glen his heart was tripping with anxiety but he needn't have worried, she went around the house looking into rooms, going up and down the stairs, exclaiming in wonder over the handsomeness and beautiful proportions, bringing light and life into places that had remained too silent for too long. In the library he lit a small fire as the evening was a little chilly, and she kicked off her shoes and made herself comfortable on the sofa, with her feet curled under her. He took out his poetry, and his hands shook as he fingered the typewritten pages, selecting what he thought might be the easiest to read to her. He braved his fears and took her into his arms and read to her, and she sat quietly and listened, her head resting peacefully against his shoulder, and there could not have been a more perfect moment in time as all his senses dissolved into a pure, grateful happiness.

And for the rest of the summer everything was brilliant, his life was transformed.

Until doubt set in.

CHAPTER FIFTEEN

In the living room, Vikki sat down opposite Alex, Jenna and Ben.

'I'll get you that wine now,' Alex said to her. 'White, isn't it?'

'Stay put, I'll look after Vikki.' Niall was already heading for the kitchen. 'Beer for you?'

'Yep, thanks.' Alex said.

The brothers were perfectly neutral, but they engaged with each other with a politeness that put Vikki on edge. Leo seemed oblivious, chatting away to Ben. He refused another drink when Niall returned with Vikki's wine and offered to refill his glass.

'No more whiskey for me, thanks,' Leo said. 'I'll leave you young ones to get on with it. I've had plenty of excitement for today, and there'll be more again tomorrow. Enjoy the rest of your evening.'

Lainey jumped to her feet and gave him a hug. 'You're welcome to join in,' she said.

'Thanks,' he said, 'but I'm going to read for a while and I'll probably go off into dreamland.' He smiled around at the group, his eyes kind beneath his bushy eyebrows, something soft and slightly wistful about his expression. Vikki wondered what it had been like for the vivacious Gabrielle, married to Leo. He must have been a striking character in his day but years of living as a widower had taken its toll.

'It's wonderful to look around and see you all here together,' he said, his voice full of emotion. 'I never thought I'd see the day – you all lead such busy lives.' Vikki was unsure as to whose benefit this was for. 'Busy lives' was certainly some euphemism for a twenty-year rift. Whatever he privately thought about it, Leo wasn't saying.

'I told you it would work out, didn't I?' Lainey said. 'We're all delighted to be here, aren't we guys?' With her arms around her father's shoulders she looked around pointedly.

'And so are the gals,' Jenna added, winking at Vikki.

'I meant "guys" in the all-inclusive terminology,' Lainey said.

Jenna looked wryly amused. 'I'm sure you did, Lainey.'

Touché. Vikki almost felt a sabre sticking into her.

Niall helped his father up from his high-backed chair, handed him his walking stick and accompanied him to his room. Vikki sat quietly, sipping her wine, as chatter went on around her, feeling slightly at a loss without Niall. She was glad when he returned less than ten minutes later.

'What's the plan for this evening?' he asked.

'Board games,' Lainey said.

'As in b-o-a-r-d, and not b-o-r-e-d,' Ben said.

'Thanks for that clarification.' Jenna smirked.

'Ben!' Lainey glared at him.

'Were you serious about playing games?' Alex frowned.

'Of course,' Lainey said firmly. 'I found some in the attic and brought them down. It'll be a bit of fun.'

'Is there nothing on that television?' Alex looked suspiciously at the big square television set in the corner as if he wasn't sure what it contained.

'There's no signal,' Lainey said. 'The network was converted to digital last year, and Lynes Glen was never connected. Even if we had the right aerial there's no guarantee we'd get anything this side of the mountain. However, I have that covered.'

'No doubt you have,' Jenna said.

'As I know only too well,' Ben quipped. 'I haven't seen my wife for months, with all her preparations.'

He spoke lightly, but Vikki heard the underlying hint of impatience in his voice, as did Lainey. She shot her husband a withering look. 'I've videos lined up for tomorrow evening, the weather forecast is for rain, unfortunately, so I'm holding them back to keep the kids entertained.'

'Monopoly will do fine,' Alex said, 'so long as there's no fighting over the rules.'

It was obvious to Vikki that he intended this as a joke, but Lainey chose to take it otherwise.

'You don't need to remind us,' she said, rather frostily. 'We always play by the rules, don't we?'

'Not the unwritten rules.' Niall said it low under his breath but everyone heard.

'I hope you're including yourself in that.' Alex's rejoinder was swift.

'How could I not?' Niall said, just as swiftly, his voice taut.

Everything went deathly still. Beside Vikki, Niall tensed, his beer paused halfway to his mouth. Lainey stood like a statue, Alex looking at his sister with a hint of startled surprise on his handsome features as though he was checking for her reaction.

Then, in the next moment, seamlessly, as though it had been rehearsed, the Blakes spoke at once and moved to cover up what appeared to have been an unexpected faux pas in the prepared script for the evening and the energy in the room shifted.

'Before we start, I'll go get some more crisps and nibbles.' Lainey got up and went out to the kitchen.

'I'll check the children and make sure they're OK,' Alex said, simultaneously.

'Can I get anyone else a drink?' Niall asked. 'Jenna? Ben? I'll get you another beer.'

It was as though the Blake siblings had agreed in advance to paper over any awkward moments that might arise between them. Vikki knew by the odd look on Jenna's face that the other woman had sensed it also and was watching her husband with narrowed eyes as he left the room.

'What the hell was that all about?' Jenna widened her eyes as she looked from Ben to Vikki.

Ben shrugged. 'Search me.'

'I wonder if Alex or Niall broke the rules,' Jenna said smartly. 'Unwritten or otherwise. Although the Blakes will hardly let us into that particular secret.'

*

Twenty minutes later, the curtains were drawn. Lamps were switched on, casting the room in a cosy light, and a battered-looking Monopoly box placed on the coffee table.

Lainey pulled a big cushion down to the floor and plopped down onto it. 'Right, everyone, I'll do master of ceremonies,' she said. 'You'll all get the chance to roll the dice, however. We might as well do it in teams and stay in our couples, OK? Vikki?'

'Yes?' She wished she didn't feel nervous with Lainey's direct gaze or the fact that she'd been singled out.

'We'll let you and Niall kick off first.'

'Oh,' Vikki said. 'I don't know how to play this.' She had spoken unthinkingly. There was a brief silence and a ripple of interest went around the group.

'You've never played Monopoly?' Trust Lainey to make it sound like a major failing.

'Nope,' Vikki said, braving her down. 'I guess it was one of those things that passed me by.'

Lainey looked at her, perfect eyebrows arched in equally perfect surprise.

Niall came to her rescue. 'You're too young, not like us old-timers,' he said. 'You escaped being part of the board-game generation in favour of video games.'

'Yeah, that was it.' Vikki plastered a smile on her face. Monopoly, video games; he might as well have been speaking in a foreign language – none of these had been any part of her childhood, except for snippets she'd gleaned from her classmates.

Niall squeezed her hand. 'We'll beat them all,' he said, raising their joined hands in the air. 'We're the A team. Bring it on.'

'Right then, Vikki, you're the perfect person to dole everything out,' Lainey said. 'No one can accuse you of cheating.' She told Vikki how to arrange the contents on the coffee table and handed her the box.

Vikki arranged the contents as instructed, beginning with a big, coloured Monopoly board, some dice, playing cards, green and red plastic buildings, and a pile of fake money. She lifted the fake money and counted through it, placing the notes on the table in their denomination. She reached into the box for the rest of the notes, disturbing the inner cardboard section when something else caught her eye and she pulled it out.

It felt heavy as it slipped through her fingers. It glinted and shimmered in the lamplight. It sparkled and dazzled, glowing the rich red colour of fresh blood. She realised she was holding the pendant Gabrielle had been wearing in the photograph on the piano, and her heart dropped. It was clear she'd caused another shock because the sight of the pendant in her hands stunned the Blake siblings into a frozen silence. She could only sit in hot embarrassment until Lainey eventually reacted.

'How did that – *Jesus* ...' she said, shrinking back, her hand fluttering to her chest.

'Let's see,' Niall said, taking the pendant from Vikki's trembling fingers, holding it aloft between his.

'We thought that was ... gone.' Lainey stared at it in alarm.

'Balls. How did that get in there?' Alex said.

'I haven't a clue,' Lainey said weakly. 'I haven't seen it since—'

'Haven't you?'

'Don't be ridiculous, how could I?'

Alex shook his head. 'I thought you organised this—' he broke off. 'Christ.'

'I'll put it away for now,' Niall said, getting to his feet and going across to the cabinet.

Lainey took a long gulp of her drink. 'What a horrible surprise and we were doing so well ... all of us.'

'Were we?' Alex shot her a look. 'Let's get on with this board game,' he said in a tired voice. 'Where's the red wine? Beer's not doing it for me this evening.'

'It's all in the utility room,' Lainey said. 'There's plenty, we won't run out.'

'Want to bet?' There was a short silence as Alex marched out to the kitchen.

Jenna let out her breath. 'Oh, wow. My husband is not too impressed.'

Lainey ignored her.

Niall sat back down beside Vikki. 'Hey, don't look so worried,' he said, putting his arm around her. 'We all thought Mum's pendant was lost. At least we have it back.'

His kind words slid off her, barely appeasing her awkwardness. The pendant had clearly been a shock, especially to Lainey, and she wished someone else had been responsible for finding it.

He reached into the box again. 'We'll sort out the rest of the money.'

Alex arrived back with a bottle of red wine.

'Right everyone, let's get this show on the road.' Lainey settled herself on her cushion.

'Show being the operative word,' Jenna said in a low voice, as she winked at Vikki.

She was right. Everything cranked up again, easily and smoothly as though nothing untoward had happened and the game of Monopoly proceeded without a hitch. There was no doubt that Gabrielle's pendant had brought back unhappy memories – and a nasty surprise – but they were firmly put to one side in favour of maintaining the perfect family façade, and Vikki couldn't help wondering what exactly was driving the Blakes this weekend.

Because lurking behind this beautiful family had to be something deep and dark.

CHAPTER SIXTEEN

'You go on up, I'll follow,' Niall said.

Vikki realised that this was Niall's way of giving her space and keeping his side of a bargain she didn't want him to keep. Jenna and Alex had already gone to bed, pleading the adjustment to their body clock for breaking up the party. As Vikki said her goodnights, Lainey – who else – said, 'We won't keep Niall up too late. Come straight back down if you don't have everything you need, there are plenty of extra towels in the big cupboard on the first floor and loads of hot water.'

'Thanks, Lainey.' Vikki was relieved to be escaping the other woman's scrutiny. She seemed to be so close to Niall that Vikki was surprised she didn't sense something was missing in their relationship, as in, it didn't exist beyond a beautiful friendship. He kissed her on the cheek and gave her a warm smile before she left the living room. Out in the shadowed hallway, the faded armchairs were empty, the doors to the dining room, sitting room, and library were closed, yet the air seemed so thick and heavy that she couldn't help looking over her shoulder as she went upstairs, hairs rising on the back of her neck as she reached the landing, and she almost expected to see someone sitting in the alcove, watching her from that vantage point, but naturally it was empty, the colourful window now darkly blank as the night pressed against it. She chided herself for being ridiculously spooked as she shut the bedroom door and leaned against it for a minute, her heart thumping.

After her shower, she pulled on a grey cotton T-shirt, thankful now she'd packed this as an afterthought, having had a last-minute panic attack over her wispy underwear and seductive night attire. That was going to stay in her case for now. The mortification of Niall seeing it would be too much to bear.

She opened the drapes a fraction, but there was nothing outside except pitch blackness pressing against the window. The ghostly outline of her reflection in the window made her jump. She left a lamp on by Niall's side of the bed and she slid between the sheets, the crisp cold of the bed taking a while to get used to, even though the radiators took the chill out of the air. Everything was deathly silent and it unnerved her. She was used to sounds of life swirling around her at all hours of the day and night in her Putney flat. Now there were no noises filtering in from a street outside, telling her that life was going on pretty much as normal, no hum of traffic or swish of tyres that often lulled her to sleep, or occasional ambulance siren she'd become so used to, she didn't really hear it any more. Nothing coming from the children sleeping in the room beyond the bathroom, and not even a voice floating up from downstairs, and everything that had happened since she arrived in Ireland replayed itself in her mind. She was still wide awake half an hour later when she heard footsteps coming slowly up the stairs, extra quiet so as to avoid disturbing the children. She sat back against the pillows, the duvet arranged circumspectly, and watched the door open, throwing a slice of light into the room.

'Still awake?' Niall's voice was low.

'No,' she joked, sudden hysteria gripping her, 'I'm fast asleep.'

'You could have switched off the lamp, I'd have found my way around.' It was clear by the awkward look on his face that he thought he'd be getting into bed under cover of darkness.

'That wasn't keeping me awake.'

'Is the bed OK?'

'It's grand. Loads of room. It's OK for me to have this side?'

'Sure.' He stood there, looking almost as stilted as Leo did in the photograph with Gabrielle. 'I'll just … um … use the bathroom.'

The conversation was all wrong and she could have wept. She'd hoped they'd be having a different type of chat. Correction, not talking at all but kissing each other instead, peeling off their clothes, the heat coming off Niall's body as he moved in closer to her, his face full of desire as he looked at her and bent to kiss her and caress her, kissing her breasts, reaching for her panties, his hands sliding inside … she knew how wonderful it would feel. She'd relived it over and over since that one night.

Stop. By the look on his face, it wasn't going to happen tonight.

She waited until Niall was settled in bed before she spoke again. He leaned over and gave her a hug and said he hoped his snoring wouldn't keep her awake. 'Thanks for being here,' he said.

'Why did you want me to come, Niall?' she said into the semi-darkness. 'Really?'

'Are you sorry you gave up your weekend to be here?'

'It's not that. I just feel a little like I'm in the way of you and your family. You all seem to be very close, especially Lainey. And I put my foot in it, didn't I, between finding the horrible birds and the pendant.'

'Hey, forget about those, please Vikki. It's grand. And Lainey – she was the glue that held us together after …' He paused.

'After your mother died?' she prompted.

'Yes. Family unity was always hugely important to her. I think she watched *Little House on the Prairie* too often when she was a child. It was before your time, I bet, a television programme about a happy family living in a big house on a prairie.'

Vikki made a noise of agreement. She didn't know the television programme but she knew the books. She'd read most of them, thanks to having a council library close to where she'd grown up. It had been her refuge and escape, immersing herself in other people's worlds.

'I wanted you here because I thought this weekend might be … a little difficult,' he said, his voice low and quiet. 'Never mind being in Lynes Glen, it's the first time since Mum died that we're together as a family, the first time since Alex and I …' he paused, swallowed, then went on, 'since we parted ways in the aftermath of Mum's accident. They were God-awful days, Vikki, days I never want to relive again. It was a horrendous time, everything went wrong and it affected us all. I was nineteen years of age and I felt my life was over. This weekend, I wanted a friendly face by my side, someone in my corner. You're a reminder of everything that's good about my life in London, but I can see now it was selfish of me to expect you to drop everything and come along to the wilds of nowhere.'

'I've got no problem being here,' she said. 'I'm glad to be in your corner.'

He'd hinted at this before, at something going wrong in his life. She thought it might have been another woman, now she knew he'd been referring to his mother's death. The family were like an enchanting Ming vase, beautiful on the outside with their compelling features, alluring eyes, and striking hair colour, but flawed; there was a hairline fracture going back over twenty years lurking on the inside. She knew why she'd felt an immediate gravitational pull towards him – he had a fracture at the heart of him, just as she had, one he couldn't talk about, just as she couldn't. Vastly different fault lines, but cracks all the same, and they always left a fragile vulnerability in their wake.

'Thanks. It's so good to have you around,' he said. He leaned across and gave her another hug, warmer this time, holding her closer. She inhaled the scent of him and wanted to melt into the solidity of his chest.

'Hey,' he said, into her hair, 'this feels ...'

Her heart jumped. 'How does it feel?' she murmured.

'Far too tempting and dangerous,' he said, releasing her. 'I don't want to break my promise. You're very special to me. Now try and get some sleep and give me a dig if I start to snore.' He kissed her forehead before he clicked off the lamp.

She lay awake for a long time, listening to the sounds of Niall breathing, the warmth of his kiss going down to her toes. So much for the lovemaking she'd pictured them having, and now that he was lying inches away from her, she felt the absence of that closeness like an ache in her heart and she had to be content with soaking up the sound of his breathing, and know that he was beside her, vulnerable in sleep, trusting her to be in his corner.

She must have fallen asleep eventually, because she awoke in the pitch dark, and knew Niall's side of the bed was empty. He wasn't in the bathroom; there was no glimmer of light coming from under the closed door. She strained to listen, reluctant for some reason to get out of bed. The darkness pressed down on her, deep and intense. The wind must have strengthened outside, because she heard it blowing around the house, rattling the windowpanes. Beyond that, there was nothing but silence.

Then she heard a noise from downstairs, a door quietly closing, a whisper, a sibilant murmur – or was it the breeze stirring up through a draughty old house? It was hard to tell. She lay in the dark for interminable moments, her body crawling with tension, until she heard the soft pad of footsteps slowly ascending the staircase, followed by a slight creak and another. She kept her eyes closed as the door opened and closed softly, then the bed dipped a little as Niall slid into it, gingerly so as not to awaken her. She sensed him lying awake in the dark for a while before she knew by his even breathing that he'd fallen asleep.

When Vikki awoke the next morning, Niall was already up. Light was pressing against the drapes, and children's excited voices and running footsteps floated up from downstairs. The dark shadows and tension of the night before had vanished. On impulse she moved across to his side of the bed, lying face down in the warm spot he'd lain in, her head buried in the indent he'd made on the pillow. She inhaled deeply through her nose, drawing in the scent of him, imagining she was lying on top of him, letting the wonderful idea send little explosions through all of her senses.

'Jesus, Vikki, are you … what's up?'

She turned around and sprang up. Niall was in the room, his

face furrowed with perplexity. Conscious of the thinness of her grey T-shirt, she grabbed the duvet and pulled it up to her neck.

'I was just ...' she said, words failing her, a red tide of mortification sweeping up her face.

He spoke at the same time, deliberately looking away from her in the direction of the window. 'Sorry, I didn't mean to embarrass you. I came up to see if you were awake and to tell you there's no rush, you can have breakfast whenever you feel like it.'

'Thanks. I'll be down in about ten minutes.'

'Right.' He stood there awkwardly for a moment, then he grinned and loped out the door, closing it quietly.

She'd need more than ten minutes to compose herself, given the way her body was crawling with acute discomfort. What had possessed her? Had he guessed what she'd been up to? Bloody hell. Her legs were shaky as she got out of bed and took a few deep breaths, trying to compose herself before she went downstairs.

She went across to the window and pulled back the drapes. It was a beautiful morning, the landscape undulating away in front, clear and pristine under high skies. She opened the window a fraction and inhaled the draught of cool, crystal-clear air that flowed into the room. Fifteen minutes later she was heading down the stairs feeling acutely self-conscious, the aroma of grilled bacon making her mouth water. In the dining room, everyone except Leo was gathered around the table in various stages of breakfast. There was a chorus of bright and friendly good mornings as everyone looked up at her, and she was struck afresh by the resemblance between Niall and his siblings, finding it unsettling to have three almost identical pairs of such unusual eyes looking at her.

Niall got up and kissed her on the cheek. 'Hi, you look lovely.

You can have whatever you like, fruit, juice, cereal, a cooked breakfast, fresh croissants.'

'It's all very casual, Vikki,' Lainey said. 'The cold stuff is laid out in the kitchen, buffet style; take a plate and help yourself. Erin and Niamh will cook whatever you'd like, bacon, eggs or whatever.'

'I'll come with you,' Niall said.

'You're still eating,' she said. 'Stay where you are.'

He took her hand. 'It'll wait for a minute or two.'

The kitchen was full of cheerful morning light, the table laid with bowls of various fruit, jugs of juices, yogurts, a couple of different cereals, breads and croissants, at the sight of which Vikki realised she was hungry.

'Good morning, Vikki, sleep well?' Erin said, looking up from the cooking range, where she was grilling some bacon. Niamh had just made fresh tea and she smiled at Vikki as she brought it through to the dining room.

'Great, thanks,' Vikki said.

'Good,' Erin said. 'There's cold milk for the cereals in the fridge, and if you want some eggs or bacon let me know. Or if you'd like porridge, Niamh is taking care of that.'

Niall poured her some fruit juice and she helped herself to a yogurt and a banana. 'I might have some scrambled egg?'

'I'll look after that,' Niamh said, coming back in.

'I bet a Saturday in Lynes Glen is a change from your usual Saturday in London,' Erin said.

'Too right it is,' Vikki said. London today would mean being at the conference now, and quite possibly she'd be doing some deep breathing in a cubicle in the ladies' bathroom, trying to take the edge off her nerves before facing Jo Morgan and the combined weight of the Rosella management. In one sense it was a huge relief not to be there. It was wonderful to be here instead on this beautiful fresh morning; the kitchen was warm and homely, she was about to have a good breakfast. Niall thought she looked lovely. He wanted her here because he'd sad memories of the last time he'd been home and she reminded him of all that was good about his life. As they went back into the dining room and passed by the end of the table where the children were sitting with juice and cereal, she heard Jack talk excitedly about the lady ghost he'd seen in the middle of the night.

No surprises there – Lynes Glen was the kind of house that leant itself quite easily to all things ghostly.

CHAPTER SEVENTEEN

How was she going to get through a full day, unscathed and undetected, Jenna asked herself, given the way she felt right now with Ben sitting opposite her? Damn and blast the man, he was gorgeous. Fresh from the shower – she'd even heard him taking it, indulgently allowing herself to imagine him naked under the spray – he was wearing a white cotton top that showed the full breadth of his shoulders. She flicked her eyes away, terrified they would betray her; this was all wrong. She took a long, slow breath, pushing away images of what had happened the previous night …

*

Alex said a curt goodnight to her. That suited her; she wasn't in the form for any kind of intimacy. He'd been cold-shouldering her for months and she hardly recognised the Lynes Glen version of her husband. Eventually he fell asleep, but she lay wide awake, like a lovesick teenager, going over every nuance of the conversations she'd had with Ben that evening, the way he'd responded with kind attention, the warm look in his eyes, the rich sound of his voice. The whole of the man.

What was happening to her? She'd never felt like this about another man before. She hardly recognised the person she'd become either. Unable to lie there any longer, she pushed back the covers and got out of bed. A glass of milk might help. She pulled on a thin robe over her fine-silk pyjamas, and holding her breath as the door creaked, she tiptoed out onto the landing. Lainey had left a lamp on in the alcove, in case any of the children awoke in an unfamiliar house, and it threw soft light down along the stairwell. She padded silently down the stairs and along the dimly lit hall towards the kitchen.

There was someone there. A figure, coming through the doorway. She jumped and put her hand to her throat.

It was Ben.

He saw her at the same time as she saw him. She absorbed everything about him in a single glance; the dark T-shirt that went down to his hips, boxer shorts, muscular legs covered with whorls of dark hair, his bare feet with perfectly shaped toes. He was carrying a bottle of water.

Shit. This couldn't be happening. So much for being nervous about the shared bathroom.

'Jenna!' he said quietly, his eyes flicking over her, making her acutely conscious of her thin night attire. 'Sorry if I startled you. Are you OK?'

'Yeah …' she whispered, feeling strangely vulnerable, 'I came down to get some milk.'

'Can't sleep?'

'No.' Her voice shook.

'Same here. Too much going on, I guess. I just nipped down to get some water.' He gave her a lopsided grin. 'I didn't get dressed up for the occasion as I wasn't expecting company.'

'It's OK.' She swallowed, hugged herself with her arms, a defensive gesture that didn't go unnoticed by him.

'Come on, I'll sort you out,' he said.

They went through into the kitchen, which was dark except for a beam of light slanting through from a lamp left on in the living room. Ben fetched a glass and opened the fridge, his face lit by the interior light. He poured some milk and handed it to Jenna, their fingers brushing. Her heart raced and she felt as if the air around them was sucked away.

He leaned back against the counter while she sipped her milk. 'We're not the only ones stirring around here.'

'What do you mean?' There was no one else about, as far as she could see.

'A figure of speech.' He shook his head slightly, amusement in his low voice. 'Whatever went on here – the memories are shifting and stirring, aren't they? You can sense it in the air. I'm not surprised you were unsettled by this evening.'

She was even more unsettled now. She started to shake.

'You must be cold,' he said, patting her affectionately on the shoulder. His touch burned through to her skin. 'Get back into bed and tuck yourself up with Alex,' he said, a small smile playing around his lips.

She really wanted to tuck herself up with Ben, and she was horrified he might read it in her eyes.

When she slid into bed a few minutes later, she tried not to imagine she was sliding in beside him.

*

This morning, she tried to shift her focus away from Ben by watching Vikki and Niall go out into the kitchen. There was something soft and vulnerable about Vikki, in spite of her dark, porcupine-like hair, which screamed 'don't mess with me'. She'd looked a little lost coming into the dining room, her big grey eyes soft as though she wasn't sure what she was doing there and she was finding it a challenge braving the might of the Blakes on their home territory first thing in the morning.

Then Jenna realised the children were squabbling.

'Mum,' Charlotte said to Lainey, 'tell Jack to stop making up stories. He's scaring me.'

'Jack?' Jenna said. 'Are you upsetting your cousin?'

'Charlotte, stop moaning,' Lainey said, in a honey-coated tone of voice that irritated Jenna. 'Remember that Jack is a guest in the house.'

'Then will you tell him to stop talking about her? 'Cos he's not listening to me and I don't want to hear any more.' Charlotte put down her spoon and put her hands over her ears.

'Talking about who?' Jenna asked.

'The lady who came into our room last night,' Charlotte said, forgetting about her attempts to block everyone out. 'Jack said it was the middle of the night and we were all asleep and she was a ghost.'

'That was probably me, making sure you were OK,' Lainey said. 'Or Jenna.' She raised a questioning eyebrow at Jenna, and asked her, rather pointedly, 'Were you up during the night?'

'I checked the children before I went to bed,' Jenna said, feigning indifference. 'That was the only time I went in to them.' She avoided looking at Ben but she sensed him shooting her a glance from across the table.

Jack shook his head so that his curls bounced around. 'It was the other lady. She came in and looked at me for ages and smiled.'

'Then it must have been Vikki, coming out of the bathroom the wrong way,' Lainey said cheerfully as though to dispel any flights of fancy. Vikki and Niall had just sat down and she looked at Vikki as if for confirmation. 'It happens. It's easy to open the wrong door, especially in the dark at night.'

'Unless I was sleepwalking, it wasn't me,' Vikki said, lifting her glass of orange juice.

'You were probably having a nice dream, Jack,' Lainey said reassuringly.

Jack's face darkened in his seldom resorted-to, pre-tantrum expression and he crossed his arms. 'I didn't dream it, I saw her.'

'Why did you think it was a ghost, honey?' Jenna asked.

'She just was – she made no noise, she didn't talk, just smiled.'

'How did you know it was the middle of the night?' Lainey said in a disbelieving voice that exasperated Jenna.

'He would, actually,' she said. 'He has a special clock, I'm surprised you didn't spot it on his bedside table. We set it when he goes to bed and it has to have a picture of the sun on the front of the clock before he's allowed to get up.'

'I see,' Lainey said.

She spoke with a faintly dismissive air and Jenna knew she didn't see at all. 'We brought it with us to help with the time-zone change,' she said irritably. 'I didn't want him waking up the whole house in the middle of the night.'

'I could do with one of those clocks,' Ben said.

This time Jenna was unable to avoid exchanging a quick smile with him.

Lainey flashed both of them a suspicious glance. 'So I did hear you getting out of bed,' she said accusingly.

Ben shrugged. 'I didn't know there was a rule against getting some water.'

Some kind of devilment made Jenna stare at Lainey with a perfectly innocent face.

'It was the lady in the photograph,' Jack said.

'What photograph, darling?' Jenna asked, imitating Lainey's honey-coated voice.

'The one on the piano,' Jack said, raising his voice.

Up to now, Alex had been ignoring the discussion. Seated at the opposite end of the table, he was tucking into a cooked breakfast, the kind he never normally ate back home, labelling it as a cholesterol-filled indulgence. Jenna decided he was being contrary in his own way and occupying himself with a big breakfast as a form of avoiding her. Now he flicked her an irritable look. 'What's going on?'

'You tell me,' she said.

'What is it, Jack?' Alex asked, buttering a slice of toast. Butter – usually another no-go. Although Jenna had to admit the Irish butter was a creamy treat.

'I saw a ghost, Dad,' Jack said. 'Charlotte thinks I'm making it up to scare her, but I'm not.'

'A *what*?' Alex's knife slid out of his grasp and clattered against his plate.

Jenna said, deliberately infusing her tone with a hint of intrigue, 'Jack saw someone – or something – in his bedroom last night.'

'It must have been one of us checking on them,' Alex said.

'That's not what he thinks,' Jenna said.

'It was a lady ghost,' Jack said. 'And she's on the piano. In a photo.'

Jenna felt suddenly out of her depth. She peeled a banana slowly and methodically. To hell with it, let Alex sort this out.

He was the one who had dragged them over here. He was the one who was covering up something, helped by his sister and brother. Anyhow, she'd enough to cope with right now, keeping Ben Connolly at arm's length – mentally and physically.

'There's only one way to solve this,' Alex said tightly, shoving his plate of toast to one side. He got up and went around to Jack. 'Tell me what happened.'

'No one believes me,' Jack said.

'I do,' Alex said patiently. 'You saw someone in your room last night. Was it your mother or Lainey?'

Jack shook his head. 'It was the lady in the photograph. Charlotte showed them to me yesterday when we were playing hide and seek. She showed me my daddy and her mummy and the lady was there too.'

'OK, we'll have a look.' Alex held out his hand to Jack, and, leaving the doors open, he brought him across the hallway to the sitting room.

From where Jenna was sitting, she heard Jack's voice clearly as he said, 'That lady, beside Grandad Leo.'

There was only one person he could have been pointing to: Gabrielle.

'Lainey, could you come here a minute?' Alex called out in a tight voice.

Lainey? Jenna found herself exchanging glances with Ben as Lainey followed him through. Charlotte and Harry scrambled down off their seats and followed.

'I'm not afraid of ghosts,' Harry said as he whirled out of the room.

'Ready for some coffee, Jenna?' Ben asked.

'If I could have a double espresso laced with brandy,' she said, 'I think I'd relish it.'

'Tut, tut, it's a bit early for that now, and we still have' – he broke off to check his watch – 'forty-eight hours to get through, maintaining cordial family relations.'

'Do you think we'll survive?'

He put his elbows on the table, and rested his chin in his hands and looked at her keenly. 'Your guess is as good as mine.'

From the sitting room, Jenna heard Charlotte's voice, 'Jack, did the ghost walk on the actual ground or float in the air?'

'I don't know, she was just there.'

'Was her face all white?'

'I can't remember her face, but she had that hair.'

Lainey came back into the dining room and called Niall. He'd been chatting quietly to Vikki, neither of them taking much notice of the proceedings.

'Must be a helluva family conference,' Ben said. 'Well done, Jack. It's a long time since I captured my wife's attention so effectively.'

Jenna couldn't help giving him a conspiratorial smile. Cool it, she told herself. 'I'd better go see what ructions my son has caused.'

'Let me know if you need me to organise that coffee,' he said.

She grinned. 'Later.'

In the sitting room, the Blakes were grouped around the piano. 'Is everything all right?' she asked. 'I hope Jack hasn't upset anyone. He was over-excited about this trip and meeting his cousins.'

She'd said the wrong thing. Lainey looked pained, Niall puzzled, and the expression on Alex's face was arctic. 'What is it?' she asked.

Lainey shook her head. 'Oh, look, we were going to keep it to ourselves, but someone has been messing with the photos ...

either during the night or very early this morning, they were fine when I went to bed last night.'

Jenna looked at the top of the piano. The photos were all askew and the frame holding the one of Leo and Gabrielle was damaged, the glass cracked into smithereens.

'What happened?' she asked.

Lainey shrugged. 'We don't know.'

'It's just a photo,' Alex said. 'There's no need to hold a bloody post-mortem.' He was trying to sound bored, Jenna knew, but his tight face told a different story.

'Daddy! I heard you say bad words.'

Alex threw his eyes up to heaven. 'Don't mind Daddy,' he said. 'Pretend you didn't hear that.'

Jack laughed. 'I can't do that. I can't close my ears, like I close my eyes or my mouth.'

Even Harry and Charlotte let out childish giggles.

'Shite,' Alex said under his breath.

*

'What was that all about?' Jenna asked Alex. They were upstairs in their bedroom, getting ready for the picnic, Jenna rummaging for a scarf, Alex changing into a thicker pullover.

'All what about?'

'Don't pretend. Something weird is going on.'

'What makes you think that?'

'Someone is trying to screw up this so-called happy family reunion.'

'That's nonsense.'

'Did I imagine three dead birds in the very place you were supposed to love as children? Did they all just happen to line up in perfect formation before they keeled over, fell neatly into a box, and died? It looked to me like someone put them there, expecting you to find them. Your mother's pendant, suddenly turning up. Then Jack. Who did he see? The lady down by the lough? Vikki saw her too, you know. Is there a ghost in Lynes Glen?'

Alex shrugged into his pullover with neat, economical movements. 'For someone who prides herself on her practical nature, your imagination is sure working overtime.'

'What about the smashed photo frame? It was very comprehensively smashed for something that could just have fallen off the piano and on to a carpet. I hate old photos anyway, and the way they bring back memories.'

'Lainey thought it was a good idea to remind us of who we are as a family.'

'How could it be a good idea to remind you of life before your mother died? How is that supposed to make you happy? Seems a bit crappy to me.' She paused and added, her tone of voice quieter, 'And it's who you were, not who you are anymore. What happened to you, Alex?'

'What do you mean?'

'The Alex in that photo – it's a person I've never known.' She shrugged helplessly. 'Your face was full of … something I can't put my finger on … you looked like you had a head full of dreams and expectations … what were your dreams then, Alex?'

'It was over twenty years ago; people change.'

'They sure do. And you're still avoiding the answer. Is Lainey trying to force your big secrets out into the open? Or is it Niall, looking for some kind of vengeance?'

'When it comes to Niall, I've as much right to vengeance as he has.'

'Oh, wow – so now we're getting somewhere.'

'We're not going anywhere with this conversation, Jenna. Niall and I called it quits a long time ago. In case you hadn't noticed, Lainey is big on family loyalty so she'd hardly do anything to rock the boat. What happened at the fort yesterday evening was unfortunate but was probably some silly hikers who weren't bothered disposing of the birds properly. One of the kids could have been messing with the photos but were afraid to own up when Lainey made a fuss. And Jack was dreaming. Now, let's forget all about conspiracy theories, I want to get through the few days as peaceably as possible, get the hell out of here, and then have a few days away from it all with you and Jack.' He marched towards the door.

'You don't sound like a man who was looking forward to returning home to the bosom of his family. Were you afraid you were going to be cut out of the will if you refused your father's invitation?' she said to his retreating back.

'*What*?' He whirled around.

Her heart was hammering; she hadn't meant to blurt it out but she'd started now and she couldn't take the words back. 'I heard you – on the phone to Lainey, soon after the invitation arrived. A no-show here this weekend meant you were going to be cut off from your inheritance.'

Alex's face was white. 'Have you been thinking this all along? All the time … we were making preparations, even when we were travelling here?'

'I have, yes. I heard you.'

'Do you really have so low an opinion of me?' His tongue was like a whiplash.

'Why else would you have come running back here after twenty years, pretending all was great with your brother?' she countered, alarmed at the turn the conversation had taken and the way his face had paled.

'You couldn't have it more wrong,' he said.

'Maybe you're the one who's trying to sabotage the weekend, for all I know.' She hadn't meant to say that either, but it was like her tongue was running away with her having been silent for so long, especially during the past few angst-ridden months.

'You sure as hell are trying to sabotage us with your wild accusations. I can't believe what I'm hearing.'

'I couldn't believe it when I heard you on the phone to Lainey.'

'Did you even stop to think for a minute that you might have got that wrong? Or were you happy to believe the worst of me?'

It was a long time since she'd seen him so angry. They were having a full-blown row – not surprising considering the tension that had been simmering between them, but they couldn't have picked a worse moment to let it erupt. In a short while they'd have to take part in the group picnic and play happy families, pretending this had never happened.

'Don't you trust me?' he asked, looking suddenly bleak.

She felt a pang inside her at the expression in his eyes, but she couldn't take any more. After the last few months her patience with Alex had worn thin. 'About as much as you trust me with the truth,' she said, her eyes daring him to speak.

They stared at each other and Jenna knew that Alex was as horrified as she was at the way things had disintegrated between them. They could hear sounds of the children getting ready in the hall, and Lainey talking to Jack in that sugar-coated voice as she took jackets and boots out of the cloakroom.

Alex glared at her. 'We'll deal with this later; this is serious.'

'Too damned right it is,' she said, feeling punched in the gut.

'Right now we have a picnic to go to.'

'Of course,' she snapped, 'the charade must go on.'

'What did you say?' His eyes were wintry.

She tried to breathe deeply and relax her rigid face so that she could summon up a suitable expression for joining the family. Then she knew she couldn't do it.

'I can't do this,' she said. 'I can't make my merry way through the forest pretending everything is perfect.'

'Fine,' he fumed. 'Stay here.'

'Right. I will.'

He walked out of the bedroom, and she knew by the controlled way he marched that he was tempted to slam the door but couldn't very well give free rein to his urge on account of where they were. She sank down on the bed and listened to the sounds of everyone being marshalled together in the hallway. She wondered what excuses Alex was making up for her no-show. Whatever he said, no one came near her, not even Jack for a goodbye kiss.

She began to cry, the look on Alex's face having scorched her heart. After a while she heard footsteps on the stairs, a light tap on her door, and Erin called out in her soft Donegal voice, 'I won't disturb you, Jenna, I'm just putting fresh towels in the bathrooms. If you need paracetamol, there's some in the kitchen, along with tea and coffee.'

'Thanks, Erin,' she said, conscious that her voice sounded husky. Alex had probably told them all she had a bad headache. She pictured him going off on the picnic, silently enraged with her. What had she done wrong? Apart from trying to have an honest conversation with him? She blinked hard and patted her face and decided she needed some coffee and paracetamol, as her head was starting to throb. Downstairs all was quiet. She knew Leo had been brought breakfast and was staying in his room until lunchtime. She went through the living room and straight out into the kitchen, where—

'Hey! What are you doing here?'

'I thought it might be a good time to make you that coffee.'

Ben turned around from the coffee machine, a warm smile on his face. Seeing him here now was a fresh shock on top of her frayed emotions.

'How come you're not gone with the others?' she asked, unable to stop herself from glowering at him.

'I got a special dispensation.'

'Why?'

'Before we even arrived in Lynes Glen, I applied for two hours off this morning to read a report before a meeting first thing Tuesday.'

'Don't let me keep you from it,' she said stiffly. 'I'll bring a coffee upstairs out of your way.'

'You'll do no such thing. What about you? How come you cried off the picnic?' He frowned, then he studied her face with gentle eyes, and realising something was amiss, he smiled apologetically. 'Sorry, I didn't mean that literally.'

She didn't mind that he'd spotted the trace of her tears. Now she'd got over her initial shock at seeing him here, she knew she felt so comfortable with this man, so much in tune with him, that it didn't bother her if he knew she'd been crying.

'It's OK, I'm fine.'

'Coffee,' he ordered. 'We'll take it out into the fresh air, while we still can, I heard there's a storm on the way.' He picked up a selection of capsules and held them out to her. 'Which would you prefer? Do you think it's too early to add any extra ingredients?'

She grinned. 'Far too early.'

'Good.' His eyes were mischievous. 'I like breaking the rules and I fancy a tiny dash of the old crathur.'

'The *what*?'

He grinned. 'That's Irish for a warming jot of whiskey, no more than a tiny drop, I promise.'

'Oh, go on then, persuade me.'

CHAPTER EIGHTEEN

Outside on the terrace, in the air that tasted cool and sweet, Jenna felt she was someone else. She'd donned another skin, a woman who was able to put to one side the upsetting scene in the bedroom, the angry look on Alex's face, her sense of outrage, in favour of just being here, this moment. The breeze riffled the tips of the grass, it gently swayed the trees in the forest, it was pleasant on her hot face, and the coffee, laced with a smidgen of whiskey, helped to unwind the knot in her stomach. Ben was chatty and cheerful.

'We'll make a pact,' he said. 'No talking about the Blakes, OK?'

'I thought you brought me out here to discuss the mystery of the smashed photo frame. It wasn't you, was it?'

'Did you have to ask?' Ben looked a little disappointed.

'Sorry.' She made a face.

'No worries. Lainey's beside herself with annoyance. My guess is that Charlotte let it fall – she could easily have reached it – only her mother is so mad she's too afraid to own up, especially with visitors around. She was curious about the photographs and asking me why there were none of the grandkids. I was trying to explain that the house hasn't been lived in for years. Leo, too, is a bit older than my parents, who would wallpaper the whole house with photos if they could.'

'My mum's the same.'

'Gorgeous woman,' Ben said.

'When did you meet her?' She was surprised he remembered.

'Last spring, when we were all out to lunch. You must remember, she was up from San Francisco at the same time as Lainey and I were over.'

Of course she did, it had been during that visit that she'd begun to feel far too attracted towards him. Lunch had been bittersweet; she'd sat on one side of Ben, her mother on the other.

'So how are things in New York?' he asked.

'Really?'

'Yes, really. I won't go running to Lainey.'

'How do you know there's something worth running to her about?'

'The way you said "really".'

'Am I that transparent?'

'That and your headache.' He smiled at her so benevolently that she felt a catch in her throat.

'Things aren't great,' she told him, her voice husky. 'Alex's business is in some kind of trouble but he won't talk about it. He brushes away my concerns, says I don't need to worry about anything. That he'll take care of it. That's no good to me, I'd like to know what's going on, for things to be upfront. But I'm being shut out, the same way I'm being shut out of his family history.'

'He probably has his pride. On both counts.'

'I can understand that to a certain degree, I shouldn't even be talking to you like this, I feel I'm letting our side down in a way, but surely love matters more than pride?'

'You're not letting him down, it's fine to bounce things off a friend.'

A friend. Not a potential lover, she reminded herself.

'Talking can help to clear your head or see another angle,' Ben said. 'Maybe he's behaving like this because he loves you? Maybe he's right; he can take care of it and he doesn't want to have you worried. And I'm not taking any sides. I'm being objective.'

'That's OK.' She paused, then she added, 'We had a row.'

'I'd never have guessed,' he said kindly.

'I said I knew he'd come home this weekend because he didn't want to be cut out of Leo's will. He went mad.'

'Go for the jugular, why don't you.' His voice was sympathetic.

She put her face in her hands for a moment, then sighed quietly. 'I did, didn't I? I don't know what possessed me to put it so bluntly. He didn't just go mad, he went ballistic.'

'No wonder you looked—' he broke off.

'I looked what?'

'In need of a good hug.'

It would be lovely to be held by Ben, with his big muscular arms. She felt like asking him if he was going to supply it. She heard the question hanging in the air as though she'd voiced it and she blinked hard, conscious of a dizzy feeling in her head.

'The coffee is helping,' she said, forcing herself to smile a neutral smile. 'Do you think that's why Lainey is here?'

'I doubt it, although I didn't dare ask her,' Ben said. 'Putting the will aside, this weekend is the culmination of everything Lainey has ever wanted. I'll never forget how delighted she was when Leo told her of his wish and she was over the moon when she heard both Niall and Alex were coming. I've listened to her often enough bemoaning the fact that her brothers live on two different continents. That's the way she puts it, going on as if there are no flight connections whatsoever between those continents.'

'What's bugging me is that I can't help feeling snubbed, as though I'm not good enough for Alex to share his history with.'

'Maybe he doesn't want to dump too much on you.'

'I thought I had married the flesh and blood man, warts and all. That's the man I want to know, not some sanitised shadow of him, who's keeping things to himself. Doesn't he trust me? Why is he afraid to be vulnerable in front of me? I don't want marriage-by-numbers. I want the real thing. I want to be there for him in the good and bad. But that's not happening. When I try to get close, he pushes me away. Even this weekend, I feel more like an observer than a participant. It's not something I can explain very well, but does that make sense?'

'Perfect sense. It just about sums up the weekend. You, me, and Vikki too, I'd imagine, are outside observers, while the Blakes are participating in some kind of elaborate charade.'

'Did you notice how careful they are being with each other? As though they are tiptoeing on eggshells around each other?'

'I think that used to happen anyway, with Lainey, when we met up with Niall or Alex. It was like there was a careful agenda to be followed as regards subjects safe enough for discussion. All very polite and mannerly. No confrontation of any kind. It's just more obvious when the three of them are together.'

They both fell silent, a silence that helped to relax Jenna a little. Although Ben was sending her pulse skittering around like crazy, on another level she felt peaceful, as though she was totally accepted by him, just as she was.

'Are you feeling OK now?' he asked.

'Much better, thanks. What's on the timetable for this evening?'

'Lainey has a couple of videos lined up. For the adults and the kids, a kind of movie night, to take our minds off the approaching storm.'

'It doesn't seem to me like there's a storm due.'

'Believe me, there is. When Lainey checked the forecast before the weekend, she was very annoyed that the weather wasn't playing ball. Things can change around here very quickly, but we're OK for another three or four hours, I'd say; it's due to hit later this afternoon.'

'I don't mind a bit of rain, we get our share in New York.'

'A bit of rain? We'll see about that.' He grinned. 'Hey, how do you feel about sneaking off for an hour or so?'

'I thought you had a paper to read?'

'It'll keep.'

'Where are you thinking of going? Driving to the village? Or is connecting with the outside world forbidden?'

'I daren't disturb the cars; it's bound to be noticed. I was going to bring you to the lough.'

'The *lough*? Isn't it out of bounds?'

'To all appearances. Lainey wants to leave it like that, to put anyone off, but there's a roundabout way to reach it through the forest. But we're not doing this at all. Deal?'

'Doing what?' She grinned at him, feeling her heart contract with a mixture of excitement and the knowledge that she was doing something a little risky. It was nothing – just a trek to the lough with Ben, not worth mentioning to Alex, given the mood he was in. 'I feel quite bold and brave.'

'It suits you, being bold and brave.'

'Does it?'

'You've more colour in your face, your eyes are brighter, you look—'

'I look – what?' Their eyes caught and held, his roving across her face, and he looked away first. She'd a strange feeling he'd been about to say she looked beautiful but thought the better of it.

'Alive, spirited, like someone, my dear Jenna, who is about to enjoy an unexpected treat.'

My dear Jenna. She hugged it to herself. Just a figure of speech, she knew, but hey.

'I'll take the cups inside,' he said, 'and give you five minutes to put on your walking shoes and a decent jacket. Meet you back here.'

*

She was wrapped in a bubble of excitement. On the surface it was an innocent trek through the forest, but in her heart it was so much more. The thoughts that skittered around her head made this all wrong. Deliciously wrong. Ben had put on a waterproof jacket and brought a big golf umbrella to use against the undergrowth. Ahead of them lay a seemingly impenetrable mix of straggling bushes, thorny foliage and tall clumps of spiky nettles.

'This way,' he said, striking off into the dense forest, hiking through the uneven terrain for a hundred metres or so. He led her through thick undergrowth and a tunnel of greenery. In places they had to duck under large branches, other times Ben used the umbrella to push back high clumps of foliage.

'Don't forget, we're not here,' he said, pausing. 'I'm reading a boring business paper and you're sulking in your bedroom.'

She burst out laughing. 'I've never sulked in my life.'

'I can believe that. You don't seem like the sulky type.' His eyes appraised her so warmly that her nerve endings were jangling. It was all in her head, she chided herself. She was imagining things like a love-struck teenager, or more to the point, a lust-struck woman approaching forty years of age whose husband wasn't paying her any attention.

'There won't be a word out of me,' she said. 'Not even a whisper.'

'Nor me.'

They were climbing now. The solitude of the forest lent an aura of intimacy as they picked their way through the shady green tunnels, Ben leading, Jenna close behind, nothing apart from the snap of twigs under their feet and occasional rustle of a hidden animal in the undergrowth, disturbing the quiet. After twenty minutes or so, Jenna saw glimmers of light just ahead, sparking through gaps in the foliage like stars at night.

'Not too far now,' Ben said. 'Wait til you see, it'll be worth it.' He used the umbrella to beat down more nettles, Jenna ducked under stray branches one more time and then they came out of the forest into the glare of sunlight on water and she blinked.

It was an area of natural beauty that took her breath away. They were standing on a high ledge, the whispery forest behind them, the folds of the mountains curving around, and below, the shimmering lough cupped in the palm of the mountains. Down to her left, Jenna saw a small sandy shore in front of the lough, and beyond that, a narrow track leading up to the blocked-off entrance from the road. It was a place of natural, pristine beauty. She could hardly grasp the reality of this being the spot where

Gabrielle had met her death. It seemed incomprehensible that somewhere so full of beauty and light had witnessed such darkness and desolation. She tried not to picture Gabrielle, alive one minute, her life bursting with hopes and dreams, only to have all that extinguished in an instant. Jenna took a slow breath.

'This is where it happened,' she said.

'Yes.' Even Ben's voice was sober as he spoke, his eyes distant. 'I was here with Lainey, the one and only time she ever spoke of it. We came through the forest, just as we did now, but Lainey was so upset that she said she never wanted to come here again.'

'When you see where it happened, being here, in the spot ... the tragedy of it all really hits you ... it must have left a terrible mark on the family. Alex was only able to tell me that his mother's car had gone off the road and he came to New York soon afterwards to put it all behind him. That has to have been total bullshit or else I'm not married to the man I thought I was. How could you put this behind you?'

'People deal with grief in different ways. Maybe that was his way.'

Slightly below her, Jenna saw the long wooden diving board jutting out from a rocky outcrop. Here, whatever way the side of the mountain had been formed long ago, the fissures in the rock made a series of natural stepping stones up to the diving platform from the shore. Up close to it like this, Jenna could appreciate the height of the board and the sheer drop down into the water. She could imagine a young Niall having the nimble ability to climb up there and execute a dive, but it would have scared her half to death even though she was an accomplished swimmer.

'It must have taken some guts for Niall to dive from there,' she said. 'This is where that photograph on the piano was taken, isn't it?'

'Yep. Lainey took it.'

'Did she?'

'So she said.'

'And that's where I saw someone sitting, on our way here on Friday afternoon. Someone with red-gold hair, just like Gabrielle.' She went on in husky tones, 'Vikki saw her also.' She swallowed hard. 'I'm not surprised it went down like a lead balloon, along with Jack's ghost. You don't think' – something that had been playing at the edge of her mind finally found a voice – 'Ben, do you think there might be a ghost? That Lynes Glen is haunted and that's what they're covering up?'

'I don't think it's haunted at all,' Ben said. 'But I think someone is stirring up trouble.'

'I thought that too, but Alex went mad when I said it.'

Ben stared out at the lough. 'It could be any one of the Blakes,' he said. 'You can feel the tension as much as I can. We don't know what kind of resentments they're hiding. Cooped up for the weekend, who knows what will happen when the shit hits the fan.'

'You mean *if* it does.'

'The way things are going, I think it certainly will.'

CHAPTER NINETEEN

1968

'Looks like I got back just in time,' Maura said.

'What do you mean?' Leo looked at her sharply. It wasn't so much what she said as the way she said it – as though she was talking to a child who'd been up to boldness in his mother's absence. And to speak to him like this in the hotel dining room, right in the middle of lunch time – it grated. He was relieved Gabrielle wasn't around to witness this small humiliation; there was no sign of her today and he guessed her roster must have been changed at the last minute.

'It's sooner than you'd planned,' he said. It was the beginning of September and Maura hadn't been expected back until the end of the month.

'Is that a surprise to you? I hope that doesn't spoil your fun. While the cat's away the mice have certainly played.' Maura wiped her hands on her white apron, drew herself up to her full height and threw out her considerable chest. 'There have been some quare goings on around here this summer,' she said. 'The minute my back is turned.'

'Like what?'

'There's no point in acting the innocent, Leo dear, I've heard all about your little summer dalliance,' she said, her eyes round with indignant mockery. 'Not from the young lady herself, mind you, but from the minute I arrived into the kitchen. Some people were only too delighted to be the bearer of the news, or, should I say, the gossip. They couldn't wait to tell me all about it. I heard you even showed your face at the dance on Saturday night. That's a proper turn up! I was convinced all the wild horses in Connemara would never drag you across that particular threshold.'

'Were you now.'

'Then again, grief does strange things to people.' She sighed heavily, leaning one hand on the table and staring into space. 'Can even send them a little batty and give them funny imaginings.'

Gabrielle. Maura had to be referring to Gabrielle but it wasn't the reaction he'd been expecting. They went back a long way, him and Maura. Even though she was the younger by a number of years, they were good friends partly because their mothers had been good friends, and he'd known Maura since her babyhood. He'd been the older brother she'd never had. Maura knew how devastated he'd been after his parents died, how much his poetry meant to him and how his inspiration had dried up in the wake of his grief. When she'd gone through a bad patch in school during her teenage years, he'd empathised with her, telling her about the gentle, rather isolated schoolboy who'd been tormented for preferring to have his head stuck in a book than brave the challenging tackles on a football pitch.

Surely she'd be happy for him instead of looking at him as

though he'd been up to no good in her absence? Still, maybe Maura was annoyed at the manner in which she'd heard about them. Not from Gabrielle herself, obviously, or from him, but from the kitchen staff. Yet the 'gossip' label she was filing it under jarred with him. The flippancy of it was far removed from the words he'd use to describe the wonderful weeks he'd enjoyed with Gabrielle. To hear their relationship reduced in such a frivolous fashion was vexing.

'How did things go for you in Dublin?' he asked, changing the subject. Maura had taken leave of absence for several weeks to go to Dublin to help take care of her sister and her small brood, as she'd fallen ill following an emergency caesarean and subsequent surgery.

'I'm surprised you remembered that's where I was,' she said. 'By all accounts your head has been rightly turned.'

He looked at her, a little puzzled as to the reason for her jibes. She must have seen something in his expression that stalled her flow of remarks because her face softened a little. 'Dublin went fine, my sister is grand, I wasn't needed anymore.'

'I'm happy to hear she's recovered,' he said.

'I'm happy I'm back now, in my rightful place. There's been some slackening around here and I'll be glad to exert my supervisory skills once more.'

He knew her return meant Gabrielle was out of a job. She'd only been helping out in the hotel dining room during the busy summer months. Did Gabrielle know yet that she was back? She'd said nothing at all to him the last night they'd been out together. They'd been to the pictures, to see a James Bond film that had finally arrived in the cinema house in Creaghbara; he couldn't even remember the name, all he could remember was the feel of her hand in his going right down to his toes, the brush of her hair against his face, the way it felt like spun silk under his fingers, his senses saturated with the golden luminosity of her when she'd leaned against his shoulder. Her kisses, later.

The staff in the kitchen – and Maura – seemed to think it was great 'gossip'.

Sudden rage gripped him. He threw down his napkin and pushed away his plate. 'I'm finished here,' he said, his appetite gone. He took some notes out of his wallet and put them on the table before stalking out.

Maura caught up with him in the lobby.

'Leo. What's on earth is the matter with you?' Somehow she managed to make it sound like he was a child having a tantrum.

He spun around. 'What's the matter? If you don't realise what's wrong then I'm not going to waste my time answering.'

She stood in front of him, barring his exit. People were coming and going through the main door and to get by her would have caused a fuss and he hated causing a fuss. He stood there silently, glaring at her.

'You do look fierce,' she said, smiling, a hint of apology in that smile. 'I can't remember seeing you that angry before. What happened to my calm and placid Leo?'

Dear God – if only he could answer that question. Gabrielle had happened; that was all, yet it was everything.

'Whatever I said, I had no intention of offending you,' Maura said, putting a placating hand on his arm. She'd done this a hundred times before, but this time it felt heavy to him. He tried to keep a straight face and not brush her hand away. 'You're my friend and I value our friendship.'

'Good,' he said.

'I'd no idea my cousin was going to be such a sensitive subject with you,' she said.

'Your *cousin*?'

'Didn't you know? You mustn't be that close to Gabrielle after all if she never mentioned it. Although there's not much of a family resemblance, I have to say.' Maura's smile was tight

There wasn't. Whereas Gabrielle was spun gold, almost ethereal, but with a filament of tempered fire inside her, Maura was bigger and broader, dark and sultry. It was like comparing the beauty of an exquisite, glowing sunrise to the heavy blanket of a warm, dark night.

*

'You never told me you were related to Maura,' he said.

Gabrielle tilted her head to one side. 'Didn't you know?'

'How could I have known?'

'I assumed everybody knew everything around here. We're not that close. Maura's father and my mother were cousins, so that makes us second cousins. So – you were talking to her?' she asked, wrinkling her nose attractively.

'Maura's an old friend of mine, she heard we were ...' he hesitated '... seeing each other. Did Maura get you the job in the hotel?'

'Her father did. He was one of the few family members still talking to my mother and she telephoned him before she left for Australia. The subject of me needing a new job came up and he suggested it to Maura, who put in a word for me. I didn't even see Maura because she left for Dublin a couple of days before I arrived in Creaghbara. I haven't seen her in years but I'll get to meet up with her now though, in the hotel.'

'Will you?'

'Yes, one of the waitresses is off to England for six months so they're keeping me on in the dining room.'

Lots of Irish workers emigrated to the big cities in England in search of better jobs and a better lifestyle, but going for six months meant only one thing. The unfortunate waitress was being banished from her family in shame because she was pregnant. The baby's father, meanwhile, would be getting away scot-free.

'Does that suit you?' he asked.

'Of course it does.'

He hadn't the heart to tell her they were gossiping about her in the kitchen. He guessed that was why Maura had been annoyed with him and had taken exception to their friendship. She didn't like her young cousin being the subject of tittle-tattle because it could reflect on her and undermine her supervisory position.

'Isn't it great?' Gabrielle said, smiling innocently. 'I'll be here for another few months and I'm looking forward to talking to Maura. Maybe we could get together, go to the pictures, or out for a meal. We could go as a foursome, if she has a boyfriend.'

'I don't think she has a boyfriend,' Leo said, casting about in his head for any references to male friends. The thoughts of a foursome didn't appeal to him in the least, especially having to make strained conversation over a dinner table with someone he didn't know from Adam. He might be feted for his lyrical skills and way with words but it was one thing for those words to come when he was sitting alone at his desk. Being out in company was a different matter. He found it easier to talk to people on a one-to-one basis and he baulked at the idea of Gabrielle witnessing his awkward social skills when it came to being in a group.

It didn't happen though. There was no boyfriend. Before he'd summoned the guts to ask Maura outright, he found out from Gabrielle, who'd tentatively suggested a visit to the cinema to Maura.

'I asked her if she had someone she'd like to bring with her and she laughed. She told me she'd washed her hands of all that romantic nonsense,' Gabrielle said. 'I think she must have been let down once too much in the past. So I hope it's OK that I said she could come with us.'

It wasn't, not when he wanted Gabrielle all to himself. He couldn't remember Maura being upset over being let down by anyone. She was always bright and breezy with him. Could be she was good at hiding things. Knowing he'd been in the depths of despair in the months after his parents' death, she probably hadn't wanted to burden him with her problems.

'Of course it's OK that she can come with us,' he said, silently deciding that cinema trips were at the back of the agenda for now.

'And maybe when we take a picnic to the lough some of the sunny afternoons? She said she'd been there before with you and would love to visit it again.'

'We'd have to see if she's free first.'

'If anyone can arrange that, Maura can. She's in charge of the roster.'

A week after Maura was back, Gabrielle's shift changed so that she wasn't there so much during lunch hour.

'I'm doing it as a favour to both of you,' Maura said. 'For Gabrielle's sake it might reduce the racy gossip that's flying around the kitchen. I know you'll miss seeing her during your dinner hour but I think you'd prefer her reputation to remain intact.'

Mother of God. 'Reputation? How could I be a threat to that?'

'Sure *I* know you wouldn't, Leo, you're the perfect gentleman. I bet you've barely kissed her, am I right?'

He stared at her, refusing to answer, appalled at the slow burn that crept through his body. The very act of kissing Gabrielle meant so much to him that it was almost an intimate thing in itself, certainly nothing to be shared with Maura.

She seemed satisfied with his silence and went on, 'It's hard to stop people talking, especially if they have notions where you're involved.'

'Me?' He laughed at the idiocy of it. 'Who'd be bothered talking about me? As for having notions …'

'Of course they'd have notions. And why not? A fine handsome man such as yourself, someone who's trustworthy and reliable, not to mention virile, doesn't come along too often in these parts.'

'Give over, Maura.' He shook his head. He'd seen more evidence of grey hairs in the mirror only that morning. Moreover, lately he'd begun to realise his dark hair didn't seem to be quite so thick. His belly hadn't rounded out like some other country men, thank goodness; he was still lean and spare-framed.

'I just hope Gabrielle appreciates what she has in you,' Maura said. 'Young ones, nowadays, don't always appreciate the … more solid and steadfast things in life. The world we're living in is changing, and not for the better, if you ask me. Meaningless pop music, vulgar dancing, women only half-dressed with skirts up to their arses, no respect for themselves, and other unmentionables I wouldn't dream of saying aloud for fear of God. I might be only a little older than my cousin but I think that you and I are of the same stock, Leo, the same generation. We understand each other. We were brought up with the similar old-fashioned values, we observe the same kind of formalities, and we speak the same old-fangled language.'

A stab of anxiety shook him. He tried in vain to push it away but it found a home somewhere inside him, burrowing itself into the very corner that had a bad habit of waking up and making itself known to him at the pitch-black, ungodly hour of four in the morning.

CHAPTER TWENTY

'It's beautiful here,' Vikki said.

Niall paused, looking around him in appreciation. 'I'd forgotten how lucky we were, to have all this so close to where we grew up. I took it all for granted. As you do. We called this Infinity Hill, because you could almost see to infinity from here. Mum used to say it should make us feel that the world was a huge and wonderful place, and we could look out to the infinity and imagine whatever we wanted for our lives.'

They were on a hill above the house, and behind them, beyond a thin drift of furze and bushes, Slieve Creagh rose up, studded with scree and shale. Directly in front, the gradient fell away sharply so that they could see over the top of the dense forest, and beyond, to where the view of patchwork fields criss-crossed by stone walls went on for miles, smudged with distance as it met the shimmering horizon. Somewhere down below, tucked into the middle of this vast and beautiful terrain, and hidden from their view by the forest, was Lynes Glen.

Vikki had found it a relief to get out of the house and into the fresh air. There had been some kind of fuss that morning, something to do with Jack and his talk of ghosts. Niall had told her to stay put while he went to see what Lainey was getting excited about. He'd come back within a short while and had told her it was fine, but she'd sensed he was holding back a wave of annoyance as he clumsily cleared his breakfast setting, and she knew by Lainey's over-smooth tone of voice that something else had backfired in some manner. And if she had been in any doubt, Alex's thunderous face as they'd gathered in the hall had spoken volumes. There was no sign of Jenna, and Alex's remarks about her bad headache didn't fool anyone. Still, the show went on and they'd set out for the picnic as though everyone was perfectly happy.

'Come on, I'll show you the waterfall,' Niall said.

He brought her around to where there was a gap in the thin layer of bushes and scrub, exposing flanks of bare mountain rock, and a tumble of water cascaded out from a cavity up high in the dark stone, crashing down for several feet, spattering off scattered boulders below. It pooled into a small natural basin and streamed out of that, gushing along a stony bed like a glimmering silvery trail, before disappearing down around the side of the mountain.

'We used to paddle in that stream,' Niall said. 'Mostly it was freezing and the stones caught between our toes but we were mesmerised by the idea of the water swirling around our ankles going all the way out to the sea and on to America. Or so Mum used to say. We used to wonder if the imprint of our feet carried over there as well.'

'That must have been fantastic to a child.' Vikki's voice softened, picturing him as a young boy. 'Did it make you dream of going there one day?'

'No, that was always Alex's dream.'

'That came true for him all right.'

'Sort of.'

His eyes became guarded.

'What about you, Niall?' she ventured. 'What kind of dreams did you have, when you were a child, growing up in this beautiful place? You must have felt the world was full of magic, waiting to be discovered.'

'I think we all did.'

'Was there anything in particular you felt you wanted to do?'

Like how about that perfect pose on the diving board? Where had that come from? Something so pure took practice and discipline, and a huge dedication, yet he'd never once mentioned that skill to her or what he might have hoped to get out of it. What was he doing spending his life cooped up in a glass cubicle in a hospital office? He'd told her his job made him feel he was doing something worthwhile and useful but how had he arrived at that place? They'd talked about lots of things during late-night conversations, aided by a glass too many of wine, but now on reflection she realised they'd only glossed over things; she certainly hadn't bared her soul to Niall in any meaningful way any more than he had to her.

But whatever about realising there were many layers to Niall she hadn't been aware of, the same applied to her. In a sense they were both players on a stage as Niall didn't know anything at all about the real Vikki Gordon. She thought of the concrete jungle with overflowing refuse bins, grilled windows, broken glass, and graffiti-covered walls, embarrassed to imagine Niall looking at it through his eyes, never mind what had gone on in the place she'd once called home.

Standing here, feeling alive in this beautiful place and breathing the clear, fresh air, a sudden moment of clarity and liberation filled her with a rush of relief. He would never find out. She didn't have to tell Niall anything at all. She didn't have to put herself in the position of being vulnerable again. She didn't have to summon the guts to bare her soul, or find the courage to pick at protective scabs and rake over yesterday's hurts, or scrabble together enough nerve to take an opener and hack away at the closed lid shielding her bleak background.

She could make the decision right now to forget her ideas of any future with him, to enjoy this weekend for what it was worth, and make the most of simply being here with him. Then, once they were back in London, she could slip out of his life just as easily as she'd arrived in it. It would be difficult, like cutting out a big piece of her heart, but it was safer.

Her new-found liberation emboldened her. 'Well, go on, what did you really dream about doing?'

He smiled at her and ruffled her hair. She allowed herself to relax and enjoy the feeling of it, instead of guarding her emotions and holding herself in check.

'Once upon a time, like most adolescents, I thought I owned the whole world.' He paused. 'Then I grew up and got real. Here, try this.' He leaned in towards the waterfall, heedless of the spray, cupping his hands together under the downpour until his clasped hands filled with water. He brought them carefully to Vikki's mouth. 'Taste that.'

It was an unusually intimate thing, sucking up the water from his hands. She dipped her head to the palms of his hands and tasted the cool clarity of the water on her tongue, momentarily dazed at the unexpected pleasure of it all.

'Incredible, isn't it?' His eyes were warm.

'Absolutely,' she said, unable to tear her gaze away from his. Now that she'd mentally detached from her worries about where their relationship might be heading, she could revel in the moment with him and it was sweet as nectar.

She heard Lainey calling them.

'Come on,' he said, 'we have a picnic to go to.'

*

They were on their way back down the track through the forest, with Niall carrying the picnic basket and Alex giving Jack and Harry a piggyback in turn, when Lainey drew alongside Vikki.

'So what's a normal Saturday in London?' she asked.

'Catching up, usually.' If Lainey expected her to reveal a few snippets about her relationship with Niall, she'd be disappointed. 'Laundry, shopping, cleaning, maybe out somewhere for brunch or dinner.' All very bland and ordinary. No falling out of nightclubs at four in the morning, with or without Niall.

'I take it home has always been London?'

'Of course.'

'I was wondering if you were from there originally or had a family home, perhaps, somewhere outside the metropolis.'

'Sorry to disappoint you, but there's no ancestral pile in Northumberland or manor house in a Cotswolds village; I'm London born and bred,' Vikki said, convinced that Lainey was fishing for information – surely her accent gave her away, considering she sounded like she could have walked straight off the set of Eastenders as opposed to inner Belgravia.

Lainey gave a half-laugh. 'Nonsense, Vikki, that doesn't disappoint me in the least. I find you ... interesting, even intriguing. Yes, I'm intrigued to think Niall has been with you for almost a year? A significant other and we didn't know.'

That's because she wasn't really a 'significant other'. Although she'd got the 'year' part right, but something about the way Lainey posed it as a question made her stubbornly reluctant to confirm it.

'If you've lived all your life in London you must find Lynes Glen quite a change,' Lainey said.

Vikki couldn't resist. 'Oh, definitely. The contrast is considerable. I find the whole setup very interesting and intriguing.'

'I suppose it's giving you a chance to appreciate where Niall has come from, his roots, his sense of place,' Lainey said. 'We spent our childhoods running wild, the three of us, it was as near perfect as you could get, especially during the long summers. Because we're so far west, the light lingers in the sky for hours. Then there were winters when we were snowbound or stormbound for days at a time and Mum would go through our school books with us.'

'A lot different to London, all right.' A world away. In every sense. Memories she no longer had to worry about resurrecting, now she'd decided to end things with Niall.

'You probably didn't know all that much about his background?'

Lainey was definitely fishing for something. How much Vikki knew about Niall's past life? Or hadn't she believed Niall when he'd told her Vikki knew nothing?

'No, not that much,' Vikki said in a casual voice, as if she was covering up something. Let Lainey add two and two together and make ten. She could make twenty, for all Vikki cared. The other woman might be Niall's sister, but she was getting up Vikki's nose with her controlling attitude towards everything. She added, recklessly, 'But I didn't know he had nerves of steel. He doesn't seem to have a fear of heights. He told me he'd climbed Slieve Creagh and then there is his diving photo. That was a steep drop down into the lough. He must have been some adrenaline junkie …' she paused deliberately and then added, 'once upon a time.'

Lainey wasn't fazed. 'People change,' she said cryptically. 'Even you—'

'Even me what?'

'Niall must have changed more than I realised because you're not his usual type of girlfriend.' Her smile flicked over Vikki from head to toe, taking everything in.

'I should hope not,' Vikki said spiritedly. 'I like being different from the usual run of the mill.'

The other woman's words had smarted. His usual type? How many girlfriends of Niall's had Lainey actually met? She was glad she didn't know any of Niall's relationship history other than he'd told her nothing had ever lasted too long. That way she had nothing to compare herself with and find herself wanting.

'You certainly are that,' Lainey said, a hint of grudging respect in the depths of those beautiful eyes. 'Most other girlfriends were far too cool and sophisticated and lucky to last a month.'

So she wasn't cool and sophisticated, according to Lainey. Before they went much further, Vikki felt the first few drops of rain plopping through the canopy of trees and their conversation was over. Lainey gathered the children to her and pulled plastic raincoats out of a bag, Alex helping to dole them out. To Vikki's delight, Niall put down the picnic basket he'd been carrying, took off his jacket and, pulling her close, he held it over both of their heads. It cocooned them in a world of their own and she anchored an arm around his waist as the rain fell through the trees in an increasingly insistent downpour. Alex marched ahead, heedless to the way his hair and jacket were becoming steadily soaked, the children pranced around in their coloured raincoats, sticking out their tongues to catch the raindrops as though it was great fun, and even Lainey was laughing with them. The wind started to strengthen, gusting through the trees, sending them swaying. It made the children laugh all the more and they hurried down the track towards Lynes Glen, pretending they were being blown away.

Back in Lynes Glen, Alex stomped straight upstairs muttering something about having a shower and changing out of his damp clothes. Lainey supervised as the children stood in the hallway and peeled off their wet raincoats, their chatter as bright and cheerful as the colours of their coats, and they scampered down to the living room. Leo was up, sitting in a comfortable chair, Jenna and Ben were chatting to him and relaxing with coffee, the room was pleasantly warm and filled with a mouth-watering aroma of baking. Vikki followed Niall as he brought the picnic basket into the kitchen.

'Something smells really good,' Niall said, pulling cups and plates from the bag.

'It's just a few cupcakes,' Erin said. 'I thought the children would like some.'

'Never mind the children, going by that delicious smell, I want to sample some as soon as they're out of the oven,' Niall said. 'If I'm ever having a party in London, I'll prise you from Dad's clutches and fly you over.'

'Och, get away with you, I'm not that great,' Erin said, in her soft, northern accent, and shook her head. Her cheeks glowed pink and Vikki told herself she was falling for the Niall effect. Charismatic, lighthearted, never taking life seriously, he had that way with women. She ought to know.

'Coffee?' Niall asked her, going across to the machine.

'Just give me five minutes, I'm going to tidy myself up,' she said, conscious of her slightly dishevelled hair.

Even in the few minutes since they'd arrived back, the storm had deepened. Walking up the hallway, Vikki was conscious that Lynes Glen, with a storm brewing outside, was very different to a Lynes Glen basking in the sunshine. From the living area, she'd already seen that the mountains at the back of the house were swathed in a murky mist and out front, through the window beside the hall door, the rolling landscape was veiled in layers of cloud and rain. The gusty wind threw large spatters of rain against the windows, sending them rattling. They seemed marooned in a world of their own. Another reason, Vikki realised, why together in the house, the Blakes seemed such a tight unit. As Lainey had pointed out, they were used to being marooned here by storms and snowfalls during the winter months, relying on each other's company.

She could have done with having some light on the staircase – it loomed ahead, dim and shadowy – but she couldn't find the switch. She stood for a moment, undecided. Alex was upstairs, wasn't he? Yet there was no sound coming from the rooms overhead, not even the hum of the shower. All was silent. Then above the sound of the wind whining around the house, she heard a noise coming from the sitting room, the sound of slow footsteps, but she didn't wait around to see who it was. Gripped by an unease she couldn't explain, Vikki hurried up the stairs, feeling stupidly relieved to reach the sanctuary of her bedroom.

Even here, the wind and rain lashed against the windows, and through the distorted glass, deep-bellied, low-hanging clouds blotted out the landscape. She was dismayed at how alone she felt. She wondered how Mia was getting on at the conference. Her absence would have been noticed, and chalked up as a black mark against her by Jo Morgan, and with untrammelled glee by other assistant editors scrambling for jobs in the reconfigured company. She hoped Mia wasn't caught in the crossfire.

Although she didn't have head space to worry about that at the moment. Deciding she'd no future with Niall was about all she could cope with for now. She would cut all ties, reinvent herself, and move on. Again.

CHAPTER TWENTY-ONE

1968

'What's wrong?' Gabrielle asked.

'Nothing.'

Gabrielle leaned forward. 'There is, Leo. You've been very quiet all afternoon, you're not really with me. Have I said something wrong?'

'No, of course not. Have *I* said something wrong?'

She looked at him, head tilted in puzzlement, and he could have wept with frustration. He didn't want any moments of discord between them and this had the potential to be one of those. He couldn't bear to have her look at him with unhappiness in her eyes.

It was the middle of September, a beautiful autumn day, and they'd spent it in Achill, strolling around the cliffs, going as far as the crystalline sea off Keem Bay. It had been an idyllic day and it wasn't over yet. At Gabrielle's insistence, because she didn't want the day to be over, they'd stopped off at Lough Lynes, he'd taken a blanket from the boot of the car and now they were sitting on the tiny strand.

He watched the sunlight play on her hair, forming a nimbus around her, the late-afternoon light mellowing the soft contours of her face so that it appeared fresh and absurdly young. He'd been quiet all afternoon because he was realising the truth in Maura's words. The gap between him and Gabrielle was more than just years, although they were considerable enough. They seemed to belong to different generations. There was a big difference between starting your schooling in the 1930s as opposed to the early 50s. What could Gabrielle see in him? He'd awoken at five that morning after a restless sleep, and when yet another new, dark thought had assailed him, he'd struggled out of bed, staring at his tired and bloodshot eyes in the bathroom mirror, turning away from his image in distaste at the idea of Gabrielle ever seeing him like this.

She laughed and twirled tendrils of red-gold hair between her fingers. 'How could you of all people have said something wrong?'

He stared at her, unable to voice the words. *It's more than that. It's the whole of me. What I really mean is, are you still interested in me? Am I speaking in a language you understand? Or are the words I say to you all wrong?*

'Leo? Are you all right?'

'Yes,' he answered hastily, wanting to reassure her and take that look out of her eyes. Then, 'No,' he admitted.

She let out a sigh. 'Good.'

'*Good*?'

'Good that you're admitting there is something bothering

you and this is not your normal behaviour. So, come on, spit it out.'

'It's us. You and me.'

'Go on.'

He took strength from the timeless beauty of where they were and voiced the dark thoughts that had pushed him out of bed. 'Does it ... still suit you to keep seeing me or did you think we were ... well, together, just for the summer? Like, to help pass the time while you worked in the hotel? You thought you were only going to be temporary. Maybe I was only supposed to be temporary also. Now that you're staying on there, I understand if you want to bring it to an end.'

'Leo!' Tears sprang in her eyes. 'Did *you* think all this was just ... temporary?'

He sidestepped her question. 'I'm afraid you might get tired of me, get bored with me, and not find me exciting enough.' He couldn't bear to mention the age difference between them. There were already more than enough barriers.

'How about you?' she countered, a determined light in her eyes. 'Maybe it's the other way around and you're bored with me.'

He couldn't answer this question without taking out his heart and putting it on the line. He gazed around at the wonder of where they were, the familiarity of this scene, his lough, rimmed by his mountains. He thought of all the years he had come here for peace, and had found it in the unwavering tranquillity of the sight before his eyes, the constant fresh air he breathed, the soft breeze that always came and riffled his face like a caress. Now he fancied all these elements were not only looking on, but were behind him, at his back, urging him to take a chance and speak his heart to this woman.

'Bored? Absolutely not,' he said. 'Never, ever ... dearest

Gabrielle, I can't even put into words how much you mean to me.' He gazed at her beloved face and reached for her hand and clasped it tightly within his, hoping his touch might convey what his words failed to.

She closed her eyes. She opened them again and he could hardly bear to meet those eyes, they were so full of a light he couldn't define except it sent shivers through him.

'Don't dare speak to me like that again,' she said. 'That part about me being bored, I mean.' She laughed, but it was a gentle laugh, like soft rain into a parched plant. She pressed herself into him and reached for his other hand, clasping it to herself, and he felt the softness of her against the hardness of his chest. Still keeping close contact with him, she angled her head away slightly so she could see his face, and looking up at him she said, 'Leo, darling, have you any idea how wonderful you are in every way? How brilliant? How I only have to look at you and my heart is full? No, you probably don't. You're far too modest for your own good, far too gentle and self-effacing, and they're just some of the things I love about you.'

It was his turn to close his eyes, a sense of dizziness washing over him as the half-life he'd led up to then dipped and swayed beneath him before dissolving away. When he opened them again and looked at her face he felt reborn.

CHAPTER TWENTY-TWO

'Where's your dad?' Jenna asked Jack, when the children erupted into the room, followed by Niall bearing the picnic bag and a slightly dishevelled Vikki, and finally Lainey, who was combing her hands through her hair, smoothing it down. She looked happy and energised, as though she was used to these elements and the rain and the wind were lifting her spirits rather than dampening them down. The children gathered around Leo showing off their spoils of unusually coloured leaves and funny-shaped twigs and pine cones.

'He went upstairs for a shower.' Lainey – naturally, as the one who kept tabs on everyone and in control of everything – jumped in with the answer. 'He got the worst of the wetting.' She went over to her father. 'Hiya, Dad, nice to see you up. You've had lunch?'

'Just finished, darling,' Leo said, looking up from inspecting the mottled leaf in the shape of a hand Harry had presented him with. 'We had a splendid quiche and side salad and these two lovely people kept me company.'

Jenna watched as Lainey's gaze travelled very slowly from Ben to her. 'All very cosy, I have to say,' she said. To her annoyance, Jenna felt her face redden as though she was guilty of some misdemeanour.

'Yes,' Ben said easily. 'We were nicely tucked up when the rain began. We were getting worried about you but you made it home just in time.'

'Didn't we just,' Lainey said, her gaze once more taking in both of them and Jenna felt her skin prickle as though there was a subtext to her words. She reminded herself that they looked totally innocent and Lainey couldn't read her thoughts.

Lainey turned her attention back to her father and the children. 'Dad, don't let them annoy you too much, I've planned a treasure hunt so they'll have some fun with that. Then a video before the evening meal, and maybe another one afterwards. I've rooted out some of our old favourites. We can forget all about the weather. Actually,' she said, addressing the room at large, a smile on her face that dared anyone to disagree, 'it'll be like old times, won't it? All of us snug together against the elements.'

Jenna stayed silent; she couldn't think of anything worse.

'Thanks for all this, Lainey dear,' Leo said. 'You've been very good to me, planning this weekend, down to the last detail. I know your life is busy enough without entertaining the indulgences of an eccentric old man.'

'Not at all, Dad, it was a pleasure.' Now it was Lainey's turn to have slightly flushed cheeks.

Then Vikki and Niall came back in from the kitchen. Lainey

went out there, and Jenna heard her speaking to Erin about the evening meal. A minute later Vikki disappeared upstairs. It's like a train station, Jenna thought, everyone coming and going, but there was still no sign of Alex.

*

Her husband didn't like storms, Jenna reminded herself when Alex eventually arrived downstairs, his face set in taut lines; they put him on edge. The breeze outside had turned into a full-scale wind that seemed to claw around the house, the noise of it shrieking through the forest outside, hissing in through gaps in the windows. Every so often it hurled spatters of rain against the windows of the living room, hitting them like a shower of glass.

She hadn't seen Alex since their row that morning. He barely glanced at her as he went across the room to say hello to his father and she felt stung. She remembered how he'd cuddled up to her during some spectacular New York storms, in the early years of their relationship and marriage. How they'd coiled together under the duvet as Hurricane Sandy had hit the city a few years ago, making space between them for toddler Jack as soon as he'd awoken. That had been the worst experience of a storm, yet the best, because everything she held dear and precious in this world had been right beside her within hugging distance, and they'd laughed and joked their way through the noise, keeping Jack and themselves entertained as they told funny stories in silly, made-up voices.

She'd asked Alex once or twice why he found storms so upsetting but he hadn't given her a direct answer and the look on his face had been enough to stop her from digging deeper. Storms in a New York apartment were one thing, where there were people above and below them in the apartment block, on a street sheltered to an extent by other similar apartment blocks, and life going on all about them, but here in Lynes Glen, they were totally isolated.

After a short chat with his father, Alex came straight across to her, put his hand on her arm in an unusually proprietorial gesture and said, his eyes boring into hers brooking no argument, 'I need you to come upstairs with me, now.'

Startled, she looked at him. 'What's up?'

His eyes flicked to the children, who had re-grouped around Leo as they examined and re-examined their various treasures. 'Not here. Excuse us,' he said, to no one in particular, ushering her from the room.

Out in the hall, they bumped into Lainey coming out of the sitting room.

'Ha, you two, trying to escape?' She looked pointedly at Alex's hand, which was still grasping Jenna's arm. Jenna felt a prickle of annoyance and realised she was desperate for another whiskey-laced coffee.

'I can't wait,' Jenna said.

'We wouldn't dream of it,' Alex said smoothly.

'Don't forget the treasure hunt will be on soon,' Lainey said.

'I hadn't forgotten,' Alex said.

'Alex knows the timetable off by heart,' Jenna said. There was a spatter of rain against the glass beside the hall door and she couldn't resist a shiver.

Once inside their bedroom, Alex closed the door and turned the key in the lock. He went through to the bathroom and closed the bolt on the door to Lainey and Ben's room.

'What all this about?' she asked. 'You're certainly making sure we won't be disturbed.'

Alex went over to the big mahogany wardrobe. Then he

flicked through the few items of clothing he had hanging up, and pulled out a casual shirt.

'Do you know anything about this?' he asked, continuing to watch her face closely as he held it out in front of her.

She was perplexed. 'No, why should I?'

He turned the hanger around so that Jenna could see the back of the shirt. It had been torn to ribbons so that it hung in strips from the hem up to the shoulder seam, hacked half a dozen times or so. It didn't seem to be the clean cut of a scissors; it had been damaged most likely with a knife of sorts.

She backed away from him, putting her hands up to her face. 'Why are you asking me? You can't think – you don't think …' she swallowed, before getting a grip on her tumbling thoughts '… did you really drag me up here to accuse me of *this*? How *dare* you.' She stared at him, appalled. Alex shoved the shirt back into the wardrobe.

'What are you putting it back in there for?' Jenna said. 'Bring it downstairs. Ask the others who did this. It didn't happen by itself.'

He sat on the bed and rubbed his face. 'No.'

'You're afraid to insult your siblings, but you're not afraid to insult me, is that it?'

'I don't want to cause any problems. Just forget it.'

'Sorry, but I can't "just forget" that my otherwise intelligent husband thought me weird enough to take a knife to his good shirt, then hide it back in the wardrobe and wait for him to find it. What planet are you on? Don't answer that. I forgot; you're on the planet of Lynes Glen.'

'I didn't mean to sound as though I was blaming you, I asked you if you knew anything about it. There's a difference.'

'Not from where I'm standing. It sounded like you were blaming me,' she flared, unable to believe they were arguing again. 'This is getting better and better. I can't understand why you don't ask the others about it. Someone did this deliberately. When did it happen?'

'I don't know. The shirt was fine when I hung it up after we arrived and I only noticed the damage now when I went to put it on.'

'So basically it could have been anybody.'

'Yes.'

'Yet you don't want to find out.'

'I don't want any confrontation. Not during this weekend. We'll be gone in less than forty-eight hours. Just leave it for now.'

'No, I won't leave it,' she said, the blood rushing to her head. 'I'm going to bring that shirt downstairs right now and find out who wrecked it.' She marched across to the wardrobe but Alex got in the way and stood in front of her.

'Don't do this,' he said.

'Why not? This is a personal insult to you, and you've already insulted me.'

'Jenna, if you bring this downstairs you'll be opening a can of worms that I don't want you to open. Please.'

Something in his voice, an odd note of desperation, got through to her.

'In other words,' she said, 'you're finally admitting that somewhere on the planet of Lynes Glen there is a can of worms?'

'There is, and I don't want to be responsible for opening it.'

They stared at each other in silence. A knot of unease formed in her stomach at the vulnerable look in his face. She moved away from the wardrobe and saw him relax a fraction. 'Why did you drag me up here?' she asked.

'I got a shock and I just needed to … tell you, to make sure I wasn't imagining it.'

It was the first time in months he'd said he needed her for anything at all. But it was coming too late and in the most ridiculous context. She hardened her heart against the soft pull she felt at the unhappy expression in his eyes. She was out of empathy right now.

'So now that you've shared this … piece of crap with me, you're ready to go back downstairs to your loving family and pretend none of this has happened? Of course it'll fall in perfectly with the family-friendly theme for the weekend – the biggest load of pretence I've ever had the pleasure to try and swallow.'

'Jenna, calm down please. We'll be out of here before lunchtime on Monday and it will all be behind us.' He looked as though he was trying to convince himself as well as her, and she realised with a sense of shock that he was on a knife-edge behind it all.

'Why can't you tell me what's going on?' she asked. 'Is this all about the will?'

'Not in the way you think. I can't say any more.'

'Your family sure have some power over you – Lainey, Niall, whoever it is.'

There was a knock on the door. 'Alex? Jenna?' It was Charlotte. 'Mum says are you ready now?'

'Your sister is summoning you,' Jenna said. 'Is she the one pulling the strings?'

'It's not like that at all,' he said, rising to his feet.

'Isn't it?' Jenna said drily.

'We're coming now, Charlotte,' Alex called out.

'Seems like the show must go on, no matter what happens,' she said. 'Although nothing is what it seems this weekend.'

'Precisely. On that we agree.'

She looked at him sharply.

Throwing out his hands in supplication, he said, 'Can't you just go with the flow and take me on trust?'

'Trust is something that vanished from this marriage a long time ago,' Jenna retorted, stalking across to the door. 'Right now I don't trust anyone in this house, and neither should you, after that act of vandalism. Seems to me you've been given a warning of sorts.'

CHAPTER TWENTY-THREE

1968

'This is a fine state of affairs,' Maura said.

Stay calm, Leo told himself, as he pushed away his half-eaten meal. In the last couple of weeks he'd avoided coming to the hotel because he wasn't inclined to face Maura and the things she might say that could put a dent in his glow of happiness. He was afraid to question too deeply why he might allow Maura to dent something that belonged to him, or how he gave her the power to do so.

'It would have been nice to have heard it from you first,' she said, 'rather than Gabrielle waltzing in and lording it over us as she flaunted her diamond ring.'

Gabrielle's innocent joy with her diamond solitaire didn't quite tally with Maura's description.

'I tried phoning you but there was no answer,' he said. He had indeed. He'd picked up the phone in Lynes Glen and called her number – twice – a tiny part of him relieved when she didn't answer. But he'd only been staving off the inevitable moment. 'And she's part of your family,' he pointed out. 'So it was right that you heard the news from her first.' He lifted the water jug and re-filled his glass, taking his time, pretending he was most unconcerned.

'Family.' Maura pursed her lips. 'I don't always set store by that. Blood ties can disappoint.'

'Aren't you happy for me?' he asked.

She seemed taken aback by his direct question.

'Happy, Leo? Of course I am. You're my dear friend. All I want is your happiness. I sincerely hope you find it with Gabrielle and I wish you the very best of luck.'

'Thank you.'

'Have you set a date?'

'Hasn't Gabrielle told you?'

'I didn't like to ask. The engagement ring was enough of a surprise. You only know each other about three months.'

Four months, actually.

'We're going to have a Christmas wedding.'

They had decided they were going to spend Christmas as man and wife. They were getting married on the shortest day of the year, the winter solstice, in the middle of the pure, savage beauty of the season. He could already picture Gabrielle's red-gold hair tumbling around a white furry hood as a splash of fiery colour on that sharply cold day. Picture it tumbling across the pillows of their bed that night. They were spending Christmas in Lynes Glen, cuddled in front of big turf fires. On Christmas Eve, they would put up a Christmas tree in the hall, decorating it together. They were also going to see in the New Year quietly, in their home, then, early in January, he was bringing her to London for a short honeymoon.

Maura's eyebrows rose almost to her hairline. 'So soon? But that's only weeks away.'

Eleven weeks. He felt impatient for them to be gone.

'Why the rush up the aisle?' Maura continued. 'If I'm allowed ask that delicate question.'

'How come it's a delicate question?' he began. 'Oh, I see.' When he realised what she was alluding to, he felt a slow burning rage that she dared to ask. Thoughts of sleeping with Gabrielle, making love to her, fired up every bone in his body, turning them to liquid. But they had agreed to wait until their wedding night and it was none of Maura's business.

'No, you're not,' he said. 'Allowed to ask, I mean.'

She lifted her chin. 'Ooh, sorry I spoke. I can see I touched a raw nerve.'

'If you weren't such a dear friend, Maura ...' he deliberately omitted the rest of his sentence, leaving the hint of his annoyance hanging in the air.

'Look, Leo' – she put a hand on his shoulder – 'it's because we're such good friends that I'm happy if you're happy. I'm overjoyed to think you've found the woman you want to spend the rest of your life with, for better or worse. I think it's great that you and my young cousin are ready to make such a lifelong commitment to each other after only a few short months. It must have been love at first sight.'

'It was, pretty much.'

'Gabrielle's so incredibly beautiful I'm not surprised you fell hard for her. I'm just surprised it's my old and dear friend who has managed to persuade her as far as the altar rails, something none of her previous boyfriends were able to pull off; then again, they didn't have your maturity. But please be happy and know that I'll always be here for you, no matter what happens.'

'Thanks, Maura, I appreciate that. Nothing's going to happen, however. You'll come to the wedding, won't you? I think Gabrielle would like to have you as a matron of honour.'

'I can't be matron of honour, Leo; that's reserved for a married person.'

'Sorry, I must have mixed it up. You'd think I'd know. *Maid* of honour?'

'I'm a bit too old to be a comely maid of honour walking back down the aisle behind the bride. I'll be there all right, on the day, but I think it's best you keep the wedding party to people of Gabrielle's age.'

She was conveniently overlooking the fact that the groom could scarcely be included in that age bracket. In his glow of happiness he decided to let that one go.

The glow didn't last. It exploded in his face the day they met for coffee before her evening shift in the hotel, and Gabrielle told him that her mother was asking questions about him, and sounding concerned that Gabrielle might be following in her footsteps by rushing into marriage with someone she scarcely knew.

'Mum had a bad experience with my father, I suppose she's bound to be worried about me, and it's not as if she can meet you that easily,' Gabrielle said, her voice soft with concern. 'I hate causing her to be anxious like this. I wish she could meet you, then she'd know I'm doing the right thing. She thinks ...' Gabrielle gave a little gulp. She pushed her coffee away and sat forward, resting her arms on the table.

A spasm of anxiety shook him at the serious look in her face. 'What does she think?'

She smiled at him hopefully. 'Maybe we should wait? Until next summer? There's no real rush, is there? In the meantime we could write to her, phone her, give her a chance to get to know you.'

His chest tightened, leaving him breathless. He was glad they were sitting in a booth at the back of Foley's cafe, with no one witnessing this. 'You want to put off the wedding until your mother has a chance to get to know me better?'

Gabrielle's eyes were huge as she stared at him. 'I can't wait to marry you. But we were always so close, Mum and me, I want her to be happy in her new life and not worrying about me. I want her to be happy and excited on our wedding day instead of full of doubts.'

He felt crushed. All his high hopes, all his joy came crashing down, leaving him raw and vulnerable. Was this Gabrielle's way of putting him off? Was she already regretting their whirlwind romance? He might have known it was too good to be true. He'd always been hopeless where women were concerned. What had made him think Gabrielle would seriously be interested in him? She'd had other boyfriends, as Maura had indirectly pointed out, probably with more experience than he had. He was still a virgin, a fact he had not yet admitted to her.

'You're annoyed with me, I can tell,' she said. 'I'll talk her around.'

'What if you can't?'

'I'll do my best.'

'And if your mother won't listen to you, does that mean you'll have a long face coming up the aisle? Or will you want to put the wedding off?'

'Don't look at me like that.'

'Like what?'

'Your eyes … you face … it's all closed up. As if you don't like me anymore.'

'I love you, Gabrielle, I always will, but I don't like to hear you talking like this. Your mother is living her life and we're supposed to be living ours. How come she feels she can tell us what to do from thousands of miles away?'

The mother who was only – he reminded himself sharply – four years older than Leo, having given birth to Gabrielle at the age of eighteen.

'You have it wrong; she's not *telling* us what do to. It was just a suggestion she made. So I could be doubly sure I was doing the right thing.'

Fear of losing her added an edge to his words. 'You've obviously listened to her and agreed with her, otherwise you wouldn't be telling me this. We'd be having a different conversation, one in which you told your mother to trust you enough to make your own decisions. Is everything in your life, in our lives together, going to be subject to your mother's approval?'

'That's not fair. She's only gone four months and we've always been close. This is a big thing, her only daughter, her only child getting married. Naturally it's harder for her being on the other side of the world. As I said, if she just had the opportunity to see you, to talk to you in person, she'd know I was perfectly right to marry you.'

'I can't go to Australia between now and Christmas so that your mother can approve or disapprove.'

'I wouldn't expect you to,' Gabrielle said. 'It wouldn't be possible for her to come back home either. Neither has she got that kind of money, even if we put the wedding off until next summer. Leo, how is this all going wrong?'

'You must have some doubt in your heart to take your mother's words so seriously.' He was pushing her and he knew it, but fear and abject disappointment made him rash, reckless. He couldn't handle confrontation; with Gabrielle, it terrified him.

'You're angry,' she said. 'Why are you angry with me?'

'I didn't expect your mother to come between us.'

'That's not fair. I told you how close we were. I don't like this side of you, Leo. Why can't you listen and understand where I'm coming from?'

'I know where you're coming from. You have your mother worried that you're rushing into marriage. Why is that? If you were all that close, should she not have realised how happy you were when you called her? Heard the joy in your voice? I think whatever way you spoke of us filled her with anxiety. So there must be some worry about us in *your* mind. That is why you want to postpone the wedding.'

They were coming out now in glorious technicolour, the demons that played in his head at four in the morning, nourished by his lack of confidence and lack of faith in himself – the age difference between them, his belief that he wasn't good enough for Gabrielle, the conviction that he was dull and boring and staid, a solitary bachelor, compared to her light, bright, glittering presence.

She twisted her ring around her finger. 'You have no trust in me.'

'This is not about trust.'

'Yes, it is. You don't trust my word, or my promises, you don't trust that I love you enough, and if you can't trust me, Leo …' she shrugged, her eyes sad but resolute.

'If you loved me enough it would have been very obvious to your mother.'

Gabrielle's eyes flashed. 'There's nothing else I can say.'

He didn't know how they had come to this. Fear clawed at his belly and sucked the insides out of him. His head was whirling, making him dizzy, making him nauseous.

'I'm going home,' she said, standing up, a proud glint in her eye. 'Don't follow me.'

'I won't.'

*

He thought he'd been in the depths of despair after his parents had died, but that had been nothing compared to this raw bleakness that bled right through to his bones. For days he couldn't eat, and the sight of his empty eyes in the mirror haunted him, a mocking voice inside him laughing at his foolishness. Of course Gabrielle had changed her mind and had been looking for a handy way out. The university term had started; he was lecturing two days a week, travelling to Galway on a Thursday morning and coming home Friday evening. Outside of that, he lived like a hermit for two weeks, wandering around Lynes Glen at all hours of the day and night. Then one Tuesday afternoon, there was an unexpected knock at the door.

Gabrielle. She'd found her way back to him. She wanted him for keeps. Never again would he doubt her. His heart lifted, a swirl of excitement rushed through his veins, and heedless of his unkempt face, he answered the door. But it wasn't Gabrielle.

It was Maura.

CHAPTER TWENTY-FOUR

Vikki watched in grudging admiration while Lainey took the living room floor in the late afternoon. She deserved a medal for maintaining her upbeat front while the deluge outside increased in intensity and the wind rattled the windowpanes and roared down chimneys.

'I'm going to give each child a sheet of clues,' Lainey said, going through the plans for the treasure hunt. 'They're simple enough, but to be fair to the children, on account of their various reading skills, they'll be paired with an adult.'

'Good,' Niall said, 'I could do with someone's help.' He winked at Vikki.

Vikki smiled back. Now that she had decided to let go of any expectations of a future with Niall, and ease herself out of their friendship in the coming weeks, she was more relaxed. She wasn't watching every word she said or being cautious about every glance, in case she appeared too eager. Somewhere deep inside she felt a little bleak and rudderless, but she'd reinvented herself before and she could do this again. She'd been right, all along, to sense Niall was different, she cared for him more than she'd cared for any other man, but his life was so far removed from hers that it would have proved far too shaming for her to take Emily Victoria Gordon out of her hiding place or have any meeting point between that girl and Niall Blake and now she was freed of this burden.

'The clues are in different orders on each list,' Lainey said. 'So everyone won't all converge in a scrummage on the same spot in the house. At least I hope not. The teams are colour-coded as well.'

'You've gone to a lot of trouble,' Niall said. 'We used to have a right free-for-all when we played this.'

'So you do remember,' Lainey said.

'I remember plenty,' Niall said, giving her a loaded look. It seemed significant, and Vikki wondered if he was alluding to anything in particular.

Lainey went through the pairings for the treasure hunt, putting Ben with Jack, Vikki with Charlotte, and Jenna with Harry.

'You're delegating this to the outlaws?' Ben remarked.

'It'll give you a chance to bond,' Lainey said, with a tight smile. 'Let the Blakes take a back seat for now. Is that a problem?' She raised her eyebrows a fraction.

'I didn't think you trusted the outlaws enough to take the lead in anything.' Ben clearly meant it as a joke, even Vikki could see that, but it was lost on Lainey.

'Didn't you?' she said, her tone of voice dripping saccharine sweetness but the look she gave her husband was quietly furious.

'Of course this leaves you free to have a family pow-wow.'

'We will not be having a family pow-wow,' Lainey snapped.

Vikki averted her eyes. It wasn't surprising that the veneer was coming away from the beautiful family façade. It was too much to expect six adults cooped up together to remain calm, especially if two of those adults hadn't spoken in years, for reasons brushed under the carpet. On top of that, the storm shrieking outside was unsettling whatever threads of tranquillity were left. Vikki glanced at Niall, wondering if he felt it too, but he was smiling warmly at something Jack was telling him and the little boy had all his attention.

'Are you ready, Vikki?' Charlotte hopped up and down in front of her, clutching a sheet of clues.

'Sure, let's get started.'

'Off you go, the winning team.' Niall looked up and winked at her and Charlotte.

'I'll share the prize with you, Niall, so you don't feel left out,' Charlotte said.

Whatever about the adults taking the lead in the treasure hunt, Charlotte was ahead of Vikki at every clue. Which was just as well, as Vikki wasn't too comfortable poking around other people's bedrooms. It was something else, she guessed, that had been designed to support the notion that they were all one big happy family mucking in together.

'I've already played two games of hide and seek,' Charlotte said, 'so I have a good idea where all the clues are sending me. We have to find the red-coloured stars and the team that brings back the most stars wins, but Mum said she's going to give out the prizes equally. I agree with that, because if we won everything there'd be nothing left for Harry or Jack. I like Jack, don't you? Even though he has a funny voice.'

'He probably thinks you have a funny voice as well,' Vikki pointed out gently.

Charlotte rolled her eyes as though it was elementary. 'I know that!'

They found a red cardboard star behind the armchair in Jenna and Alex's room. They found another star, a yellow one, between the folded towels in the bathroom shared between the children and Vikki and Niall.

'We can't take the yellow ones, to give the other teams a chance,' Charlotte said, sticking it back under the towels. 'Or the green ones. They're the rules. Mum likes everything fair and equal.'

To her surprise Vikki felt a tug in her heart thinking of Lainey and the trouble she'd gone to, trying to be fair to all the children as she painstakingly planned this game in advance of the weekend, devising it to make sure they enjoyed it equally and were made to feel like a winner. She must have been very upset when her other carefully laid plans had backfired.

'What's the next clue?' she asked Charlotte.

'It's says where Niall's feet rest. It could be your bed. Don't his feet rest there?'

Uneasy at the thought of the treasure hunt making its way around their bed, poking and prodding, and Lainey there before them, scattering her clue, Vikki reminded herself that it was just harmless fun as Charlotte began to search around the cushions and pillows, and burrow under the duvet. But it wasn't harmless fun when Vikki checked under Niall's side of the bed. There was something resting on the carpet, something gleaming. It wasn't an innocent star awaiting their discovery. She got down on her hands and knees, reached in, and slid it closer to the edge.

It was a knife; a steak knife with a wooden handle and a long, shiny, serrated blade.

Why the hell was she making a habit of finding trouble?

Charlotte heard her sudden intake of breath. 'Can you see a star, Vikki?'

'No, it's just a stray tissue.' Vikki slid the knife towards her and carefully up the sleeve of her jumper, hiding it there, pulling down the cuff and curling her fingers to secure it so that the blade sat flat against her forearm. She got to her feet a little unsteadily. 'I'm going to use the bathroom while we're here,' she said brightly. 'Why don't you look in Niall's shoes? They're over near his travel bag.'

She heard Charlotte's cry of triumph as she went into the bathroom and looked for a safe place to store the knife. The top of the cabinet would do, it would be out of the reach of any of the children, although she had to stand up on the side of the bath and balance herself while she shoved it as far back as she could. Outside, the wind reached a crescendo before pausing momentarily to gather pace in a fresh onslaught.

By the time she rejoined Charlotte, who was gleefully clutching a red star and trying to figure out the next clue, all the fun of the game was lost to her. The knife couldn't have been lying there for any length of time as the surface of it hadn't gathered any dust. There had to be a reasonable explanation. Did Niall always sleep with such a weapon close by? If not, why had he hidden it there? The knife had probably been in too far under the bed for any of the children to reach, but, still, it shouldn't have been there in the first place.

Had Niall put it there because he felt in some kind of danger?

CHAPTER TWENTY-FIVE

Jenna thought she'd never get the gin and tonic into her system fast enough so that she could forget everything in a warm, alcoholic fuzz. The treasure hunt was over, Niall and Ben were organising pre-dinner drinks, and the children were clustered around Lainey as she doled out goodie bags filled with small games, crayons and puzzles.

Since they'd rowed about his shirt, Alex hadn't met her gaze let alone spoken to her. He went out of his way to avoid being within her radius, but, funnily enough, instead of feeling mad with him and embarrassed at the way he was ignoring her, her heart felt heavy that they had come to this.

Was this how it ended? A love affair begun with so much exhilaration and desire? Flickering out in the face of mistrust, detachment, a sense of resentment, as they gradually eroded warmth, passion and togetherness? She took large gulps of her drink, uncaring if everyone noticed she was knocking it back rather quickly. She caught Ben's eye and tilted her glass a fraction. He knew immediately what she wanted and obligingly refilled her glass with the minimum of fuss. If only Alex was half as responsive to her.

'I've sent Erin and Niamh home in view of the weather,' Lainey said. 'We'll manage without them this evening.'

Jenna couldn't believe the stab of visceral envy that streaked through her at the thoughts of getting away from Lynes Glen. 'That's what I should have done,' she said, alarmed at the edge of resentment in her voice, 'escaped into the town instead of being trapped out here in the storm.'

'Trapped?' Lainey rounded on her. 'You sound as if you're a prisoner of sorts. Alex, have you anything to say to your wife?'

Alex didn't even glance at Jenna as he said, 'I'm sure my wife didn't mean it quite like that.'

'Maybe I did,' Jenna said, flashing him a look that he ignored.

'Don't leave us, Jenna,' Ben said. 'Think of the fun and games we'll have here, marooned out in Lynes Glen.'

'Jenna, dear,' Lainey began in her sugary-sweet voice, as if she was placating Harry, 'I agree the storm is a bit of a nuisance but we'll all feel better after we've had some food. Erin and Niamh left everything ready, we just have to help ourselves. Ben, can you give me a hand, please?'

In the dining room, Jenna made a semblance at eating her meal, her appetite gone. So what if Alex didn't want to cause a scene by asking about his shirt, but why couldn't he take her into his confidence? It didn't help that Ben was sitting beside her, sensing her disquiet. They had moved onto wine now, and he made sure her glass was topped up. At every turn she was acutely aware of the nearness of him, the rich tumble of his laughter, the relaxed kindness of him so much at odds with the forbidding demeanour of her husband at the far end of the table that she had an incredible urge to weep into his chest. She caught Lainey studying her at one stage with a calculated glance, and she lifted her glass and swilled her drink, holding Lainey's gaze until the other woman looked away.

Vikki was paler than usual, the younger woman also downing her wine as though she too was finding the going tough. Niall, sitting beside her, seemed to be more attentive to her, but Vikki seemed distracted, playing with her food as much as Jenna was. Looking at the faces around the table Jenna found it impossible to believe anyone would have damaged Alex's shirt, yet she had seen it with her own eyes. Someone had wanted to offend Alex. Or threaten him. Aided by the alcohol zinging around her bloodstream, her thoughts flew in all sorts of directions as questions.

What could Alex have done in the past to have caused such resentment? Had it anything to do with Niall? They were the only two people present who'd had a major falling out, weren't they? Surely Alex suspected that, but why was he so determined to keep the peace at any cost? Then again, they must have pissed off Lainey big time, letting her run between them for years. A can of worms, he'd said. The way things were going, the lid would surely be blasted off before the weekend was over.

'We've got a special dessert this evening,' Lainey said, her eyes expectant as she looked around the table for approval. 'Bread and butter pudding with custard and cream …'

Jenna could almost have written the script and averted her eyes and quietly murmured the words at the same time as Lainey continued, '… one of our favourites when we were growing up.' Beside her, Ben turned a snort into a cough. Still, Jenna forced herself to take a few bites lest she incur Lainey's wrath. She had to admit it tasted delicious.

*

After the meal, Leo went to his room for the night, leaning on Niall's arm. Lainey and Alex cleared off the table and set everything to rights while Ben topped up both Jenna and Vikki's wine as soon as they went into the living room.

'There are plenty of spirits if you want anything else – gin, vodka, brandy …' he said.

'Aren't there enough spirits going around the house as it is?' Jenna quipped. 'I'll let you know as soon as I need something stronger.'

'Sooner rather than later, I bet, the way things are going.'

Lainey came in from the kitchen. 'Right, everybody, we'll get started in half an hour, that'll give everyone a chance to get settled in for the night. Feel free to change into something more comfortable, the children can get into their pyjamas and be ready for bed. I'm going to lead the way and get into mine, this weekend is all about having a chill-out, so please just relax as if you were having a cosy Saturday night in. Ben, can you sort out the nibbles, please?' she called out over her shoulder as she ushered the children upstairs. Alex went with her to help with Jack, and Ben dutifully went into the kitchen.

'How are you, Vikki?' Jenna asked, picking up her glass and going over to sit beside her. She sank into the cushions, noticing that Vikki was still pale.

'I'm not about to get into my pyjamas,' Vikki said, 'so I hope I don't spoil the party.'

'Me neither,' Jenna said. 'Personally I don't care if I spoil any party.'

Vikki shivered, and something in the younger woman's face made Jenna ask, 'Are you feeling all right?'

'Just about.' Vikki grinned, but Jenna sensed it hadn't been without a determined effort to look OK.

'Not the kind of weekend you were expecting?' Jenna ventured.

'Absolutely not,' Vikki said. 'A haunted house, a scary storm, creepy incidents, I can't help wondering what'll happen next.'

The lights overhead flickered, shadowing the room momentarily.

'There you go,' Jenna said. 'The ghost is listening.'

'You didn't find out whatever happened between Niall and Alex, did you?' Vikki asked in a rush.

'Nope.' Jenna shook her head. 'That's still top secret. Why? Any theories?'

Vikki shrugged. 'Just curious.'

'It's all behind them, isn't it? Or so we've been told,' Jenna said.

'You don't believe that?' Vikki asked.

'I don't know what to believe,' Jenna said. 'The only thing I know for sure is that we'll be out of here on Monday morning.'

'I wonder if anything else will go wrong before then,' Vikki said.

'Don't let that worry you, Vikki, if it does it's entirely the fault of the Blakes. They're the ones in cahoots.'

*

The children arrived downstairs in their PJs and slippers. Lainey followed them into the living room, and Jenna did a double take. Her sister-in-law was totally transformed. In place of her dark trousers and blue top, her figure was muffled in a thick, fluffy pink robe and she was wearing equally fluffy pink slippers with matching knee socks. Jenna didn't know whether to laugh or cry. Whatever about the children looking cute and cuddly, surely this was taking the concept of relaxing in the bosom of a family reunion a bit too far? Still, she had to admit there was something touchingly vulnerable about Lainey's efforts to bring relaxation to a whole new level.

'We're going to ignore all that bad weather and have a cosy night in,' Lainey said in her soothing voice. 'Did you microwave the popcorn, Ben?'

'All done,' he said, coming out of the kitchen.

It was another fifteen minutes before everyone was settled. Wine and beer had been topped up as well as cordials for the children. Lainey asked Ben to bring the goodies in from the kitchen and lay them out on the coffee table. The children sat on a rug in front of the sofa, where Lainey joined Jenna and Vikki. The men manoeuvred armchairs around. Ben had the video tape ready. It wasn't an original version; it had been recorded at some stage from the television onto a blank video tape as Jenna saw the title 'ET' on the handwritten label stuck along the side of the cassette in block letters, along with the warning 'Do not tape over'.

'*ET* was one of Mum's favourite films,' Lainey said, with a slight catch in her throat. 'Nice to think all her grandchildren are watching it together, gathered in her favourite spot. She loved Lynes Glen,' she went on a little wistfully, speaking to no one in particular.

It was as if, Jenna thought, she had let down an invisible guard to reveal a softer Lainey in conjunction with her attire.

'Ben will do the honours,' Lainey said. 'The television is

already set up for the VCR. I tested it out last weekend and Ben double checked it yesterday afternoon.'

Ben pushed the video tape into the slot and pressed a button on the side of the television set. The screen went fuzzy for a few seconds, then it sprang into life, but it wasn't the opening sequence to *ET* that appeared.

Even though the picture quality was poor, there was no mistaking what it was; a stretch of shore line, the camera held by an amateur as it swung wildly from the golden sand beneath up to a sky mottled with fluffy clouds, and then it panned around showing a rim of grey-blue mountains encircling calm, silvery water before dropping down to where small, lacy waves rolled up against a patch of shiny wet strand.

The lough. Jenna held her breath. Everyone else seemed transfixed.

There was the sound of laughter and the partial image of a woman appeared in a corner of the screen: a softly curving cheek, a smile playing across her lips, the camera travelling up towards her emerald-green eyes while tendrils of long red-gold hair drifted across, lifted by the breeze. The camera panned back and the woman filled the screen, golden, dazzling, laughing for the sheer joy of it; Gabrielle.

She spoke. 'Hey, give it here,' she said in a musical voice. The camera showed an expanse of sand, Gabrielle disappeared, and the screen went from dark pink to black. She'd taken the camera into her hands because it was now pointed at another person; a man who was using a long, thin arm to shoo the camera away, who, even sitting down, appeared to be tall and lanky, his dark hair thick and wavy and almost down to his shoulders, and to Jenna he looked like an earnest, romantic poet, a sort of George Harrison without the moustache: Leo, much younger.

The camera moved once more, to another woman, also waving her hands back and forth in front of her face in an attempt to prevent herself from being captured on film.

'Ah, come on, Maura, just one smile, please?' Gabrielle said in a coaxing voice.

The other woman relented because she finally took her hands away and smiled an exaggerated smile, lifting her head to emphasise the curve of her neck, leaning back on arms that were outstretched behind her, her red bikini doing little to cover her full figure. The camera panned along, she was taller and heavier than Gabrielle and she even wiggled her toes, showing off toenails painted in varnish to match the colour of her bikini.

The screen went dead. There was a tense silence. Even Lainey sat there, unable to talk. Then Alex got to his feet and strode out of the room.

'What was that all about?' Niall said, turning on Lainey. 'Another crap joke?'

Lainey stared at him for a moment, and everyone seemed to be holding their collective breath until she managed to speak. 'It was no joke,' she said, her voice thin and wavery. 'I've no idea how that got there. Ben, give it to me.'

Ben was already ejecting the video tape and he handed it to Lainey. She inspected it, turning it around in her hands, clearly mystified. 'Somebody must have switched the labels,' she said eventually, in a small voice. 'I'll go talk to Alex,' she said, putting the video tape down.

Jenna stood up. 'He's my husband. Surely if anyone deserves to know what's upset him it's me.'

'Let me look after this,' Lainey said, holding up her hand in a stop signal like a policeman on point duty. 'It's family stuff.'

'And I'm not family?' Jenna felt the blood rush to her face.

'You are, of course,' Lainey said. She stared pointedly at the children, who were beginning to realise something was amiss, and then back to Jenna. 'We can talk about this later, OK?'

'We certainly will,' Jenna said, deciding not to push it with Lainey for the sake of the children.

'Ben, can you check the other videos please?' Lainey continued. 'There should be a few suitable ones there. Niall, check the drinks please. Alex and I will be back in a sec.'

The hell they would, Jenna decided, subsiding onto the sofa. Alex in a mood was not someone who could be placated easily and Lainey would find it difficult to get him to return to the room. Niall silently topped up her glass, doing Lainey's bidding, but his face was set in taut lines and it was obvious he'd had a shock. Vikki seemed to have had a shock as well because she went out to the kitchen and came back with a glass of water. More, Jenna suspected, to give herself something to do rather that sit there numbly.

Ben gave her a reassuring wink before he checked through the videos, slotting one in, and there was a general lightening of the atmosphere when *The Muppets* appeared. Instantly the children were engrossed. Even Vikki pretended to be watching it, although Niall was sitting with his legs stretched out and Jenna knew by him and the pulse in his cheek that he wasn't seeing anything except the video clip of his mother down by the lough.

To Jenna's astonishment, Lainey reappeared shortly afterwards with Alex in tow. Her husband's face gave nothing away as he sat back down on the chair he had vacated and picked up his bottle of beer. Lainey gave Jenna a soft smile as she sat down beside her on the sofa.

Je*sus*. What kind of a hold did Lainey have? It was as if she had some kind of power over Alex, now that they were together on home territory. Whatever it was, it went far above and beyond the family solidarity she'd experienced between them in New York. God knows what was putrefying in that can of worms. The sooner they got out of here, the better.

Outside the wind moaned around the house, shrilling like a madwoman, hurling itself against the window along with a deluge of rain. A bang and a crash sounded from outside and beside her, Jenna felt Vikki jump, the younger woman keenly affected by the tense atmosphere.

Niall got up, went to the window and peered out. 'I think that was some garden furniture falling over.'

'Are you sure? I don't know how you could see that between the dark and the rain,' Jenna said, heedless of whether she sounded provoking.

'There's still some light in the sky,' Niall said, taking her literally. 'And there's nothing else out there that could cause that noise.'

'I hope not,' Jenna said. 'That wind is like some kind of monster, roaring around the house. I hope the roof isn't about to blow away because that's what it sounds like.'

'Sure that's nothing,' Lainey said. 'You'd want to be here during a real storm.'

'If this isn't a real storm I don't know what is,' Jenna said crossly. She meant more than just the weather and wondered if anyone had picked up her implication. Alex was staring at the television with a laser-beam attentiveness as though the story of *The Muppets* had the most profound meaning for him. Once upon a time he used to look at her like that.

Then there was a flash and all the lights went out.

CHAPTER TWENTY-SIX

I wonder who'll crack first. Not me. I'm made of sterner stuff, a quality that was learned the hard way.

I like the way the storm has been boiling around the house, setting everyone's nerves on edge. The taint of old resentments is slithering through the atmosphere, although everyone is still pretending it's fine. The wind is whistling through gaps in the windowpanes, blowing through crannies in the frame of the hall door, making a high-pitched screeching sound, like someone lamenting a death.

Hah – that makes me want to laugh, because it seems to me that it's lamenting in advance. Nobody's dead – yet.

The house is creaking, shuddering under the onslaught of the gale, doing its best to withstand it. You could imagine it might just lift up and blow away, but it was built square and solid, put together to withstand storms of this nature. Outside, a shed door bangs, like an erratic drumbeat, and even though it's irritating, no one has gone out to secure it, as no one wants to face the battle across the back garden in that torrential rain and howling gale. Something rolls around outside on the terrace, one of the ancient planters, slamming against a table leg every so often, hurling itself on the rebound against the wall of the house, and the grinding noise of terracotta on concrete sounds like a slow, medieval torture weapon.

The raw, unbridled strength of the storm suits me. It mirrors the pent-up anger and sadness choking my insides; anger that has been boiling in my head since I found the diary, along with sadness that has scourged my heart and inflamed every nerve in my body. Just when the wind is at its zenith, the rain pummelling the windows so ferociously that even inside the house you can feel the cold moisture of raindrops trickling down the back of your neck, there is a flicker and a pause, and then another flicker, longer this time, and everything is plunged into darkness.

A slight complication. I hadn't been expecting the electricity to go. I hadn't planned for this but I should have known it was a possibility. It might be a problem, but I've waited too long for what I want to let it fall apart now.

Saturday night; only a matter of hours before I have my beautiful revenge.

CHAPTER TWENTY-SEVEN

In the sudden, shadowy darkness Vikki sensed rather than saw Niall leaping to his feet.

'What the f—' he said, cutting short his expletive when he remembered the children.

There were cries of disappointment from them when the television screen went dark at the same time as the room was plunged into blackness.

'Don't panic, we'll get this sorted,' Lainey said, in a panicky voice. 'There should be candles, plenty of them. We always kept a stock in case of this eventuality, we just need to find them.'

'And matches,' Niall pointed out.

'And how do you propose we find them in the dark?' Alex asked.

'Try the main light switch first,' Lainey said. 'It might be just a couple of fuses.'

'I doubt that,' Alex said tautly. There was the snap of a switch but nothing happened. 'No joy.'

'Of all the rotten luck,' Lainey said. 'Just when things were going so well.'

So well? Vikki was glad no one could see her face.

'Kiddies, stay exactly where you are,' Lainey said. 'You're not used to this house and I don't want any of you bumping into the furniture. The last thing we need is an accident.'

'You OK, Vikki?' Niall asked.

She tried to think of something funny, to be her usual devil-may-care self, but it failed her. 'I'm OK.'

There was a rattle as Lainey pulled back the heavy curtains, but there was little to see apart from thick ropes of rain streaming down the darkened windows. The sky wasn't yet pitch black, there were streaks of dark grey visible in between the low-hanging, full-bellied clouds and it gave them a glimmer of light, enough to make out the shapes of people moving around the living room.

'This is a new kind of game,' Ben said to the children. 'We'll have some fun with this as soon as we get sorted.'

'I think there's a flashlight and a couple of torches in the cloakroom,' Lainey said. 'Has anyone a mobile down here? It might give me enough light to find it.'

Alex gave a short laugh. 'Thought mobiles were banned.'

'They were until now,' Lainey said impatiently.

'I've a torch on mine, but it's upstairs,' Niall said.

'Has anyone got one nearby?' Lainey asked, sounding decidedly tetchy.

'I have,' Vikki said, feeling foolish as she took it out of her back pocket. She'd kept it close by on the off-chance that she might have been able to receive a text from London. From Mia, as opposed to any conference gossip. Right now Rosella Inc seemed like a different planet, but something from Mia, a few nuggets of wisdom reminding her to hold on to her kick-ass attitude would have been welcome.

'Can I borrow it?' Lainey asked. 'Just until I find some torches. And we need to check on Dad.'

Vikki felt she was surrendering part of herself as she keyed in her pin code and passed the mobile across to Lainey. Holding the glowing screen in front of her, Lainey went out into the hall, along with Alex and Niall. The children scrambled after them, despite Lainey's protestations, wanting to help find the torches.

'Thanks, Vikki, you jumped in ahead of me,' Ben said, producing his mobile. 'This is just as important as finding a torch.' He held the tiny screen light over the coffee table, picked up the wine bottle, and refilled both Vikki and Jenna's glasses. 'OK, ladies?'

Vikki listened to Ben and Jenna sparring off each other, both of them a little more relaxed now that the Blakes were out of earshot.

'Ben!' Jenna said, sounding amused. 'You of all people should have been obeying the mobile rules! Now if you could just order a cab to take us off this mountain and back to civilisation, we'd be laughing.'

'I'd have to climb halfway around Slieve Creagh for a signal.'

'Why didn't you impart that vital information before now?' Jenna said in mock exasperation. 'I'll go. I've good climbing shoes and a head for heights. Although "halfway" in Ireland probably means about five or ten miles. I think it's a rescue helicopter we need and not a taxi, it wouldn't manage the roads in this storm.'

'I don't think a helicopter could land in this either.'

'So I was right, we are trapped,' Jenna said.

'Seems we are. But don't say that again.'

'Trapped? Is it upsetting you?'

'Everything about this weekend is upsetting me.'

'You'd never think that to look at you.'

'Good.'

A short time later, Lainey appeared with the children, ahead of Niall and Alex. The children were using a small torch to light the way, but whatever way Lainey was directing the big flashlight between her hands, it cast a glow upwards onto her face that made her look sepulchral.

Vikki jumped and put her hand to her mouth. Lainey pretended not to notice, merely taking Vikki's mobile out of her pocket and handing it to her. 'Thanks, Vikki. Right, let's get this show on the road. I've checked Dad and he's asleep. If we find another torch I'll leave it with him. We need candles in here, and in the kitchen. I'm not sure how many there are, some of us might have to go to bed in the dark or take turns with the torch.'

Vikki tried in vain to visualise how that final option might work, but it was Jenna who commented dryly, 'Some of us might prefer to grope our way around in the dark rather than creep around the corridors in our frilly negligees,' she said. 'So long as we're careful who we grope.'

'And it depends on who's creeping around the corridors,' Ben said.

'I wasn't suggesting that,' Lainey said frostily, directing the beam of the flashlight so that it fell squarely on Jenna's face. 'We'll work out something but we need to plan for the power being out for the night, I can't see repair crews getting out in this weather.' She slid the beam around the group. 'Alex, if you hold the flashlight for me I'll check the sideboard for candles, and then we can try the kitchen presses. Niall and Ben, will you use your mobile light and have a look in the library and the sitting room?'

'Yes, ma'am,' Ben said.

'Can we play hide and seek?' Charlotte asked.

'I'd prefer you to stay here, you might trip over something,' Lainey said.

'Aw, Mum, you're spoiling the fun. We want spooky, don't we, Harry and Jack? We might even see Jack's ghost. What did she look like again, Jack?'

'Quiet!' Lainey said, sounding for once, Vikki thought, like she was coming to the end of her patience. 'That's enough, Charlotte. You're staying here with Vikki and Jenna. We'll just be a few minutes, then we'll have a couple of games and bed.'

There was the sound of disagreement from Charlotte, who flung herself onto the sofa beside Jenna, but she seemed to know better than to argue with her mother. Vikki decided she was best staying quiet for now. Eventually, candles and matches were found, Niall and Ben even arrived back with a packet of tea lights from the sitting room, and there was shadowy light cast around the living room and in the kitchen. A fat candle was put on the landing for anyone going upstairs, and tea lights on saucers were left ready.

Vikki observed all this activity, slightly detached, but not detached enough to see there was something bothering Niall. The video clip had been a shock; she'd felt his startled reaction and even though she'd still been trying to figure out what a sharp knife was doing under his bed, her heart had gone out to him when the image of a beautiful and laughing Gabrielle had appeared.

He still seemed to be in a sombre world of his own as the candles and matches were organised, and once when he met Vikki's glance she smiled reassuringly, as though to let him know she was fine, but he gazed at her unseeingly, his eyes drifting instead to where Lainey was coming back in from the kitchen with small treats for the children.

'Why don't we have a little concert?' Lainey suggested, her voice anxious despite the note of cheer. 'A sing-song, with the children? Charlotte has a lovely, sweet voice. Would Jack sing, Alex?'

Charlotte put her hands up to cover her face. Alex looked at Lainey in annoyance. 'A sing-song? What brought this on? I thought we had games to play, or haven't we?'

'It'll be like old times. Remember? On nights like these, we'd hold a concert and do our party piece.'

'You mean you would,' Niall said, addressing his remark to his sister.

Vikki was surprised at the coldness in his voice. What had happened to the amazing Lainey?

'You joined in too,' Lainey said, not seeming to be perturbed by him.

'I didn't have much choice, did I?' he said. In the flickering candlelight, Niall looked as though he was challenging his sister. It was the kind of look that Vikki would have quailed under. She had the strange feeling he was alluding to something else besides a sing-song. What choice could he have been talking about? And what had happened to the tight-knit Blake unity? Between Alex, and now Niall, it seemed to be unravelling a little at the edges. She glanced over at Alex, who was leaning back against the sideboard, observing his siblings, an inscrutable expression in his eyes.

'None of us had much choice, Niall,' Lainey said, and now there was definitely a hidden meaning in her words. They stared at each other; it was a stand-off of sorts, Vikki realised. Six-year-old Jack must have sensed something in the atmosphere because he went across to Jenna and whispered in her ear.

Jenna reached out and smoothed his hair. 'It's OK, love, you don't have to do anything like that. No one is expecting you to sing. Why don't we play one of the games?' She turned to Lainey. 'What have you got that's suitable for the children?'

Lainey shrugged. 'We've quite a selection, snakes and ladders, ludo, Kerplunk …'

'Snakes and ladders,' Jenna said.

Lainey pulled out the game from the storage box and Jenna got off the sofa and knelt by the coffee table, organising the counters and the dice. Niall used that opportunity to sit down beside Vikki.

'Hi,' he said, squeezing her hand.

'Hi, yourself,' she said. *Where have you been?* she wanted to say. *You've been lost to me. Had you forgotten I was here? And what the hell is really going on?*

Typically, the words died in her throat. Niall was smiling at her, his eyes warm and appreciative, and all she wanted was to soak that up and not disturb the moment. His thigh was pressed against hers, sending ricochets of pleasure shooting through all her cells, and she revelled in the moment when he brought up his arm and curved it around her shoulders. She wanted to sink back into his embrace, absorb the feel of him beside her, and relax into it in the flickering candlelight.

'Thanks for being here,' he said.

'You seemed to be getting on OK,' she replied.

'Yeah, well' – his voice was soft – 'it might seem like that.'

Then she remembered the knife, the cold, hard shine of the serrated edge under his side of the bed and she sat bolt upright.

'What's wrong?' he asked.

'Nothing,' she said, her heartbeat galloping. How would she tell him? He was bound to notice it was missing … if he'd put it there. Anxiety formed a hard ball inside her and in the shadowy light everything took on a slightly menacing, surreal air; Lainey watching Jenna play snakes and ladders with the children, Ben down on his hunkers helping Jack and Harry, Alex watching too, slightly apart from everyone else, an observer with narrowed eyes flicking from Lainey to Niall as though he was trying to figure something out.

What, though?

CHAPTER TWENTY-EIGHT

Even after three games of snakes and ladders, giving everyone a chance to win, the children didn't want to go to bed in the darkness. Sitting with Niall's arm around her, Vikki couldn't blame them. The living room was cosy in the dim lighting and she wouldn't have fancied braving the dark hall or stairwell.

'I've changed my mind about Jack's ghost,' Charlotte said. 'I hope we don't see it.'

'You won't, promise,' Lainey reassured her.

'It's not *my* ghost,' Jack protested.

'I didn't see it, *you* did,' Charlotte pointed out. 'So it is your ghost.'

'You didn't see it 'cos you had your eyes closed.'

'I never went asleep in the dark before,' Harry said.

'Do we really have to go asleep in the dark?' Jack sounded worried.

'It won't be quite dark,' Ben said reassuringly. 'I'll tell you some stories.'

'I'll be there too,' Jenna said.

Lainey clapped her hands in full schoolteacher mode. 'Right, kiddos, going to bed in the dark will be a big, huge adventure. You'll remember this for years and years. And it's way past your bedtime. We have all of tomorrow and you'll want some energy for that.'

'Why? What are we doing tomorrow?' Charlotte asked.

'It depends on the weather,' Lainey said. 'We'll see in the morning.'

'You mean you haven't got it all planned out?' Alex said. It was the first time he'd spoken in a while and Vikki noticed that even Jenna looked up, surprised at the harsh tone in his voice.

'I've got a few ideas,' Lainey said vaguely. 'I was leaving tomorrow a little loose, depending on how today went. Dad wants to talk to us so we'll have to see what time suits him.'

'That should be interesting,' Niall said.

There was a heavy silence, during which the shed door outside, buffeted by the wind, gave an alarming slam. Vikki jumped slightly and Niall tightened his hold of her. She tried to recall what he'd said to her about the weekend, and his father wanting them all together. Family business, perhaps the future of Lynes Glen. At eighty-three, Leo wasn't going to go on indefinitely.

There was a short discussion as to how they'd safely manage the candles and the children. Lainey suggested leaving a couple of tea lights on saucers up high, out of reach, with the adults taking it in turns to check on them regularly.

'I'd prefer to have a torch left on,' Jenna said. 'I think it would be safer.'

'I'm not sure how long the batteries will last in this.' Lainey pointed to the big flashlight.

'Oh, for God's sake,' Niall said. 'Surely they can have it for now, and we'll deal with it later if we have to.'

Surprised at Niall's uncharacteristic irritation, Vikki took a large gulp of wine. She saw Lainey lift her chin and looked at her brother meaningfully, her mouth in a thin line, her face set as though she was trying to send him a silent message. He stared back at her, his eyes dark pools of hostility until something rippled across his face, a hint of sadness and regret, and everything was shuttered, like a mask going on. Lainey gave a tiny shrug and for a moment her face was filled with regret and she looked punctured, as though some of her fighting spirit had faded.

As though she was totally oblivious to the charged atmosphere, or she didn't care about it, Jenna stood up. 'Right, that's sorted. Who fancies a bedtime story in the torch light?'

There was a happy chorus of assents and Vikki spotted the grateful look that Ben directed at her. He too, got to his feet. 'You relax, Lainey, I'll look after this.'

Vikki was tempted to follow Ben and Jenna as they trooped out with the children. It would have been far preferable to sitting here, alongside the combined weight of the Blakes and their secrets swirling in the shadowy air. Lainey busied herself tidying an already tidy snakes and ladders box. Niall poured more wine. Alex disappeared into the kitchen and came back with a whiskey. Outside, a fresh gust of wind caught a plant pot so that it ground noisily across the terrace. It crashed against something and he swore.

'That's it,' he said. 'I'm going out there to sort it out. That and the shed door.'

As if on cue, the shed door banged.

'You'll be drowned,' Lainey said.

There was a taut silence.

'Remind me, why don't you,' Alex said in a hard voice. 'It won't be the first time someone in this family drowned.'

'Alex! I didn't mean it like that!'

Even Vikki couldn't help feeling sympathetic at the note of desperation in Lainey's voice. Clad in her fluffy pink dressing gown, she seemed defenceless.

'Didn't you?' Alex said. 'I think someone, this weekend, is doing their very best to remind us of what happened.'

Lainey flinched. Vikki shrank back into the sofa. Niall seemed to have forgotten she was there, as had the others.

'That's mad,' Lainey said, her voice shaking a little with uncertainty.

'Is it?' Alex said. 'One by one, reminders of what happened, of what we were and what we did to each other, are popping up all over the place.'

'Like what?' Lainey asked, her voice quavering.

'Even before we got here, Jenna saw something out at the lough. We managed to dismiss it – I think – but Jenna's not given to fanciful imaginings, or stupidity of any kind. She's bright and clever and the most down-to-earth woman I know. She says it as it is. It's a wonder she put up with me for so long, all the baggage I'm carrying. If she said something was there, then it was there.'

Vikki was sorry Jenna was upstairs with the children. Alex's face had changed when he was talking about his wife and his voice had softened. There mightn't have been any overt displays of affection between them this weekend, but there was no doubt he loved her.

'You shouldn't be carrying any baggage, Alex,' Lainey said. 'At least not from Lynes Glen.'

'Oh yeah? Did you seriously think any of us could ever forget?' he said, staring at his sister.

Forget what? Vikki wanted to ask.

'And by the way,' he continued remorselessly, 'don't try to distract me and ignore what Jenna claims to have seen. Then there was Jack. And his ghost, who sounded remarkably like what – or who – Jenna saw.'

'Jack? But he's only six.'

'I know, I know, and he could have been dreaming, out of his normal routine, never mind a transatlantic flight, excited about his cousins, etcetera ... how come he picked his ghost out of a photo he had never seen up to yesterday?'

Vikki didn't dare breathe. She waited for Niall to say she'd also seen someone down by the lough en route here, but he didn't. He seemed to be totally stilled by the exchange between Lainey and Alex.

'Why are you trying to blame me?' Lainey asked. 'And what reminders are you talking about anyway?'

She was stalling, Vikki guessed. She knew full well what incidents Alex was alluding to. Even Vikki knew something was definitely 'off'.

'Things like where did the dead birds come from?' Alex spat. 'Who goes up to that godforsaken place anyway? They didn't just fall into that box and assemble themselves in a row; they looked like they'd been carefully arranged.'

'You're being spooked over nothing,' Lainey said heatedly. 'You said it yourself yesterday, someone must have left them there by sheer coincidence. You get ramblers around the mountains occasionally who are too lazy to clean up after themselves.'

'I dismissed it yesterday because the children were all ears and I didn't want to upset them any further. Who knew we were going to be there? Who planned that trip?'

'You sound like you think *I* put them there. On purpose.'

'You would have had the opportunity. You were here before any of us.'

Lainey shook her head and laughed. 'This is ridiculous. Besides, you and Niall knew what I had in mind. I checked it with Dad to make sure he was OK with everything and ran the ideas by you first, remember?'

'The idea of arranging old photos across the piano was mad. You didn't run that by us first; it was your clever idea, Lainey, designed to remind us, you said it yourself.'

'Yes, remind us of the time we were happy as a family.'

'Who wants to go back in time to that particular summer?' Alex snapped. 'I certainly don't. And the smashed photo – just, like, out of thin air?'

'The children – Charlotte must have been messing with that.'

'As if she'd be bothered. So who interfered with the video? Charlotte could hardly have done that. Where did the ruby necklace come from?'

'You hardly think I set all that up? Any one of us could have done that since Friday afternoon. I wasn't here all that long before anyone else. Your flight got in at five yesterday morning. What were you doing all that time?'

'You know we stopped off in Galway to catch our breath. I knew once we got here it would be full-on.'

'You weren't a million miles away. You could have done a round trip and set up those dead birds yourself.'

'Now you're being crazy.'

'No more crazy than you are,' Lainey said heatedly. 'You still blame Niall and me for what happened. Next you'll be blaming me for the storm and the power cut. The weekend was all Dad's idea, not mine. I was delighted you both accepted and we had the chance to be together, like a normal family again. Why do you think I'd scupper this?'

'He didn't leave us with much choice, did he? Following up his kind invitation with an ultimatum of sorts.'

'Does that matter in the grand scheme of things? We're here, and it's about time we were all together; he can't have many years left to live, and now you're conveniently avoiding my comment. Why do you think I'd try and spoil a family reunion I've wanted for so long?'

'Because you haven't forgotten, because you still blame us, or more precisely, me, for the way everything was ruined. So you're throwing reminders in my path all the time. Jenna hasn't a clue what's going on this weekend. It was a wonder she agreed to come with me at all, I've cancelled so many things this last year on account of work, yet she came and I feel stupid and guilty that I'm not coming clean with her.'

Vikki could hardly breathe. They had forgotten she was there. Even Niall had forgotten she was sitting beside him.

'We agreed. All of us,' Lainey said. 'Remember?'

'This weekend someone has broken that agreement. There have been too many off-the-wall hints and innuendos all set up to rattle us. I haven't even got to the part about my shirt.'

'What shirt?'

'My torn shirt.'

Lainey stared at him blankly. To Vikki's eyes, she either didn't know what he was talking about or she was a consummate actress.

'I put it hanging in the wardrobe when I arrived on Friday evening,' Alex said. 'Between that time and this evening, it's been slashed to ribbons.'

Slashed? Something icy ran through Vikki's veins.

'I don't believe you,' Lainey said.

'Do you think I'm making it up?' Alex said, his anger palpable. 'Someone went to the wardrobe, took out my shirt, and damaged it. Deliberately. It wasn't a coincidence, or a mistake. I very much doubt if it was a stray hiker who just happened to wander into Lynes Glen. I was so ... gobsmacked I even asked Jenna if she knew about it. Jenna ...' he rubbed his face, shook his head. 'I'll never forget the look in her eyes. She was totally insulted I could even ask her such a thing. She's barely talking to me now and I don't blame her. So between that and everything else, how can I *not* think someone is playing me for a fool?'

His gaze swung from Lainey to Niall.

'Hey, you don't think I had anything to do with all this?' Niall finally spoke.

'You're the one who could have had very good reason – aren't you?' Alex squared up to him.

There was a sharp intake of breath from Lainey and she dropped her head into her hands. Even Alex seemed surprised at the words coming out of his mouth. His eyes widened a fraction as they hung in the air, but it was too late to take them back and the tension fizzed between them, all pretence of family unity gone.

Vikki sat frozen to the spot. *Niall*? What could Niall have had to do with Alex's torn shirt? Her London-Irish guy with the quirky smile? Was there any connection between Alex's shirt and the knife she'd found under Niall's side of the bed? A knife that could have been tossed there in a hurry. There was a tightness in her chest that pained her.

Then Lainey gave a funny little gulp and began to cry.

CHAPTER TWENTY-NINE

Jenna found something restful about putting the children to bed with Ben. He was patient with them as they cleaned their teeth by torchlight, the relaxed atmosphere in their bedroom so different to the tension shooting around the living room walls downstairs. His unruffled calm seemed to transfer itself to the children because there was no fretting about going to sleep in the shadowy darkness or the prospect of a ghostly visit later that night.

After he tucked the children into bed, Harry and Jack into a double bed and Charlotte into a small, single divan, he made himself comfortable beside the boys and proceeded to make up a story about Luke Skywalker and Hans Solo visiting Lynes Glen, trekking to Infinity Hill and the fairy fort along with the children, and they joined in, adding further exploits to the tale.

Jenna relaxed alongside Charlotte. She could stay there forever, listening to his mellow voice, glancing at him occasionally, his face in the dim light, his warm eyes meeting hers, and although the children were between them, they could have been in a world of their own. She could quite easily have lain alongside him and slipped in under the curve of his arm, turned her face into the warmth of his chest and listened to his heartbeat. The prospect of this felt so right, she was quietly amazed. Yet Ben couldn't have been more different from Alex. And he was someone else's husband.

Worries that had nibbled around the edges of her heart over the last year came to the surface once more. Would Alex have married her had Jack not been on the way? Did he regret their hasty wedding or resent her for putting him in that position? What about her – would she have married someone like Alex had she not been pregnant? Still, being here now, in the room with Ben was so soothing to her jangled insides that it was like being cast under a spell and it was easy to ignore her anxieties. Nothing seemed to exist outside this room and the sense of connection she felt to this man.

Harry fell asleep first, lulled by his father's voice, then Jack. Ben smiled across at her over their sleeping faces and her heart leapt.

'You can go,' Charlotte said in a drowsy voice.

'Are you sure, pet?' Jenna asked her.

'Yes, I'm going asleep now.'

Jenna kissed her forehead, and Ben came over and kissed his little daughter, tucking her in. 'We'll leave the torch on in the corner,' he said, 'and the door will be ajar.'

Outside a candle was lighting in a glass bowl in the alcove, giving a faint glow and casting long, flickering shadows along the landing down the stairwell. Jenna paused by the banisters. 'You were right,' she said, her voice a murmur. 'You do a mean story. I got so relaxed listening to you that I forgot about the storm outside, never mind the storm on the inside, and I could have fallen asleep too.'

'The storm on the inside?'

He was standing right beside her, hands on the banisters, too close for comfort, but she was powerless to move.

'Alex is hardly talking to me, we've had another row. I wish to God we'd never come here. Lainey seems to be—' Jenna shook her head, conscious she was talking about his wife. 'Then on top of all the weird things happening, there's Alex's shirt ...'

'What's wrong with Alex's shirt?'

'Someone took a knife to it, and he had the gall to ask me if I knew anything about it.' Suddenly she was fighting tears. The bitter-sweet proximity of this man unnerved her, so close and yet a million miles away.

Ben looked mystified. 'I don't get you. A shirt?'

'Come on, I'll show you,' she said, feeling like they were two conspirators as she picked up the candle and went into her bedroom. She set down the candle and took out the shirt from the back of the wardrobe, bringing it over to the flickering light so that Ben could see the damage. He gave a low whistle.

'Jeez, what happened to that?'

'I don't know, Alex found it like that this evening, asked me if I knew anything about it, and we had an almighty row.'

'That happened here? In Lynes Glen?'

'Yes, but I've no idea when. It could have been any time after we arrived and it could have been anyone. We've all been up and down the stairs.'

'This is ... serious stuff. Does Lainey know?'

'No. Alex said he doesn't want to open a can of worms. His exact words.'

'Christ. This is unreal. If Lainey saw this ...' Ben subsided on the side of the bed. 'I'll be glad when this weekend is over, I can't believe so much has gone pear-shaped and I fear for Lainey. It's been so much of an obsession with her that I ...' He paused, thought the better of what he was about to say. 'If we can't pick up the pieces of a normal marriage after all this, I fear for that also.'

Jenna sat down beside him. 'We're the same ... Alex and I ... we've been so living on the edge this last year that I felt Alex coming back to his roots and facing whatever demons he left behind would make us or break us. Right now it seems more of a breakage.'

It was easy to talk to Ben in the dim lighting. She could have sat there all night, talking to him. She could have turned around and kissed him, allowed herself to fall into his arms, allowing herself to fall back across the bed. Her body was crying out for a warm hug, a tender touch, for a man to appreciate her as a desirable woman. She was appalled at how effortlessly she could imagine herself making love to Ben.

'What do you mean about demons?' he prompted.

Jenna sighed. 'Alex won't talk about them, and he'd probably hate me for telling you this, but he has nightmares every so often. Sometimes, in his sleep, he's even trying to fight me, in bed. When I wake him up, he says he doesn't remember anything, hasn't a clue what the nightmare was about, but he must know something.'

'Why do you think they'd have anything to do with here, though?'

'I've heard him muttering "Niall" and "Lainey" in the middle of his nightmares.'

'Oh dear.'

'So you see, it's all about the Blakes, isn't it?' she said, her hands twisting over and around together in her lap. 'They seem to be protecting each other … or something. We're just the supporting cast in this charade, aren't we?'

'I don't know what to say …' He fell silent for a moment and put a comforting hand on her agitated fingers, quietening them. They gazed at each other in the flickering candlelight, Jenna's heart hammering. She had a powerful longing to close her eyes and melt into this man, and she was terrified she might betray how she felt.

Above the wind and the rain, there came another noise. Jenna strained to hear. 'What's that?'

It sounded like someone crying, and it was floating up the stairwell. Her scalp pricked. As she stared at Ben, she knew by his face he'd heard it also.

'If this is some weird kind of ghost,' she said, her voice shaky, 'we're not imagining it. We've both heard it.'

'I don't think it's a ghost,' Ben said, getting to his feet. 'I think it's Lainey.'

CHAPTER THIRTY

1968

When Leo opened the door to Lynes Glen, he knew instinctively he should have turned Maura away. But he faltered and was lost.

Her face wreathed in concern, she looked much as she had when she'd called in the aftermath of his mother's death. Doing much as she'd done then. Embracing him in a comforting gesture, her eyes gentle and compassionate. Going back out to her car to bring in some shopping; milk, eggs, fresh soda bread, butter, rashers and sausages, a beef casserole, already cooked, thick with meat and fresh vegetables, steaming with flavour.

A bottle of whiskey.

That was a new departure, it hadn't been brought the last time.

She sent him up for a bath first, lighting a cosy fire in the living room while he wallowed in hot, sudsy water, and the scent of the turf fire along with the aroma of the casserole being heated upon the stove assailed his nostrils as he came downstairs in fresh clothes.

The small table drawn up to the fire and a deep bowl of succulent casserole put in front of him along with some buttered, crusty bread. Second helpings washed down with a glass of creamy milk.

Then a small glass of whiskey and another … and another … falling into it comfortably, becoming relaxed in a way he hadn't been for days, the slow draining of the tension in his stomach, the softening in the rigidity of his bones, leaving him empty and weak.

Maura's calm, slow smiles. Her hand on his arm. Her face next to his, blurry in the firelight. The warm familiarity of her, different now that she was so soft and yielding, her breath on his face, the ache in his heart crying out for human contact.

A moment of hesitation and then she kissed him, warm and lingeringly. His mind slowed down, stopped, in the background something hazy flickered, but it was far away and easily disregarded in this restful bubble of heat and soft skin and comfort and total ease.

A moment of protest when her hand brushed past the front of his jeans.

His automatic, reflexive reaction. *God, no!*

'Ssh, relax,' she murmured, kissing him on the mouth. 'You want this as much as I do.'

Did he? He was powerless to stop an unbearable ache of need; that was all he knew.

Somehow her blouse was opened to the waist – had he done that? – and her creamy skin was brimming over a nest of white lace. She pulled his head down to her cleavage and undid something at the front of her bra so that the lace fell away and heat engulfed him when his face was pressed against her full breasts.

There was no turning back. He was on fire, with need, with hunger, with lust, with an ache deep inside him that cried out for fulfilment. He heard himself groan, heard her sighs of pleasure, her gentle whispers of encouragement; he was surrounded by a dark, intoxicating heat, knew it was scorching him indelibly, but he fell into it and allowed it to consume him.

*

Maura didn't wait for breakfast the following morning.

Leo woke early, a heavy regret weighing him down and pinning him to the spot while he thought feverishly about the polite necessities of getting her out of his bed and home. Polite? Hah! Who was he kidding? That had gone out the window hours ago. There had been nothing polite about the way he'd responded to her last night and his face flamed.

Maura made it easy for him. 'Good morning,' she said, turning to face him in bed, a satisfied smile curving across her face, as though it was the most ordinary thing in the world to wake up beside him.

'Good morning,' he said, feeling frozen with dismay and self-disgust, unable to handle this and hoping it didn't show on his face.

She stared at him for a moment, then she slid out of bed, gathered her clothes unselfconsciously and went into the bathroom. In the few minutes she was in there, he hastily made himself decent. A shower and a shave would have to wait until later.

'I have to go,' she said, when she came back out of the bathroom, not making any reference at all to the previous night.

It was clear from the guarded way her eyes flicked over his that she sensed his deep disquiet.

Too late. The damage had been done. That was how he felt – damaged goods in some way.

*

In the immediate aftermath of Maura, Leo's days took on a surreal air, split between beforehand and afterwards. He was going through the motions, afraid to think too deeply or analyse what had happened. He couldn't bear to think of Gabrielle. Whenever she slammed into his thoughts, which was every other second of the day, his heart felt scalded. He'd thought he would have come to her as a virgin, but that would never happen now.

It had happened with Maura, but he didn't feel happy or satisfied as he imagined people must after such a night of passion – they'd made love at least three times, him shocked at the need unleashed in his body, and full of self-loathing that he'd been unable to contain it. Maura had even supplied the condoms, bought across the border in Derry. Quite clearly she'd planned it – she scarcely went around carrying condoms on a daily basis. He was annoyed to think he'd been reduced by loneliness and a fog of alcohol, but still, when he rose above his self-loathing, his memories of Maura that night were her softness and warmth, the good food, the comforting bath, the ease of the whiskey slipping down his throat and warming his belly, the care she'd taken of him, the way she'd loved every inch of his body, unrolling the condoms almost reverentially as though he was some kind of sex god instead of a clueless virgin, the words she'd murmured soothingly afterwards: *We understand one another, we're two of a kind, you and me.*

It hadn't been the first time for her, she'd known her way around a man's body too well: how to touch, how to excite, exactly where to stroke to bring him to the brink of desire. She'd been so sure of what she was doing, it didn't matter that he'd been a novice, she'd made it easy for him to follow her lead.

A week after he'd slept with Maura, he finally braved the town. It was a matter of necessity, as he needed to go to the bank. The town looked different, the rooftops and outlines of buildings sharper, light bouncing harshly off the walls as though everything was cast in a more unforgiving light, but he knew it was an outward reflection of how he felt about himself. He was seeing everything through guilty eyes, convinced everything about his night with Maura was shrieking out through his pores.

He was coming out of the bank when he saw her across the road, walking briskly towards the supermarket. She was wearing a white top and jeans and her beautiful hair rippled down her back, the colour of burnished gold. He'd picked a time she was usually at work in the hotel, but here she was and he feasted his eyes on her, his heart clenching. Everything had changed irrevocably in the last week and now she seemed unattainable and out of reach. He'd intended going to the supermarket himself, he was short of essentials, but now he decided to walk up the road in the opposite direction, where his car was parked. He would wait in the car until he was satisfied that she was finished doing her shopping and there was no risk of bumping into her.

Fate had other things in store. Even though he waited a full thirty minutes before venturing back down the road, relieved and disappointed there was no sign of her as he did his shopping, when he arrived back at the car, she was sitting on the low wall in front of his parking spot.

'Hi, Leo,' she said, her voice subdued.

'Gabrielle.'

'I'm sorry,' she said, 'so very sorry for upsetting you so much. Can we start again? Pretend we never had a row? Go back to the way we were the first night I showed you how to jive? Better still, go back to the first night you read your poetry to me? I miss you, Leo. I'm not eating or sleeping, and there's a pain in my chest that won't go away. There's a pain behind my eyes with the tears I'm holding back all the time.'

She was pleading with him. He'd never had a woman plead with him before. To experience this now, and from Gabrielle, who sounded as though she was suffering as much as he was – apart from that one night, that one lapse, his conscience reminded him.

He struggled for words. They felt like boulders in his mouth. 'I don't think … we can go back …'

'Do you still love me?'

'Of course. I never stopped.'

'That's all that matters, isn't it?'

He shook his head. 'You don't understand.' He couldn't bring himself to put it into words. *I've slept with someone … your cousin Maura, by the way. We had sex three times in one night.* As it went through his head, he was astounded freshly by the magnitude of it. Gabrielle looked so beautiful, so sparkling, that the words roaring in his head made him feel sick. 'I can't.'

'Can't what? Can't love me anymore?'

'You deserve better than me. Go home, Gabrielle. Forget you ever knew me.'

Something in his face connected with her, and with a stifled sob, she got up off the wall and walked away.

*

'You needn't look so scared, Leo, I'm not going to tell her.' Maura stood in the hallway in Lynes Glen. She'd called with a small parcel of books that had arrived in the post office for him. He hadn't asked her into the library or the living room. It was a wonder he'd answered the door to her, he felt so sick.

'It makes no difference now,' he said. 'We're over.'

'You know she lost her job?'

'What? How?'

'Not concentrating on her work, dropping plates full of food, hanging round like a pale ghost as though she was going to faint and running off crying in front of customers. I didn't sack her, the manager did.'

'God.'

'So you'd better kiss and make up, hadn't you? The sooner the better.'

'How can I, after what we did?'

Her mouth curled. She looked at him disdainfully. 'For God's sake, don't be such a prude or take life so seriously. It was just a quick ride, a little bit of sex, another notch to my belt. I've forgotten all about it already. That's how much it meant. It wasn't even all that …' She shrugged, and left the rest of her sentence hanging so that he could only guess what she'd been about to say – further humiliation for him.

'I thought …' he stumbled for words, a peculiar relief coursing through him. 'I thought you had ideas about us.'

'Ideas?' She made a dismissive sound. 'In my dreams. It'll never be "us". I knew by your face the morning after that you didn't want to wake up beside me. That freed me from any silly notions I might have had.' She straightened her shoulders. 'But I've more pride than to let that kind of nonsense get to me. I'm not about to be anyone's second best. I'll be sorry to say goodbye to the prospect of running Lynes Glen,' she said, her glance roving around the hallway. 'It's a fine house. Any woman would be delighted to make this her home. And now that Gabrielle will be homeless …'

'Homeless?'

Maura raised her eyebrow. 'Without a job, how can she afford to pay her rent?'

'But – what is she supposed to do? They can't throw her out on the street.'

'Can't they? Anyway, as I said, our little secret is safe with me.'

'I thought you'd be delighted to spread the word.'

'And have my cousin, and the whole town, know that you rejected me for her?'

'I didn't do that.'

'No? Who were you thinking of when you woke up to find me in your bed? Who were you wishing was there instead of me? It's OK, you needn't answer that,' she went on, obviously taking pity on his flustered face. 'But if you think I'm going to admit to anyone that you turned me down in favour of her, even though I went all the way with you? No thanks.'

'Gabrielle wouldn't see it like that.' He sprang to her defence.

'How do you know what she's capable of? You only know her a wet week. I'm not risking it. I don't want to be the laughing stock of the hotel. I have my pride.'

'You wouldn't be a laughing stock, and it wasn't like that – you were kind and generous with me.'

'Kind! Generous! What happened to sexy? Jesus, I don't know whether to laugh or cry. I don't hear you saying you can't live without me, that you're mad about me, that I send your heartbeat racing …' She looked at him, a question in her eyes, while silence stretched between them, a silence he was unable to break.

She raised her chin. 'Gabrielle won't hear anything from me, I promise you that, but you never know, word might leak out, eventually, sometime. I'll relax in the knowledge that you might have chosen her, but you'll be looking over your shoulder from time to time. Anyway, besides bringing your post, I came to tell you that I'm off to England. For good.'

'How come?'

'I'm not sticking around here to watch you two love birds walking back down the aisle, or stepping out as a married couple.'

'Who says that's going to happen now?'

'I'm saying it. I know you're mad about her and you better go and make up before she fades away completely. I'm shaking the dust of this narrow-minded country off my shoes and making a brand-new life for myself, beginning next week. The whole world is waiting for me. There are far better things out there for women these days besides small-town Ireland and Lynes Glen.'

'I don't know what to say.'

'Wish me luck – that's all you have to say. But remember one thing, Leo' – she smiled crookedly – 'I'll always know that I had you first. You'll always know that too.'

*

In the end it didn't matter that he'd lain with Maura first. It turned out to be insignificant in the wonder of emotions that Gabrielle stirred inside him. The pleasure of making up with her and holding her in his arms was so perfect that the row had almost been worth it. In Maura's absence, Gabrielle was rehired in the hotel dining room, which gave her some independence in the weeks leading up to their wedding. Leo arranged for Lynes Glen to be painted and decorated, cleaned and polished from top to bottom. He bought a new bed and bedding, sleeping in one of the spare rooms so that it would be pristine for their wedding night.

They married at midday on a December day that glowed with winter solstice sunshine. Some of Leo's relations on his father's side came from Dublin, and his mother's two sisters and husbands along with cousins travelled from Limerick, the same group who had attended his parents' funerals. Colleagues also came from the university. Gabrielle had some family there and Maura's father gave her away.

Leo scarcely noticed any of these, apart from being surprised they came, patting him on the back, happy there was something good to celebrate. He only saw Gabrielle, a vision of startling beauty in her classic, unfussy wedding dress. Over that, she wore a white woollen cloak, the hood rimmed with fur.

They had a wedding meal back in the Creaghbara Hotel. The manager and staff did them proud, decorating the room with winter flowers, candles and holly, good silverware and glittering crystal, and there were speeches and toasts, as well as music and dancing. It slid along the surface of his senses as though it was someone else's wedding and his face ached with the effort of talking to other people. At six o'clock that evening, Gabrielle changed out of her wedding dress into a green velvet dress, and, still wearing the cloak she'd been married in, they left in a rush of best wishes, telling everyone that they were headed to a secret location.

At last they were alone together.

Leo drove them back to Lynes Glen, where he lit cosy fires, switched on lamps, poured some wine, and in the library – not wanting the first time to be in his bedroom – he drew Gabrielle down onto the big rug in front of the fire and they lost themselves in the wonder of each other.

*

Their lives were perfect, each year bringing some new joy to celebrate.

There were the babies, Alex first. He stared down at his tiny son, amazed that his love for Gabrielle and hers for him had produced this miraculous human being. Gabrielle sat back against the pillows of a hospital bed, exhausted but triumphant, pale-faced but luminous. He was afraid to hold his son at first, but Gabrielle encouraged him to pick up the sleeping infant, and as he steadied the warm weight of him in his hands, his heart swelled and he knew he was holding the very meaning of life itself.

His joy was doubled the following year when Lainey arrived, a quick birth this time, and his tiny daughter stared at him with unfocussed eyes as though she already knew him and he felt he had always been waiting for her, but hadn't realised that until now. Then a few years later, Niall arrived, and their family was complete. He loved that they were all tiny replicas of their mother, and that he was surrounded by constant reminders of her.

Their home life was content, fun even, Gabrielle filling the house with her effervescent joy, putting all her energies into loving him, and loving the children, giving them a happy childhood, giving him time and space for his poetry. Giving him inspiration that fed the spring inside him so that it was easy to find the colour of the words in his head and land them on paper, one after the other, building them up as you would oils on a canvas. Occasionally the dark moments he'd endured during their brief separation came back and acted as a foil for the glory days. He began to be successful, to win awards, but it meant nothing to him without her.

After ten years of marriage, he loved her more than he ever had, delighting in the way she made life in Lynes Glen an adventure for the children and a total bliss for him. Right up to the end, he still took her hand and they jived together across the living-room floor if a suitable song came on the radio or television. When the children were young they laughed and clapped their hands. In their teens, that laughter turned to embarrassment, and as they left adolescence behind and finally transformed into communicable adults, they watched their parents dancing across the living room floor with soft indulgence.

Sometimes he is still there, holding Gabrielle's hands in his, she as light as thistledown, twirling under his arm, strands of her hair flying around like filaments off a dandelion clock in the breeze, her face alight with happiness. When he awakes and stares at a pitch-black, four-in-the-morning ceiling, he feels the pain of his heart breaking over again.

Because just when he least expected it, when his children were starting to make their own way in the world, and Gabrielle and he were about to write a new future together, the life they had built together over the years, lavished with layer upon layer of love and care, came crashing down around him.

CHAPTER THIRTY-ONE

Jenna hurried down the dimly lit staircase behind Ben. Alex was already in the hall, his arm around Lainey. In the candlelight, their reflections threw monster shadows on the opposite wall. A fresh gust of wind hurled itself against the hall door, shrieking through tiny gaps like a coven of witches. Jenna shivered. From what she gathered, Alex was trying to calm Lainey, but however gently he was trying to placate her, it wasn't working. Lainey had stopped crying but was shaking her head at Alex even as she dried her tears.

When Ben reached the end of the stairs, Lainey went into his arms.

Ben stroked her head. 'Hey, don't go upsetting yourself.'

Lainey drew back slightly. 'I can't help it, my beloved brothers seem to think I'm out to scupper the weekend.'

Ben rubbed her arm. 'I'll have a word with them.'

Lainey blew her nose. 'Thanks, but I'll do my own talking. I want to sort this out once and for all.'

'Alex?' Jenna said. 'What's going on?'

'I don't know. That's what we're trying to figure out.' His voice was unusually subdued. He wasn't pretending everything was fine and that chilled Jenna. 'Are the children settled?' he went on, as Lainey and Ben went into the living room.

'Tucked up and fast asleep,' Jenna said.

Alex stood there, momentarily at a loss. 'I wouldn't mind being tucked up in bed right now. With you.' To her surprise he cradled the side of her face in the palm of his hand in an affectionate gesture. There was something tender in his eyes as he gazed straight into hers that brought a lump to her throat. It was too much, coming on top of the rainbow of emotions that had whirled about her, back in the bedroom with Ben.

'Really, Alex?' Her voice was sharper than she'd intended.

'Yes, really. I'll be glad when the business here is done and it's just the three of us.'

'I'll be glad when I have a better idea of what's going on in your head,' Jenna said. 'There have been too many secrets and silences between us. I don't even know what kind of business you're talking about.'

He caught her hand. 'Look, Jenna, I—' Then he paused, as though he'd checked what he'd been about to say.

'I can't stand here any longer if you can't bring yourself to talk to me. I might find out more from your sister.'

In the shadowy living room, Ben was refreshing drinks with the aid of the candlelight.

Jenna went into the kitchen to get a glass of water. Out here, a tea light flickered on the table and the room seemed alive with dancing shadows. She poured her glass, relieved to return to the living room. That too seemed surreal, with the family grouped around like figures on a stage, the guttering candlelight wavering around their faces, the tension almost tangible.

'I don't know why anyone could think I'd try to spoil this weekend,' Lainey said, her voice quivering with emotion, her words directed to her brothers. 'Surely you know this family has always meant everything to me? How could I, or any of us, forget the wonderful years we had growing up here? They were just perfect. We had great parents, a magical childhood, and such hopes for the future, until it all' – she gulped – 'went mad.'

She paused; no one dared say anything. Jenna's gaze slid around the room. Vikki had shrunk back into the sofa and seemed frozen to the spot, Niall sat forward with his elbows on his knees, frowning as though he was trying to figure out where his sister was going with this, and Alex was bolt upright near the bookcase. Although Ben was standing close to Lainey, his arms were folded across his chest, his head bowed as he stared at the floor. In her puffy dressing gown, Lainey seemed alone and defenceless.

'Like you both, I forgot about my hopes and dreams after Mum died,' Lainey said. 'Like you both I put them to one side, and I stayed on here for almost five years, trying to keep some kind of life going on for Dad, and the semblance of a united family.'

'You didn't have to do that,' Niall said.

'Didn't I?' she challenged him. 'Someone had to,' she said bitterly. 'Dad couldn't be left on his own – he was devastated – and both of you were gone.'

Niall seemed about to protest but Lainey jumped in. 'Not that I blamed you. All of us ended up with our lives in ribbons and our dreams in tatters. At least I made it to Dublin, but London must have been a let-down for you after your plans for South Africa.'

Jenna caught the startled look that rippled across Vikki's face. The younger woman sat forward as though she was trying to catch Niall's attention but he studiously avoided making eye contact with her.

'And as for you, Alex' – Lainey turned to her elder brother – 'the streets of New York must have been a far cry from your Hollywood dreams.'

It was Jenna's turn to be jolted. Pinpricks of unease skittered about in her head. When had Hollywood featured in Alex's plans? *Hollywood*? What the hell had happened to make him forgo that kind of dream? Alex was staring at Lainey as if willing her to shut up, but there was no stopping her.

'So we all have reasons to be resentful,' she said, wrapping her arms around herself. 'But if I blame anyone for how I feel or where I am, I blame me. Because I'm stupid and silly enough to care too much about this family. I've spent years being pulled between the two of you, standing in the middle, trying to be the glue that holds everyone together, walking on a tightrope between you two, afraid of saying the wrong thing, trying to keep the lines of communication open, instead of looking after my own marriage and family. Isn't that right, Ben?' She wheeled around to face him. 'You need to hear what I'm saying just as much as my brothers do.' She paused, but nobody spoke.

'It's a wonder Ben stayed married to me for so long,' Lainey went on, her voice shrill. 'It's a wonder he didn't tell me to cop on to myself, to put less energy into the Blake family and more into the Connolly family. Right from the start, he knew how much my family meant, how much I was always trying to keep the peace. We even' – she swallowed – 'got married in Rome, although Ben would have far preferred a big Irish country celebration with all his relations and cousins. Instead to suit me, we had a small wedding, abroad, because I didn't want to rock the boat with either of you. I knew you wouldn't both come home together, so I thought it was best to take the decision out of your hands. I've been trying to keep everyone happy, but I know now it just doesn't work like that.'

All of a sudden, Jenna's thoughts were running wildly in different directions. Lainey seemed so totally honest yet utterly vulnerable as she stood there. Why had Ben allowed Lainey to be pulled between her two brothers, fretting about keeping the peace? He might appear to be a man who was relaxed and very much at ease, and she'd found that restfulness attractive compared to Alex's edgy tension, but maybe he was too laid back for his own good, and the good of his wife. Then again, he'd probably been ultrasensitive to Lainey's sad circumstances, afraid to interfere or take a stand.

'So now, here we are, all together again, for the first time since that summer,' Lainey said tremulously. 'Wonder upon wonder, everything I'd ever wanted was happening, and guess who organised getting the house ready, and the food, and all the preparations, big and small, and yet someone thinks I'm trying to *sabotage* the weekend?' Her voice rose as she looked from Alex to Niall. She pulled a tissue out of her dressing gown pocket.

Darts of unease slithered around Jenna in the face of Lainey's upset.

Ben, at last, took action. He put a hand on Lainey's shoulder. 'Hey, it's fine. *You're* fine, you're brilliant, we'll sort it,' he said, ushering her over towards an armchair. Lainey shook off his hand but nonetheless, she sat down.

Alex blinked and shook his head. 'Jesus, Lainey,' he said, his voice husky, 'I wish you wouldn't get upset. I'd no idea you felt … that strongly.'

'Didn't you?' Ben said, a touch of belligerence in his tone.

Alex looked vaguely surprised at Ben's intervention. 'Sorry if I made you feel torn in two, sis, or accused you of messing up the weekend. I was out of order.'

'Same here,' Niall said. 'But maybe I'm missing something – didn't we all agree to forget what happened that summer and move on?'

'You make it all sound so glib, Niall,' Alex challenged him. 'Did you find it that easy to forget? Or is it still there, eating away at you? Lainey certainly didn't forget, nor me. How does it feel to be around me again after all this time? Were you tempted to finish what you started?'

Lainey looked at him indignantly. 'Alex, for God's sake—'

Jenna's patience finally dissolved. 'Alex, darling, I'm not sure what this is all about. Apart from the obvious power cut, and I'm not trying to be funny, but I'm totally in the dark as to what happened that summer, as I guess Vikki is, and probably Ben?' She threw a glance at Ben. His face was expressionless as he looked at her. She remembered how she'd been tempted to melt into his arms a short while ago and her stomach churned. She'd have to process that later.

Her husband gave her a defeated look that wrenched her heart. 'I'm sorry, Jenna, the three of us agreed to stay silent on what happened. We were all in it together.'

'Except,' Lainey said, 'one of us seems to be trying to break that silence with all the fun and games that are going on this weekend. It's not me, I can assure you.'

'Nor me,' Alex said. In that moment, Jenna believed him.

'Certainly not me,' Niall said.

Lainey lifted her chin and looked at her brothers in turn. 'Then one of us is lying.'

CHAPTER THIRTY-TWO

14 August 1995

Lynes Glen is more magical than ever this summer.

Alex, Lainey and Niall are like exotic movie stars fizzing around against the perfect backdrop of glittering sunshine days and long, warm evenings. Lainey wants to capture as much as she can with the new camera Leo bought her for her birthday. She coaxes Alex into a photo leaning by his car – not that he needs much coaxing, his car is his pride and joy. She begs Niall to pose on the diving board down by the lough, and comes home gleefully saying she has the best photo ever. To her amusement, Niall and Alex have a play fight over this, each claiming their photo is the more superior. I can still hear the musical sound of her carefree laughter echoing around as they argued the toss.

Then Lainey asks me to take one of her by the curving staircase in the hallway when she's all glammed up for a party, saying her photo will blow her two brothers out of the water.

She loves the photos so much that she goes into the town and has them framed, putting them up on the piano in the sitting room, making room alongside other family photographs. The sight of them all lined up together is so beautiful it gives me a funny kind of ache in my heart and I don't know why.

We are dining outside on the terrace this evening, something that's not always possible in this part of the world, so we are making the most of the good weather while we can.

Every single word of this diary entry is scorched on my brain. I know it off by heart. It sounds so happy and innocent yet it wasn't long after she'd written these words that she left this world far too soon and in a manner no one should ever leave. It pains me to realise she probably didn't know then how soon it would all be over.

In less than twenty-four hours, this will be avenged …

CHAPTER THIRTY-THREE

Summer, 1995

If he was to choose one word to describe the summer of 1995 – up to the day before his life became a desolate hell – Leo would choose the word 'shimmer', because it seemed to him that for a few wonderful weeks the world around him and everyone in it glowed with that luminous quality.

The weather was unexpectedly sunnier and warmer than normal, and there was a succession of days when the gardens around Lynes Glen, the terrace to the side, and the landscape unrolling off to the west of the house shimmered under a band of thick heat. The air was mild to begin with in the misty early mornings, then hotting up during the day, and staying sweet and warm into the long, scarlet twilights, carrying the scents of the flowers on the terrace mingling with the resin from the forest.

The heat held the forest in a silent grip; the thickly rimmed trees were still and stationary and hushed with languor, silhouetted with intense clarity against the sky; the sky itself, changing from soft morning baby blue to a deep afternoon blue, to a faded pearly evening glow before it bloomed with red and purple sunsets. The mountains soaked it up, the hazy blue summits and veiled green valleys relaxing into the languor as though it was their due, the peaks of Slieve Creagh basking benignly as though they'd been cast under a spell.

Against all this, his wife and children shimmered.

It seemed fitting that the weather had chosen this summer to show off what it could do best, because it was quite possibly the last summer that the family would all be home together.

His sons shimmered; it was in Alex's glinting eyes and sparkling joie de vivre as he moved about the house. After three years of living and working in Galway, when he'd come home for regular weekends, he was back under the roof of Lynes Glen, arriving in early July with all his worldly goods jammed into a rather snazzy-looking car – Leo was hopeless with makes and models – relaxing at home before he embarked on a new career and headed for America to follow his dream of acting. Although he had qualified and worked in IT consulting, his part-time theatre work had finally paid off and he had screen tests and casting appointments set up for early September in Hollywood.

Leo thought he was being very brave and courageous to follow this path.

Niall had a different drumbeat to follow – from a teenager, he had spent his spare time freediving and scuba diving around the Killary fjord, but having stayed close to home for most of his nineteen years he was off to South Africa and beyond, also in September, to improve his skills, gain further qualifications and spread his wings at the same time. He too shimmered with expectation, and his enthusiasm for the coming months and the adventures before him was like a contagious glow.

Leo soaked up the sparkling presence of his sons, letting it flow through to his bones, as if he was trying to imprint it there forever, whether it was their footfall on the stairs, the low rumble of their laughter on the terrace, Niall standing in the kitchen, his mouth full, yet another bowl of cereal in his hands, the roar of Alex's car reverberating around a countryside held captive by the heat as he took the precarious bends along the narrow road to Lynes Glen.

Then there was Lainey, his precious, beautiful, only daughter. He was selfishly relieved that although she too planned on moving out for good, it was only to be as far as Dublin, and not America, like Alex, Gabrielle's secret favourite. Lainey wafted through the house, trailing scent like the sweetest of flowers, the glisten of her freshly washed hair, the tinkle of her silver bracelets – his amazing daughter. Hugged into her dressing gown in the early mornings, she looked like an innocent, transparent teenager in her clean face, bare of make-up; fashioned like a beauty as she prepared for a night out, sparring mischievously with her brothers as though their combined energies lit a spark inside her, the twinkle in her eye as she sparred with him.

It was the summer when Gabrielle glittered and glowed and looked amazingly beautiful. The summer was her element; she blended into the season seamlessly.

'It's going to be a wonderful few weeks,' she said at the beginning of it all. 'We're going to enjoy this special time. I'll have all my beautiful darlings back together in the nest for a while. Oh Leo, it'll probably be the last time we're all together like this, what with all their great plans to conquer the world. Won't you miss them terribly?'

'Yes, I will. We'd better make the most of every day.'

'I'm going to wrench every good moment out of it and forget about September. I can't bear the thoughts of saying goodbye to them all.'

'It's not really goodbye, and it was only us in the beginning,' he said. 'We were perfectly happy. We will be, still, if we want to be. We can do different things with our free time.'

'I wonder where our sons got their itchy feet from. Not you Leo, anyhow.' She laughed gently. 'Wild horses wouldn't tear you away from your beloved Lynes Glen. I hope Alex doesn't find his time here too quiet and boring after Galway.'

He took her hand. 'It's not quiet and boring, it's incredibly beautiful and peaceful, and every day here with you is a bonus.'

'Even after more than twenty-six years of marriage?'

'Especially after that. You mean more to me now, as though every day has added to that joy.'

'I hope I can prise you out of your study some of the time, so you can talk to your sons.'

'Of course.'

This summer, surrounded by her family, the love spilled out from Gabrielle's pores and radiated about her so that she glided about the house like a fairy godmother. Always the nurturer, she kept the fridge, larder and drinks cabinet full, she had spruced up the house in anticipation of these weeks, adding little touches here and there, candles in nooks, fragrant wildflower arrangements in jugs, big fluffy towels, new cotton sheets. She delighted in buying new garden furniture, a table and chairs, squashy cushions, lanterns for thick pillar candles, an awning over the terrace to provide shade from the sun, and a couple of sun loungers, happy in the knowledge that they would get plenty of use out of them.

She filled terracotta pots and arranged trellises with colourful plants and fed and watered them judiciously so that they spilled over like a joyous chorus and formed a multicoloured backdrop to the lazy breakfasts and coffee breaks held on the terrace, and the blooms exuded warm-scented air during evening drinks in those sultry summer evenings. Gabrielle moved between the terrace and the garden in a swirl of iridescence, in floaty kaftans and flat, jewelled sandals, her hair caught up so that tendrils floated around her face, and her fine skin covered from the sun so that the scent of coconut sunscreen always plunged him back to that time.

It was a near-perfect few weeks, a bubble in time during which his children laughed and joked and talked about their hopes and dreams for the future, their plans and big ambitions, confident with the optimism of twenty-something youth that everything would work out, and there was no sign of the catastrophe about to be unleashed. He moved around his wife and children and Lynes Glen in a circle of burnished light, unaware of the darkness that had to follow as surely as night follows day.

Because, at the beginning of August, Maura came back.

And three weeks later, Gabrielle was dead.

*

'We have a visitor, Leo, you'll never guess ...'

He'd just arrived back from the town, where he'd been to the stationers, selecting some pens and notebooks. He'd been glad to get home to Lynes Glen, out of the hot stuffiness of the car, and he'd been looking forward to the cool of his library. As he crossed the gravel driveway, the welcome sound of Lainey's laughter and the waft of music from her ghetto blaster reached him from the sun-warmed terrace. It was the day after her birthday, and they'd had a lovely celebration for her the night before.

In the hallway, Gabrielle diverted him. She was smiling and happy, and looked beautiful in a flame-shaded kaftan that floated around her calves. Her toenails were painted in a soft pearl colour.

'... she's come all the way from London, home for a visit,' Gabrielle went on, laughter and excitement bubbling in her voice.

Something faltered inside him, began to tumble down – it was the sensation of his heart dropping to his feet, but he realised later it was the walls of his life as he knew it, tumbling down and collapsing in a heap.

Gabrielle was ahead of him moving back down to the living room, a swirl of exquisite, scintillating beauty. He wanted to stay forever in this moment, as they were, perfect and complete. It flashed before him: all the mornings he awoke beside her, calm and tranquil, all the nights they fell asleep in bed together, relaxed and at ease, taking the ordinary succession of their days in between for granted, not appreciating the absolute treasure they represented.

Through the window overlooking the terrace he saw Lainey lift a languid arm, silver bracelets glittering as she picked up her drink. He wanted to freeze this moment also. But his gaze was drawn to the armchair by the window and she smiled at him, a dark, voluptuous, provocative smile.

Maura.

CHAPTER THIRTY-FOUR

21 August 1995

I'm finally admitting it – I don't think I can bear it anymore, the way Leo looks at her, his eyes like hot coals, his gaze following her around at all times. What has she got that I haven't? No one else seems to exist for him right now.

This was a big mistake.

My heart is in ribbons. Can jealousy kill you? That's what it feels like, a thick black tide of envy scouring through my head and my limbs. Sometimes it suffocates me, when I can't take it any longer, I go blank all over and it recedes slightly, leaving me weak and empty.

It's hard hiding my feelings from Alex, Lainey and Niall, but that's what I must do. Put on a good face. Keep smiling. I don't want them to witness my pain – it would reduce me in their eyes and ruin everything. They say the summer is finally going to break and thunderstorms are on the way. That suits my mood because there are times when I feel agitated and turbulent.

Then there are moments when I'm tempted to do something wild and reckless …

It was so difficult to read this entry. It squeezed me dry. I felt her pain. I felt her dark, stormy mood and the last few words jumped out at me like a horrible premonition …

CHAPTER THIRTY-FIVE

One of us is lying.

In the oppressive semi-darkness, the words echoed in Vikki's head, the casual yet convincing way Lainey uttered them leaving no room for any doubt. She froze as Niall flung himself out of the chair and disappeared out the door. She was unable to react, while the wind whined outside and Lainey began to cry again, soft sobs that made Ben scoop her into his arms and induced Alex to mutter something about needing a stiffer drink before he disappeared into the kitchen.

'What's up with Niall?' Jenna said to her quietly, sitting down beside her.

'I'm just about to find out.' Vikki stood up, her legs shaky, her mouth dry.

'Good luck. He seems a nice guy.'

Vikki took a saucer with a tea light and went out into the hall. The flickering candlelight from the alcove on the landing threw eerie, elongated shapes that danced across the darkened hall, in conspiracy with the shadows caused by the tea light. Gusts of wind pummelled the hall door as though they were trying to break in.

With fingers the consistency of jelly, she pushed open the door to the sitting room holding her tiny light aloft, and she called Niall's name softly. He wasn't there. The photo frames on the piano gleamed silently where the candlelight licked over them and she jumped. She went back out into the draughty hall and through to the library. Niall stood by the window, hands in the pockets of his jeans, looking out to the black, turbulent world outside.

'Niall? Are you OK?'

He didn't turn around. 'Vikki. Sorry about all this.'

'What's the matter?'

Nothing but silence. Dense, impenetrable silence, coming from Niall, surrounding him like an invisible wall. Her words seemed to bounce off that wall like ping-pong balls against the might of Slieve Creagh.

'You can tell me what's bothering you,' she tried again. 'I'm happy to listen.'

'Forget it,' he said, his voice rough. 'You're better off staying in blissful ignorance.'

'Why?' She couldn't walk away and let this go.

'I shouldn't have brought you here, it was another mistake.'

Another mistake. Her heart bled. There was no sign of the warm intimacy of earlier that day, when she'd sipped water from his cupped hands up on Infinity Hill. He was a stranger to her in a way he'd never been before.

'I thought you wanted me here; a friendly face, you said.'

'It was wrong of me,' he snapped. 'I should have kept you away from this shite. You don't want to know what I'm capable of doing. Just leave me, Vikki.'

Even though she quailed at the tone of his voice, she stood her ground. 'Why, what are you capable of doing?'

He remained silent but she felt the turmoil emanating from him in waves. She sensed a terrible darkness within him and knew if she went out of this room and left him to it, he would be trapped there still. Images of all the times they'd spent together – laughing and talking, joking, playing it light and easy, while they skittered around the surface of both their lives – spun through her head like a swiftly turning kaleidoscope. What had he been hiding all that time? But it didn't matter what he'd done. This man's happiness and peace of mind was more important to her than her own and nothing he could say would change him in her eyes.

'Didn't you hear me? I asked you to go.'

'Where exactly can I go to?' She lifted her chin and tried a different approach. 'There's a wild storm outside, or hadn't you noticed? I'm stranded here.'

'You'd hate me if you knew the real me,' he said.

'Would that bother you?'

'I'm dangerous.'

'I figured that out a long time ago.' Dangerous to her heart.

'I'm not being flippant, I mean it.' He finally turned around from the window.

'Niall,' she began, hesitant, 'we all have our dark side.'

'Go away. I know you mean well, but you haven't a clue what you're talking about. Or who you're dealing with.'

She'd nothing to lose. It was already over, whatever they'd

shared. She'd be fading out of his life soon enough, come their return to London. She moved closer, her heart hammering, blood pounding in her head. 'I'm not going anywhere, Niall Blake. I want to know why you consider yourself dangerous because I don't think you are, not for one minute. Tell me why I'd hate you – go on, I dare you.'

To her shock, he pulled her close, his arms on her waist, his mouth pressed against hers. Her senses reeled with the physical contact of his lips on hers, with the solid familiarity of him and she would have fallen down, only for his arm clasped her tightly to him. As suddenly as he had pulled her to him, he let her go, and she had to grab the top of an armchair for balance.

'I almost killed a man, right?' he said, in a strangled voice. 'I'm not a good person. I should have kept miles away from you, but you were so lovely to be around, so nice, funny and kind … I couldn't resist you.' His voice broke. 'Christ, Vikki, do yourself a favour and get the hell away from me as soon as you can, you deserve better.'

'Who did you almost kill?' she said softly, already guessing the answer as a few pieces of puzzle fell into place for her. 'Don't worry, I'll get out of your life if that's what you want, so you can tell me anything, it won't make any difference.'

There was a charged silence. Niall sank down into the armchair she was leaning against and rubbed his face with his hands.

'Alex,' he said, his words blurred through his fingers. He took away his hands and looked up at her, his face a pale oval. 'I almost killed Alex.'

She'd half-expected that answer. She stayed leaning again the armchair and spoke into the semi-darkness. 'But you didn't.'

'Only because Lainey risked her life and jumped between us.

She saved both of us, Alex from being killed and me from being a convicted murderer.' He drew a long, shaky breath.

'I can't imagine you hurting your brother in any way, not in a million years. You would have stopped in time.'

'That's the thing … I don't know.'

'Niall – what you're saying … something terrible must have driven you to this.'

'It was just after Mum died. We were all over the place, the three of us. Angry. Guilty. In shock. Our heads melted.'

'How did it happen?'

'You don't need the details, it's a whole load of crap.'

'Tell me about the crap,' she said gently, taking the risk of reaching out and putting a hand on his shoulder. 'It was after your mother died – how did it start?'

'We were in the kitchen, we had a big argument about … how Mum died,' he said, in a low, monotonous voice. 'It became physical. I was in some kind of blind fury and after punching Alex around the face I picked up a knife and wrestled him to the floor. I had him pinned down and was holding it against his throat. I didn't see him at all; it was as if I was consumed with this rage and nothing else existed. Another minute and I would have cut his jugular, only Lainey stopped me. Don't ask me how, she managed to squeeze between us, shouting and screaming. She nicked her own hand getting the knife off me. Alex broke his collarbone when I pushed him to the floor. So you see, that's the kind of man I am. That's why you're better off steering clear of me. That's why I don't want to get close to you … After what I did to Alex, how can I trust myself?'

'But you said yourself you were in a bad place after your mum died. You were nineteen and mad with grief.'

'That doesn't excuse anything. I nearly killed my brother.

How do I know I won't lose it again? Sometime, somewhere? Knowing what I almost did, how easy it was at the time, what happens if there's another lapse? How do I know I won't reach for a knife again and lash out? I don't think Alex has ever forgiven me.'

'Of course he has,' Vikki said. 'You were all in bits at the time.'

'We both owe Lainey. Big time. She took a huge risk because I was in such … a fury … that I could have turned the knife on her.'

'But you didn't,' she said desperately. 'You stopped in time.'

'I should have left you safely tucked up in London. You're part of my new life, the one that has nothing to do with Lynes Glen. Anyhow, Vikki, if you're still talking to me when we're back in London, you know why I am the way I am. I decided long ago that I'm not fit for anything much and I'm afraid to commit to anyone. That's why I've found you to be such a good friend; you accepted that without question. Other women saw it as a challenge, but they didn't get very far.'

'Is that why you broke off contact with each other?' Vikki asked. How crazy was it, to be having a conversation like this? Just a short while ago she'd dismissed the idea of Niall damaging his brother's shirt. Now he was telling her that he'd almost killed him.

'More or less,' he said. 'It wasn't something we consciously set out to do. We needed space apart to lick our wounds, but ignoring each other became the new norm over time. I went to London, Alex went to New York, days turned into weeks, which turned into months, and the more time went by the less inclined I was to lift the phone, or send an email.'

She knew from personal experience how easy it was to turn your back on the past, to close a door and excise it all away. She'd never even felt guilty, as if some inner self-defence mechanism had kicked in and activated itself, freeing her from any kind of remorse.

'The years ran in quickly,' he said. 'We were living on different continents but Lainey kept us up to date with family stuff, so we weren't totally disconnected. I knew what was going on in Alex's life and vice versa.'

She risked asking, 'Was this why you gave up on your travelling dreams? Whatever Lainey meant about you not heading out to South Africa?'

'We all had dreams we left behind. Alex – Jesus, he had great plans to conquer Hollywood. He'd always been interested in drama, joined all the groups in college, and then a director saw him in action during the Galway Arts Festival and invited him over to a casting … but he didn't get going. Lainey was due to go to Dublin in September, to take up a scholarship post in English literature, but that didn't happen, and me' – he sighed – 'I had ideas of travelling through South Africa, then on up to the Seychelles … we weren't short on ambition …'

She thought of how bright and shiny they had all looked in the photographs on the piano, how full of passion and confidence they'd been, and her heart bled. She sensed there was more – there had to be more to this. Beyond being devastated after their mother died, something else must have happened to have impelled the gentle and mild-mannered Niall to act as violently as he had. With a shock, she remembered the knife she'd found under the bed, the steak knife with the wooden handle.

'Niall? Vikki? Are you in here?' It was Ben's voice. The door opened and a glow of light from the candle he was holding pin-pricked that side of the room.

'What is it, Ben?' Niall asked, sounding so defeated that Vikki wanted to wrap her arms around him, to hug him and kiss him and make him feel better.

'Sorry to interrupt, but the storm has disturbed Leo,' he said. 'Lainey has given him something to settle him but he wants to see the family for a few minutes. All of us. I'm doing a quick check of the children and I'll follow you in.'

'Is that OK with you, Vikki?' Niall asked.

'Yes, sure.'

She couldn't leave Niall's side right now, even though she was as raw and emotional as he was. But she knew worse was to come when a few minutes later, Leo looked around at the group gathered in his shadowy bedroom and said, in a whispery voice, 'I have a confession to make.'

CHAPTER THIRTY-SIX

What he had to say was so difficult that Leo felt he could have been speaking through chunks of broken glass.

The storm had woken him. The crashing and banging of the wind sounded as if the world was coming to an end. He had lain awake, his conscience so heavy that he'd welcomed every one of his aches and pains as a fitting penance. When Lainey came in to check on him, she'd given him more painkillers, but something had urged him to speak up and he'd asked her to bring in all the family.

After Gabrielle was gone, life became intolerable, yet to Leo's astonishment and disgust he was still very much alive. He couldn't understand how a collection of physical cells and organs conspired to keep him in this world when the meaning of his life had vanished. He couldn't understand how he felt hunger and tiredness and rain on his face when his mind was numb and flat-lined. The only decision he was capable of making was to have the lough barricaded – once his most beloved place in the world outside of the house – so robustly that no one could go near it again.

In time, he read about other tragedies far greater than his, and eventually grief gave way to a heavy, dispiriting pain at the general unfairness of life, only relieved by the arrival of his grandchildren, when his world exploded into a startling new and colourful dimension.

He could have retired very gently into an old age, with nothing much to concern himself with except enjoying his new blessings, but in recent months, now that the end of his earthly existence was surely drawing closer, his troubled guilt could no longer be supressed. Gabrielle! What would she have to say about the way he had lived? Then there was his failure to do anything constructive to bridge the rift between his sons, even though they'd assured him down through the years that everything was fine. He'd been afraid that any pushing or prodding by him might alienate them further. Needing to unburden himself, he'd gathered his family this weekend, but as he gazed at the faces of his children in the dim lighting, he knew it was going to be every bit as difficult as he'd imagined. Growing old did not mean resignation and acceptance of one's path in life, it did not blunt or soften the senses. He could have been fifteen on the inside, and teeming with adolescent angst.

Apart from his children, what consequences would his words have for his wonderful little ones, the precious blessings he'd been granted late in life? Charlotte, Harry and Jack carried his and Gabrielle's blood, and the blueprint of his parents and grandparents in the shape of a nose, the tilt of their smile, and, in little Jack's case, the colour of his hair – so like Gabrielle's it made his heart twist and rejoice all at once. They meant more to him than life itself.

'I brought you here to tell you something important,' he began. 'I thought it was only fair that you hear it all together and not from each other. But now I find my courage is fading away.'

Lainey took his hand. His little peacekeeper, she had willingly taken on the role of family mediator, and kept the family torch burning. Thoughts of telling her upset him the most.

'It's fine, Dad, don't be afraid,' she said.

'I can't help being afraid, Lainey, in case you turn away from me when you hear what I've done.'

'What is it, Dad? No matter what you have to say, you're still our dad and we love you. That'll never change.'

To Leo's surprise, this came from Alex. His firstborn son, Gabrielle's golden child.

'We'll see,' he said heavily. 'It's about when your mother died … you need to know I was responsible for her death.' He paused, unable to continue for a moment. The words echoed around the room like the sad, oppressive tolling of a funeral bell. There was a thick silence. He was afraid to look at his children; he could only imagine the horror-stricken expression on their faces. The silence became overpowering, so he gathered his courage and went on, 'I couldn't tell you at the time, I would have magnified your loss a thousand times. You would have lost your father as well as your mother. So I buried it away.'

Still, the silence. He braved a glance at their faces but his children looked more puzzled than anything else.

'That couldn't be.' Lainey was the first to speak.

'I see this has come as a shock to you all,' he said, his heart aching. 'It was impossible to speak of it at the time, and as the years went on, it became more difficult. But now I'm coming to the closing stages of my life and I need to … resolve certain things before I come face to face with your mother again.'

'We all thought we had something to do with it,' Alex said, looking at Lainey and Niall as if for confirmation.

'What? *You*?' Leo shook his head. 'Your mother loved you all unconditionally and worshipped the ground you walked on. As I do. There was nothing any of you could have done to cause her death. It was me. I haven't been a good father. Or a good husband. Gabrielle's death might have seemed like a terrible accident, but I was behind it, as surely as if I'd driven her car into the lough myself.'

'I don't understand, Dad,' Lainey said.

The words, rehearsed in his head since he'd known this weekend was happening, came from somewhere outside of him. 'Years ago,' he said, 'before your mother and I were married, I slept with her cousin, Maura.'

He'd agonised over his choice of words. They'd hardly 'slept', spending most of the night doing other things. But it hadn't been an affair as such and 'having sex' conjured physical images he didn't want to inflict on his family. Still, even in the dim candlelight, he noticed the sudden tautness on Alex's face. Although he had expected this, his heart fell. His eldest son, his high achiever, would not be impressed with him.

'*Before* you were married?' Niall said. 'How could that matter so much?'

His gentle son. Niall had always been of a soft, temperate nature.

'Your mother and I had been engaged to be married but we'd had a row and it was all off – temporarily, as it turned out. I – there's no excuse for my behaviour – I slept with Maura, one night. It was a dreadful mistake.' Leo closed his eyes. He opened them again and looked at the tableau around the bed. Lainey had a hand up to her mouth, pressing hard against it to prevent what might come out. Alex, his arms folded in front of him, looked into space as though he was afraid to meet anyone's eyes. Leo was glad they were here with their spouses and partners, which was why he'd asked all of them to come in as they would need that support.

'A couple of weeks later, Gabrielle and I … we made up and it was wonderful. I tried to tell her … there was something she needed to know, something I'd done, but she wasn't having any of it, she wanted to start afresh and forget about the row, just focus on the wedding and the rest of our lives together. So we continued with our plans and I said nothing. Maura left for London before the wedding, she told me she'd already put our night together out of her mind, that it hadn't been' – he searched for words – 'worth remembering, and for the sake of her pride, she'd no intentions of enlightening anyone as to what had taken place. She didn't want the whole town or her cousin to know that she'd slept with me and I'd passed her up—'

Lainey was shaking her head. 'No, Dad.'

He could see the words weren't making sense. Or else she was thoroughly offended by what he had to say and that thought saddened him. Still, what else had he expected?

'Things were very different for women, you see, in 1968,' he went on, trying to explain. 'Anything outside marriage was strictly frowned upon, especially for the woman involved. I put my night with Maura behind me as best I could, and Gabrielle and I got on with our lives.'

He felt immensely tired all of a sudden, and a great wave of exhaustion washed over him as the drowsiness caused by the painkillers finally kicked in. He closed his eyes against the ton weight of his eyelids. He was tempted to succumb to the warm blanket of sleep, but he had more things to say, and he grappled for words.

'I thought it was over and done with,' he said, his voice slurring with fatigue. 'But years later, during that last summer, Maura came back …'

He sensed a disturbance amongst his children, and heard a door open and close, but that was as far as he got before he sank beneath the thick wave of sleep.

CHAPTER THIRTY-SEVEN

If only he hadn't been so beguiled by Maura that summer. If he hadn't been so captivated by her lush curves, her dark, mascaraed eyes filled with sultry promise, her throaty laugh …

From the moment she'd arrived in Lynes Glen, he'd been unable to take his eyes off her; the way she moved in her red dress, her hips swaying suggestively, the swell of her full breasts pressing tightly against the lace, his fingers itching to slide down into the soft cleavage thrust on display in her low-cut tops. Then there were her figure-hugging white shorts, with the faint suggestion of her lacy pants visible beneath. Other times it was apparent she was wearing a provocative G-string. As for her halter-necked tops … he knew she wasn't wearing a bra and the more he fantasised about opening the strings tied behind her neck, the more painfully aroused he became.

The hot days and warm sultry nights, and the pop song Lainey played on constant repeat – Bryan Adams throatily crooning 'Have You Ever Really Loved a Woman?' – the lyrics and the beguiling tempo weaving a seductive spell around them both, Maura's eyes taunting him as to whether he'd ever really loved a woman whenever it came on.

If only he hadn't felt like a teenager on heat ...

The sexual tension had simmered between them while they eyed and circled and brushed off each other under the roof of Lynes Glen – where there was no question of anything happening. Until it had become unbearable, and in a voice unlike his own, he suggested a walk one hot afternoon. He led her to a sheltered spot, deep in the tangle of the forest, under the cover of thick summer foliage, not far from the fairy fort.

'Is this safe?' she asked, her eyes dancing with merriment, leaning back against a tree, raising one knee and rubbing it provocatively against his thighs.

'Safe for what?' He pretended ignorance. He caught both of her hands in one of his and held them up over her head, against the tree trunk, leaning in to kiss the side of her long white throat, his mouth trailing kisses along her collarbone.

'Don't pretend,' she said, twisting her head away. 'Safe for what you and I are both panting after. Safe for the consequences.'

'What consequences?' he said. He kissed her on the lips, feeling victorious when she kissed him back.

'One afternoon will not be enough,' she said, her voice hoarse. 'Who cares – I can't wait any longer.' She wiggled out of his hold and reached around, pulling at the ties of her halter-necked top. He watched, dry-mouthed, while her top fell down to her waist, baring her breasts. Then she opened the top button of her shorts, licked her lips, and looked at him with thick desire in her eyes. He pulled her roughly to him and lost himself in her body.

Three times in quick succession that first afternoon, while they took the edge off their hunger. There had been consequences, because if anything, it had only fanned his desire. Maura had no inhibitions, and she surprised him with her raunchy sensuality. The depths of the forest behind Lynes Glen and the shelter of leafy branches, somnolent in the heat, were a silent witness to their moments of shared pleasure. And when Maura moved out of Lynes Glen into a rented holiday cottage, there were more opportunities.

If only he hadn't felt like the next James Dean waiting in the wings, trying out his acting skills by wooing a more mature, sophisticated woman, imagining himself on a Hollywood set as they heaved together.

Or that conversation when he'd blown her out … if only he'd handled that differently.

If only he hadn't swaggered around in front of Lainey and Niall, high on a cocktail of lust and adrenaline, causing cracks in the close sibling unity that had defined the summer up to then.

He felt a hand on his shoulder. He was standing in the darkened hallway in Lynes Glen and when he turned around his wife's concerned face swam into his vision.

'Alex? What's the matter? Don't you think it's time you told me?'

'My father is mistaken,' he said, baldly. 'He wasn't responsible for our mother's death. *I* was.'

CHAPTER THIRTY-EIGHT

Alex

Sitting on the side of the bed in their shadowy bedroom, his mouth full of the bitter taste of pain and regret, Alex finally spoke, stumbling over his words, while images of the summer of ninety-five and beyond continued to flash in front of him in rapid succession and he was back there once more:

The next James Dean waiting in the wings found it more difficult than he'd thought to make the break with Maura. She wasn't impressed when he called to her rented house and told her they had to finish; in less than a week he'd be leaving for America. The summer storm that had been hovering on the horizon had finally broken. Sheets of rain poured down, darkening the day, the sky illuminated by nothing except the odd flash of lightning.

'Take me with you,' she said. 'I can't bear to say goodbye. I can't get enough of you. Let's start a new life over there, the land of the free.'

'*What*?' He laughed. 'That, my dear Maura, will not be happening. No way.'

'What about us? Our relationship?'

'*Relationship*? It's been fun and games, sex – no more. What did you expect? We always knew it was just going to be a summer fling. Don't kid yourself.'

'Let me go with you; we don't have to set up home together, we can just be friends. Sex friends.'

He told her to fuck off.

'That's very nice, I must say,' she said. 'You weren't saying that when you were deep inside me, were you now?' Her eyes were alight with indignation.

'You're forgetting one thing,' he said. 'By the time I'm forty you'll be sixty-five. I'll be coming into my prime and you'll be—'

'Thanks. So now you've had your fill of me, I'm to be discarded like an old rag doll?'

'This whole conversation is to be discarded,' he said, unable to believe he'd got it so wrong.

'I'm very hurt. Didn't I mean anything to you beyond a fling?'

'We both knew this was nothing but sex – good sex, mind you – but that's all.'

'I'd watch out if I were you, Alex Blake. A woman scorned and all that.'

'What do you mean? Ah here, you're only taking the piss.'

'Just telling you to watch out.'

'You're not the only one who's after my blood.'

'Don't tell me you've another woman on the go…'

'Other woman as in Lainey – she's fed up with me strutting my stuff and going AWOL.'

'Do they know about me?'

'Yeah. Niall told her.'

'Niall?'

'They knew there was something going on. When he asked me where I kept disappearing to and who was putting the gleam in my eye, I couldn't resist a few boasts. I think I ruffled him up big time.'

'Who cares about your precious family; you'll all be scattered soon.'

'Yeah, but Lainey seems to think I broke up the party too early – it's like I defected.'

'So now I'm the enemy as well – thanks.'

'I didn't mean it like that.'

'My heart bleeds for you. It's my turn to tell you to fuck off. Fuck off home like a good little boy and make up with your siblings.'

He stalked out of her house, feeling her eyes bore into his back, and, despite the thunder roaring overhead and the relentless rain, he drove to Galway and met up with an old and accommodating friend, spending the night with her – anything to get the taste of Maura out of his mouth.

The following day, his mother was dead.

*

Then there was the last conversation he had with Maura, less than a week after his mother's death – even that had gone wrong.

'What did you say to my mother?' he demanded, standing in her small porch.

'None of your business,' Maura said.

'You must have said something to upset her.'

'How dare you.'

'She was coming back from here when she crashed and went into the lough. On a road she knew like the back of her hand.'

'Do you think I don't know that? Before you lose the head altogether with your wild accusations, remember I'm as gutted as you are that Gabrielle's gone. Anyway she already knew we'd had a fling.'

'I know. I got up Lainey's nose a bit too much and she couldn't resist popping my balloon and letting the cat out of the bag. None of us expected Mum to hotfoot it over here.'

'She didn't. She dropped in for coffee and your name came up in the conversation. That's all.'

He stared at her, trying to gauge if she was speaking the truth, but Maura's eyes were dark and shadowed. 'This has torn us down the middle,' he said. 'We're all blaming ourselves for what happened.'

'All of you?'

'Me especially. If I hadn't hooked up with you, if I hadn't bragged to Niall or irritated Lainey, who told Mum, who came over here …'

Maura shook her head. 'It was an accident.'

'That's no consolation to me, or Lainey, or least of all Niall.'

'How is Niall?' Maura's tone softened. 'Poor divil. Of you all, he had a horrific experience.'

The sequence of events on that desperately tragic day flashed through Alex's head. He'd arrived back from Galway to find no one at home, a hastily scribbled note in the sunlit kitchen urging him to go straight to the hospital. There, a deeply traumatised Niall had attempted to tell him what had happened down by the lough, groping for words, the pictures he was conjuring up in Alex's head agonising beyond belief.

'I know,' Alex said. 'He's taken it very badly. I don't think he'll ever be right again after what he went through. We had words in the kitchen the other night, all of us stupefied with grief, and it led to a fight. He grabbed a knife and even tried to kill me; Niall – who wouldn't hurt a fly.'

'Is that what happened to your face? You look like you've had a run-in with a grizzly bear.'

'Two black eyes, a broken collarbone, bruising to my neck and a gash where the knife nicked me. Not that I blame him. He's still crazed with shock thanks to what he experienced and if anyone's to blame for that it's me.'

'Jesus.'

'You might have been at my funeral, only for Lainey pulled him off me.'

'Shite.'

'I've missed my casting appointment in Hollywood, but I don't care. I couldn't do it anyhow, between Mum and … everything else, my heart has gone out of any kind of acting career.'

'Everything else?'

He didn't answer her. Playing the part of the next James Dean had brought him nothing but trouble. He couldn't stomach anything like that ever again.

'How's Leo?' Maura asked.

'Still in shock. Numb. In a trance. He hasn't even noticed my face. Just as well.'

'Does he know about us?'

'Hell, no.' He stared at her, trying to decipher the inscrutable look in her eyes. Maura stared back, unblinking.

'If you hadn't come back here in the first place, stirring up trouble, none of this would have happened,' he went on, lashing out.

'Do you think I don't know that? I'd never have wished that

awful tragedy on Gabrielle, not in a million years. Inside, I'm cut to pieces.'

A long silence. Both of them looking defeated and devastated.

'Are you still going to the States?' she asked.

'I'll be gone as soon as I can get out of here. I might have lost my big opportunity but I've other plans.'

'Don't worry, I won't be following you over. I know when I'm not wanted.'

'Get real. That was never going to happen.'

'I *am* getting real. You didn't want me in your life once you'd had your fill of me. I'm going back to London on Saturday morning. There's nothing here for me now. Not that there's much over there either.'

It was the last time he saw her.

*

The following week, Lainey drove him to Shannon airport.

'Will you be OK?' she said, tearful at the departure gate.

'I'll manage. Eventually. At least I'll be away from it all. How about you?'

'I'm staying put for now. I can't leave Dad on his own, not at the moment. Not that he'll even notice if I'm there or not.'

'After all your hopes for Dublin …'

'It doesn't matter, it's not important right now. I'll get a teaching job in a school, hopefully within an hour's commute.'

'Teaching. After all your dreams.'

'Did you say goodbye to Niall?'

'No.'

'He's still in bits, almost killing you on top of the disaster with Mum. He said he's never going to dive again.'

'I know. That's why I couldn't face him this morning. I don't blame him for attacking me, I started all the crap by hooking up with Maura, but not diving again? He can't turn his back on that.'

'He feels he was to blame for Mum's death.'

Alex shook his head.

'He won't talk it through,' Lainey said. 'He's clammed up. But none of us will talk about this ever again, right? I can't bear any more blame game conversations. No matter how much we scourge ourselves, nothing will bring Mum back.'

'Agreed.'

It was a pact Lainey had made with both himself and Niall, late the previous night in Lynes Glen, in an attempt to start healing their wounds; irrespective of who felt they were to blame for their mother's death, they would never talk of the events of the last month again, not ever, not to anyone else at all, not even amongst themselves. It was a painful episode in their lives that was far too distressing to resurrect and best left buried.

'Niall told me he's going to London,' Lainey said. 'In a way we're all quits, all our dreams in ribbons.'

'This is a horseshit conversation to be having in the middle of an airport.'

'It is.' Her eyes were welling up again and he cursed himself.

'I have to go through,' he said. 'I hate leaving you like this.'

The effort Lainey made to force a smile on her pale, damp face caused an ache in his heart. 'I'll be over to visit sometime,' she said.

'Bring Dad. When he feels like it. One day, sis, we might look back on all this and while it'll still be sad, it won't seem as horribly sore.'

'I don't know if I agree,' Lainey said. 'It's not something I ever want any of us to look back on.'

'It might do us all good to put a bit of space between us.'

Lainey smiled sadly. 'We'll see.'

He spent thirteen years in New York, using his IT qualification to find work, pulling a tight shutter down over the past, finding his feet, the years blurring together in a haze of sadness and regret, working hard, playing equally hard, and keeping in touch, just about, with Lainey and his father. He set up his own company, working harder than ever again to keep the memories of that summer at bay.

Then one Monday morning he slept it out following a broken sleep, thanks to being disturbed by his recurrent nightmare about Lainey and Niall, mixed up with his mother and Maura. He was late, exhausted, and unprepared, hurrying into the offices of Thomas Price, the large multinational where he was bidding for a contract.

In the big shiny conference room, with huge windows looking out onto an impressive view of Manhattan, a woman got up from the conference table and brought him up to the podium, organising him with his presentation, offering tea or coffee, her blue eyes warm and attentive, her voice musical, her whole demeanour one of composure. That's all she had to do for him to feel an ease deep in his soul. He couldn't take his eyes off her during the presentation and subsequent discussion, soaking up the sight of her and the sound of her voice.

It didn't take him long to work out what was happening to him. It was as if the unfathomable, silent core of him that had been constantly churning with agitation since he'd left Ireland was now soothed, and deep below the rush of hot desire she caused in him, under all the games lovers play in their coming together, he knew this woman would make him calm again.

Jenna.

CHAPTER THIRTY-NINE

When her husband finally stopped talking, Jenna curved her arm tighter around his shoulder and leaned into him. For a long time he simply sat there, at the edge of the bed, his head buried in his hands, and she was glad he seemed reluctant to move out of her embrace.

'I hear what you're saying,' she said eventually, 'but you shouldn't blame yourself for your mother's accident, even if your fling with Maura was a little inappropriate.'

'Inappropriate?' He laughed. 'She was over twice my age and Mum's cousin. That would have sunk like a bomb in Irish society in those days, sticking like foul mud to both my parents. They didn't deserve that. Maura was different – she was dangerous in a way, an exotic animal, watching and waiting, you sensed undercurrents about her, although on the surface she was fine, laughing and joking, teasing our dad for being a little out of touch with modern life – which he wasn't; he was reserved and preferred his own company to the bright lights and he loved his wife and family more than anything. These were his guiding values; anything else was superfluous. Mum's accident ...' He paused. 'Had Maura been bragging about us to her? I dunno, but Mum must have been upset enough to lose concentration on the road ... a road she could have driven in her sleep, so well did she know the twists and turns ...'

'You've been carrying that all this time.'

'Yes.'

'You can't torture yourself with imaginings, Alex, you don't know for sure what your mother was thinking. You can play as many guessing games as you like, and spend the rest of your life driving yourself mad with all sorts of assumptions, but you'll never know what was in your mother's thoughts or what caused her to swerve off the road.'

He listened to her words and leaned back into her, reaching up to squeeze her hand. 'The blame game went around in a circle between me, Niall and Lainey. We were all distraught. Especially Niall.'

'I can well imagine,' she sighed. 'What a catastrophe. You still have nightmares about that row,' she went on. 'I've heard you in your sleep.'

'I was frightened of Niall. He had such strength, I don't know how Lainey pulled him off me. None of us have ever worked this through. We were wrong to agree we'd never speak of it, we were all trying to protect each other because we all felt we'd been at fault in some way. I know now there are some things you can't just draw a line under and expect them to resolve themselves, they run too deep.'

Another pause, both of them silently acknowledged the truth of this.

'I also feel I haven't been fair to you,' Alex continued, 'bringing baggage like this into our marriage, but I had my pride and I'd hoped I could forget about it and start over with a clean sheet.'

'Is that the real reason you came home this weekend? Did you want a chance to resolve things?'

'It was the note from Dad. The invitation came first – you saw that, it was very straightforward – but before I had replied another note came, which I didn't show to you, and this was a little different. It said he dearly wanted us all together, and he wanted it so much that, if anyone didn't show, the other two siblings would be taken out of his will.'

'In other words, if you hadn't shown up here, Lainey and Niall would have been disinherited and vice versa? I can't imagine your father writing something like that.' How mistaken she'd been, how quick to judge. Wrongly as it turned out. She wept silently.

'He probably guessed it was a surefire way to bring us home, and he was right. No matter how much I might have wanted to stay away, I couldn't do that to Niall or Lainey.'

She let the silence stretch as they held each other. Then, speaking as gently as she could, 'Things aren't going well in New York, are they, Alex?'

'No. I haven't been fair to you about that either, keeping you in the dark. I had my pride about that too, and I didn't want to worry you, I didn't see the point in both of us having sleepless nights. I hoped I could have sorted it out but it's gotten too big and it's out of my hands now.'

'I think you'd better tell me now before I imagine the worst.'

'This is as bad as it can get.'

He told her that his business was being sued for information getting into the wrong hands. One of his trusted staff had lost an unencrypted data stick containing hundreds of business-sensitive files: a silly and careless error, one that had the potential to wipe out the business he'd worked so hard to develop, as well as his reputation.

'We'll face this together,' she said. 'So what if we have to start again? You should have told me before now. There were times when I felt shut out between your silence around your family and the business problems,' she admitted. 'There's no point in pretending I didn't. Sometimes, in my worst moments, I wondered if you'd only married me because Jack was on the way, because that was also a matter of pride with you.'

'No, Jenna, never just that. I've loved you, always. If I've been distant, it's been my silly, stupid pride. Sometimes I used to lie awake in the dark thinking terrible things, then when I listened to your breathing, I was glad that at least you were having a good sleep. I was glad I could let you have that much, in the nightmare things were. Even you lying next to me made me feel less alone.'

'You should have woken me up to talk to you.'

'Keeping everything to myself was a salve to my pride. It also meant I wasn't a failed businessman in your eyes.'

'Hey,' she said, hugging him tightly, 'never think that. No way. We both bring different things to this marriage. I love your silly, stupid pride, your energy and passion, it turns on something inside me and makes me feel I can be more, bigger, better than I am. Without you in my life I think I'd only be half the person I am. Let me love you in the way you deserve to be loved, even if that means waking me up at four in the morning because you can't sleep.'

Her heart swelled. She closed her eyes momentarily,

profoundly grateful that nothing stupid had happened with Ben. She shivered when she thought how close she had come to stepping over a line. It had been nothing but an indulgence, brought on because she'd felt so totally at odds with both Alex and herself, but thankfully, it had gone nowhere.

She kissed the side of Alex's face and he pulled her into his arms.

CHAPTER FORTY

Vikki fumbled with the handle of the back door. It flew open, slamming back against its hinges, hurled in the teeth of the wind. The rain lashed down, drumming on the terrace, gurgling down the drainpipes, the wind lifting sheets of it so that she felt it spitting into her face as she stood in the doorway.

Niall was out there somewhere.

By the time they'd left Leo's room, Alex and Jenna had already disappeared. Vikki and Niall had followed Ben and Lainey back to the living room. Some of the tea lights had gone out so Lainey had lit a few more while Niall had sat staring into space, a heavy stillness radiating from him that had unnerved her.

After a few moments he'd flung himself out of the chair and gone into the kitchen. Vikki had expected him to return with a beer but instead, to her alarm, she'd heard the noise of the back door opening, the increased howl of the wind as it had surged into the hall outside the kitchen, then the door had banged shut again.

Without giving it any thought, she had followed him.

She stepped outside into the deluge, managing to pull the door closed behind her. It was pitch dark and the force of the gale almost took her breath away. She stood for a moment, gasping at the sheer relentless rain pounding into her, running coldly down her face and into her eyes, trickling down the back of her neck. The trees in the forest were bending and twisting and bashing together, the wind keening through them eerily.

'Niall? Where are you?' she shouted, the wind wrenching her words away.

This was mad. Totally crazy. She turned to go back inside. Then she heard his voice above the slam of the storm.

'Vikki, what the hell are you doing? Go back inside.'

'What are you doing out here?' she called.

'Never mind. Go in.'

His voice was coming from the rear of the house. She ran around from the terrace, and here the storm's intensity was slightly reduced, the front and side of the house taking the brunt. She saw a glimmer of light and tried to recall the layout of the rear garden. There was a shed, wasn't there? A small wooden potting shed with windows. The door had been banging in the wind. She saw a flash of light again and ran towards it, her feet squelching on the wet, tufty grass.

The light was coming from the potting shed. In the hazy shadows she was able to make out that the door had finally stopped flapping because it had been wedged open by a heavy planter that had rolled up against it. Niall was sitting on the floor of the potting shed, partly sheltered from the storm, his elbows on his knees, a small torch caught on a nail giving a tiny beam of light.

'Hi,' she said, sitting down beside him, heedless of the puddles of water.

Niall ignored her.

'I understand if you're upset with your father,' she said. 'It must have been a shock and he seems to have deep regrets, but—'

'You don't know what you're talking about,' he said gruffly.

She shivered. 'No, probably not, I'm just trying—'

'Don't bother.'

'Right then, I won't.'

They sat staring out into the pitch blackness, listening to the sound of the wind buffeting around the house and tearing through the trees in the forest. Just as Vikki was beginning to feel disorientated, her wet clothes seeping into her skin, raindrops plopping down from her hair, Niall spoke.

'I used to come here as a child,' he said, in a flat voice that dismayed her. 'I'd watch my mother potting up little seeds, tiny flower buds; I thought it was amazing the way they grew. I still remember the rich, earthy smell, her hands dusted with clay. Mostly I remember the feeling of peace.'

She made an encouraging noise, hoping he might continue speaking, but he didn't. 'No matter what you want to talk about, or not talk about, I'm here,' she said eventually.

Silence fell between them again, and she stole a look at him in the thin light. He was staring straight ahead, his hair and his face damp with rain.

'You shouldn't be here, it's all wrong – everything.'

'So what if it's all wrong,' she said. 'We're all just muddling our way through, and sometimes it's a pile of crap.'

He gave an exasperated sigh. 'You haven't a fucking clue.'

'Obviously fucking not,' she said smartly, responding in kind. 'I don't know why I'm sitting here, getting wet, in the middle of a storm. I must be mad.'

'I was the mad one, asking you to come here. It's more than just a pile of crap.'

Her jangled nerves got the better of her. 'Oh, for God's sake, Niall, I know what happened was awful, I know it was horrible to lose your mother the way you did, I'm sorry about that, I know you must have got a shock tonight but, come on, your dad and Maura was years ago. It must have been' – she tried to work it out – 'nearly fifty years ago?'

Slanting a look him, she saw his face drop into his hands.

He lifted his head again. 'I don't give a shit about my dad and Maura,' he said tersely. 'Sleeping with Maura before they got married? Jesus. Mum might have been annoyed to find out but not enough to do something silly. They were crazy about each other, Mum and Dad. Mum loved him to bits. He was her hero. When Maura came back that time ...' he paused. 'When Maura came back that time, it was Alex she went for, not Dad.'

'Alex ... and Maura?' Vikki said.

'Yeah,' he said roughly. 'She stayed with us for a while, she was full of it, I saw her eyeing up Alex, I saw what she was up to, then he changed ... he was missing a lot, stayed out nights. I challenged him. He boasted about what they were up to, proud as punch, so cocky he pissed me off. He thought I'd keep it to myself but I made the shitty mistake of telling Lainey.'

She sat there, hugging her knees, too anxious to say anything.

'Lainey and I were so ... sanctimonious,' he said. 'Annoyed with him ... he thought he was a hotshot, it was a mini-scandal ... I was jealous that he was having loads of sex. Alex was always Mum's golden son, the firstborn, and even she was beginning to wonder what had happened to him. Then the day before she … the heat was sweltering, it was hot, there was thunder. Alex was missing again. The next day Mum asked Lainey if she knew where he'd got to, and in a moment of devilry, Lainey let slip that he was seeing Maura. Mum went to see Maura and when she was coming home … aaah, fuck me …' That last expletive was drawn out long and loud.

She tried to get her head around what he was thinking.

'Dad's wrong.' His voice was thick. 'He can't blame himself for Mum's death. It was my fault.'

She edged closer to him, she dared to put her cold hand on his arm. 'Are you blaming yourself for your mother's death, because you told Lainey about Alex and Maura, and she passed it on?'

He brushed her hand away. 'No.'

'Then … what?'

'You don't get it, Vikki,' he said, his harsh words almost a shout.

'Don't I?' she shouted back.

'It was me. *See*?' He was still shouting. 'That's why I haven't dived since, that's why I hate myself.'

'*What*?' She was shaking. So was he.

'Dad, Alex, or Lainey – it was none of them. It was me … my fault. I was there that day … at the lough … I tried but couldn't do it. I couldn't save her.'

She gripped his arm. 'What happened, Niall? *What happened*?'

CHAPTER FORTY-ONE

Niall

He sat with his head in his hands. Even now, years later, it tortured him. Images of that afternoon taunting him, revisiting him in the night. And, as if he hadn't done enough damage that day, he'd followed that up by almost killing his brother in a fit of black, self-hatred rage. He very much might have, only for Lainey.

These were dark things that had lain silently across the centre of his heart all these years, driving him from job to job, woman to woman. He daren't allow anyone in who might find out what he was really like behind the mask of the fun-loving Irish guy with the laughter and the jokes. If at times he felt lonely, he welcomed it. There was no one else he could hurt.

He would never have returned to Lynes Glen but for the terms of his father's summons.

He hadn't meant to ask Vikki to come with him this weekend. They were friends, he couldn't allow it to be anything more, but the words had slipped out of their own accord when he'd thought how good it might be to have her around when he came face to face with his brother. The agreement with Alex and Lainey, to never again speak of those dark days, still held. Lainey said she'd planned a relaxing, free and easy weekend, with fun and games for the children, and only good memories of the way it had been. Only that hadn't happened. Right from the start, the past had burst out of its hiding place with a vengeance.

And now he was here, sitting on the wet floor of an old potting shed, a woman was holding onto his arm, while the rain drummed on the roof and the wind banged and bashed its way through the forest. He was squeezing words out over the ache in his throat and it was like a dam breaking loose, the words coming out of the darkness within him, painting pictures against the black of the night so that he wasn't here, he was … there.

*

It was 29 August 1995, and this afternoon it was as if the thunderstorm of the previous day had rinsed everything squeaky clean, all the dust that had gathered over those dry summer weeks, because the sun was more sparkling than ever, the world around him polished and shiny, the sky arching above like a fresh blue cloth.

He'd come down to the lough to get away from Lynes Glen, where all he could visualise was Alex and Maura carefully and deliberately sidestepping each other. Even though she'd moved out, the sexual tension between them had been so strong it was still fizzing in the air.

He'd never been jealous of Alex before, the six-year age gap had been enough space to allow them both to get along quite happily. But he was jealous that Alex was enjoying his fling with Maura, looking like a sleekly satisfied cat – a jaguar perhaps – and getting up Niall's nose with his swaggering walk and the way he flung his BMW around the corners of the approach road to the house. His own latest girlfriend had recently blown him out after they'd practically gone all the way, so he was feeling particularly sensitive to all things carnal right now.

He also wanted to get away from Lainey – he was sorry he'd told her about Alex and Maura. She'd jumped on the information with a glee that had surprised him. It had quickly turned into a state of affairs where Niall and Lainey considered themselves to be judge and jury about Alex's behaviour. The feeling of unity that had bonded the three of them during the warm summer days had vanished.

And then Lainey said she was going to tell Mum.

'What do you want to do that for?' he asked, annoyed with himself for saying anything to her in the first place.

'She's been asking me if I know where Alex is, so the next time she asks, at least I'll know.'

'I don't think that's a good idea.'

'I think it's a great idea,' she said, tossing her beautiful hair. 'He's spoiling the end of our last summer together, why should he get away scot free?'

'You're just bored from hanging around here. The sooner you go to Dublin, the better.'

Then Alex had been missing the previous night, when the thunderstorm had struck, obviously keeping Maura safely tucked up from the thunder and lightning, and he still wasn't home.

'Mum was looking for Alex,' Lainey said to him out on the

terrace after lunch. 'So I kind of let it slip where I thought he might be,' she went on, with an impish grin on her face.

'Where's Mum now?' he asked.

'I think she's gone to see Maura. Oops. I hope Alex isn't still there, he'll be caught in that flagrante thing.'

'Lainey, I wish you'd—'

'What?'

He'd been about to say grow up when he remembered she was older than he was.

So he was here now, seeking escape on this glorious afternoon, not wanting to be at home in Lynes Glen when his mother arrived back. He tried and failed to imagine her going into the library in high dudgeon to tell his father what Alex had been up to. He tried and failed to imagine her gossiping with Lainey about her visit to Maura; then he realised he couldn't visualise these things because his mother was above that kind of carry-on. Neither did he want to be at home when Alex arrived back from wherever he'd gone, only to find that, thanks to him, Lainey had let the cat out of the bag.

He'd already dived three times, flying out into the space between the water and the sky, before breaking the surface of the water, falling down, down, down into the icy cold, clear depths. He was catching his breath before he dived one more time when he saw the approach of a car glinting in the sunlight, and then he saw the geese. Two of them, gliding in perfect formation across the sky. They were slightly off course, and they were early. He watched their progress across the sky, and then he heard the bang.

It seemed to happen in a millisecond that went on forever.

He would never clear from his head the horrible sucking sound, like a gulp, or the final gleam his mother's car sent out, a last sparkle in the beautiful afternoon, before it slipped under the water; he would never forget running along the diving board as though he was running on air because his legs felt like jelly; the dive down into the waters before he'd taken a proper breath, his heart about to be wrenched from his chest cavity, struggling to hold back his terror, the nightmare sight of his mother's frantic face through the glass, inches away from his, unable to open the door, he signalling for her to roll the window down – she waving and gesticulating wildly with her hands, the terror of it all in her eyes, so unreal it couldn't be true, it couldn't be happening – his burning lungs forcing him to leave her and break the surface to draw in gulps of air.

'I couldn't open the door, get her out …' he heard himself say. 'I couldn't … just couldn't … I saw the water rising but I came back up for air – had to – and rushed back down again but it was too late … I couldn't do anything to save her …'

When he dived down again, he saw that she was gone.

When he resurfaced, the day was still as beautiful and incandescent as ever. His raw, rough howl tore from his mouth, bouncing off the encircling mountains, echoing down the valleys.

'It was my fault,' he said, his voice loud and rough. 'My fault she died, no matter what anyone says. It will never leave me … the guilt … I was useless … I still see the desperate look in her eyes in my nightmares …' He closed his eyes and he could see her face again. And her eyes.

Someone was holding him tight. There was a hand clutching his arm, another arm around his torso, someone pressing into him. He realised his clothes were wet, he felt a chill. He was sitting on a wooden floor and it was damp. There was a woman pressing into him, she was shouting. Eventually the words coming out of her mouth infiltrated his brain.

'It's OK … *it's OK*, it wasn't your fault. You didn't kill her. It was an accident … an *accident* … It's OK, you're OK, it's fine, you're fine, it was an *accident* … I'm here, right here … right here …'

He turned to her blindly, her face was there, pale in the dim light. It was Vikki. It was OK. He pressed his face to hers, it was cold and damp, but her mouth, when he found it on instinct and clung to it, was warm.

Beautiful, lovely Vikki.

CHAPTER FORTY-TWO

Vikki woke up, gradually moving from sleep to consciousness, wondering why she felt so warm. And uncomfortable. One of her arms was trapped underneath something heavy. Her other arm was also caught fast. She opened her eyes and found herself staring at the broad expanse of Niall's shoulders, clad in a black T-shirt, and everything that had happened the night before came back to her in a rush.

They'd made it in from the shed, dashing together across the garden through the dancing sheets of rain. Upstairs, they'd hurried between their bedroom and the bathroom, peeling off wet clothes, muffling themselves in thick, fluffy towels, feeling heat coming back into their bodies, and then they'd got into bed and slept.

They'd fallen asleep spooned together, one of her arms was still caught underneath his torso, her other arm was looped across his chest and he was still holding fast to that hand. Then she realised she was jammed up so tightly to him that her breasts were pressed against his back, with only his T-shirt and her cotton top acting as a thin barrier. She held her breath, unable to move, the heat in the bed overpowering. Then she relaxed and decided to luxuriate in the moment and enjoy the feeling of being so close to him.

Without knowing the time, she sensed it was early; the house was silent, not a sound coming from the children's room or the connecting bathroom. There was no sound of raging wind or squally rain – the storm must be over.

After a while Niall stirred. She felt him freeing her hand and she saw his arm snaking around to check what – or who – was behind him. It touched her shoulder and in that instant Niall turned around to face her.

His face was relaxed with the residue of sleep, his hair rumpled, and up close like this, she absorbed every minute detail of him; the texture of his skin, the shade of his eyes in the early morning, watching the way his face changed, became alert, recollections of the night before rippling in his eyes until he was looking at her with gratitude.

'Thank you,' he said.

'You're welcome,' she said.

'You saved me from ... falling down into a terrible black hole that I mightn't have been able to get out of.'

She was tempted to deflect the gravity of the moment and respond with a careless remark, about that kind of thing being her speciality, but the words stuck in her throat at the expression in his eyes.

'You were amazing,' he said.

'You're not so bad yourself,' she said, finding her voice. Then a little softer, 'I was glad to be here. I'm still on your side. I want you to know that. I meant everything I said last night.'

His eyes roved slowly around every detail of her face, as if studying her from a new perspective, and she didn't flinch, not for a second.

'Niall, you have to be kind to yourself for a change,' she said, meeting his eyes with a determined look of her own. 'What happened to your mother was awful, truly terrible, and for you to have been there – I can't imagine how dark you must have felt, then or since, but what do you think she'd want the most for you? A lifetime of regret? Or a lifetime where you let in some peace and happiness that would help to ease the sore spot in your heart?'

His gaze didn't waver. 'I haven't dived since that afternoon,' he said. 'I haven't even been in a swimming pool. My dream was to go to South Africa and the Seychelles to dive, to get more qualifications, but I forgot all about that.'

'You didn't kill her, it was an accident. You did your best. None of us can perform miracles.'

'Being here, this weekend, it's bringing everything back. The funeral … everything about the next few days was a nightmare. Dad's face, Lainey, Alex himself. We were speechless, shocked, it was beyond comprehension that Mum was gone. After the row, we vowed never to talk about it again. Dad knew none of this, he was tanked out with sleeping tablets. We never spoke to him about it, we agreed there was no point.'

'You've been far too hard on yourself. You'll have to learn to live your life, despite what happened. You'll have to start seeing things in a different way.'

'What way?' he asked.

'You did all that was humanly possible to save your mother,' she said. 'No one could have done any more. That afternoon by the lough, look at it another way. You showed great courage when you tried to save your mother. You put your whole life on the line, where – if you hadn't obeyed your instincts – two of you could have died and not just one. It would have been double the devastation for your family.'

He sighed. 'I suppose …'

She moved a little closer. 'It's hard to turn around the thoughts of a lifetime,' she said. 'Don't let the bad side of that day fill up all the good spaces in your mind and heart, and define the rest of your life. Supposing it had been Alex who'd dived in, Alex who was in your shoes, Alex who hadn't been able to save your mother. Would you want him to spend the rest of his life cracked up with guilt? What if Alex was feeling exactly as you are now, what would you say to him?'

'I wouldn't say anything,' Niall said.

'Wouldn't you?' She was disappointed.

'I'd give him a big hug.'

'Why?'

'Because I'd want to let him know it's OK, he tried, and I still love him anyway.'

She put her arms around him. 'Let me give you that hug.'

He looked into her eyes for a long moment. Then, 'Thank you again. You've been very good to me.'

Good?

'I mean that in the nicest way possible,' he said. 'I'm not explaining myself very well. Just know that you being here is everything.' They stared at each other, and something leapt inside Vikki, a need, a desire, a longing, almost painful in its intensity.

He sensed it. She knew by his face. He moved nearer until his face was but inches away from hers, and then he kissed her on the forehead. But instead of drawing away, his lips stayed there. She could hardly breathe with the nearness of him in the bed, the whole solidity of the man, and she lay very still. After a while he kissed the side of her face, the tip of her nose, her closed eyelids, with an infinitely tender touch, and she sensed him pulling back and felt a dart of dismay, but it was only to make himself more comfortable and move closer again, because in the next moment, she felt the strength of his hard thighs pressing against her legs and he put his arms around her and kissed her mouth.

Her heart hammered in her throat as she kissed him back. She was suffused with heat; it came from within, it radiated from his body, and under the duvet, it encircled both of them. The kiss went on forever, deep and strong; she was dazed, she was on fire, everything fell away except for the glorious sensation of kissing him, she never wanted this to stop and it was difficult to surface when it came to an end.

'Wow,' he murmured, leaning up on his elbow, smiling at her as he stroked her cheek. 'That was … even better than the way you kissed me last night.' There was a question in his eyes as he traced the outline of her lips with his index finger.

'Yes … it was,' she said, her head spinning, a wonderful feeling of certainty sweeping up from her toes.

She didn't care what she was doing; she forgot the past, it had no place here, she forgot her worries about the future, it didn't exist right now; feeling this man inside her was the only thing that mattered. She sat up long enough to pull her cotton top over her head, watching his beautiful eyes darken with desire as he looked up at her. She lay back down again, her skin burning all over, aching for his touch.

He pulled off his T-shirt and shrugged out of his boxer shorts.

He laughed gently and hitched the duvet up around them both, and in the cocoon of warmth, he gathered her close so that they were clinging together, skin to skin, kissing and touching, tangling their limbs, tasting and stroking, her body soft and tender, his, lean and rock hard.

She melted into the heat, in the fever-pitch moment when he slid his hand under her pants, cupping her intimately, and she heard his swift intake of breath. Hers had stopped momentarily because his fingers were doing exquisite things. He pulled her pants away and she waited for a long, aching moment. He gazed at her at the same time as he began to push inside her, his face trusting and vulnerable, and there was nothing in the world she wanted more than the pure joy of this man filling her up.

Later, they heard the children waken, scampering in and out of the bathroom and across the landing, eventually going downstairs, their voices excitable and high-pitched. She listened to them, loving the way Niall stroked and teased her under the cover of the duvet, stopping her moans with kisses until he was satisfied the children were all downstairs.

'You're very special,' he said softly to her. 'You're funny and beautiful. I hope you know that, Vikki Gordon.'

'Sure I do,' she said, stretching herself like a languid cat, feeling free and uninhibited. And happy. And tingling, still, all over. And loving the feel of his face next to hers as she absorbed the sleepy scent of him and then the moment when she felt herself being wrapped once again in his arms, enjoying more ripples of pleasure that were almost painful in their intensity.

Downstairs, so much had happened the night before that no one seemed to notice the new closeness between them or the glow Vikki felt wrapped in, thanks to the way Niall was looking at her, holding her hand, touching her waist. As they passed from the kitchen into the dining room, she could hardly take her eyes off the way he moved his body, whether it was the set of his head, the breadth of his shoulders in his grey jumper, his hand pouring juice for both of them, the touch of his fingertips as he handed her a glass. The children were chattering away, Alex and Jenna were in a world of their own being extra attentive towards each other, and Lainey was much quieter and more subdued than normal. Only Ben was much the same, and he was in and out of the kitchen helping Lainey with the cooked breakfast. The electricity was still gone and they were dependent on the solid fuel cooker for cooking and to heat the water for tea or coffee.

'No Erin or Niamh this morning?' Niall asked, as he replaced the carton of juice in the fridge.

'I wasn't expecting them,' Lainey said. 'The last time we had a storm like this we had landslides, fallen trees and we know there are some power lines down as well.'

'I hope we can get to the airport in the morning,' Niall said.

'It's hard to say,' Lainey said. 'It depends on whether there are any more landslides or toppling trees.'

'I need to get back to London. So does Vikki.' He smiled at Vikki to include her. His smile was so tender that it gave her a small hint of what he visualised might happen when they returned, and, for the first time that morning, she felt a tiny sliver of hope mixed with a nibble of anxiety rippling across her heart.

Could they have a future together, even if she couldn't bring herself to talk about her past? Would Niall accept that and understand? She pushed her worries away for the moment because she didn't want hard reality to intrude on the warm glow that now surrounded her.

They were just finished their breakfast when Lainey announced that Leo wanted to see the family again.

'We can go in as soon as I organise the children to keep them occupied,' Lainey said. 'He said it won't take long, but he needs to see us all. I hope—'

'Hope what?' Niall asked.

'He seems very down,' Lainey said. 'I hope it's not anything more dramatic than what he had to say last night.'

CHAPTER FORTY-THREE

Propped up against pillows, Leo watched his family gather around. His bedroom was sunny this morning, a thick band of pale-yellow light slanting across the walls, bringing a cheerful brightness to the room after the dim candlelight of the night before. There would be no hiding in the shadows today, no falling asleep before he said what he'd gathered them here for – no avoiding the unforgiving truth.

Funnily enough, despite his confession of the night before, they seemed more relaxed today, with no sign of any animosity towards him. For the first time that weekend, Alex looked at ease, standing behind a seated Jenna, his hands on her shoulders, her hand covering one of his protectively. Niall, too, looked as though he was in good spirits, his arm curving around Vikki's waist. Only

Lainey, sitting on the side of his bed, looked as though she hadn't slept very well, her face was pale and she had shadows under her eyes. His heart contracted in anxiety, for she would, he guessed, be the most upset of all.

'I have something to tell you,' he began, mentally preparing himself for stripping away any final illusions his children held. 'About the summer your mother died—' He choked on the word; it was still so difficult to think of his vibrant Gabrielle gone.

Lainey gave a sigh. 'Don't look so worried, Dad, it can't be that bad.'

'It is. When I said I held myself responsible for your mother's death, it wasn't just because of Maura,' he began. 'There was something else … I can only guess it was the undoing of her …'

Those days rolled through his head with perfect clarity: every nuance of every scene, the emotions that pulled and sucked at him, even the same waves of sunlight that set his bedroom walls aglow this morning had shimmered around Lynes Glen, winking and glimmering, paying no heed as his world plunged into greater and darker depths.

*

To his immense disquiet, Gabrielle invited Maura to stay for a few days.

'We've so much catching up to do, I can get a bed ready for you,' Gabrielle suggested. 'It's just a divan in an attic room but you're welcome to it for a few nights. Isn't she, Leo?'

'Of course.' The words were wrenched from him, leaving a tightness in his throat. He saw the flash of triumph in Maura's eyes before it was hidden by her lowered lashes and slightly bowed head. Fake humility didn't suit her.

'We've far too much food and drink in, as it is,' Gabrielle said.

'With all the children at home, I stocked up. I've never forgotten that it's thanks to you I have all this …'

'What did I do?' Maura asked.

'If you hadn't left a vacancy in the hotel, I'd never have met Leo in the first place.' Gabrielle came over and kissed his cheek. Judas Iscariot in reverse. Over his wife's shoulder, he saw the cool way Maura was observing them. He wanted to weep. Didn't Gabrielle realise the Trojan horse she was admitting into the peaceful beauty of Lynes Glen?

'That's settled, then,' Gabrielle said. 'Come on out to the sunshine, the children are all relaxing on the terrace. Leo' – this to him over her shoulder, her face happy and innocent – 'will you get the drinks?'

Later that week, Gabrielle had to go to a meeting in the hospital outside Westport where she acted as voluntary secretary to the fundraising committee.

'Do something nice while I'm gone,' Gabrielle said, as they sat on the terrace with morning coffee and fruit scones.

'Is the fairy fort still there?' Maura asked.

He listened to the chat as if from far away. Gabrielle gone for the morning filled him with nameless dread.

'Yes,' Lainey said. 'You should pay a visit. If I wasn't going into Galway with Alex I'd go with you. Make sure you make a really good wish.'

They were all conspiring to desert him, leaving him unattended with Maura. Even Niall had asked to borrow his car to go diving in Sligo.

'I'll make a wish for you, Lainey,' Maura said. 'I'm not so good at making them for myself.'

'Your wishes aren't big enough,' he heard Alex say. 'We Blakes only make huge, wonderful wishes. The fairies get scared when they see us coming.'

'And do your wishes come true?'

'All the time,' Alex boasted. 'They wouldn't dare to hold out on us.'

'Isn't it well for you then, having even the fairies at your disposal,' Maura said, flashing him a smile. He had a sudden urge to scratch that smile off her face.

'Go on, off you go up to the fort,' Gabrielle said. 'It's a lovely day for a walk. I'll be back by lunchtime.'

*

It was up in the fairy fort that his world crumpled. The magical place that was supposed to be the keeper of dreams, part of his children's innocent childhood, became instead the nightmare spot that haunted him for years.

They walked in silence for a while, Maura wearing cut-off shorts and a red top, the sun flickering between the trees, the breeze kind and gentle.

'I wish you'd stop looking at me as though I'm the devil incarnate,' she said eventually. 'I'm amazed your family haven't noticed your attitude towards me yet.'

'Why are you back here and what do you want?'

'That's not very welcoming now, is it?'

'Sorry I don't extend the same welcome to you as Gabrielle has.'

'I take it she doesn't know.'

'Know what?'

'That says it all. Do you even remember? You've hardly forgotten, have you?'

'I thought you would have long forgotten, seeing as it was largely irrelevant to you. I thought you had far more exciting men to remember.'

'No, actually, I never forgot.'

'I find that hard to believe.'

'Some of us have certainly moved onwards and upwards. Look at you, and the setup you have. And your success. I bet you never expected that for a mountain man.'

'I owe everything I have to Gabrielle.'

When they reached the clearing, fond memories of his children running freely about the fort swam in front of him in the incandescent afternoon.

'What do you want, Maura?' he asked, disgusted with the note of desperation in his voice. 'You're hardly here to make a wish. Is it money? Are you about to blackmail me?' In the depths of the night, he had wondered if this was the case, feverishly trying to figure out how he could pay her off.

Maura looked as though she wanted to slap him. 'How dare you, you arrogant man! How dare you think I've come here for money. I've never been so insulted in my life.'

'What, then?' He was suddenly nervous, realising with a sickening sensation that there was more to her homecoming than just a casual visit. 'Why have you come back now, after all these years?'

'Twenty-seven years minus nine months.'

'I don't understand.'

'No, I didn't think you would,' she said smartly. 'You might be terribly clever with words, but you're not so good at the maths. You can be very obtuse at times, Leo.'

'My family wouldn't agree. I love them more than anything.'

'I know you do, but isn't that partly because they're an

extension of yourself? Think about it. Anyway, you don't love all of your family. You haven't met your other child yet.'

'What other child?' At first he was numb, as if his mind was warding off the blow.

'Ours. Mine and yours.'

'What are you talking about?' The breath was knocked out of him. He couldn't believe the afternoon was going on much as normal, the birds chirping, the breeze whispering in the trees, while something terrible was waiting to pounce. How could this be? He began to walk away, back down the path to the house but she pulled at his arm.

'You're going to listen to me,' she said.

'I am listening,' he said, his insides dissolving into a liquid mess.

Her words, delivered calmly and without emotion, shattered his life. She spoke of her shock at finding herself pregnant soon after she arrived in London, despite them taking precautions. Adoption was the only option, and by far the best for the child. She put her heartbreak behind her – eventually – and got on with her life. Now she was head of Customer Relations in a Covent Garden hotel, she had friends, holidays, a good life. But no love, and no one to call her own. And the child had finally contacted her through social services.

'If I decide to respond,' she said, her voice subdued, 'I can't pretend you don't exist.'

'What am I supposed to say to that?'

'I'm not asking for an answer now, I know this has come as a shock. I've been living with it for twenty-seven years. I know you need time to get your head around it.'

'Hah.'

'I have two more weeks' holiday leave. I was supposed to be

going to Italy but when the letter arrived I cancelled those plans and came here instead. I'd no intentions of staying in Lynes Glen but I couldn't resist it for a few nights, after Gabrielle's warm welcome.'

'I don't want her hurt, I don't want any of them hurt.'

'I'll get out from under your feet, give you some head space. I need time to think myself. I'm going to rent a holiday cottage outside the town, it's already arranged.'

He stopped and faced her. They were approaching Lynes Glen and never had the sight of the chimney pots torn his heart so much. 'No matter how long or short you stay, Maura, I can't see how I can bring myself to tell my wife and family that I have another child as a result of one night with you.'

'You sound so cold … shame on you, Leo.'

'Do you want to destroy Gabrielle's life? And my children's?'

Nothing was resolved between them that day. Maura moved to her rented cottage and it wasn't until the hellish days following Gabrielle's funeral that he spoke to her once more. She arrived unannounced at Lynes Glen and he brought her into the library.

'What are you doing here?' he snapped.

'I have to talk to you. Please, Leo.'

He hadn't seen her at the funeral. Then again he hadn't seen anyone. Similar to their wedding day, when he'd had eyes only for Gabrielle's beauty, on the day of her funeral, he'd only seen the flower-laden coffin, unable to understand how this had come to be, every cell in his body shrieking that Gabrielle couldn't possibly be in that wooden box, lying cold as marble. Seeing it being swallowed up by a hole in the ground had driven him demented with grief.

It took a monumental effort for him to look Maura in the eye.

'I don't want to see you. Or talk to you. Gabrielle …' his throat closed over at the mention of her name '… had come from your house when she had the accident. What did you tell her about us?'

'Very little,' Maura said quietly. 'She turned up unexpectedly … she'd a funny look on her face and I was full sure you'd spoken to her.'

'I hadn't.'

'We talked about a few things … whatever way I spoke, she guessed we'd slept together.' Maura paused and gulped.

'You told her about the child.'

'I didn't.'

'I don't believe you.'

'For God's sake, Leo, listen to me. I didn't say a word. But whether you believe me or not, it won't make any difference now. I was the last person to see her alive. The last person she spoke to. Oh God, is there anything I could have said differently? I keep going over it in my mind … I feel so bad about this I can't bear it.'

'*You* can't bear it? How dare you – get out of this house. I don't want to see you again.'

'Please, Leo…' She kept talking but her words danced in front of him. Eventually she realised it was useless and backed away. 'Don't worry, I'm going,' she said sadly. 'I've messed up everything. I love you, Leo. I always have. You were always and ever the only one for me. I hate to see you in such pain and your family … oh God, I didn't mean to cause this.'

'Just go.'

'I've a flight out of Knock in the morning. I'll be in London by lunchtime and I won't be back.'

There was a finality in her tone that saddened him.

'Let me know what you decide to do,' he told her.

She gave him a heavy-hearted smile. 'You'll find out one way or another ...'

*

Leo was so caught up in the events of 1995 that it took him a while to re-orientate himself. In the bedroom in Lynes Glen, looking around at his family, he could see they had been stunned into silence. He felt a curious emptiness.

'So now you know,' he said. 'That's the sorry story. I have another child, whom I refused to acknowledge. My conscience is getting heavier and I want to make amends before it's too late. I'll need your help. But I don't blame you if none of you have the inclination to help me after what I've done.'

Lainey looked at him wide-eyed. 'Are you saying that Mum found out? And she was so upset she lost control of the car that day?'

'I can't think of any other reason,' he said, sighing heavily. 'Maura denied telling her about the child but she was as inconsolable as I was, so she mightn't have remembered clearly.' Leo took out a handkerchief and wiped his brimming eyes. 'That was the last time I saw Maura. I'm sorry I didn't have the courage to tell you before, I was too ashamed of myself. At the time you were all brokenhearted enough as it was. How could I twist the knife in further? I preferred to live with my guilt and let it drive me mad. I tried to keep some distance from you all, I couldn't bear to witness your unhappiness or heartbreak, or confess I was the cause of it. I know it was weak and selfish of me.'

Alex and Niall were clearly stunned. The silence in the room intensified.

Eventually Lainey said, 'So why now, this weekend?'

At least she was still talking to him. She hadn't walked out. Neither had his sons.

'I want to make reparation, if it's not too late,' Leo said. 'Maura did what she thought was for the best under the circumstances. I did nothing. That's something else on my conscience. I don't think Maura ever managed to respond to social services ... poor Maura, she was distraught ... hers was another tragedy in its own way ...' The distress on her face the last time he'd seen her was something else that had haunted him.

Lainey clasped and unclasped her hands. 'I thought you were – God forbid – dying or something, and you wanted to see us all together one last time.'

Leo summoned a smile. 'I'm most certainly dying, but not just yet, I hope. The little ones have given me a reason to stay alive. Having everyone together again is wonderful, apart from my upsetting news. I was surprised when you all accepted my invitation. I was expecting at least one refusal, maybe two ...' He couldn't help looking from Niall to Alex.

Niall shook his head. 'After your second invitation, it was impossible to refuse.'

Leo was momentarily confused. 'Second invitation? I might be in my eighties but I only recall sending out one. I was very proud of my computer work and clip art.'

'There was a second note,' Niall said, 'to say that you were so anxious to see us all together, that if one of us decided not to come, the others would be taken out of your will.'

'*What*? Definitely not. As if I'd do anything as unfair as that. Come on, now.'

His family stared at him as though he was gaga.

'That's strange,' Lainey said. 'I thought you were so desperate to see us you were resorting to blackmail. Isn't that right, Alex, Niall?' She looked around at her brothers.

They clearly thought he was in his dotage. He felt too drained after his confession to process this confusion. He seized on the one positive thing that jumped out at him. 'It's good you all made the effort to come home and ensure your siblings got their share of the estate, and that none of you thought to stay away and take the opportunity to try and grab it all for yourself – not that it would have happened anyway. My will is fair and equal.'

'You mean it's good we all came home, to be together this weekend,' Lainey said, speaking slowly. She leaned closer to him. 'Dad? Do you know what happened to Mum's ruby pendant? The one you gave her for her birthday? She hardly ever left it off and she'd been wearing it the day of the accident … we all thought it had been lost.'

'It wasn't lost,' he said heavily. 'Gabrielle left it in Maura's that day. Maura said the clasp was loose and it had slipped off your mother, but I thought Gabrielle had taken it off and left it there on purpose. To send me a message of sorts. That she didn't believe in my love anymore. When Maura tried to give it back to me I told her to get rid of it. I never wanted to see either it or her again. Why?'

Lainey's face flooded with anxiety. 'It turned up here last night.'

CHAPTER FORTY-FOUR

I've been to the graveyard. Curiosity, I suppose. An urge to know she's still well and truly buried under the cold hard earth. I hate her by default. If it hadn't been for her, my life could have been so different.

The graveyard is in a windy spot overlooking the Atlantic ocean, bounded by a meandering straggle of low stone walls. It's ancient. Some of the crumbling headstones date back to the early 1800s but a lot of them are so old they're illegible. It's weird to think of all the people buried here, several generations gone, one after another, all their hopes and dreams, rivalries and passions reduced to nothing but a layer of dust, trapped in a stagnant, airless box, untouched by the fitful sunshine or the fluttering breeze.

I'd say there are few visitors. The breeze coming in off the foaming sea is sharp, it skitters around, dancing between the stones, twisting and flattening tufts of unkempt grass. In this desolate place they are the only signs of life and movement. Close to the ruins of an old church there is a small black marble headstone with a simple inscription in gold lettering: Gabrielle Blake, beloved wife and mother, born 1 June 1947, died 29 August 1995. There are no memorabilia, prayerful or otherwise, adorning her grave, nothing to indicate the kind of life she led or the bright vivacity of the woman now buried here.

In death Gabrielle is silent and anonymous. No ghost writhing up from the layers of maggoty soil in a shimmer of golden hair and translucent skin. No flowers or plants even, just pebbles covering the surface. Then again no blooms would last for any length of time in this godforsaken, wind-whipped corner of the world.

I look again at the date of death; two weeks before my mother met her untimely end, dropping in front of a Paddington-bound express train in the middle of London rush hour.

I hadn't known about it at the time. I found out years later, long after I had given up hope of hearing any response to my letter. Not that I had expected much of a response, given the irate nature of the letter I had written when I was in a totally black frame of mind. Even after I sent it, I still felt angry and I hated the thoughts of my natural parents so much that it was cracking me up. I tried to forget about them and get on with my own life as best I could. Surely all my bad luck, all the crap, was behind me now?

It wasn't. It had left a scorching mark on my heart. One that had scarred me for life.

Then in the way fate can twist like a hairpin bend, the social services were clearing out old offices prior to demolition and they came across a small package addressed to me. My mother had posted it to them but it had been misfiled and had languished for years in a pile of storage boxes containing bundles of old records. It took them a while to find me, as I had moved a few times after my initial enquiries. I had to travel to London in person to confirm my identity before they handed over anything. The small package contained the diary, a few faded photographs, a ruby pendant, a video tape, and my mother's birth certificate. They apologised profusely for the mix-up and offered to help in the search for my mother.

I needed help. There were thousands of Maura Kellys out there, but the details in the diary helped. Then they called me back into their spanking-new offices with a view of the Thames, putting a glass of water and a box of tissues in front of me. They told me they'd traced her and, as delicately as possible, explained what had happened. I wanted neither the tissues nor the water. The pain in my heart was too deep to be mopped up.

I managed to get a copy of her death certificate and the coroner's report. Her death was ruled an open verdict. Witnesses gave evidence that she'd seemed perfectly composed as she'd moved beyond the yellow line, but no one had expected her plunge into the path of the oncoming train. At her father's wishes, she'd been cremated – whatever was left of her – and interred into the memorial wall of a London cemetery. I haven't been there yet.

It was only a matter of time before I traced the Blakes and Lynes Glen and made sense of everything. The final, real-time entries in the diary plague me, it's like I can hear her actual voice calling – no, crying out – across time and distance:

I must speak to Leo … and Alex; an entry that was dated the fourth of September.

Then the final entry, three days later, a week before she plunged to her death:

I told Alex I know when I'm not wanted … He's off to the States. I'm going back to London. The family are blaming us for Gabrielle's death and Niall tried to kill him with a kitchen knife. Even Leo is distraught. I hate to see the look on his face. There is nothing here for me now … my heart aches like it never has before and I can't bear it …

Between them, they fucked her up, Leo and Alex. Those bastards are both to blame for what happened to my mother and now they will pay. Any time this morning. I wonder how long it will take for the awful realisation to kick in …

CHAPTER FORTY-FIVE

Vikki was glad of the weight of Niall's arm around her shoulders as they filed out of Leo's bedroom. It meant he was still connected to her despite his father's bombshell. Leo had admitted to being exhausted and he'd asked to be left alone so he could rest for a while. He'd give the family time to absorb the shock and chat to them later. Even though Niall's face was subdued, he met her eyes and smiled.

'I'll get Dad a glass of water and make sure he's settled, but I'll be back,' he said, going ahead into the kitchen.

In the living room, Vikki saw the top of Charlotte's head peeking over the sofa before she hurriedly ducked down out of sight.

'Charlotte, what on earth are you doing there?' Lainey asked sharply.

Even Charlotte seemed surprised by her mother's harsh tone, looking abashed as she poked her head back out.

'We're playing hide-and-go-seek, Harry has to find me and Jack, but now you've spoiled it. He'll know where I am.'

'Oh, for God's sake,' Lainey snapped.

Alex and Jenna walked in, arm in arm. 'Where's Jack?' Alex asked.

'He's hiding too,' Charlotte said. 'It's Harry's turn to be on.'

'Play it upstairs, darling,' Ben said, going across to ruffle her hair. 'I'll go up and we'll arrange some more games in a few minutes, Mummy just needs a little time to herself. OK?'

Charlotte pulled a face and stomped upstairs.

'I'll put the water on for coffee,' Vikki suggested, knowing it was one way of making herself useful.

'Good idea,' Ben said.

Alex disappeared out onto the terrace with Jenna, to talk privately, she guessed. Ben was trying to put on a good face but she could see he'd been as much affected by Leo's words as Lainey had been. She filled a pot with water and put it on the stove. She saw him take Lainey to one side and hug her, murmuring in her ear, Lainey clinging to him while she mopped up her tears. Ben put his fingers gently to her cheek to stop them from falling and in a tender gesture he wiped them away. Lainey wrapped her arms around his neck and leaned into him. Vikki looked away, feeling she was intruding. She felt hands on her shoulders and Niall turned her around to face him.

He kissed her on the forehead and gave her a hug. 'What a weekend. Family drama. Silly pranks. Old secrets, confessions. You've certainly had an introduction to the family, and there was me, afraid you'd be bored.'

'Bored?' she said. 'I think this weekend has kicked Barcelona into touch.' Then on a softer note, 'All families have secrets. I hope you're OK.'

'Dad's news was a shock. To say the least. I can't take it in. All these years … all this time … who knows …' He left the sentence unfinished and ran a hand through his hair so that it stuck up in small unruly tufts.

She resisted the urge to reach up and smooth it down. 'Such is life in all its multicolours.' She knew at first hand, didn't she? Nothing was ever black and white.

'Thanks,' he said. 'You've been brilliant. I thought I'd scuppered our beautiful friendship.'

'You haven't, anything but.' She hoped she wouldn't scupper it when he found out she'd no plans to introduce him to her family. 'I'm even making myself useful,' she said, ducking away from him. 'Coffee coming up.' She took some mugs and a jar of instant coffee out of the press and set them on the counter.

'Coffee time – good,' Ben said, arriving into the kitchen. 'I think we could all do with it. Thanks, Vikki, you're a star.'

'I hope it tastes OK, it's not exactly state of the art.'

'It'll taste beautiful,' Ben said, spooning instant granules into the mugs. 'I think Lainey needs this more than I do,' he said.

'How is she?' Niall asked.

'She's a bit fragile. She never expected this.'

'It's not over yet,' Niall said. 'We still don't know who's been messing us about with their silly pranks.'

'I don't think Lainey can take any more shocks or pranks for now,' Ben said. 'I'll bring this out to her and make sure the children stay out of her hair for a while.'

Niall picked up two mugs. 'Come on, Vikki, we'll go and chat in the library.'

*

Out on the terrace, the air tasted cool and fresh, and Jenna loved the crystal sharpness of it on her tongue as she drew in large gulps. Pools of rainwater, overturned planters, and a layer of debris from the trees in the forest were the only signs of the previous night's storm. The sky arched overhead, remnants of puffy, white clouds drifting across the blue expanse. Even though they'd talked at length, and made tender love the night before, she'd feared for Alex back in Leo's bedroom, because his face had gone so pale. Since they'd left Leo's room, he'd been silent and withdrawn.

'Talk to me, Alex,' she urged. 'Don't shut me out this time.'

Her attraction to Ben had been a cold wake-up call. What had she been thinking of, allowing herself to wallow in flirty imaginings? It would have been all too easy to let Alex and her marriage slide away from her, but last night had given her a renewed determination to fight her corner of their marriage and not allow him to shut himself off. She'd been on vulnerable ground before, unsure of the depths of his love, afraid to rock any boats in case they flipped over. She should have had more faith in herself.

'I won't shut you out, promise,' he said. 'I'm still stunned. Dad and Maura, and a child, for God's sake. How the hell did I let myself get messed up with her?' He sat forward on the stone seat and put his head in his hands.

Jenna sat on her hunkers in front of him, and peeled his hands away from his face. 'It's in the past, Alex, it was a different life. Look at me,' she said forcibly, as he closed his eyes. 'Open your eyes and look at me. It doesn't matter what you did. I mean this. Get it into your head that the important things now are you, me and Jack. Being alive and well and there for each other. Right?'

He opened his eyes and looked at her and her heart melted with the expression in his.

'As soon as we're back home,' she continued, 'whatever stuff you have to sort out with your company, we'll do it together. We can still take a glass of wine out onto a balcony, but we'll do that together too, and so what if we need to re-locate, it doesn't have to be a tenth-floor balcony with a view of Battery Park or the Hudson. Alex' – she squeezed his hand – 'no matter what's going on around us, your family, the business, you and me are going to take time to relax and talk to each other, and to go out every Friday night, as lovers on a date, even if it's cheap and cheerful. I don't want to go through anything like the silence of the last few months ever again. I want my passionate Alex back. I know he's still there.'

She was rewarded with a smile. She sat up beside him. 'Hey, give me a hug.'

He gave her a hug and kissed her hand. 'You're cold,' he said.

'Only on the outside, and it's good to get out into the fresh air. It's so clear and pure you could nearly drink it. On the inside I'm feeling lovely and warm. Happy. Good. Excited for us and the future. It'll work out once we have each other.'

'We'll be on our way as soon as we help Dad get sorted, and we have to find out what's happening with the power one way or another today. And get to the bottom of those weird incidents. It's strange that Mum's pendant—'

Alex paused as Ben came out through the French doors.

'Is everything all right?' Jenna asked, alarmed by his sober face.

'No,' Ben said. 'Jack's missing.'

CHAPTER FORTY-SIX

Vikki's heart sank as they went around the house and there was no sign of Jack. She couldn't bear to look at Jenna's white face, never mind Alex's. They raced from room to room and up and down the stairs, calling out his name. She and Niall went over every inch of the ground floor, while Ben and Lainey searched the attics and gardens. Everyone arrived back in the living room, their faces tight with anxiety, the air swirling with tension.

'Tell us exactly what happened,' Ben said to Charlotte.

'We were just playing, that's all,' Charlotte said, half crying, half gulping in her distress.

'It's OK, nobody's blaming you,' Ben said, his voice reassuring.

'I thought Jack was a very good hider, we couldn't find him for ages.' She let out an explosion of sobs.

'Try and stay calm, Charlotte. Relax. We need you to help us. OK? Now think for a minute, what time did you last see Jack?' Ben asked.

'But that's what I *am* saying, it was ages ago.'

'What was he doing the last time you saw him?'

'It was Harry's turn to find us. He was upstairs at the end of the landing counting, with his eyes closed.'

'Just to be clear, who was counting? Harry or Jack?'

'I *said* Harry. He had to count up to fifty. Me and Jack tiptoed downstairs and I hid behind the sofa. I thought Jack was going to hide in the kitchen.' She stared wildly towards the kitchen doorway as though he was suddenly going to walk through it.

'Was that when we were coming out of your grandad's room?' Ben asked, his voice very calm, belying the fact that some ten minutes had passed since then, and more time had passed since Charlotte had seen him. 'Remember we came out and you were behind the sofa. Was Jack in the kitchen then?'

'I think so 'cos I said you were going to spoil the game and I knew that if you saw me in here then you'd see Jack in the kitchen and send him upstairs as well. I went up and hid under the bed. I didn't hear Jack coming up so I thought he'd hidden really well or was just being quiet as a mouse.'

'I'll check the kitchen again,' Jenna said, starting towards it.

Ben shook his head. 'He's not there, or anywhere downstairs. Or with Leo. We've checked.'

'Still, I'd rather have another look myself,' Jenna said.

They all heard her voice, softly cracking in two, as she called out, moving across the kitchen, opening the pantry door, checking the utility room once more, 'It's OK, Jack, you can come out now, the game is over.'

'He's not in the house,' Ben said to Alex.

'He's not in the gardens either,' Lainey said. 'How far outside could a six-year-old get in twenty minutes?'

'You don't think he's wandered off outside, do you?' Jenna had come in from the kitchen in time to hear this and she put a fist to her mouth, looking as though she was biting back a full-scale scream.

'I think it's worth checking the places we've taken him to,' Alex said.

'We'll have to organise ourselves properly,' Ben said. 'No point in everyone rushing out in all directions without some kind of plan.'

'I'll check Infinity Hill,' Niall said. 'Vikki, are you on for a hike?'

'Sure,' she said.

'I'll do the fairy fort,' Alex said.

'I'll come with you,' Ben offered.

They moved out into the hall and fetched jackets from the cloakroom. Alex shook his head when he saw Jenna reach for her jacket and scarf.

'No, Jenna, please wait here.'

'Are you afraid of what you might find?' she asked in a trembling voice.

'Not at all,' Alex said, the anxiety in his eyes as he pulled on his jacket belying his reasonable tone of voice. 'He's probably out looking for rabbits. I'd like one of us to stay here in case he comes home in the meantime. Maybe Lainey will stay with you?'

'Sure,' his sister said.

'Alex and I will check around the gardens outside one more time before we head to the fort,' Ben offered. 'Charlotte, why don't you play Snap with Harry?'

'Are we in trouble?' the little girl asked, her eyes big as saucers.

'You're not in trouble.'

'But Jack must be. He told us he saw the ghost again last night. But he asked us to promise not to tell.'

Jenna stifled a gasp.

'There is no ghost,' Lainey said, sharply enough for Charlotte's eyes to fill with tears. To her brothers she said, 'Come back here as soon as you've checked those places.'

Alex gave Lainey a quick hug and then they were all outside.

*

Vikki and Niall trekked most of the way hand in hand and in silence, a tacit silence as they both had their ears attuned, listening to any sounds of a small boy. The track was muddy and dotted with puddles, making it slippery in parts. After the rain, the scent of the pine trees was intoxicating, and the bulk of Slieve Creagh, visible through gaps in the trees, thrust into a sky rinsed clear of all rain. But the further they went from Lynes Glen, the less convinced Vikki was that a six-year-old had ventured this far.

They were dispirited when they got back to the house to find out that Alex and Ben had drawn a blank also.

By now Jenna was standing in the hallway with her jacket on. 'I'm going out, I'll find him.'

'Jenna, please,' Alex said.

'You can't stop me,' she said, desperately. 'He's our son. He's lost. We can't even phone anyone for help. Or keep in touch with each other when we're out searching.'

'I don't like what I'm thinking,' Lainey said.

'What is it?' Jenna hissed, grabbing her arm. 'Tell me, Lainey, don't go all secretive, this is our *son*, he's *missing*.'

'I don't know what to think,' Lainey said. 'My head is all over the place. Never mind all the shitty things that have happened this weekend, this is a nightmare. But you'd almost think it had been planned.'

'Planned?' Jenna's voice rose. 'Do you think he's been abducted?'

'You said it yourself, we can't even phone for help, it's all very clever. Who could have been so clever?'

'What are you saying?' Alex's face was white.

'We were all in Dad's room when Jack went missing,' Lainey said, her words pouring out. 'Coincidence? Or was someone waiting for that chance? I was caught up this weekend thinking either Niall or Alex were up to tricks, trying to upset everyone, and you two were convinced it was each other or me, getting some kind of stupid revenge for breaking up the family when Mum died. But what if it was someone else all along … someone else with an interest in provoking this family?'

'Like who?' Niall asked.

'Our father has another child out there, who'd be a little older than Alex now. A child he pretended didn't exist… I'd be very hurt if that were me. I'd probably come looking for him. I might even want to harass the family.'

Jenna grabbed her shoulders and shook her. 'What are you talking about, Lainey?'

'There was someone who was clever enough to use blackmail to make sure we all turned up this weekend by sending a second invitation,' Lainey said, her voice shaking. 'Someone whom Dad entrusted to post his invitations, who would have found it easy to use his computer, who had all the address details to hand… who would have had the opportunity to set up all the crappy things before we arrived … I'm talking about Erin. When I think of it now, sweet Jesus – she just happened to appear at the right time, when I was badly stuck for help with

Dad. Because Helen, his assistant, had just broken her hip in a mugging incident down in the town. Helen was attacked from behind and the assailant was never found. Coincidence? Or planned?'

Alex swore. 'Erin,' he said. 'You're joking. You hardly think she's Dad's …'

'She could well be, she's about the right age. Did she just happen to arrive in a small town like Creaghbara at the right time by pure chance? Or had she deliberately tracked down Dad? I was so glad to take her on I didn't question too much. She was good with Dad, and good with me. Was she biding her time? She knew exactly what was planned for the weekend. She helped with the preparations. She has a set of keys, she knows this house like the back of her hand.'

'Why, though?' Niall asked.

'Why? It's obvious. I know exactly how I'd feel if I were her; she was rejected and now she wants to get back at this family…'

'We're wasting time,' Jenna said. 'I don't give a flying fuck about Erin. I want to find Jack.'

Vikki hated making the suggestion, but it had to be said. 'I think we should check the lough.'

'That's all blocked off,' Alex said.

'Not quite,' Ben replied.

Niall rubbed his face as though he was trying to wake up from a bad dream. 'Vikki's right. Both she and Jenna saw someone down by the diving board the first day we arrived. Someone with long red hair … like Jack's ghost …'

There was a cold silence.

'Fuck.' Alex put his hands up to his head. 'We need help. How far is the nearest mobile signal?'

Ben zipped up his jacket again and checked his pockets for

keys. 'Back towards the town. You come into range about two miles down the road. You pass the lough on the way. I'll take the jeep. See how far I can get. Niall, come with me. I'll drop you at the lough.'

'I'll go with Niall,' Vikki said immediately.

'So will I,' Alex said.

'Alex, there's a way to the lough through the forest, around the barricades, you best go that way with Jenna,' Ben suggested. 'Never mind how I know, just go. If anyone is heading to the lough from here, that's most likely the route they'll take – we didn't hear any cars. They could be anywhere along that trail. Lainey, please stay here. We need someone at home just in case.'

Vikki noticed that he didn't say what the 'just in case' was and nobody dared to ask. Just in case something happened to the other children? Or Leo? Outside, she shivered with apprehension as she climbed into the jeep, Niall in front. Ben reversed down from the side of the house and spun out onto the road. Vikki saw Alex and Jenna already sprinting hand in hand across the garden to the gate in the wall and the edge of the forest.

'How long is it going to take them?' Niall asked.

'Fifteen or twenty minutes,' Ben said. 'Long enough for us to get there first and make sure Jack is safe.'

So he wasn't just a great big cuddly bear, Vikki realised. He was thinking clearer than any of them.

'You don't think he's in any real danger, though?' Niall asked.

'I don't know,' Ben said tightly. 'I'm not good at fathoming people, I usually take them at face value, because you never know what's going on behind the scenes unless you're in their shoes. But if Erin happens to have Blake genes in her veins, and she's anything like Lainey, she'll be single-minded to a fault and passionate about her beliefs. Whatever beliefs she might hold.'

There was silence in the car and Vikki supressed a shiver.

They were out through the gates and turning left onto the narrow road, but Ben had only driven halfway to the lough when they came to a halt, the road blocked by a fallen tree.

CHAPTER FORTY-SEVEN

Lainey

Ben's words echoed in her ears as she closed the hall door on the chilly morning, the noise of the jeep fading away.

'We need someone at home.'

The house settled silently around her. She went down to her father's room, but Leo was dozing lightly. Coming back into the living room, there was no sign of Charlotte and Harry. Sudden anxiety gripped her. If anything happened to them, her life might as well be over. Conscious that she was on her own in Lynes Glen, without any able-bodied adult around, her heart thumped as she hurried upstairs, and relief poured through her when she saw her children sitting on the carpet in their bedroom, playing with Lego.

But only two children, where there should have been three, and her heart ached.

'Will they find Jack, Mum?' Charlotte asked her worriedly.

'They will, of course,' she said.

'Do you think the ghost has taken him?' Harry asked.

She sat down on the floor and gathered the two of them close, wanting to wipe the anxious look off their faces.

'I'm not sure who or what Jack might have seen,' she said, as calmly as possible. 'I don't know where he's gone or if he went with someone, but there's no such thing as a ghost. They only thing I do know is that between your daddy and Alex and Niall, they'll bring him home. Honestly they will. The best thing you can do is stay here and play with the Lego while I do one more check around upstairs, and then we'll all go downstairs together.'

Even though the bedrooms and bathrooms had been checked already, she looked around them again because she needed to do something to distract her, besides torturing herself with imagining what Alex and Jenna must be going through, never mind six-year-old Jack. She went up to the attic where there was a large storage area and two small bedrooms that had been used back in the halcyon days to accommodate friends and visitors. The bedrooms were blank and silent, but she thought there was something indefinable in the air, a stirring, a slight disorder, perhaps a scent, that hadn't been there before. It could have been from Alex and Jenna, sweeping through the rooms when they'd checked every corner and cranny, but the feeling of disturbance seemed heavier than that and it could have come from something else – someone who had been hiding up here, perhaps, awaiting the perfect opportunity.

She went over to the window, wondering what was happening outside in the clear, bright day, frustrated that she was unable to contact anyone. So much for her determination to persuade everyone of the benefits of a WiFi-free, digital-detox weekend. If anything had backfired, that certainly had. She turned around and an icy chill slipped down her spine. She saw it from where she was standing just now, shoved in under the small space between the bottom of a chest of drawers and the floor, out of sight from any other part of the room. It gleamed mockingly, it flashed vulgarly, she felt it was slithering around her throat, tighter and tighter, such was her inability to breathe for a moment. She knew what it was, without touching it or pulling it out, because she couldn't bear to put a finger to it.

It was a bright-red wig.

She left the attic room, shuddering as she passed the spot where the wig was hidden under the chest of drawers. She closed the door as if to contain its revulsion within, and came down the narrow staircase to the first-floor landing. She sat on the armchair in the alcove for a few minutes, trying to compose herself before she faced her children. If anything happened to Jack, it would be too much to bear, but the wig was proof beyond a shadow of a doubt that it would be partly her fault.

*

She loved this house, she loved Lynes Glen with a passion. The long, untroubled, privileged years of her childhood glittered like a golden bubble in her memory. All linked to this house, to her mother, and her brothers, and her tall, gangly, beloved father. To being one of the Blakes of Lynes Glen.

How often had she fed titbits of those wonderful years, embellished with the rose-coloured glasses of time, to Erin? Coming down to visit her father, chatting over a cup of coffee in his Creaghbara apartment, extolling the wonders of Lynes

Glen and her beautiful, glittering mother, whom her father loved to pieces.

Sharing an occasional bottle of wine with Erin on a Friday evening before Erin finished up and went home. Erin, the capable, soft-spoken woman from Donegal she'd hired when her father's previous carer had been injured in a mugging just outside the town, breaking her hip in the fall, leaving Lainey in the lurch. She'd welcomed Erin with relief and gratitude, the woman with excellent references.

'Your father ... I don't quite know how to put this, but he seems sad from time to time ... I hope I'm not doing anything wrong, or saying the wrong thing ...' Erin's soft smile, inviting confidences. Her father tucked up in bed, the kitchen warm and homely with the residue of baking and freshly laundered sheets. The wine slipping down her throat with ease.

It didn't happen in Dublin. Lainey had always kept the sad part of her life private from her circle of friends and acquaintances. She'd lived with it by drawing a veil over it and carrying on as best she could, unwilling to appear vulnerable with her academic colleagues, never mind the neighbours and acquaintances she mixed with in the middle-class Dublin suburb. She'd never indulged in family gossip or heart-to-hearts after a book club meeting or Pilates class. How could you explain a family wrenched apart in the way theirs had been? It would be like picking a thick scab off a still-festering wound. Here in Creaghbara it was different, there was a more relaxed rhythm to her Mayo visits, and in the familiar landscape of her youth, where her life in Dublin didn't exist, the pull of Lynes Glen and the surrounding townland, the magic of those years, was stronger.

'Dad was never the same after my mother died,' Lainey had

admitted. 'She was the only woman he loved and he loved her passionately. He was devoted to her.'

'She died, when?' Erin had prompted.

'Twenty years ago. I still remember her like it was yesterday.'

'Twenty years ... good memories?'

'Oh yes, I have wonderful memories of my mother and growing up in Lynes Glen.'

'It must have been very special, to go by some of the photos Leo – your father – has shared with me.'

'He has? He must be feeling nostalgic. It was fantastic, a fairy-tale childhood, but like lots of fairy tales it had a dark side. There was a wolf waiting in the woods.'

'A wolf?'

'A wicked witch of sorts ...' Lainey had said, allowing herself to shiver. 'And whatever about my fairy-tale illusions, it all fell apart during one of the most beautiful summers imaginable, which, in the end, turned out to be the blackest.'

'That sounds sad.'

More wine.

'It was. Very sad. A summer of two halves. Unexpectedly warm and sunny, everyone was home, and we had an absolutely fabulous few weeks until it all went wrong.'

'Oh dear, in what way?'

'I can't talk about it ... the family don't talk about it, it was upsetting even before Mum died.'

'It must have left a terrible mark if you can't talk about it twenty years later ...' Erin's voice had been soft, encouraging. 'I'm not surprised, I know by Leo, and the way he looks at the photographs ... you've all been through so much. It's not easy to revisit those dark places.'

'No, it's not.'

'Sometimes you just want to keep them covered up.'

Lainey had felt something give inside her; she was tired of keeping it all bottled up, maintaining appearances, putting a good face on it all. 'It is a dark place because we were all to blame ...'

'All?'

'Alex was a bit stupid about something ... someone. Then I made it ten times worse ...'

'You, Lainey? You couldn't have.'

'I did, believe me. Oh, never mind ... it's best left alone, we pretend it never happened. At least we try to. Up until my birthday, that summer was brilliant. After that ... well, things changed, life turned very sour, but then even worse was to come, because three weeks later Mum was gone.'

'Tsk, tsk.' Erin had looked at her, tilting her head as though she was expecting to hear more. But Lainey had remained silent on that.

Now, sitting in the alcove in Lynes Glen, one of her mother's favourite spots, Lainey allowed herself to remember.

Her birthday: the last night everything was perfect. All five of them on the terrace in the sultry evening after a celebration meal, candles guttering in the lanterns, light slanting across the ground from the uncurtained windows, her favourite song coming on her ghetto blaster, feeling so free and relaxed and so certain of a glittering future ahead that she had been on a high, she was kicking off her silvery sandals and dancing across the terrace in her bare feet, swaying and shimmying her body in time to the music, pretending she had castanets in her hand. Throwing a cushion at Niall when he made a just-about-to-puke face. Dragging a reluctant Alex to his feet. Her father, laughing, taking her mother's hand and twirling her across the terrace in the soft light, their shadows dancing and mingling as one, her mother's hair flying out like a spangled flag when they went into a spin. Watching her tall, lanky father, and how her petite mother fitted perfectly into the protective curve of his body as he bent towards her. Taking the joy of it all for granted, feeling nothing could touch the Blakes.

Then the next day Maura arrived and nothing was ever the same.

Annoyed with Alex and the way he'd taken up with Maura – twice his age, and Mum's cousin as well – following her around like a dog in heat and now the glorious summer was soured and the siblings at odds, it had been far too tempting for her to take her sometimes swaggering, occasionally irritating older brother down a peg or two by dropping hints as to what he was up to.

If only she'd kept her mouth shut …

If only.

Not that they would ever know what precisely had caused her mother to drive off the road, or what she'd been thinking in those last few moments, but it was thanks to Lainey's catty remarks about Alex that she'd taken the car that day to visit Maura in the first place.

How much did Erin know? When word of Maura's death had reached Lynes Glen, they were still in such shock after Gabrielle that they had barely taken it in. Yet Erin must have found something, traced something, known something. She hadn't just coincidentally arrived in this part of the world, she'd come on purpose, managed to get the job with Leo – just how had she managed this? Lainey shivered with apprehension – and had used a chance remark of Lainey's to put the idea into his head of the family getting together.

Snippets of another conversation roared into her head.

'I'd love to see all the family together in the house. One more time,' Lainey said, thinking there was about as much a chance of that happening as the family going to Mars.

'Leo, did you hear that?' Erin said. 'Wouldn't it be nice to have your family all around again? Just the way they used to be in happier times? Before—'

'Before what?'

Erin smiled and shrugged. 'Sorry, I wasn't implying that anything might happen to you. It's just – well, you never know what's around the corner in anyone's life.'

'I know that only too well, Erin,' Leo said, pausing for a moment, his face shadowed. 'But I can assure you nothing's going to happen to me any day soon.'

'You're invincible, like the rest of us,' Erin joked. 'Everyone thinks, including me, that death won't happen to them. However, the saddest people I've cared for are not those who think death lurks around the corner, but those with regrets. When it's too late to do anything about them ... nothing more heart-wrenching than seeing a person too helpless to do anything about their regrets at that stage. Gosh, is that the time? I'd better fly ... I'll be late for my date.'

*

When she felt a little more composed, putting her good face on everything as usual, Lainey went back into her children and, making a game of it, she brought Charlotte and Harry downstairs to the living room, along with their Lego and other toys. Once again she looked out the windows, opening both the hall door and the French doors, standing outside in the still, calm air, in case any sounds carried to her. But all was silent except for the birds calling to each other, swooping and gliding amongst the treetops in the forest. There was no sign of

Ben or the others returning, and no sound at all of Jack's high-pitched voice.

She tidied an already-tidy dining room and kitchen, heating water on the solid fuel stove to use for washing the few remaining cups. She rinsed the cups and set them on the drainer to dry. God knows what Erin had been saying to Leo when Lainey wasn't there, filling his head with dangerous thoughts about regrets and guilty consciences. And Leo fell right into her carefully, delicately spun web. As did Lainey.

Fidgety and uneasy, she went up to the sitting room, feeling sick when she looked at the photos she'd lined up with so much hope.

'*We need someone at home* ...' Ben had said.

But this wasn't her home, it hadn't been her home for almost twenty years. No matter how much she wanted to hang onto the memory of perfect family life at Lynes Glen, how much she wanted to relive it, it belonged to the past. She had to let it go. She'd seen that straightaway this weekend. Her brothers had new lives. Time and distance had given them an indefinable air of belonging somewhere else. They were now a different fit to the house. They moved around like visitors. It wasn't their home any more than it was her home. Niall had lived in London more than the length of time he'd lived in Lynes Glen. Alex and his family were rooted in New York. No matter how much she'd wanted to put the clock back to the good old days, they could never go back.

Her home was in Dublin, her life was there with Ben and the children; it wasn't here, with the ghosts of the past. She'd married Ben because he was a patient, easy-going man, the kind of man to give her plenty of space within their marriage. Maybe he'd given her a little too much space and been too undemanding and she'd taken advantage of his kind nature, but that would have to change.

She stared out the window, willing his jeep to appear with everyone safe and sound. Especially Jack. Three big strong men would surely have no bother rescuing him from the likes of Erin.

CHAPTER FORTY-EIGHT

Vikki watched, dry-mouthed, while Ben and Niall dragged the fallen tree across to the ditch, once they'd ensured there were no electrical wires caught in the branches and it was safe to do so. Then they were back in the jeep and Ben gunned the engine as they tore down the mountainy road towards Lough Lynes, all of them spilling out of the jeep as soon as it slew to a halt, sending a flurry of stones flying up from the ditch.

'I think I saw someone out there all right,' Ben said. 'Looks like she's waiting for us.'

Vikki also thought she'd seen someone – it had just been a quick blur through the gap in the trees as Ben had sped by, but enough to send hairs rising on the back of her neck. Up close, she saw how solidly the track to the lough was blocked off. A thick gate barred the way behind which a fallen tree trunk was trapped.

Over the years the surrounding landscape had encroached, sending out roots and tentacles, wrapping itself around the gate and the tree trunk, solidifying and strengthening the barrier further. Her heart sank. She tried not to imagine how terrified little Jack must be if indeed Erin had him in her clutches.

'Is there any way around this barrier?' she asked.

Ben gave it a kick. 'The jeep and a rope will make short work of this. I just need to reverse.'

Niall stood by the barricade, his face white and tense, while Ben manoeuvred the jeep into position.

Vikki touched his hand. 'How are you?'

'After Mum, I swore I'd never come back here again,' he said, his eyes like flints. 'But if that bitch does anything to Jack … I'll do whatever I have to do.'

A tremor ran through her at the look in his eyes. 'I know you'll do whatever is humanly possible,' she said. 'So will I.'

Ben took a thick coil of rope out of the boot and tied it to the towbar. He and Niall secured it around the gate and with Ben in the jeep, tyres spinning, engine protesting, it was finally wrestled from its mooring place and dragged to one side. They did the same with the tree trunk, parts of it splintering, vegetation crumbling and scattering into the air as the rope strained and they hauled it away.

Then they were past the obstruction and hurrying down to the small sandy shore, where, in the clarity of the morning, the lough shimmered before them, silvery and alive, dappled by the sun, cupped like an offering in the curving embrace of grey-blue mountains under the infinite, arching sky. The breathtaking beauty of it caught in Vikki's throat.

Only today that perfection was marred. Up high, and over to her right, was the diving board, the long plank of wood extending out from a mountainy outcrop over the lough. Erin was sitting close to the end of the board, with her arm around Jack, who was slumped against her, his eyes closed.

'Holy shit,' Niall muttered, grabbing Vikki's hand.

Ben shook his head. 'God, no.'

'Well, hello!' Erin cried out. 'I thought you'd never get here.'

Niall helped Vikki up as they began to ascend the rocky part of the shore, but when they reached a narrow plateau, a few metres from the diving board, Erin called out again.

'Now that you *are* here, don't attempt to come any closer,' she said. 'Or else I'll fall in and bring Jack with me.'

Even though she'd half expected this, the words slammed into Vikki's head, making her reel with fright.

CHAPTER FORTY-NINE

'What do you want, Erin?' Niall asked.

Vikki was glad he sounded in control and that he was holding onto her hand. The whole scene was so threatening, she felt incapable of doing anything except cling to him.

'Don't you know who I am?' Erin said.

'Maura's daughter?'

'Wrong!' she shouted triumphantly.

Niall and Ben exchanged glances.

'I'm *Leo* and Maura's daughter,' she shouted. 'Leo and Maura – how does that sound? Better than Leo and Gabrielle, don't you think? In other words, your half-sister. As for what I want, that's easy – revenge, plain and simple. I want to make you suffer the way our bollix of a father made me suffer.'

'What's that got to do with Jack?' Ben asked. 'And what have you done with him?' His tone was calm and reasonable in spite of the fraught situation they were in.

Erin pulled him closer. 'I gave him something to make him relax. Wasn't I clever? That way I won't have any trouble with him. He's a strong little lad.'

'Please don't harm him,' Niall said. 'Whatever has upset you, it's nothing to do with him.'

'Upset me? *Upset*?' Erin cackled, the soft Donegal accent long gone, replaced by a voice tinged with a mixture of London and Northern Ireland accents. 'You morons haven't a fucking clue. That doesn't come anywhere near describing the fucked-up train wreck my life has been, thanks to your father. I want you all to feel the pain *I've* been feeling all these years. I had no one who loved me. *No one*.' Her last few words were more of a scream and Vikki flinched.

'Ben,' Niall muttered, 'get help.'

'I don't like leaving you.'

'I'll be fine. I have Vikki. Go!'

Vikki's heart sank. Niall thought he had her there for support – little did he know she was far too shook up herself to give him the support he needed. It shouldn't take Ben too long to find mobile coverage but she wondered how long it would take for help to arrive.

'Erin,' Niall said, 'Ben's going back to get Alex and Jenna. Maybe you'll listen to what they have to say.'

'Go ahead, Ben,' Erin called out. 'Alex is the one I want to see. He was another prick for the way he treated my mother.'

'What happened to you?' Niall asked.

'Do you really want to know?' she shouted. 'I bet you don't give a flying shit. You're only saying that now because you want something from me. You're scared of what I might do – aren't you? Scared that I might just happen to fall in. I don't care if I do.'

'Erin, we do want to know,' Niall said.

'I bet you were a much-wanted baby,' she said, her voice almost a snarl. 'A darling sibling for Alex and Lainey, lucky for you. I was the discarded one, given away at birth, to a family who treated me like you wouldn't even treat a dog – how would you like that to happen to you? I bet you can't even visualise it; you had the perfect family, the beautiful Blakes with the world at their feet.' She paused for a moment, before continuing, the words pouring out of her as though they'd been damned up for too long. 'I heard all about you, and your wonderful childhood. How would you like to have had a so-called father who was a pillar of the community, but who abused you from the age of eight, who raped you time and time again, only you didn't know what it was, and when you tried to run away at age ten, age twelve, you were simply brought back and told you'd been given one more chance and this time you'd better behave? Or else?'

Niall and Vikki were silenced while Erin's words echoed around in the clear air, all the more shocking for the gulf between the desolation of the life she was describing and the incandescence of the morning.

Out here, close to the edge of the rocky plateau overlooking the lough, there was a vibrancy to the day; it was in the light breeze playing with Vikki's hair and buffeting the surface of the lough, in the wheeling birds calling to each other, and in the sun, peeping between fluffy clouds, casting a fitful, translucent glow over everything.

But as she listened to Erin, Vikki felt her world spinning off its axis. Because parts of what Erin described could have been her life. She hadn't been raped – she'd escaped that ultimate trauma – but it had been very close and nasty. She listened to Erin in growing horror, as pieces of her own past unravelled in front of her, the dark past that had kept her paralysed with shame and guilt. For the sake of her sanity, Emily Victoria Gordon had closed a door on it all and reinvented herself. Opening that door would require courage she didn't have.

'Oh, they covered their tracks well, my so-called parents,' Erin said. 'No one could have guessed what they were capable of. I got away as soon as I could, and moved from London to Belfast, and then to Derry, but I didn't really escape it. I found myself hanging out in all the wrong corners with all the wrong people, unable to make a decent life for myself, or make any kind of life – but I do a mean Donegal accent, don't I?'

'We didn't know any of this,' Niall said. 'You can't blame Leo for the actions of your so-called father. Come in from there, give me Jack, and we'll talk about it.'

Erin shook her head. 'Fuck off. I do blame Leo. He didn't want to know. He brushed off my mother when she came home to Ireland that summer. She only came because I'd written to her through social services. I told her I'd had a crap childhood, thanks to being abandoned. Even then I spared her the gory details because I couldn't even face writing them down at the time – maybe I should have … social services told me they'd passed the letter on, but I heard nothing at all for years and years. I went from one poxy life to another. And then lo and behold, it all changed last year.'

Vikki tried to breathe to keep a grip on herself. She blinked, unable to believe they were still in this nightmare. She guessed Niall was keeping Erin talking to stop her from doing anything stupid, but she didn't know how Alex and Jenna were getting on in their trek through the woods or from where they might appear.

'What happened last year?' Niall asked.

'Social services contacted me again because they'd found a package addressed to me and guess what? Maura's diary was in it.'

'What diary?'

'She must have had a guilty conscience after abandoning me and she was upset about Leo, but she very kindly wrote it all down before she jumped under that train. I found out about Leo and how he'd rejected both of us, about the fabulous lives you all enjoyed – something I could have had from my mid-twenties onwards, if he'd so much as acknowledged me. There were other items in the package as well, a video tape and a necklace. They came in very handy for rattling you lot.'

'Erin, what happened to both you and your mother was very sad, but—' Niall began.

'Shut *up*!' she screamed. 'She tried, you know? She tried to get your father to come around and acknowledge me, that last summer. I was twenty-six then, maybe I could have salvaged something of my life if I'd been wanted and loved. He didn't want me or my mother; he only wanted his precious Gabrielle, so Maura was as much a victim as I am.'

Vikki felt she was in a bad dream. Erin could have been telling parts of her sad, sorry story, the one she never wanted to share with Niall. Her father was dead, he hadn't jumped under a train like Maura, but off a bridge when he'd been stoned. Her alcoholic mother, who had replaced her father with a succession of boyfriends, was still very much alive. She clung hard to Niall to stop herself from swaying as the past she'd tried so hard to forget came screaming back in front of her.

Niall was talking again, sounding perfectly reasonable. 'Look, Erin, we can see how tough that must have been. But we can work this out, talk it out between us, and find some way to make up for the past. Come in from there and we'll go back to the house and have a good chat. Only this morning while you were taking Jack, Dad called us all together and told the family he wanted to find you.'

'Bullshit. You're just making that up. And it's too little, too late.'

It was obvious to Vikki that Niall wasn't getting through to Erin. He was trying hard, saying what he thought he should be saying, but his words meant nothing to her. She knew more than anyone that the damage Erin had suffered couldn't be appeased so easily. She had lived with similar scars for far too long. Erin's scars ran far deeper, however, and Vikki could only guess as to the horror she'd endured. In spite of the fraught situation they were in, she understood what demons had driven Erin to do this.

'*I know how you feel*,' she wanted to say. '*You aren't alone …*'

Suddenly, out of the corner of her eye, Vikki saw Alex and Jenna hurrying by the edge of the forest where the trees thinned out, then coming into the clearing at the far side of the diving board, stopping abruptly as they took in the scene. If they moved closer, anything could happen given Erin's frame of mind.

Niall must have realised this also. He deliberately stepped forward and Erin shouted out, inadvertently warning the others as well. 'Don't you dare move any closer or I'll fall and take Jack with me,' she roared. 'I can do this you know, I've nothing to live for.'

Vikki saw Jenna put a hand to her mouth and Alex grabbed her and pulled her close into his chest, muffling any cries.

'I mean it,' Erin called out. 'Any funny business and we're both gone into the lough. I don't think you get me at all. I hate each and every one of you. Leo wouldn't acknowledge me because of you and your wretched mother. I hate Gabrielle too, for driving into this lough. It was the last straw for my mother. Any chance Maura might have had of changing Leo's mind and rescuing some of my life was gone. I would have jumped under a train myself years ago but the thoughts of getting some kind of revenge kept me alive. And here we are. This is it. The sweetest moment of my life so far.'

Alex wrapped his arms around Jenna's head as though to anchor her.

'If your fight is with us and our father, why Jack?' Niall said. 'What has he ever done to you? He's only six.'

'Can't you see?' she laughed. 'It's obvious. Your precious Leo keeps telling me how wonderful his grandchildren are, the greatest gifts in his life, blah, blah, blah. I'm going to ruin that for him just as he ruined my life. I want to hurt him where it pains him the most. And taking Jack with me, rather than Charlotte or Harry, is a bonus.'

'Why is Jack a bonus?' Niall asked.

'Because he's Alex's. His cruel snub was the final straw for my mother.'

'You don't know anything for certain,' Niall said. 'You don't know what went on between them.'

'I know what my mother wrote down.'

'It was a brief summer fling, that's all. Temporary fun. For both of them. So let Jack go, it's got nothing to do with him. What happened to your mother has nothing to do with Alex.' He chanced taking a step forward but it was too much for Erin. She inched further down the diving board, holding Jack tightly to her.

'You'd better not come any closer or we'll fall. Both of us.'

Alex's face collapsed in anguish. He loosened his hold on Jenna and took a few steps forward, scattering loose gravel, sending stones and grit rolling down the shale slope, alerting Erin to his presence.

Erin turned her head around. 'Ah, Alex,' she said. 'You're there. You've probably been there all along. I've been waiting for you to arrive with your lovely wife. It's a pity Ben had to leave. He'll miss all the excitement. If he's gone to get help, it'll be too late. I didn't want to do anything with your precious son until I knew you'd be here to witness it in all its glory. When we fall, I want you to be haunted by this, every single moment until the day you die.'

Erin inched further down the board.

'*Wait—*' the word was out; it had left her mouth and was ringing in the air before she realised she'd said it.

Vikki put her hand up to her face, but it was too late to take it back. Everyone's attention switched to her – Erin's, Alex's, Jenna's, and the last person in the world who needed to hear the words whirling around in her head … Niall.

CHAPTER FIFTY

For a long, charged moment Vikki froze.

The memories were there, pulsing at the edge of her vision, fresh and colourful, filling her with loathing, strong, as though it had all just happened yesterday. The succession of images from her childhood and adolescence that she'd fought so hard to strike from her mind came silently, swirling around her as though they were performing a war dance, before slotting into place, like playing cards in a deck, one on top of another.

'Well, well, Vikki,' Erin said, in a malicious tone of voice, a false smile on her face. 'What have you got to say for yourself that you think I might find interesting?'

It would have been so painless to say nothing, to simply ask Erin to reconsider what she was threatening to do, but that would have been taking the easy way out. Feeling lightheaded,

Vikki gathered scraps of her courage and said, hoping her voice wouldn't sound too shaky, 'I have some idea of how you feel.'

Erin's artificial smile changed to a snarl. 'Do you now? That's *very* interesting. How dare you presume to know how I feel.'

'I know because … something similar happened to me.'

She sensed Niall's sudden start.

Erin gave her a big, cynical grin that said she didn't believe her. 'Something similar? Oh dear. Yeah, right.' Across the divide, Jenna and Alex were staring at her and seemed to be holding their breath.

'Vikki, darling, is this true?' Niall asked in a quiet voice.

Darling. 'Yes.'

'Ah, dear God.' He tightened his grip on her hand.

'Hey,' Erin called out, 'are you two love birds finished whispering to each other? You're being very rude.'

'I'm not presuming to guess exactly how you feel, Erin,' Vikki said, hoping the other woman would be curious enough to want to listen. 'Everybody has their own story, but like you, I had a difficult childhood. I was abused by my father for years while my alcoholic mother turned a blind eye. After he fell off a bridge, Mum's boyfriends very kindly took his place.'

Without letting go of her hand, Niall looped her arm around his waist so that it curved around him, and he put his arm around her shoulders. She felt the solid weight of it, holding her securely, and knew they were anchored together. She was thankful; all of a sudden she felt faint and thought she might cry.

'You're one brave lady,' he murmured softly.

She wavered, just for a nanosecond. 'Thank you.'

He turned very slightly towards her and she felt the barest touch of his mouth on the side of her head. 'I should be thanking you,' he said.

'Shut the fuck up talking to each other!' Erin roared. 'You had a crap childhood, but what's that to me?'

'Not much, apart from you hate Leo, and I hated my father and my mother. And her boyfriends. You have scars, I have scars. Out of us all here today, I have some idea of how you might feel.'

'Scars!' Erin scoffed. 'From where I'm sitting you don't have any.'

'They're well hidden. But they sure messed me up. They still have me messed up.'

'Yeah, so much that you managed to hook up with the Blakes.'

'I felt like damaged goods for a long time,' Vikki said, pausing for a minute, seeing that Erin was paying attention, trying to think of how best she could put her words in order to connect with her. 'I thought there was something wrong with me, some horrible flaw, that everything that had happened was my fault, that I was ugly and useless, and when I began to meet men, I got in with all the wrong kind, the kind who hurt me, who had no respect for me, because I had no respect for myself. I was messed up big time.'

'And then you met your Mr Fix-it,' Erin drawled. 'Lucky you.'

Vikki shook her head. 'Niall's not my Mr Fix-it. There are some things you can never fix, they're too badly broken, but you can push the broken bits to one side and step over them. I became friends with Niall when I said to myself what the hell, I'm going to kick the shit out of my crappy past, I'm not going to let it get the better of me. Instead of men walking all over me I'm going to walk all over my past for a change and stamp it into the ground, and have me a decent life because I deserve it, right?'

There was silence for a moment.

Erin cackled with laughter. 'Aw, what a sob story, Vikki. For a moment there I thought I might feel *sorry* for you, but guess what, I don't.'

'What I'm trying to say is, you deserve better than this,' Vikki said. 'There's nothing to stop you from hooking up with the Blakes. Niall has already said they'd be happy to talk to you. There's nothing to stop you from stamping all over your past, kicking the ass out of it, making the most of the years you have left, and turning them into good years.'

'Oh wow – good years? That sounds exciting.' Erin's face grew darker. 'You listen to me for a change, you pompous do-gooder, bright and chirpy, butter-wouldn't-melt little missy-miss, I don't give a flying fuck about your life, or mine. It's over, it's worthless. I don't give a rat's ass if you think you have some idea of how I feel, because you don't. I came here for one reason – revenge. Nothing is going to change that, no matter what anyone says.'

She moved down along the diving board, clutching Jack to her.

'Erin, for the love of God …' Jenna begged.

'Give Jack to us, please, Erin,' Alex said.

'Shut the fuck up. Don't take one step nearer, either of you!' Erin screamed, inching further down the board, maintaining her grip on Jack. 'I'm warning you.'

'What are you going to do?' Alex asked.

'If you come any nearer I'll topple into the water with Jack.'

'I hear you and I understand your threat,' Alex said, his voice slow and measured. 'I meant, what are you going to do anyway. Do you plan to sit there all day with us standing here. Is there anything we can do to persuade you to come in off that board and talk to us? I'll go out there right now and talk to you if you like.'

'Don't attempt to move any closer or I'll jump. There's nothing you can do, the damage is already done. I've no intention of sitting here all day. I want to savour this moment for a little while longer. I've waited so long to find out about the father who abandoned me, that I don't mind hanging on for a few more minutes to enjoy the moment I pay him and his family back.'

'And after you've savoured the moment? What is your payback plan?'

'Just you watch and see,' she said, her laughter echoing around.

Jenna collapsed, weeping, into Alex's arms.

'I'm scared,' Niall said quietly to Vikki.

'Of course you are,' she said. 'So am I.'

'I think she might jump.'

'So do I,' Vikki said. Something that had been holding her back broke free inside her and rose up, light as a feather, yet strong and true. 'When you dive in after her to rescue Jack, I want you to remember one thing and one thing only.'

'What's that?'

She turned to face him. 'I love you,' she said. 'No matter what happens now, or what happened before, or what happens in the future, just remember that I know you, I know what happened, and I love you. You are wonderful and precious and funny and caring. A good person. A kind man. A man I am proud to know and love. Always. No matter what happens. OK?'

'OK. Thank you.' Their eyes met and the world about them stilled as a look of total understanding and acceptance passed between them. Then she saw him bring his whole attention to where Erin sat on the board with Jack. She felt a chill on her neck when he slid his arm away, released her hand from where it curved around his body, and almost imperceptibly moved a slight bit away from her.

There must have been something in Niall's stance, in the tilt of his head, in the line of his shoulders, because Vikki saw Alex stare across at him, and give him a tiny nod of acknowledgement.

Erin began to inch down the board.

'Watch and see, watch and see,' she called out in a singsong voice, stalling when she was a dangerous four feet from the end.

Beside her, Vikki felt Niall tense.

'Don't do this, Erin, please,' Alex called out. 'I'll give you whatever you want, money, holidays ...'

'There's nothing you can give me, nothing you can do, I'm already all smashed up.'

'We can help,' Jenna said desperately. 'You just need a little faith and hope.'

'Faith and hope!' Erin shouted in a shrill voice. 'You must be used to an easy life if you still believe in that kind of mumbo jumbo. I've gone beyond all that. You'll soon find out what it's like to feel black and hopeless.'

'Please, Erin, you can have anything you want, anything in the world, if you just bring Jack back safely to me and his mum,' Alex said. 'Blame me for whatever you like but he's a little innocent in all this. Please, I beg you.'

'Don't come near me, you fucking wanker!' Erin screamed. 'I'm warning you.'

She began to move further along the diving board, dragging a drowsy Jack with her. There was the sound of a car coming around the bend, the brakes jamming on, a door slamming, then Ben came hurrying across to where Vikki and Niall stood.

'Christ Jesus,' he said. 'Help is coming. I hope it's in time.'

'Go back for the rope. Come down to the shoreline with it,' Niall told him quietly. 'I'll need you there.'

'How can I leave—'

'Go!'

Vikki saw Erin shift again, staring tauntingly at Alex as she inched down the board.

Whether it was intentional or not, Erin lost her balance. For a long, frozen moment, she teetered on the edge of the board, then she went freefalling into space, bringing Jack with her, both of them tumbling over and over as they fell towards the lough in a tangle of arms and legs. There was a huge splash as they hit the water and it swallowed them up. Jenna screamed and Alex rushed down the slope towards the board, stumbling on the loose scree in his haste.

In two seconds flat, as though he had already rehearsed the steps in his head, Niall pulled off his boots and jacket. Vikki watched him run down to the end of the board, stopping briefly to compose himself. In a vivid millisecond of pure vitality and aliveness, silhouetted against the sky, she saw him draw a long breath of cool air into his lungs, reach out his arms, focus, and then he was arrowing down into the lough.

CHAPTER FIFTY-ONE

In that moment, as he went to the rescue, his long, lean body slicing cleanly into the water, Niall was the most beautiful, heart-clutching sight Vikki had ever seen.

She'd said it – the L word – despite her firm intentions. She'd told Niall she loved him, but it had seemed so right in that moment that she would never regret it. She closed her eyes, finding it agonising to watch for a break in the now-smooth surface of the lough, waiting to see a head or an arm emerge. It wasn't hard to imagine the impact of the water; the iron-hard mass of it shocking him, the coldness, the weight of it pressing on him, sucking him down, down, into blue-green depths. The battle he'd have finding anyone in the shadowy waters, never mind the strength and energy needed to bring them to the surface. She found herself counting seconds, afraid to guess how long he was able to hold his breath.

'Here, Vikki, this is something we can do.' She opened her eyes at Ben's voice. He was tying a section of the rope around his waist, knotting it fast, the end of it secured to the tow bar on the jeep. He'd already taken out a blue picnic rug and a towel, leaving them ready on the hard section of sand. Alex and Jenna had joined them, Jenna shaking and crying.

'I'm going to be the anchor man along with the jeep,' Ben explained, 'and Alex is ready to wade out as far as he can go in case Niall needs help coming in with Jack.' The calm way he said it took the hard edge off her anxiety.

Alex took off his jacket and sports shoes. He left some slack, and, picking up the mid-point of the rope, he circled it around his waist, leaving a length of rope free, and making a tightly knotted loop at the end. He coiled the rope into loops and walked down into the shallows until he was waist deep in the water, holding the rope up out of the water.

'How can I help?' she asked.

'Have you ever done CPR?' Ben asked.

'No, not in real life, but I trained.'

'Good. Me too, but be ready, just in case I need you to help with that.'

'I trained as well,' Jenna said, her voice husky.

'All the better,' Ben said.

They seemed to be waiting a long time, standing on the shore, Vikki giddy with fright, Alex a suddenly lonely figure as he waited in the water for any sign of his son or brother. Then, at last, Jenna shouted.

'There! Look!'

Over to the left, away from the shadow of the diving board,

something broke the surface of the water. A hand. It disappeared almost as quickly and Vikki's heart dropped. Then there was more, the sight of a small, wet head appearing above the surface. Jenna coiled over, hugging her stomach. Alex lifted the rope over his head. Seconds later, Niall's head appeared and all Vikki's insides turned to liquid.

'Wait, Alex, not yet,' Ben called out. 'He's too far out.'

It was an agonising wait, while Niall seemed to tread water, holding Jack's head clear. Then he began to make some progress towards the shore, slowly closing the gap. Eventually Ben roared, 'Now, Alex, throw the rope.'

Alex's first attempt went too wide. He hauled the rope back in again, looping it around his arm. Threw it again, but this time Niall failed to grasp it before it sank. One more time Alex hauled it in, coiled it and threw it, and this time, Niall managed to grab hold, manoeuvring it around both him and Jack. Alex and Ben pulled on the rope, walking backwards for further leverage, helping Niall to come closer and closer to the shore until he reached waist-high water. He got to his feet, carrying Jack in his arms. They dropped the rope and ran forward into the shallows to help. As if in slow motion, Vikki watched Niall hand Jack over to Alex, the little boy's body limp in his father's arms as he hurried back to dry land and laid him down on the rug.

Ben dropped to his knees and checked for a pulse, nodding at Jenna and Alex. He began CPR with chest compressions, counting aloud, stopping briefly to blow air into Jack's airways. Jenna knelt down beside him, ready to take over. In the taut, tense moment, she seemed eerily calm and focussed on the job of resuscitating her son. Alex took off Jack's sodden trainers and trousers, rubbing his limbs and folding the towel and rug around them. Niall staggered across, breathing heavily, and Vikki ran to him and threw her arms around his saturated body.

He seemed distant, his mind elsewhere. He didn't put his arms around her.

'I'm going back in,' he said, already moving back towards the water's edge.

She hurried after him. 'You can't.'

'I have to. If there's any chance for Erin … She's already been through enough wars.'

She put a hand on his arm. 'It's too much to expect.'

'I won't do anything stupid,' he said. 'Where exactly did I come up?'

'Over there,' she said, indicating. 'About thirty feet left of the diving board.'

'Right. As soon as Jack comes round, have someone ready with the rope.'

'Niall, please—'

'I have to do this.'

'Come back to me,' she said, 'I love you.'

She felt his kiss on her forehead, and then he was gone, splashing through the shallows, diving beneath the water as soon as it reached his chest. She wrapped her arms around herself and stared out at the space where he'd disappeared, apprehension twisting her stomach. Behind her, she heard a cough and a splutter and then a cry of relief from Jenna.

Jack would be OK.

'Where's Niall?' It was Ben. 'Don't tell me he's gone back in?'

'He has. How's Jack?'

'He'll be fine, he's cold though, he needs to get to A & E and be checked over. But Niall … for God's sake—' Ben shook his head.

'He asked that someone be ready with the rope.' She was

beginning to shake so much from nerves she could hardly get the words out.

Ben sighed heavily. 'We'll be ready. Alex?'

Vikki looked around at the small tableau on the shore. Jenna was sitting down on the strand with Jack in her arms. Alex was tucking his jacket around the small figure of his son, who was coughing and crying all at once, and still deathly pale. When he was satisfied that Jack was as good as he could be for now, he hurried across to Ben.

'What's with Niall going back in? I saw it out of the corner of my eye. I can't believe he did that.'

'Neither can I,' Vikki said.

'We'll do our best,' Alex said, giving her a hug. 'Are you a good swimmer, Ben?'

'Not really, no.'

'Then it's me, so.' He shrugged off his jeans and picked up the rope that had been dropped on the ground. 'Here, get this around me, I'll swim out as far as I can, there's no time to waste.' Alex played out the rope, judging the amount he'd need, looping it around his waist at the halfway point, Ben securing the end of it around his waist. Alex coiled the remainder of it loosely around his neck and went into the water. 'Shout when you see him and tell me where he is. If I put my hand in the air or go under, you'll have to pull me in,' he said, glancing across to his wife and child.

'Absolutely, I will.'

Vikki couldn't bear to watch. Neither could she bear to imagine what Niall might be experiencing under the water, his lungs at bursting point. Surely Erin was too long submerged by now to have any chance of survival. Alex made slow progress, his head bobbing up and down as he swam out, while Ben dug his feet into the sand to anchor himself and played out his end of the rope, until it grew taut. Alex could go out no further; he swam slowly on a course parallel to the shore, first one way then the other.

Then, after what seemed like forever but was only a couple of minutes, Niall's head surfaced above the water, a few yards away from Alex. Both Ben and Vikki yelled to him and were rewarded when Alex threw the rope so that the looped end fell just beyond Niall and he caught it first time. Then he disappeared under the water again, pulling Alex out to him, and the sudden tug on the rope drew Ben down into the shallows and for a while he looked as though he was going to be swept off his feet.

'Vikki, the jeep,' he yelled.

It took her just a second to realise what he meant. She ran up the shore and climbed into the jeep, her legs and hands like jelly. The keys were in the ignition. From somewhere she found the strength to block out all her terrors and start the engine, letting off the handbrake at the same time as she inched the jeep forward. She watched the drama unfold in the rear-view mirror, Alex making efforts to swim back to the shore, but hampered by the drag of Niall at the far end of the rope. Ben fought ground with all his might, slowly moving back up out of the shallows as Vikki drove the jeep forward. She didn't know if she was imagining it, but Alex seemed to be coming in closer, and – her heart leaped – she saw Niall again further out, the top of his head just visible above the surface. She couldn't see if he had anyone with him. She tried not to panic when Niall disappeared again under the water, focussing on the feel of the accelerator under her foot as she inched the jeep up the incline. She checked the rear-view mirror once more and saw Alex reaching the shallows and Ben stepping out of the rope to help haul him to his feet, and together they pulled on the rope until Niall came in closer and closer.

Vikki cut the engine, pulled on the handbrake and ran down just as Ben and Alex half lifted, half dragged Niall up to the dry shore, lying him down carefully on his back. He was unresponsive. His eyes were closed and his face had a blueish tinge. Ben dropped to his knees and began CPR, as Alex ran back out to the water's edge and hauled in someone else. Erin.

Then, in the distance, they heard the sound of a helicopter.

CHAPTER FIFTY-TWO

The day took on a surreal quality. Sitting by Jack's hospital bed, Jenna felt she had lived a million days in a couple of hours. Some images of that morning would never leave her mind, so sharply had they sliced a dividing line between the old Jenna, shearing it completely away, and the new Jenna, who knew her life from now on would be underpinned by a deep and abiding gratitude that Jack had been saved. She would never forget the heart-stopping moment that Niall had come out of the lough carrying their son in his arms and handed him over to Alex.

It was now late afternoon. After Jack had been whisked off to the county hospital in the helicopter with a stretchered, unconscious Niall, and an equally unconscious Erin, the police had brought her, Vikki and Alex around by road and Ben had gone back to Lynes Glen. Together Ben and Lainey had gathered a change of clothes and overnight essentials for everyone, and with Lainey driving Leo and the children in the jeep, and Ben taking Alex's hired car, they'd locked Lynes Glen and come straight to the hospital. Ben had already booked rooms in a nearby hotel for that night; no one was going back to an out-of-mobile range, out-of-power Lynes Glen.

Jack was fascinated by the hospital, by the bed with all the equipment around it, the curtains that swished closed, the funny and tickly things that the doctors and nurses pulled out of their pockets or off a trolley to check him out with. He didn't want to stay in bed where they were keeping him in for observation. Full of chatter and energy, he wanted to tell everyone about his exciting helicopter journey. Then his dad had arrived at the hospital in a police car. A real police car with a siren and blue flashing lights. Wait until his friends in school heard about this!

Then Ben and Lainey and his best cousins ever, Charlotte and Harry, had come to see him, along with his Grandad Leo, Harry wanting to get into a bed as well, so that he could taste the hospital water in case it was different, and read the comics Jenna had bought in the shop – they even had a shop here, Jack told him, selling different kinds of sweets and comics that he'd never seen before. And food came around on a little tray and he had to eat it in bed. Food. In bed. In the middle of the day.

Jenna listened to his endless stream of chatter, soaking it into the pores of her skin as though it was as vital as her life's blood. Right now, satisfied that Jack was going to be fine, Alex was up in the Intensive Care Unit with Vikki and Lainey where Niall was being treated for lung complications.

Erin was somewhere in the hospital as well, fighting for her life, whatever quality of life she might have left after her near drowning. Jenna didn't want to know anything about her at the moment. Lainey had told her about the red wig, tucked away in the spare attic room. It would account for the person she'd seen by the lough the afternoon they'd arrived, and the nights Jack thought Gabrielle had been in his room. Ben had spotted Erin's car tucked into a ditch on the approach road when he'd gone to call for help that morning, which suggested she'd returned to Lynes Glen sometime after leaving yesterday evening, making the latter part of the journey on foot so as not to alert anyone.

There were lots of questions to be answered. The police too were waiting to talk to them.

Jenna looked up to see Ben coming down the ward, a figure of warm familiarity in the clinical hospital. 'Any updates?' she asked him.

'They reckon Niall will make a good recovery, although no one has been allowed in to see him yet,' Ben said.

Jenna closed her eyes. 'Good. We owe him everything.'

'I've brought Leo back to the hotel,' Ben went on. 'He's upset about Erin, but relieved that Niall and this little one will be OK,' he said, ruffling Jack's hair.

'And how is Lainey now? She seemed to be very anxious when I spoke to her earlier.'

'She's blaming herself for hiring Erin in the first place, but I'm not going to allow her wallow in that. As soon as we get back to Dublin I'm going to put my foot down, even if it means giving her some tough love.'

Jenna smiled. 'Ben Connolly and tough love is a contradiction in itself.'

'I might surprise you, Jenna.' His eyes gleamed. 'I've already talked to Lainey and as it happens, she agrees with me. Other things besides the Blakes and Lynes Glen are going to come first from now on. I'm going to make sure of that.'

'Hey, Ben, can you help me with this puzzle?' Jack said, holding out his comic towards him.

'Sure I can.' Ben sat down on the other side of the bed, and the two of them pored over the puzzle page of Jack's comic. After a while he met Jenna's eyes over the little boy's head and gave her a warm smile. 'This little fella seems to be fine, so no harm done.'

'No harm done whatsoever,' she echoed, her eyes scanning his face, half wondering if she was sending both of them a subliminal message. Ben was one of the nice people in life and the world needed people like him to help oil the wheels. No wonder she'd felt attracted to him. No wonder Lainey had married him; he'd tucked her into his big strong arms and made her feel safe after her world had collapsed.

But it was Alex whom she loved, who torched her senses – driven, quickfire Alex, Gabrielle's eldest son, in whose blueprint she still lived on, genes he had in turn passed on to Jack. Jenna looked down at her son's deep-red curls and put her arms around him. She felt such an overpowering connection to that vibrant woman that she could have been in the room with them and she wondered if maybe, just maybe, Jack had seen her after all ...

CHAPTER FIFTY-THREE

29 August 1995

'You know, don't you? He's told you,' Maura said. 'I've a feeling you didn't just drop in for coffee.'

Gabrielle looked at her cousin as she sat at a tiny formica-topped kitchen table and fingered the ruby pendant around her neck. 'Yes, I know,' Gabrielle said.

For a long, charged moment, they stared at each other.

'What are you going to do about it?' Maura asked, looking tense and uneasy.

'Do? Nothing,' Gabrielle said.

'*Nothing*?'

Gabrielle gave a half-laugh. 'What do you expect me to do? Alex is an adult. What he chooses to do with himself is his own business, not mine. Anyway, he's off to America soon so …' she shrugged.

'Ah,' Maura said, 'the lovely Alex.'

Gabrielle noticed her visibly relaxing. Calling for coffee had probably not been a good idea, but she'd been curious. Now she was sorry she'd come.

'I was bold,' Maura said, her eyes dancing with mischief. 'Sorry, Gabrielle, but I enjoyed teasing him, he takes me so seriously ... you should have seen his face when I asked him if I could go to America with him. You brought your children up too well, they're far too perfectly mannered and respectful. But I'm not sure if they're selfish enough for the harsh world we're living in nowadays.'

'You call my son going to bed with you respectful?'

'Yes, actually,' Maura said, moving around the tiny kitchen of her rented house, taking out mugs, coffee, milk. 'In the sense that he didn't want to upset or embarrass you or Leo and insisted that nothing happened under the roof of Lynes Glen. Alex and I ... I didn't mean it to happen, he didn't either, but I couldn't resist making a play for him. I couldn't help trying out my seductive charms one more time, it was fun pretending I was twenty again. He's gorgeous, all that red hair and deep-green eyes. Movie star looks. Jesus, how could I resist? And he's fiery, like you. It just ... happened, helped along by the hot summer nights and the chilled white wine. I think he got a little carried away, boasting about it to Niall, but I enjoyed his attention. My last fling, I expect, before I become a dull and invisible fifty-something. Which is something you'll never be, either dull or invisible.'

'We're all getting on,' Gabrielle said.

'Yes, but some are getting on better than others,' Maura said tartly. 'You're a lucky woman, to have so much, your adoring Leo, and three fabulous children.'

Gabrielle's fingers played with her pendant again. 'I know. Believe me, I count my blessings every day.'

'I'm quite jealous, actually,' Maura said frankly.

'You? Jealous?'

'I think that, in another life, it could have been me. But the reality is, I know Leo would never have loved me half as much as he worships you.'

Something in her eyes, her tone of voice, alerted Gabrielle.

'You loved my husband.'

'How could I *not* have loved him?' Maura said. 'I felt selfishly passionate about him once, and I was insanely jealous when you married him, but we grow and we change and London took the edges off me in more ways than one I can tell you, and I'm different now. At least I thought I was, until I came back here.'

'You slept with him,' Gabrielle said flatly, the look on Maura's face causing an old memory of Leo trying to tell her something rising to the surface.

'Did he tell you that?'

'Not quite.'

'What did he tell you?'

'Why, is there anything else I should know about?'

'I didn't think he'd mention it to you.'

'So you did. Sleep with him. Leo didn't say a word. I knew by your face.'

'It was just the once. Well, one night,' Maura corrected herself. 'Years ago, before you were married.'

'I see. Is there anything else going on, while we're on the subject?'

The pause was a little too long for Gabrielle's liking.

Eventually Maura spoke. 'I've nothing else to add.'

'You haven't really answered my question.'

'There's nothing to say, Gabrielle, other than I'll be out of your hair by the weekend, you'll be glad to know.'

'I don't think I'll wait for coffee after all,' Gabrielle said, 'but I'll see you before you go.'

*

She drove back to Lynes Glen in glittering sunshine, enjoying the peaceful beauty of the familiar journey. It would soon be autumn, flaming, beautiful autumn, her favourite season. The mountains would be carpeted with purple heather and yellow gorse, the deciduous trees in the forest would be on fire, their colours rivalled only by the scarlet and tangerine sunsets in the west. Leo had even written a poem for her, comparing her beauty to that of the season.

Leo! Sleeping with Maura. Once upon a time that would have stung deeply, but now, twenty-six years of love and marriage, caring and sharing, ups and downs had created their unique history and had welded them together so strongly that nothing as inconsequential as that would cause much damage.

As for Alex, she'd seen him impatient to leave the quiet of Lynes Glen and begin his new life. It wasn't all that surprising that he'd dallied with Maura. London had given her voluptuous cousin a cosmopolitan aura that he was bound to have found attractive.

All summer long, she'd had the sense that things were changing at a visceral level, that the pattern of their lives was in flux, and come the autumn, nothing would be the same. The warm summer had been an oasis of sorts, between the old and the new, and she'd thrown herself wholeheartedly into that magical time with all her energy and love. Soon, all her children would fly the nest, making their own way in the big wide world.

She would miss them far more than anyone realised, and, for her, the wonderful days and nights of the last few weeks had been tinged with her feelings of impending loss and the occasional secret bout of tears.

It was in the natural order of life that her children would leave home, she'd told herself sternly, trying to get a grip. She was lucky to have had them around for so long, and she would still have them at a remove, but the house would be deathly quiet without them. There would be no more Lainey gossiping at the breakfast table in the mornings, no more seeing her all beautified up for a night out with friends; no more big, gentle Niall raiding the fridge, using his shoulder to close the door, thanks to his laden hands; no more Alex tearing up the road in his car, bursting into the house like a ball of intoxicating energy. Their presence had always filled her with a deep-seated sense of peace and joy and she would feel the lack of that sharply.

Not that anyone knew. She'd been very careful to keep her feelings to herself. She wanted her children to go off and explore the world unencumbered. Even with Leo, she'd glossed over it, in case her super-sensitive husband felt in any way inadequate.

She came around her favourite bend in the universe, where there was a view of Lynes Glen in the near distance, followed by the first glimmers of the lough. Her attention was caught by something arrowing across the sky – geese, a pair of them, making their graceful way across the heavens, their silhouettes gilded iridescent by the sun. They usually arrived in the autumn to winter in this part of the world, so these were unusually early.

All of a sudden she was filled with the soothing knowledge that her children would come back, like the returning geese. They all loved Lynes Glen and their homing instincts would bring them back to her and Leo. They would, in time – and her heart lifted at this thought – bring little ones of their own to the magical places of their childhood: the forest trails and Infinity Hill and the fairy fort and the lough. She could see them in her mind's eye, little ones who were but blank silhouettes waiting to take form and shape in the fullness of time. She watched the geese for a moment longer, caught up in the spellbinding grace of their homecoming flight and the thoughts of what was to come in the years ahead.

Then, distracted for a split second too long, she hit the ditch on the next bend and the car flipped over, sliding down the incline on its back, directly towards the small shore and the lough. It happened so quickly she barely had time to register the jolt or the sensation of being whirled upside down or the scrape of metal against shale. In a split-second fragment of time she saw how perfectly wonderful the world – her life – was just at this moment: the steadfast backdrop of blue-grey mountains, the sun flaring off the surface of the lough so that she could have been sliding into a bowl of dappled sunshine; Leo, writing wonderful words in his library; her children, poised on the edge of great new adventures.

Her love for them all flowed out and around her like a living thing.

CHAPTER FIFTY-FOUR

In the small waiting area outside ICU, sunshine pressed through the corridor windows, slanting across the walls like blocks of lemon drizzle cake, the only beacon of cheerfulness in the grey hospital environment. An orderly rushed past with a small trolley, wheels squeaking on the linoleum, as Lainey pushed yet another cup of coffee into Vikki's hands.

'It shouldn't be too long now,' Lainey said.

Vikki shivered in spite of the warmth emanating from the takeaway coffee. It was early evening and she still hadn't seen Niall since the paramedics had whisked him away into the bowels of the hospital. Lainey had joined her, keeping vigil as they'd waited for news, hoping they'd get in to see him before that night. Alex had eventually come up from the ward where Jack was under observation, once he'd been reassured that Jack was OK and likely to be discharged that evening. Lainey and Alex had spoken to the consultant. Vikki was incapable of putting together a coherent sentence. They'd been told that Niall was responding well and expected to make a complete recovery. As soon as he was able for visitors, they'd be allowed in to see him one at a time. Now Alex was over at a dispensing machine, doing his best to extricate a soft drink can. At last it fell from its place and thumped to the bottom of the dispenser and he scooped it up and turned around to them, grinning boyishly as though he'd won the prize.

Vikki sipped her coffee, hoping it might thaw her out a little, because, for some reason, even though on one level she was deeply thankful and relieved that Niall would be OK, her limbs felt stiff and frozen solid. Inside, she felt terrifyingly empty as though someone had scooped out her innards, leaving just a raw and brittle shell. From the time the helicopter had arrived at the scene, she'd been on autopilot, as though something inside her had shut down.

'We owe you a huge debt,' Lainey had said to her earlier.

Vikki had shaken her head.

'Alex told me what you did, what you said, trying to delay Erin, trying to talk her out of it. It was very decent and brave of you. We can't thank you enough.'

Feeling blank, Vikki had been unable to respond. Sensing this, Lainey had put her arm around her.

'I hope my brother doesn't let you get away,' she'd said. 'I'll never talk to him again if he does.'

Vikki had tried to put on a fake smile, but her face had felt as though it might crack. Alex had also thanked her profusely, and said that Jenna would also want to show her deep appreciation as soon as she could tear herself away from Jack. For starters, he'd said, she was to come to New York as their guest, with Niall, as soon as it could be arranged. It all slid over Vikki's head, her sensation of being in a frightening void merging with the flurry of activity along the corridor and the overlapping minutes and hours of the passing day.

At last a nurse came through the doors and spoke to Lainey. Vikki heard her talking about oxygen levels and heart monitors and then Lainey turned around and said, 'We can go in now, one at a time. He's out of ICU.'

'How is he?' Alex asked the nurse, coming over to join them.

'He's doing quite well,' she said.

'Go on, Vikki, you first,' Lainey said. 'I'm sure you can't wait to see him.'

Once she knew Niall was going to be OK, Vikki could have walked away. She was in no hurry to see him whatsoever, she didn't need to see him, but Lainey gave her a gentle push, propelling her after the nurse. She felt she couldn't breathe, she would have preferred to have been a million miles away as she followed the nurse along the shiny linoleum floor through the swing doors, through a maze of corridors.

It hit her then, what was wrong with her and why she felt so blank. He knew. Niall knew all about her sad and sorry past. Everything she'd sworn to keep hidden from him, all those tawdry, shameful details, had been dragged out of their hiding place and presented in full technicolour not only to Niall, but his family. She'd given voice to that screwed-up young girl, so that every part of her, every inch, every dark secret that had paralysed her, had been stripped bare and exposed. The nurse led her to a small side ward, and, in spite of the heat of the unit, Vikki felt chilled to the bone as she moved across to the bed.

But when she saw him, everything changed.

It came to her with the force of a juggernaut and the gentleness of a gossamer whisper; the past was over and had no power, she had unblocked that plug and it had flowed through and was gone, leaving a vacuum. This was her life in all its colour and glory, what had happened years ago had nothing to do with this present moment. Maybe in time she could go back and find proper resolution with Sally Gordon, but the only thing that mattered now was that she was here, in this room, moving across to the bed, to this man, his eyes smiling at her over the mask covering his nose and mouth, his hair sticking up against a mound of pillows. She put her hand in his and was jolted by a sense of belonging, and all her empty spaces began to fill up at the sensation of his hand enclosing hers. She sat by the bed, their eyes locked on each other, while life went on around them: the murmur of voices coming from the nurses' station, the rustle of paperwork, light footsteps on the corridor, the aroma of tea and toast, the bleep of a machine.

Niall took off his mask.

'I bet you're not supposed to do that,' she said.

'That's why they wouldn't let anyone in before now,' he said, mischief in his eyes. 'They knew I'd want to talk. I have to tell you something – two things, actually.'

She waited, absorbing the look on his face and the aura of peace surrounding them, allowing both to infiltrate every cell in her body.

'I saw her … in the water …' His face was serious and he drew a shuddering breath.

'It's OK. You don't have to talk now.'

'I know she's dead but I saw her. The second time I went down.'

'Shh,' Vikki soothed, 'we don't know about Erin yet, and no matter what happens I'm going to keep reminding you that you did everything you could. You risked your life.'

'She was looking at me,' he said. 'She was beautiful, all gold and luminous even in the water …'

Her heart snagged. He must have been having a hallucination.

'She came to me out of nowhere,' he whispered. 'She stared at me and her eyes told me to go back, I knew by her eyes she wanted me to get out of the water and go back. She wanted me to save myself. She was cross with me for being down so long.' He paused for a moment and Vikki could only wait, a lump in her throat.

'It was my mother,' he murmured, 'I saw my mother – Gabrielle – she was more beautiful than ever, glowing, and the look on her face … Oh, Vikki, I can't believe I didn't see it, didn't understand it before now – as she stared at me, she had the exact same look in her eyes as the day – as the day she went into the lough … she wanted me to save myself.'

'Of course she did,' Vikki said gently. 'She loved you with all her heart. I can only imagine how much.'

His gaze slowly scanned her face. 'There's something else,' he said.

'Take your time …'

'I loved what you said to me just before I went into the lough after Jack,' he said, his voice a little hoarse. 'I was sorry I didn't have the chance to respond to you then, but I was a little busy.' He gave her a small grin. 'The moment I dived in, as I was going down, I swore to myself that if I got out of this alive, I wanted nothing more than to bring you to a quaint little pub on Achill island, by the edge of the sea.' He paused for a moment, his eyes holding hers. 'And drink chilled beer, and sit on rickety chairs and watch the sun go down, and tell you how much you mean to me, and talk to you of all the lovely possibilities we might have … together … how does that sound?'

She didn't realise she was crying until something wet splashed onto her hand. She grinned through her tears. 'You're on, but you're talking too much.'

'I know. Sit close so I can just look at you.'

She replaced his mask gently and kissed him on the forehead. She sat closer and held his hand, lacing it between both of hers. Then feeling strong and powerful, she told him again exactly what she'd said to him before he dived in to save Jack.

ACKNOWLEDGEMENTS

I would like to pay a huge tribute to the wonderful people I am privileged to know and work with, whose support, encouragement and enthusiasm is invaluable to me throughout the whole writing process, from the beginning of an outline draft until a fully polished and beautifully packaged book eventually arrives at the finish line: my inspirational agent, Sheila Crowley, and the hard-working team at Curtis Brown, London, also my super-talented editor, Ciara Doorley, along with the equally outstanding team at Hachette Books Ireland.

Thanks to all the dedicated booksellers and book bloggers, who work tirelessly to promote books and a love of reading and who rally around whenever a book hits the shelves. I don't know where writers would be without your energy and commitment.

I am particularly grateful to my amazing circle of family and friends, for endless love and patience, understanding and kindness, and for steadfast belief in me, all of which enable me to do the work I love.

Last but by no means least, thanks to you, dear reader, for picking up this book. I sincerely hope you enjoy it.

Zoë x

In her heart, Grace knows the reliable, good-looking Gavin isn't right for her. Then she meets Danny. Unpredictable and spontaneous, he turns her world upside down. All of a sudden, Grace is seeing life differently and doing things she never thought she'd do.

But tragedy strikes when Danny dies in a motorbike accident, shattering Grace's world. As she struggles to come to terms with her loss, she becomes more and more convinced that she's being followed – sighting a motorbike exactly like Danny's everywhere she goes.

As more and more sinister things begin to happen, Grace voices her suspicions – that his death was not an accident – but no one seems willing to believe her. Was Danny hiding something from her? And what kind of danger is she in now?

Also available as an ebook

The artisan bakery Ali and Max Kennedy own isn't just a successful business – it's a second home, a dream come true. But when bad luck begins to stalk the couple, Ali worries that her fear of losing it all is becoming a reality.

Across the city, Max's brother Finn and his wife Jo long for the carefree happiness they had when they first met in Australia over twenty years earlier. But when Finn loses his high-profile TV job and becomes more bitter by the day, Jo starts to suspect that he's hiding something from her.

While both couples navigate their marriages, little do they realise that Max and Ali's daughter, Jessica, harbours a dark secret which threatens to destroy the whole family.

Then it happens – the accident. And the Kennedys will never be the same again.

Also available as an ebook

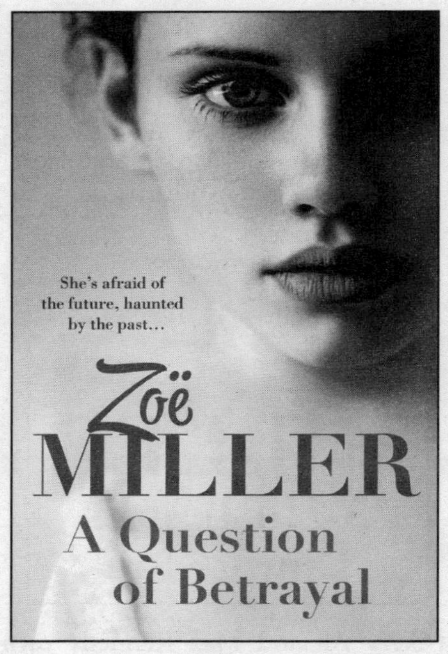

Ever since the deaths of her adored parents, Carrie Cassidy has avoided risk and commitment, fearful of bringing something precious into her life only to lose it again. So now she finds herself working in yet another uninteresting job, and the love of her life, who wanted more than she could give, has left her. Will she ever move on?

Then, a mysterious woman visits Carrie and reveals a secret that forces her to delve into her mother's past. As Carrie learns more about the woman she thought she knew, she finds herself looking at her own life and wondering if she's living it the way her mother would have wanted her to.

Meanwhile there is someone watching Carrie who would rather the past stay buried . . .

Also available as an ebook